BY

JT BLUNDELL

★ ★ ★ ★ ★

FOOL~
WHISKEY
~HERO

A NOVEL

BY JT BLUNDELL

FOOL-WHISKEY-HERO

A NOVEL

NEWPULP PRESS

Published by New Pulp Press, LLC, 926 Truman Avenue, Key West, Florida 33040, USA.

For information contact:
Publisher@NewPulpPress.com

ISBN-13: 978-1945734052 (New Pulp Press)
ISBN-10: 1945734051

Printed in the United States of America
Visit us on the web at www.newpulppress.com

ONE

The scrawny guy in the Hawaiian shirt was in trouble. You didn't have to be a genius to figure it out. He couldn't cower any further into his seat in the corner booth unless he started digging into the plastic upholstery.

Granted, the Dirty Pickle wasn't exactly a classy pub. Most of the chairs had been broken during one brawl or another and glued, wired or taped back together. The tables were old barrels with plywood nailed on top. It was dark because they couldn't afford the electricity, not for ambience or any pretentious crap like that. The bar had been slapped together with whatever wood had been handy and the many layers of paint were all that kept it from collapsing. My stool wobbled and bowed as I sat on it, I'd covered it with my jacket for fear of splinters and leaned on the bar to keep balanced. The glass I was guzzling whiskey from was chipped, and the only cleaning it received was when it was filled with booze.

No, The Pickle was not pretty, but the bartender still wouldn't be happy if the Hawaiian shirt guy tore the Hell out of the cushions in the booth.

The guy was stoop shouldered, weak chinned and had lost more of his black hair than he'd kept. Fringes poked out around his ears like unkempt bushes. His shirt was a Hawaiian thing they sell to tourists, blues and oranges that may have blinded me if it wasn't for the dimmed lights. His back was to the wall and he was trying to sink into himself.

Hawaiian shirt guy was scared out of his mind.

It probably had something to do with the behemoth beside him. A no-neck monster with a long beard and even longer hair and massive arms, he had a belly but there was no mistaking the muscle underneath or the fact he knew how to handle himself. He had two big handfuls of the Hawaiian guy's shirt and was almost choking him with it.

The guy with the backwards ball cap sitting across the booth was slightly smaller, but still big, just in better shape. He had the same beard, but had gone with shorter hair and was the one in charge. I couldn't hear from the bar, but the way snot and spittle splattered the chin on the ball cap guy, and how red his face had gotten as he spoke, they weren't just telling the guy how ugly his shirt was.

This was going to get bloody, and the Hawaiian shirt guy looked too scared to talk his way out.

But I had my own problems

My glass was empty.

If I didn't remedy that I'd wind up sober, and then where would I be?

I waggled my glass at the bartender. "Fill'er up."

Bertie, a short squat guy, with a thick moustache and even thicker hair on his arms shook his head. He was the owner and only employee. He placed the bottle of cheap rye in front of me but didn't let go.

"Don't you think you're drunk enough?"

"You sound like my wife," I said. "But you're not as pretty."

"So why don't you go home to her then?"

"If you can convince Marin to let me in, I'll owe you for life."

"And drinking more is going to help?"

"Isn't your whole business model about assholes like me drowning their sorrows?"

"You want more you pay for it," he said and lifted the bottle away.

I snatched a hold of his wrist and held firm. "When I'm done."

Bertie stared at me for a moment, rubbed his

2

moustache and then nodded. I let go of his wrist and he filled my glass. He nodded over to the guys in the booth. "Do you know what that's about?"

"I don't know and I don't care."

Bertie set the bottle down beside my full glass. "I've never seen the guy in the ugly shirt before, but the other two are the Webber brothers. The fat one is Sam and the other is Jack." He sighed. "My guess is the guy can't pay his debt."

I took a drink and smiled as the rye burned my throat. "They're loan sharks?"

Sam, the fat one, slapped the Hawaiian shirt guy hard enough across the face that his nose started bleeding.

"They're bookies." Bertie frowned. "Well, technically, their Momma is, the boys just collect for her."

"A family business? That's sweet."

Grabbing the Hawaiian shirt guy by the face, Sam drove the man's head into the paneled wall, twice. The faded pictures hanging around them shook. Sam thought about it for a moment, and smashed the man's head into the wall a third time. The guy's eyes were rolling in their sockets.

"They're going to wreck my place," Bertie said, reaching down under the counter to where I knew he kept a baseball bat.

"So why don't you tell them to stop?"

"Cause they're regulars and I owe Momma Webber myself," Bertie said. "You should do something because they're going to kill that guy."

"How is that my problem?" I took another drink.

"You're the boy scout

"What talking about?"

Bertie laughed. "Are you so far into the bottle that you forgot you were in the army?"

"Are you so stupid you forgot they kicked me out?"

I swirled the rest of the rye in my glass. I'd done five years with the Princess Patricia Canadian Light Infantry. I'd gotten only as far as Corporal. It was a good gig. They fed me, paid me and trained me all to get me to shoot and fight a bunch of assholes across the ocean. I'd had worse jobs.

"Yeah, you punched a cop," Bertie said. "So you can handle those two."

"It was an MP," I corrected. "If you can believe it they're even dumber than a cop."

"So you're scared of them, then?

Turning on my stool, I appraised the Webber brothers again. Sure they were big and mean looking, but so was I. I'm a big guy, like get-out-of-my-way big and at least six inches taller and with twenty pounds more muscle than those two bullies. But that didn't mean I had to get involved.

"No, I just don't care."

Draining my drink, I left the glass upside-down on the table.

Sliding off my stool, I stumbled to the bathroom to take a leak. I bumped into the door frame on the way in, and had to put a hand on the wall as I relived myself to keep my balance. I zipped up and washed my hands, trying to avoid my reflection in the mirror. It didn't work. I stared back at the hard, scared face and the light blue eyes rimmed in red. My hair had grown out a bit and was in need of a buzz. My jeans and t-shirt probably needed to find either a garbage can or a washing machine. I looked like the shit pile my life had become.

When I walked back out into the bar, it was empty. The Webber brothers and Hawaiian shirt guy had taken their disagreement elsewhere. Bertie was probably in the back grabbing more booze or on the phone.

I needed another drink, but checked my pockets and came away with only a handful of bills. There wasn't enough to pay for what I'd already had let alone any more liquor. Bertie still hadn't come out from the back. Grabbing my jacket from the stool, I snuck out the side door. I could settle up with Bertie later, but keeping the few bucks I had meant I'd be able to go somewhere else and drink.

The door exited out into an alley right beside a dumpster. The sweet rotten smell curdled my stomach. The door slammed shut behind me, and I sidestepped an old rusted bike that had been chained to the dumpster. The tires had been long since stolen, so the frame hung like a necklace from the bin.

Further down the alley was an old sofa with no cushions. It was up against the wall next to where the two Webber brothers were kicking the crap out of the Hawaiian shirt guy. Fat Sam had the guy's arms pinned as Jack punched away. The guy's head hung limp between strikes and Fat Sam was the only thing keeping the guy standing.

My fists clenched as I stood and watched. I put my fists into my pockets and turned away, heading for the street.

There was a smack of knuckles crushing flesh.

"Where's our money, Marty?"

Smack.

"You told us you'd pay last week."

Smack.

"You don't pay us and it makes us look like fools."

Smack.

"Momma told you what would happen."

Smack. Thud.

I stopped and looked back from the entrance to the alley. Hawaiian shirt guy Marty was sprawled on the ground. He was out cold. It was over.

Or it should have been.

Sam and Jack started kicking, laying their boots into the ribs and stomach. They were going to kill him.

I closed my eyes and sighed. "For fuck sakes."

They were still kicking as I walked back towards them. The guy's ribs were mush. If he took any to the head he'd be dead for sure.

I called out. "Hey, fellas, I think he's had enough."

The Webber brothers stopped and looked up in unison. Fat Sam was sweating, panting and welcomed the break. Jack wiped his face with his ball cap before putting it back on and taking a step towards me. I stopped, my hands held loosely at my sides.

"This ain't got nothing do with you," Jack said.

"Yeah, I know," I said. "Except you're going to kill him, and that's not cool."

Jack stopped five feet from me, and Fat Sam was right behind him. "That's his fault," Sam said. "He owes us money. Are you gonna pay it?"

I laughed. "Not fucking likely. How about you let him go, I take him to hospital and he gets you your money later?"

The brothers exchanged a look, grinned, and took another step towards me. "Or how about we just kick your ass right now?" Jack asked.

"Then we're going to have a problem," I said. "And it won't be pretty for you two."

They laughed and started to circle, trying to outflank me.

"You're drunk, I can smell it on you," Jack said. "You think you're tough just cause you've got a few drinks in ya?"

"Now you're just hurting my feelings."

"We're gonna mess you up, asshole," Sam barked.

I turned with them, trying to keep both in my vision. "Last chance boys, think about your Momma, and her having to push both of you in wheel chairs," I said. "First she'll push one and then stop and have to go back to get the other. It'll take her all day to get down the street."

"Shut your mouth," Sam growled.

And then Fat Sam swung.

I slipped the punch, and as he moved past I smashed my elbow into his face. I drove my heel into his knee and

6

Fat Sam went down. Jack rushed in already swinging, but I spun and his fist only glanced off my jaw. He took my left hook to his mouth. I grabbed the back of head and brought it down as I raised me knee. Once. Twice.

As Jack dropped to the ground, Sam found his feet. But two quick rights sent him down on top of his brother. Jack was fumbling to pull a knife from his pocket, but my foot to the side of his head ended that idea. The Webber brothers were finished.

Marty tried to crawl away, but only made it a few feet before falling. His Hawaiian shirt was ripped, barely clinging to him and covered in his blood. His face was an unrecognisable swollen lump.

"It's okay Marty, it's over," I told him. "I'm going to get you to the doctor."

He mumbled, but I couldn't make out the words through his swollen mouth and busted teeth. I reached down to pick him up, and help him breathe as I suspected he's got a chest full of broken ribs. There was a squawk of a siren and the alley was washed in blue and reds.

"Damn it."

A big, broad shouldered cop with a square jaw and a buzz cut stepped out of the cruiser and moved right for us. His gun out at the low ready, his eyes kept watch on us while searching the shadows. His gaze fell on the Webber brothers and the gun was raised and pointed right at me.

I raised my hands because I was drunk, not stupid.

"Don't move," he ordered. "What the hell is going on here?"

"Those two," I said, nodding to the brothers. "Were kicking the crap out of Marty here. I stopped it."

"Why would they do that?"

"His shirt is pretty ugly."

"Funny how everyone is injured except you."

"They did call me names." I shrugged. "It hurt my

feelings if that counts."

"No, it doesn't." He moved closer. His uniform was clean, pressed, and his epaulets announced he was a Patrol Sergeant. His name tag said, "Quill," and he wasn't amused. "Name?"

"Grady Fisk."

"Hello Grady, you've caused a bit of a mess here, and I'm not sure I buy your story," he said. "We're going to have to see if we can put an end to this little misunderstanding."

"How do we do that?"

"Well, you're going to turn around and put your hands behind your back, for starters." When I did, I instantly felt the cold steel of handcuffs snapping across my wrists.

That's what you get for being a good guy.

TWO

The girl slowly closed the door behind her, allowing a barely audible click as the latch caught. Crossing the room quickly, her footfalls stirred up the odours embedded in the carpet fibres.

It smelled of sex.

It reeked of perfume.

Incense failed to mask anything.

The decay began with the carpet but spread to the walls, which had long been yellowed by decades of cigars and cigarettes, except in the corners where the mould had started its slow crawl forward. The dresser leaned far to the left, and was only useful as a place for empty beer bottles. A milk crate served as a night stand next to a bed whose frame groaned in protest at the slightest movement. The lumpy, musty mattress had enough bugs living on it to overwhelm someone while they dreamt. Except, the bed wasn't for sleeping.

The blonde girl opened the closet door and pushed aside the negligees, tattered silk robes and skin tight dresses which revealed more than they hid. The stench of perfume was heaviest in the closet, and the girl reminded herself to wash her hands when she finished.

She was not in a bedroom but an office.

The small run down bungalow would never be mistaken for an office building, but it was home to many businesses just the same.

There was a crack den in the living room.

A grow op in basement.

They ran a numbers racket in the attic.

And the main floor bedrooms were used by the ladies in

the whorehouse division.

Crouching down into the closet, the girl pushed the plastic high heels out of the way and pulled off the baseboard. From a hole in the drywall she withdrew a long metal box. She opened it, checked that the money was still there with the necklace left to her from her Nana, the brooch from her Aunt and the other trinkets and keepsakes that the sixteen-year-old girl valued. She placed her cell phone with the treasures, closed the box and stuffed it back in the wall. After the baseboard was replaced, she scattered the shoes to hide her trespass. As she backed out of the closet, the door to the room opened.

The hallway light painted a halo in the woman's bleached blonde damaged hair. Her threadbare red dress was tight against her belly but loose around her sagging shoulders. Her thick make up nearly cracked as the woman took a deep drag of her cigarette. She closed the door and leaned against it, a smile found her face at seeing the girl.

"Nyah, what are you doing here?" The woman sighed. "This is no place for you."

Nyah stood and wiped her hands on her jeans. She fixed her bright blue eyes on her mother. "This is no place for you either, Delores."

"Don't start with the Delores crap, and save the sermon. We need money and that's that."

"Are you for real, Mom? Go be a housekeeper or work at McDonald's. I'll help you find something, I promise."

"It's more complicated than that." Delores sat down on the bed. The lamp highlighted the track marks on her arms. "But I don't want to talk about it now."

"We have to talk about it now, Mom, you're better than this."

Delores took another drag of her cigarette and hung her head. Tears ran through her thick mascara and streaked her cheeks. "I'm not…"

"You were." Nyah tugged on the tattered sleeve of her sweater. "If Dad was here he wouldn't let you... let you... do those things with men for money..."

"He's not here is he?" Delores rose from the bed and lit the candles on the milk crate.

"And Nyah, don't think you're going to get away without telling me what you're doing here."

"I just came to see you."

"Don't lie, I always know when you're hiding something. You know damn well your father is looking for you."

"I don't have anything to say to Vern."

"You know he doesn't like it when you call him Vern."

"I already have a Dad and it's not Vern. I can call him Douche Bag if you want."

"Why were you in his office?"

Nyah laughed. "Office? It's the spare room, and it's my house too. Besides I was just using the computer."

"Whatever, Nyah, but you really shouldn't touch his things."

"I was just downloading some music, there's no harm in that."

"You know that Vern gets angry when his private things are touched."

"I noticed." The girl held up her arm with the fresh red and purple bruise across her wrist. "If I hadn't bolted, there'd be more."

Delores walked to the closet, crossing in front of her daughter without looking at her.

Especially not at the damage done to her arm.

Not at the disgust on Nyah's face.

The disappointment.

Instead, the woman opened the closet and sifted through the dresses. She chose a silver strapless number, with a plunging neckline and lace worked around the hem.

She laid it on the bed. "Vern is under a lot of pressure."

"Are you making excuses for him? You're my mother, you should be pissed he even dared to touch me."

"Well, you did upset him..."

"You're unbelievable."

"Just tell me you didn't take anything."

"Is that prick calling me a thief?"

"You need to stop upsetting him. If you'd just learn to ..."

"Don't you even go there. You don't care about me. All you care about is your douche bag husband and sticking a needle in your arm."

Nyah rushed for the door. Her mother reached out for her, but Nyah pushed her hands away. Delores gasped, and started to say something, but Nyah slammed the door behind her as she ran out into the hallway.

THREE

Sitting on the front steps of my apartment building, the wind swirled newspapers around my feet, rotten food spilled out of the garbage bags heaped around the crumbling front steps and piss smelling puddles filled the sidewalk. Rust and grime covered the brick work, and the window sills sagged. I'd been doing serious damage to a forty of Crown Royal when a familiar black Jeep turned onto my street.

Davis Parsons parked his Jeep at the curb right in front of me and got out with a big smile on his acne scarred face like he and I were old friends. We weren't. Still, I let him sit down beside me and even passed him my bottle. He downed a quarter of it before handing it back.

"Suppose you're wondering why I stopped by," he said.

"Figured you'd get to it."

"Not working tonight?"

I checked my watch. I was two hours late for my bartending shift at The Red River Pub. Everyone calls it The Rub. "I still might stop by."

"You know, after I bailed you out I waited outside the jail like an idiot for over an hour. Now that I've found you, let's go upstairs to your place so we can speak in private."

"I didn't have reason to talk then and I sure as hell don't now." I took a deep pull of the whisky. "So why walk up all those stairs when I can tell you to fuck off fine right here?"

"This is the thanks I get? I spend my good money to bail you out after you kick the shit out of two guys ..."

"We both know your money is dirty as shit. You want me to say thank you? Then, thanks, but I don't owe you anything."

"Grady, this is serious. I really need to get in touch with your brother."

"Reece?" I took another drink. "Why?"

"I sent him on a job and he should have been back hours ago."

"Not my problem."

"I need your help. It's a big job and dangerous people are expecting results."

"You're talking to the wrong guy. I'm no thief."

"I'm not either."

"No, you just get idiots like my brother to do the dirty work for you."

"You're not worried?"

"I'm not. He's probably just passed out somewhere with a needle in his arm. You're a dumbass for sending him on a job alone."

"I don't think so," he said and stood. He reached into his coat pocket, pulled out a slip of paper and dropped it into my lap. "Here's the address. Do what you want."

I had no intention of touching that address as I watched Davis drive off. I sipped from my bottle, trying to concentrate on the beautiful liquid warming my belly. It was no good. The paper felt heavy on my lap.

The front door opened behind me. I didn't turn around; I knew my wife looked beautiful.

"Have you come to say sorry?"

She snorted. "It wasn't me who got arrested, Grady."

"For not bailing me out."

"Call me crazy, honey, but it doesn't look like you're in a cell."

"You're unbelievable." I swallowed a mouthful of rye. "Part of the deal is as my wife, you're supposed to be there for me."

"I guess that rule doesn't apply to husbands." A long, heavy moment of silence floated between us. "What are you going to do about Reece?"

"You were eavesdropping""

"I came down to tell you I was going to my father's."

"Figures."

"Reece is your brother. Go get him Grady, no one else will."

"Everyone else has figured out he's a waste."

"Fine, maybe I should have bailed you out, but I was just so mad at you. Happy?"

"Just so you know, all I did was help some poor sap that was getting his ass kicked. I saved his life and now you're mad at me and the judge gives me six months probation. No one said thanks."

"You want a medal for putting two bullies in a coma? How about explaining why you were at the bar in the first place?"

I shook my head. "When are you going to realise getting mad at me is a waste, it doesn't change anything."

"Loving you doesn't work miracles either, but it doesn't mean I'm about to stop doing that."

"Love? I love you too, Marin, but it doesn't fix what's broken."

"Maybe that because it's not me you need to love." She sighed. "I thought maybe if I didn't come this time you'd smarten up."

I sat there, turning the bottle over in my hands. "I can't change, and neither can Reece."

"The difference between you two is I knew you'd make out all right."

"And I did."

"Can you say the same for Reece? Can you say you won't find him dead in some ditch?"

I answered with silence.

"Just go get your brother," she said and slammed the door.

I waited until I was sure Marin was gone before I picked up the slip of paper. I had some pride. My first instinct was to crumple up the address, toss it on the ground and piss on it. Instead, I stumbled over to my rusted out Chevy Bel Air and drove off.

The address was for a house on Magnus Avenue just off of McPhillips. It wasn't Winnipeg's worst neighbourhood but it was right next door to it.

I stared up at the small red brick house. All was quiet, the street was empty and it was dark inside. I heard no music and saw no one moving around. I hadn't come upon a gang war, spontaneous civil uprising or any of the chaos Reece usually incited.

It looked like Davis had seriously overestimated the amount of trouble Reece was in.

I checked the piece of paper, and the address was right. As I knocked on the front door, I wondered if I should have brought the tire iron from the Chevy's trunk, if only to smack Reece with it. No one answered. I turned the knob and the door swung open.

"I wouldn't go in there if I were you," a voice said behind me.

I looked back, a girl stood on the path behind me. She looked around sixteen, seventeen tops. Her eyes were bright blue, and they didn't look the least bit intimidated by me. She tucked her thin blonde hair behind her ear and waited.

"Thanks, but you're not me," I said.

"Obviously." She clicked her tongue. "I'm also not the one who pays women for sex."

"That's an odd statement from out of nowhere."

"You're standing outside a whore house."

"Whoa, I'm not like that."

"Sure, none of you are."

I descended from the front porch back down to the path, stopping a few feet from her. "Listen, I'm here to get my bother and then leave. That's it."

"Really? Your brother? Who's he?"

"One of the degenerates you just described."

"Oh, well, then just tell him what I told you."

"I have. Many times. It never works." I held out my hand. "My name is Grady Fisk."

She looked at my hand but didn't move. "I'm Nyah."

I dropped my hand. "Well, Nyah, you heard my story, what are you doing here?"

"I'm waiting for my mom. She doesn't listen either."

"What's she doing here?" The look she gave me made me want to crawl into a sewer. "Sorry. Fuck, I'm an idiot."

Just to get her eyes off me, I turned and climbed the front steps. I put my hand on the door knob and turned around to throw out another apology. She was gone.

FOUR

I waited for the monsters to jump out of the shadows. None did. I braced for the gunshots and ear splitting screams. There were none. I crossed the threshold and the smell hit me like a slap. Empty beer cans, take out containers and milk cartons lined the hallway and the carpet was soggy under my shoes.

Two bums, with half-drunk beer bottles in their laps, slumped against the wall. I stepped over their splayed legs and towards the first doorway on the left. It led to the living room. The greenish light from the TV illuminated a young couple with tattoos covering almost every inch of their visible skin. Their eyes were black and dulled by a billowy cloud of crack. His pants were around his ankles and her dress hiked up above her waist as she rode him with skill but no passion. The man offered me his crack pipe. The girl offered me a blowjob if I had any drugs to share. I refused them both and moved on.

On the floor of the first bedroom, a business suit was neatly folded next to a pink fringed dress. A heavily made up hooker had her legs high in the air as a red faced pot bellied sales rep pumped away. I walked in on an older hooker in a silver strapless dress, the next room over. She and some biker whose huge arms and massive shoulders were covered in tattoos that screamed jailhouse were just getting started.

He threw a boot at me and told me to go fuck myself. The lady told me to wait in the hallway like a good boy and I'd have my turn.

I closed the door and a girl, not much older than Nyah, stood beside me. She told me I didn't have to wait, pulled on my belt, leading me towards the shadows. She scurried off when I told her there was crack in the front room.

Down the hall, I found a man passed out on a bed, his sleeve still rolled up and his necktie wrapped around his arm. His beard was long and shaggy, and his suit might have fit him forty pounds and a million needles ago. He was the source of the smell, which he couldn't have made worse even by shitting himself.

A second man lounged on a couch; drool seeped out of the corners of his mouth. His thick black sweater and rumpled khakis were stained. His shoe laces were untied, his hair was greasy and plastered to his skull.

I looked at him and tried to see the little brother I used to play Lego with. Where was the kid who chewed his nails when he was nervous? Reece had killed that kid with heroin, crack, and any other poison he could cram into his body. Now he only chewed his nails when he needed a fix.

My brother was fixated on the pretty blonde hooker in the miniskirt and halter top beside him cutting lines of coke on a mirror nestled in her lap.

Reece looked up and saw me in the doorway. He stretched, a sleepy smile rose to his face. "Hey, Grady, what's shaking, man?"

I made eye contact with the girl. "Beat it, honey."

"I'm not going anywhere until I have mine," she said.

"He doesn't care, Emma," Reece said. "Ain't that right, Grady?"

I smiled. "Emma, consider me kicking you out the best favour anyone ever did you."

She turned her big blue eyes to Reece. "This guy a cop?"

"No, he's my brother."

"Go join the couple down the hall," I told her. "I'm sure they'll cut you in."

"Jenny? Hell no." Emma laughed. "That bitch got the alphabet."

"What?"

"HIV, HEP C, HPV," she said, ticking each one off on her fingers.

"You keep this up you'll join her."

Emma pouted, bent over and snorted one line after another, even as my brother moaned, "Hey, bitch you ain't leaving me any?"

"It's what you deserve for being a drag," she said, tossed the mirror on the floor and strutted out of the room, all the right parts swaying.

"Why did you have to do that?" Reece whined.

"Davis said you were in trouble."

"There's no trouble, I'm having a beautiful time, man."

"I see that, but now it's time to go"

"Can't go, bro. The job's not done, man."

"What exactly has Davis got you doing?"

"He didn't tell you? No, I guess he wouldn't have." Reece stood up and stretched. "He said it would be easy, but it ain't. The whole deal is ..."

I held up my hand and cut him off. "Really, I don't care. We're leaving. Now. I'll drag you out if I have to."

Reece sorted through the beer bottles on the floor, but they were empty. He looked over at the bum passed out on the chair, who still hadn't roused. "Okay, man, we'll leave with you."

"We? There's no fucking we."

"Yeah, this guy's gotta come with us, he's part of the job, man."

"What are you talking about?"

"This dude's got some info for Jacob."

The man let out a groan, leaned over the arm of his chair and barfed on the floor. My brother and I jumped back to avoid the splatter.

"What could he possibly have to say?"

"Just a name, that's all. When we get it, we take her and

be gone."

"Her? What her?"

Reece leaned down and slapped Watson. "Okay, man, you had your good time, now tell me the girl's name."

Watson burped. "I know lotsa girls."

"Seriously, dude, you don't want Davis to come down here, man." Reece slapped him again. "Tell me about the girl, asshole."

"The place is full of girls, it's a whore house," I said.

"This is serious, Grady, Davis is counting on me for this."

"I don't care."

"Listen, one of the girls here has got something Davis wants. I've got to get it before she does something stupid." He scratched his head. "Actually, I thought it was Emma ..."

"And you were going to fuck it out of her?"

Reece opened his mouth to answer but stopped, his eyes locked to something over my shoulder. I turned around to find a man and a woman in the doorway. The guy wasn't much over five feet tall, with blonde hair gelled and spiked in a hundred different directions. The lady was a stunner with long, wild red hair and a painted on black pantsuit that gave us a great view of her boobs.

The guy marched up to me, a right arrogant look plastered to his face. "Where the fuck is Delores?"

"How the fuck should I know?" I asked. "Do I look like a Delores to you?"

"Do you know who I am?"

"Let me guess, she's a hooker and you're the pimp."

His face went crimson. "Don't ever talk to Franny like that."

"A hooker? Seriously?" Reece said.

Franny shook her head. "I'm not on the game."

I shrugged. "Whatever, then he's the hooker and you're the pimp, lady, I'm not here to judge."

She laughed. "You think Shamus is a prostitute? Oh, that's funny."

"Yeah, you're a real fucking clown," Shamus snapped. "Now beat it or you'll end up in the middle of something you don't want to be."

"Listen, buddy, I'm grabbing my brother and getting the hell out of here. After that I don't care what you do."

Shamus jabbed his finger into my chest. "No one goes anywhere until I talk to Delores."

I looked down at his finger, still touching my chest. "Move the hand or lose it."

"You ain't got the balls."

Maybe his ego blinded him, or he'd contracted some weird genetic thing that messed with his perception, because easily I was a foot and a half taller and a hundred pounds heavier than Shamus.

I also don't like people touching me. I get that from my father. The round puckered scars on my arms, legs and back are from his cigarettes. The thick ropey scar above my left eye was from a belt buckle that was meant for Reece.

So I dropped him. One punch. I caught Shamus right on the jaw and the pretty boy crumpled to the carpet.

Franny screamed and lunged at me, her long fingernails aimed right for my eyes. I grabbed her by the wrists and flipped her harmlessly onto the couch. Shamus staggered to his feet and pulled a gun out of his waistband. He levelled the Glock at my brother.

I backed away, keeping myself between the gun and the two addicts. "Easy buddy, just calm down," I said. "We can talk this out."

"I'll fucking kill you," Shamus screamed. "You fucking suckered me."

"You put your hands on me first. Let's call it even."

"Sure, after I put a bullet in your head."

"Just kill the bastards, Shamus," Franny shrieked.

23

Beads of sweat tracked down from Shamus forehead and over the swelling that was growing on his face. The barrel of the gun swivelled back and forth between me and my brother. When the gun tracked towards Reece I grabbed Shamus' arm with both my hands and turned it away from us.

Shamus squeezed his hand to pull back and the gun went off. Watson's head exploded. Blood painted the wall behind him and his body crumpled onto the carpet. Two more shots slammed into the ceiling as I wrestled with Shamus. I pushed him back, swept his legs with my foot and we both toppled onto the floor.

I heard a click over my left ear, and out of the corner of my eye I caught the barrel of a Colt .45. Reece was holding a gun and it was aimed right at Shamus' head.

"Stop it, Shamus, and drop the gun," Reece ordered.

I stole a glance at my brother. "Where the fuck did you ..."

Franny wasn't intimidated. She jumped on my back and tried to grab my hair, but I keep it short. She went for my eyes next and I was now wrestling her and Shamus.

Reece fired. The gun bucked in his hands and his eyes went wide with surprise. He grazed Franny in the shoulder, and she spun off me. Blood sprayed my face as Franny wailed in pain.

I screamed at Reece to stop shooting and Shamus brought his knee up, sending my testicles rocketing into my stomach. Stars filled my eyes. I rolled off and puked on the carpet.

Shamus fired, the bullet sung as it whizzed past, splintering the doorframe. I scrambled to my feet, hands cupping my boys, and stumbled into the hallway. Reece followed, firing back at Shamus who charged down the hallway after us. Bullets flew everywhere and the drywall was shredded.

The biker stormed out of his room. He was naked and

pissed off. I dragged Reece with me as I slammed into the biker and drove past him. The biker crashed into the wall, turned to take a swing at me when a bullet tore through his neck. He pitched forward, blood spurting onto the floor.

Shamus sprayed us with bullets as I bowled over the old hooker. We tumbled into her room, her legs and arms intertwined with mine and Reece's. I stood, pulling myself free from the human web. When Reece got up his shirt was covered in blood. The prostitute's dress was around her waist. In the middle of her chest was a big bloody hole. Reece did a frantic search of himself but none of the blood was his.

I knelt beside the woman. Fear filled her eyes. I pulled her dress up and held it over the wound. Warm blood seeped through my fingers. Her mouth worked, but no words came out.

"Save your strength," I said softly. "We'll get you help."

She tried to smile, but there was no helping her. The light in her eyes grew dim and her skin turned to grey.

"You okay brother?" Reece asked.

"Just fucking peachy. What the fuck is going on?"

"I told you it was a big mess, man. Davis needs Watson's help."

"He doesn't have a face. He won't be helping you with shit."

Gunfire lit up the hallway once more. Reece rushed to the doorway to return fire just as a blonde haired streak flew into the room. Reece stuck his arm out, pumping off shots. Nyah stood over me and stared down, her eyes wide with fright. All her toughness was gone; she looked every bit the scared little girl.

"You need to get out of here, Nyah," I said as the fire fight continued.

"What did you do to my Mom?"

"Your what?" I looked down at the lifeless woman in my

arms. "Your Mom? I'm sorry, she took a bullet. It was..."

"You shot her?" Nyah pushed me and I fell meekly back on my ass. She cradled the woman, kissing her cheeks. "You shot her? What's wrong with you people?"

"It wasn't us. It was an accident, this maniac was firing and she got hit by mistake."

Nyah had stopped listening. She knelt over her mother, trying with all she had to breathe life back into the one who'd birthed her. As Nyah pushed air into her, bubbles rippled in the woman's wound. I didn't have the heart to tell her it was useless.

I went over to Reece and ducked down behind him. Shamus and Franny were both firing at us, keeping us pinned down. Over Reece's shoulder I peeked out into the hallway. I gazed into the dirty faces of the tattooed couple peeking out of their doorway across from us. The guy was still holding his crack pipe. Their eyes were bright and faces masked in horror as they watched the blood spread from the woman onto the carpet. The girl grabbed her boyfriend and dragged him back into the safety of the dark room.

Down the hallway, Franny laid cover as Shamus inched his way towards us. I took the gun from my brother and he slunk back into the room and sat on the floor between me and Nyah, not wanting to be too close to either.

Sirens emerged in the distance.

"Hear that, Shamus?" I called out. "The cops are coming, what are we going to do?"

"I'm going to kill you fuckers," Shamus screamed.

"I don't even know you. Let's all just get the hell out of here."

"You can tell Davis he's dead too. I'm going to kill every fucking one of you."

Reece rocked back and forth on his knees, his face buried in his hands. "Grady, we're so fucked, man."

"I got no time for your shit, Reece." I poked my head

out the doorway. "Shamus, be fucking smart. Let's all just go before the cops get here."

"Fuck the cops," Shamus spat. "I'll kill them too."

I dove back into the room as Franny put three bullets a foot over my head. "Reece, we're either dead or arrested if we stay, so we only got one choice." My brother was already nodding in agreement. "Get ready to run when I say so."

I bent over the girl, and pulled her hands off her dead mother. Nyah was covered in blood, and her eyes were wild and full of tears. I hugged her, and she buried her face in my chest. "This is a shitty thing, Nyah," I said. "But we can't stay here. In ten seconds, when I make my move, you have to run out of here and make for the front door. You don't stop running, got it?"

Nyah shook her head, and reached down for her mother.

"You can't do anything for her now," I said. "But she'd want you to get out of here alive. Right?"

The girl nodded.

I kissed her forehead and then hunkered down behind the door. My brother grabbed Nyah's hand and pulled her to a crouch behind me. I felt their breath on my neck as I whispered the countdown. At ten, I rushed to the hallway and fired wildly. Shamus and Franny ducked down as the lead filled the air. Reece and Nyah broke for the door and I squeezed that trigger until the clip was empty.

Dropping the gun, I spun on my heels and bore down, pushing for all I was worth. I was halfway to the door before Shamus and Franny started to return fire. Pieces of drywall and ceiling exploded around me as I rushed through the front door and out onto the porch. A cop stood there, looking back to where my brother and Nyah, both blood soaked, had just ran past him. For a moment, the officer and I locked eyes, his hand still reaching for the doorbell.

Quill?

What the Hell was he doing there?

Quill, too surprised to defend himself, ate my punch. He stumbled back, and I drilled him with an uppercut that left him splayed out cold on the front lawn.

I caught up to Reece a block away. He was bent over, wheezing with phlegm dripping down his chin. "Girl... Gone... Too... Fast..." he sputtered.

I grabbed Reece by the arm and pulled him along. "We gotta keep moving, no idea where Shamus or those cops are."

Reece and I sprinted to my car, hopped in and sped away. We made it a block and a half before we ran out of gas. We left the Chevy parked in an alley and ran off. We caught a cab two streets over, hopped in and threw whatever cash we had at the driver. We told him to take us to the nearest bar. I needed a drink.

FIVE

The tears blurred her vision, turning the city into a kaleidoscope of traffic lights, neon signs and passing cars. Nyah ran, the stones and heaved concrete stabbing at her feet through the thin soles of her second hand sneakers. Her lungs burned and legs were numb. She pushed past it, creating as much distance as she could from that house.

From the men with the guns.

From the bullets.

From her mother's corpse.

From the blood.

Oh my God all that blood.

Nyah ran on, still soaked in her mother's blood. She smelled it, and her sweater stuck to her, heavy with it. Her legs finally gave way, and she swerved off the sidewalk and ducked down in some big, leafy bushes at the edge of a property that had fallen into disrepair. Nyah sat down, bringing her knees up to her chin and hugged herself. Struggling to process what had become of her world, Nyah's brain throbbed as it spun inside her head, her equilibrium had been ripped away.

Delores had been her last link to happiness. The last person who had known Nyah when she had been allowed to be a kid, to laugh, have fun and play with toys.

Her mother can't be dead. First her Dad, and now her mother, both gone, both snatched away through violence. Bullets and crazed gunmen had taken away her parents, and now Nyah was an orphan. What was she going to do? Who was she now? She had no parents, no one to watch over her. No one to love her or protect her. Nyah had lost everything. She cried so hard she lost her breath.

Nyah shook her head. She needed to focus. Crying wasn't going to solve anything, and Nyah was sure there'd be more tears to come so there was no point wasting them all now. If she stayed there too long they'd find her and she'd be seeing her parents sooner than she was ready for.

Taking off her sweater, Nyah was careful to avoid letting the blood touch her face. She tossed it on the ground and covered it with dirt and leaves. She stood and brushed off her pants and wiped her hands. The autumn winds picked up and the cold knifed right through her. Nyah shivered, her skin rippling into goose bumps.

Stepping forward, Nyah spread the branches with her hands and peeked out into the sidewalk. In a blur, two figures rushed past before stopping not more than five feet from her. It was the two from the house, the short man with the gelled hair and the redhead with the pretty face. Shamus was hunched over, breathing deeply through his mouth. Nyah guessed his nose had been broken. The lady was breathing hard too, her breasts threatening to pop out of her shirt. Nyah was impressed she'd kept up in those heels.

Dropping to her knees, Nyah inched backward from the bush. She held her breath, worried they'd hear her heart hammering at her ribs. Nyah forced herself to remain motionless and listened while she searched the abandoned yard for escape.

"Are you sure she ran this way?" Franny asked Shamus.

"For fuck sakes, how did we lose a fucking kid?" Shamus wheezed.

"Do you think she was the one?"

"All I know is the bitch we need is some dirty hooker. It could have been any of them."

"You sure it was one of the girls?"

"My guy said she was supposed to be there."

"Well, we lost this one."

"We lost them all. They just fucking scattered. If I find

that asshole who suckered me, I'm gonna fucking kill him."

"Focus on the big picture Shamus, that guy can wait. Do you think we can track them all down?"

"We have to. If not, we're done."

Shamus and Franny gathered themselves and ran off down the sidewalk. Nyah only exhaled when she no longer heard their footsteps. She was shaking. Why were they looking for her? What did they want with any of the girls? Had they come looking for her mother? Was this all because of what she had done? Nyah felt more lost with every question. Visions of her mom, bloody and ruined pushed themselves back to the surface. With effort, Nyah fought back and stuffed them back to her subconscious, no doubt to return late at night among the shadows.

Grady had been right, she couldn't fix any of that now.

She'd made a decision, and she had to keep on track. Nothing changed. In fact her choice now felt more right than ever. Nyah had too much taken from her, now it was time for her to take back. People were going to pay, because someone just had to.

But first, she needed her phone.

Slowly, sticking to shadows and side streets, Nyah picked her way back to the house. She ducked behind parked cars and hid behind trees whenever she heard a car or footsteps. Each time sure that Shamus and Franny had found her. Nyah had a dozen panic attacks in a two-mile trip.

Nyah stopped a block from the house. It made her skin crawl, it was some sort of monster that slowly sucked the life out of her mother. As though the house were alive and fed off the souls of those forced to sell their bodies. The house had finally devoured her mother whole.

There were a dozen cop cars parked outside. Officers in uniform and detectives in suits milled about on the front lawn. An ambulance was parked further down the street, but it was in no rush. Everyone left inside the house was dead. No doctor was saving anyone.

No doubt those cops were going to tear the house apart. The last thing she needed was for them to find her phone; she couldn't trust anyone, the cops least of all.

Nyah turned down a side street and approached the house from the back. She slipped through a hole in the neighbour's fence, and cut across the lawn until she was standing in the backyard of the small bricked house. She'd come that way often when she was avoiding Vern but still needed to see her mother. The back yard was the final resting place of a rusted out pickup, and Nyah hid behind it, watching the house until she was sure no cop was lurking around. She rushed for the hedge that grew wild and untamed by the basement window. She jimmied the lock and slipped into the basement quickly and quietly.

From the furnace room, Nyah made her way up the stairs slowly, careful to avoid the third last stair that always creaked. Nudging the door open just a crack, Nyah scanned the hallway. Her stomach lurched into her throat, the hallway looked like it had been hosed down in blood. Splatters of crimson rose up from the carpet and even painted the ceiling. The biker's body still lay right where it had dropped, and a tech in a white hazmat suit knelt over it, a black bag full of test tube and other gear on the floor beside him. Others in similar garb, dusted the walls for prints, took samples from the blood and moved around like a swarm of albino bees. If they weren't enough of a deterrent, a cop stood in the doorway, guarding the entrance.

There would be no sneaking past them to grab her phone. Her only hope was that they'd have no reason to give the closet more than a cursory glance. She was going to have to come back later when they'd finished. But even then, people were looking for her.

The phone was no more than twenty feet away, and to Nyah it might as well been at the bottom of the ocean.

Nyah carefully let the door shut and backed slowly down the stairs and slipped out of the house. She hurried out the backyard and down the back lane. Nyah found a tree house in the backyard near the end of the street, climbed the rope ladder and curled up inside. A kid had left some blankets and stuffed animals, and they were soft enough that she couldn't help but lean her head back.

She hadn't planned to sleep, only rest her eyes, but when she came to, it was dark outside. Nyah climbed back out and took to the sidewalk, headed for who knew where. Home? What if Franny and that slimy Shamus knew to look there? What if Vern was there, and now she didn't even have her mother for a buffer. Nyah wrapped her arms tighter around herself, freezing in her t-shirt. Where was she going to go? Her friends had disappeared not long after her Dad died and her Mom had taken to drugs for comfort.

She had no phone.

No money.

No family.

No friends.

And fuck Vern.

The only person who'd been any help to her at all in months had been Grady Fisk. She believed him when he said he hadn't killed her mother, if he had he wouldn't have saved her. He was obviously no friends with Shamus either, and no one liked Vern. Grady wasn't obligated, but he made sure Nyah got out safe.

She knew that she was grasping, but it was the only connection she had, and she couldn't think with her mind such a complete mess. Grady didn't belong at that house, he wasn't one of them, which is why Nyah had to talk to him. At worst, it looked like he was on the same side. Grady was her best chance for help because he was her only chance.

Sometimes that was enough.

Now she just had to find him. Nyah prayed he hadn't lied about his name. It wasn't much but it was more than she'd had five minutes before.

SIX

When the cops busted into my apartment, I was still shit-faced. My wife hadn't been gone for a day and the place was already a disaster. I found her note on the coffee table when I stumbled in.

Reece and I closed down the bar the night before, trying to blur the images of dead bullet ridden bodies with whisky. I drank enough to forget my name, but the booze couldn't dull the sight of Nyah holding her mother in a pool of blood with half her chest missing.

The cops found me passed out on the couch surrounded by drained bottles of rye and empty cans of beer. Pizza boxes and fast food wrappers spilled off the coffee table onto the floor. I wasn't any more presentable with dried vomit covering the front of my shirt. They cuffed me, took me downtown and launched me into a holding cell. I was arrested for the murder of Harris Watson.

The couch was not an inspired place to hide. Winnipeg is a big city and I hid on my couch. Being such a criminal mastermind it's a wonder the cops ever found me. Maybe it was the snoring.

I sat on a steel bench, gripping it so hard my knuckles went white, just to keep the room from spinning. My shirt was stuck to me with sweat and I wouldn't open my mouth for fear I'd hurl. The voices in my head were screaming.

Sobering up sucks.

Two straight days in lock up would be added to the pile of reasons my wife hates me. As my father-in-law is a retired cop, it'll be the reason he wishes I was dead.

The drunk tank was always full of colourful people and usually entertaining. Sometimes we'd even sing, mostly to annoy the cops. That cell wasn't as fun as the drunk tank.

However, it was a carnival of laughs compared to the Detention Barracks back when I was in the army. Punching that MP got me six months in the Detention Barracks before they kicked me out. That was hard time. You marched, cleaned and got yelled at from the moment you woke up until you passed out from exhaustion. Everyone knows how tough basic training is on a new recruit, but the DB made that look like a wet dream. There were only three or four guys locked up there at a time with a dozen MP's on duty to abuse and humiliate you. The fact that I was there for kicking the crap out of one of their own garnered me more personal attention.

You'd think I'd learn.

Two cops cracked my cell door and twisted up my arms in some kung fu grip. My left arm was behind my back up by my ear and they tried to wring water out of my right. I left the cell on my tip toes.

They marched me down a hallway, as my guts churned hard. I made the mistake of opening my mouth to warn them and ended up painting the cop's shoes in last night's meal.

The fists flew and my headache got worse. The swelling closed my left eye.

Paint was peeling from the ceiling of the interrogation room where a naked bulb hung, giving off a harsh light. A mirror took up an entire wall. I'd seen enough movies to know there were detectives watching from the other side. The table in the middle of the room was bolted to the floor. I was handcuffed to a chair and left.

My brother was chained to the chair beside me.

Reece smelled like he'd been fished out of a sewer, which was a more imaginative hiding place than my couch. His cheeks were wet from crying and Reece begged. "Please man, I can't do this. I can't go to prison."

"We'll walk if you don't say anything stupid."

"We got no alibi, man. Big, hairy, bastards will be making me their girlfriend, man."

"They have nothing, just keep your mouth shut."

"Oh fuck. My gun. I don't even know where it is, man. The cops must have it and ..."

"Reece shut up..."

"We were so stupid, Grady. I didn't mean to shoo..."

I kicked him in the shin. "Shut the fuck up! The cops aren't even in the room and you're fucking confessing."

"But..."

"We have no idea what happened, Reece. That's your fucking alibi."

"Sorry, man, I gotcha."

"I need you to say it, Reece."

"Sure, man. Just like you said, I don't know what they're talking about. My head gets kinda whacked out sometimes." He licked his lips. "We ain't done ..."

The door opened and Reece's denial died in his throat.

A tall detective walked in. Thin with short red hair, he had a thick ugly scar on his lip. "I'm Detective Rogan, my partner, Jian will be right in. Let's not fuck around here; you two are in a lot of trouble."

I snorted. "We hadn't noticed. No wonder you made detective."

Another cop, a shorter Asian guy stormed in. He was a walking ball of muscle with no neck to speak of and forearms the size of man's thighs. I guessed he was Detective Jian.

He dropped a thick file on the table. "I miss anything?"

Rogan pointed at me. "I was just about to smack the lips off his face for trying to be funny."

"I was just making an observation," I said.

"Is that so?" Jian asked. "You seem pretty comfortable for a guy who's been arrested for murder. Aside from a few fines for being intoxicated in public, you've got a clean record, Grady. I'd have thought you'd be pissing your pants right now."

"Easy to be comfortable when you're innocent."

"Oh that's right, you're the tough soldier boy, right? Bet you think killing is nothing new, like it's your right."

"Only a moron would think you ever learn to like killing."

Jian kept talking like he hadn't heard me. "Your brother, Reece here is another story. He's been arrested five times for breaking and entering and four times for possession with intent to traffic. Odd thing is he's not done a minute of jail time. How can that be?"

"I'm just lucky, man," Reece said.

"Smells like a rat to me," Rogan said. "Worried your brother might roll on you, Grady?"

"We're family, that won't happen," I assured him. "Besides, we didn't do anything wrong."

"Your family isn't something to brag about." Jian flipped through the file. "There isn't a cop here who hasn't arrested Fergus Fisk for something. He's spent twenty years of his life in prison, so I'm surprised he had time to father you two. He did eight years for attempted murder, six years for armed robbery, three for fraud, two years for home invasion and one for aggravated assault."

"I don't need you to tell me my father was an asshole," I said.

Jian closed the file. "Where is dear old Dad now, boys?"

"Dead," I said.

"Oh, so sad to hear," Rogan sneered.

"It wouldn't be if you knew him."

"Looks like you're both following in his footsteps," Jian said. "If either of you give me anything less than a full confession, you'll both do a life bit."

Reece moaned. "Fuck, Grady, we're done, man."

"If they had anything on us they wouldn't be threatening us, we'd already be getting charged. These two are lucky they found the room."

Jian waggled his finger. "Watch your mouth or you'll lose teeth."

"Not now junior, the adults are talking."

Jian's slap almost unhinged my jaw. Those muscles weren't for show.

Rogan grabbed my throat. "Tell us another joke, Grady, and you'll get more of the same."

"Are you two dating?" I asked.

Rogan's first punch caught my ear and the next two almost put me out. My brain rattled around like a pinball.

Reece screamed. "Grady, I can't watch this, man. They're gonna kill you."

Rogan straightened his tie. "Keep up the lip and it'll only get worse."

I didn't see how. I was about to move into an eight by ten room with bars for curtains. What could they do, cancel Christmas?

Jian reopened the file. "Where were you last night?"

"At home, drunk."

"Can you corroborate that?"

"There's puke on my damn shirt."

Rogan drove his fist into my stomach. It felt like he reached my spine. "Feel like answering that again smart guy?"

"You going to keep asking stupid questions?" I croaked.

Tears rolled down Reece's face. "Please, man, just leave us alone."

Jian moved in. "Tell us what we want to hear, Grady, or this goes to a whole new bloody level."

He drove his heel down on my foot. The pain shot up to my balls. "We ain't done shit," I hissed.

"Then let me tell you a story," Rogan said. "Last night

you went to Harris Watson's house to rob him, he resisted so you killed him. On your way out you shot the place all to hell and killed one of his whores, Delores Tynes, and her john, wannabe biker Max Jackson to eliminate the witnesses. Luckily most of the other girls managed to escape. Regardless, we have three corpses resting in the morgue and you two put them there."

"It sounds like you're making this up as you go."

Jian poked me in the chest. "Do you think this is a joke?"

I shrugged. "Kinda."

"Do you think it'll be so funny once they have you up in Stony Mountain and your cell mate is pimping you out to all his buddies?"

Reece gasped. "Please, no, I can't do that. Please. I'll tell, man. I'll tell..."

"Reece, you fool, shut up," I snapped.

"Tell us what?" Jian demanded.

"Reece, don't say a word," I said. "They don't have shit for evidence. They're praying they can either beat a confession out of us or cut some shit deal."

Rogan flipped through our file. "We have plenty. We have a statement from a Miss Emma James who says she left you both with Mr. Watson not more than a half hour before he was killed. We have testimony from two of Watson's girls, a Sara Silo, who might I say is too ugly to be paid for sex, and a Tammy Smalls who is too young to be doing it either." He shook his head. "Anyway, they both swear they saw two men fitting your description running out of Watson's home right after they heard gunshots. The statements we took from Jenny and Mark Brooks put you in the house when Watson was shot and standing over the dead bodies. You also assaulted a cop as you made your escape." He tossed the statements in front of me. "A fucking cop, Grady? How dumb are you?"

He didn't wait for an answer.

"Harris Watson was shot twice in the face," Rogan said, holding up Watson's morgue photo. "Delores Tynes had a hole punched right through her chest, and we pulled twelve bullets out of Max Jackson's body." Rogan added more photos to the pile. And we have the gun."

"It was found in the stairwell of Reece's apartment building," Jian added. "Ballistics says it's the same Colt .45 that fired the bullets we pulled out of the walls at the house."

"Was it used to kill Watson?" I asked. "Does it even have our finger prints?"

"Do you want to talk fingerprints?" Jian asked. "We pulled over a hundred prints out of Watson's house that belonged to Reece. So we have the gun, witnesses and we have your fucking fingerprints, all which add up to a life in prison without parole."

"How do you explain all that, Grady?" Rogan demanded.

I couldn't. The words and weight of the evidence hung in the air. Eventually they'd drop like a guillotine, with my neck on the block.

"You know, Grady, we also received reports that you are in business with Jacob Poole," Jian said.

"I know him, if that's what you're asking," I said.

"So you're just friends with the biggest drug dealer in Winnipeg?" Rogan asked.

"I doubt he'd call us friends."

"Major Crimes told us that you owe him almost fifty thousand dollars." Jian pointed at Reece. "I thought he was the addict."

"He is," I said.

"Then how do you owe Jacob Poole money?"

"None of your business."

"Are you paying Reece's debts? That's mighty nice of you."

"My wife doesn't think so."

"This is all starting to make sense to me." Jian leaned against the table. "Watson was a known drug dealer and Reece owed him money. Rather than pay off another debt for your low life brother, you killed him."

"Watson looked like a user not a dealer."

"I didn't say he was good at it, but it's the only scenario that makes sense."

"Of course it would, you're not very bright."

Rogan grabbed me by the shirt, pulling me forward so his face inches from mine. "You killed him, asshole, just say it."

"I didn't kill him, I didn't touch the gun." I turned and spit on the floor. "You got the wrong guy."

Jian smirked. "So then you're saying it was Reece."

I opened my mouth to tell Jian to go fuck his hat, but my brother spoke first.

"Enough of this shit, man." Reece shook the hair from his face. "I'll talk, man. I gotta end this."

A slimy grin slithered onto Rogan's face and he released me. "How nice."

"No, Reece, keep your mouth shut," I told him.

"I think I want to hear what Reece has to say," Jian said.

"What are you playing at, Reece?" I demanded.

"I'm so tired, man. I want this shit to be over." Reece hung his head, his eyes glued to his untied shoes. "We talk now and maybe we keep our bit short."

"Don't admit to anything, Reece. Let's get a lawyer first. Don't do this."

"I'm not admitting to nothing, man."

It felt like he'd just slapped me. "You mean you'll rat me out and save yourself. At least be man enough to say it."

Reece said nothing. That told me everything.

The addict wouldn't look at me as the cops led him out. I winced as the door slammed shut behind them.

Insanity circled me, gradually and steadily building momentum. Voices screamed in my head, and there was no way to quiet them.

The cuffs dug into my wrists, like razors, biting and slicing my skin. My guts churned and my bones ached from the need to drink. The chair was hard and unforgiving, causing bolts of pain to shoot up my back. The room stunk. The lights were too bright. A migraine exploded behind my eyes, like someone had stabbed me there with an ice pick.

Reece was across the hall lying his rat face off, blaming me for everything. But jail was not an option for me. Five years, ten years, it wouldn't matter. There would be no place in this world for me to come back to. Marin wouldn't believe me when I told her I was innocent. She knows how well I lie.

The voices in my head, screaming my fears, grew louder and louder.

The door opened and Jian walked in, crashing my pity party. "Your brother says the most interesting things. My ears are actually getting tired, Reece just goes on and on."

"What the fuck do you want?"

"Hey, relax. The tough soldier routine is impressive, but while you're in here being cool, Reece is telling us how you killed three people. You need to get in front of this before it rolls over top and buries you."

"I got nothing to say."

"Your brother doesn't feel the same way."

"He's a liar."

Jian shrugged. "He's the only one talking."

"Don't let me keep you."

"You're stupid if you don't try and help yourself. We have witnesses, the murder weapon and as soon as Reece finishes flapping his gums we're going to have a signed confession."

"Fuck me." My plan had been to play it cool and let the

truth come out on its own. That had been a shitty plan. "I didn't kill anyone, a guy named Shamus did."

"And now you suddenly have a name." Jian laughed. "All the witnesses say it was you."

"Who? A bunch of hookers and crack heads? Who's going to believe that collection of fuck ups?"

"I'm not here to try the case, but here's what I'm wondering," Jian continued. "Part of the information we've collected is that your brother was there looking for some girl. What do you know about it?"

"There's lots of girls, it's a whore house genius."

"There was one girl in particular. Did your brother say who? Did he mention a name?"

"I have no fucking clue what you're talking about."

The detective smiled, stood and walked towards the door. "Better think hard, Grady, because the first one to give us the truth gets manslaughter. The other asshole gets first degree murder and a life time stay in our finest maximum security prison."

A young cop burst into the room. "Reece Fisk's lawyer is here and threatening to sue the whole police force. He claims he should have been notified hours ago."

Jian swore and pushed the kid out of the room.

When the door opened a minute later I expected Jian and Rogan to strut in and formally charge me. Maybe if I resisted they'd shoot me.

But the man who entered was no detective.

The young cop had returned with a thin man in an expensive black pinstripe suit. His briefcase and shoes were both Italian leather and I didn't need anyone to tell me he was a lawyer. They say crime doesn't pay, yet there are millions of rich attorneys.

The lawyer ordered my cuffs removed and the young officer couldn't do it fast enough before scurrying out of the room.

Maybe I don't hate lawyers so much.

I rubbed my wrists; the skin was red and raw. The man sat at the table across from me. I stretched my limbs and rolled my neck, my body cracking and groaning. The lawyer waited for me to talk, and I was fine with letting him wait. He'd come to see me.

A smirk curled his lips. "My name is Conner Drake, and I am your attorney."

"I didn't ask for you."

"Davis Parsons indicated you needed help."

Hard to argue that.

Drake's nose wrinkled. "You smell."

"It's puke."

"I know what it is. I just wonder why it is there. No matter, I am here to assist you in dealing with your predicament."

"It is quite the fucking pickle, but unless you perform miracles I'm not throwing what little cash I have at this."

"Miracles are not my forte. However, if you wish to avoid jail, I am your man."

"I'm willing to bet you're dead wrong on that buddy."

"Wager accepted." The lawyer opened his briefcase, pulled out a silver flask and laid it on the table before rising. "I must have a word with Reece." He motioned to the flask. "That is yours. You won't be disturbed until I return."

My liver cheered. "Is that what I think it is?"

"Twenty-five-year-old rye to ease your nerves. I'll return shortly."

He left and it was just me and the booze.

I twisted the cap off the flask and the sweet oak and caramel aroma filled the air. I put the flask to my lips and allowed the first drops to flow over my tongue. It took effort not to guzzle. Warmth spread through me, and I settled. I was exhausted and the booze hit me hard. I took another pull, my brain went lazy and my vision blurred.

When Drake returned I was plastered. He sat and removed some papers from his briefcase. I toasted him and took another swallow. "Thank you for this."

"I give people what they want."

"And you can get me and Reece off?"

The lawyer folded his hands on the table. "Without question the case against you is purely circumstantial. The witnesses were high during the incident and hardly reliable. The hand gun was found on the stairs in a very busy building with absolutely no fingerprints on it. The officer was knocked unconscious and his memory of the event is spotty at best. The police have little proof so they've resorted to extracting a confession by force. By the look of your face, Grady, it appears they are doing an excellent job."

"I bruise easy. I don't think I can afford you."

"Davis assured me that payment would be a non issue."

"He's paying?"

"No, he's not. I am working for you, so you're on the hook."

"How expensive are you?"

"It is all relative, isn't it? If you have billions a million is nothing. If you are homeless, twenty dollars is a fortune."

"The longer you don't answer, the more fucking expensive I think you are."

"Let's both lay our cards on the table, shall we? I work for Jacob Poole, and by extension, Davis Parsons. Let's just say I'm on a permanent retainer."

"So I won't owe you, I'll owe them."

"Basically."

I took a long draw from the flask, letting the alcohol clear my mind. "Since you just explained to me how easy it's going to be to get me off, I guess it'll be a teeny tiny favour I'll owe them."

"We both know that you'll owe Jacob Poole whatever he says you owe him. Please don't be so stupid as to underestimate the seriousness of your situation. Circumstantial or not, your case still presents a myriad of complications."

"Of course it does."

"The chief problem is they have witnesses saying you killed these people and we have none saying the opposite."

"What do you want me to do? Brainwash them?"

"Let's say for argument sake that you are innocent ..."

"I am, dumbass."

"Then if I were you, Grady, I would devote the rest of my waking hours to finding one of the girls who'll verify that."

"How the Hell am I going to do that? Seems to me all those girls are saying the same thing, and I'll bet that's because Shamus got to them first and scared the shit out of them."

"We only need to find one to raise doubt, Grady." Drake pulled a note pad from his briefcase and flipped through it. "When I spoke to your brother a moment ago, he told me that he was at Watson's house to meet up with some girl."

"Funny, everyone seems to know about that. Yeah, Reece said this girl had something of value to Davis."

Drake leaned forward in his seat. "Which girl?"

"I have no fucking clue. People starting dying and I was ducking bullets so it kinda slipped my mind to ask."

"If this mystery hooker is in business with Davis, maybe she is a friend as well. She might even be willing to tell the truth."

"So I gotta find this girl, who no one knows but everyone is looking for? This is bullshit."

"Just look at it as helping yourself, Grady," Drake said. He reached out his hand. "So can I tell Jacob Poole that you've agreed to become my client?"

I nodded and we shook hands. "It's not like I ever had a choice. Now when do I get the Hell out of here?"

"Patience. It won't be long," he assured me and left.

The door barely closed before it flew open again. Rogan and Jian came in, their teeth grinding. They hauled me to my feet and I ducked my chin, bracing for the flurry of punches. None came. They dragged me out of the room and down the hall.

"What the fuck is going on?" I demanded.

Jian growled. "You're going home you lucky piece of shit."

"What? Just like that?"

Rogan snarled. "Give us time and I promise you'll be back for good."

A big, broad shouldered cop with a square jaw and a buzz cut stepped in front of me. His forehead sported a goose egg and his lip was split. Sergeant Quill didn't look happy to see me.

He leaned in, his nose inches from mine. "They say you're the one that sucker punched me and killed that man. They also say because you went and got yourself a fancy lawyer you'll skate on this."

"Sometimes 'they' get it right."

"This isn't over. We'll be seeing each other again." He turned on his heels and marched off.

Rogan and Jian plopped me on a worn, wooden bench by the front desk and tossed a plastic bag in my lap. I took a peek; my wallet, keys, watch and other crap were inside. I was too drunk to bother, so I stuffed the whole thing in my jacket pocket.

I stood up to leave when an old friend sat down beside me. His name was Carl Lynch. He's a few years older than me, but we'd grown up on the same street.

Instead of walking by, pretending he didn't recognise me drunk and puke covered, Carl said hello. He didn't laugh or act smug at how pathetic I was. Instead he asked me a question.

He asked what I'd done.

I told him I'd been detained by mistake and I asked Carl the same question.

I wished I hadn't.

His wife had been murdered. Carl had come to identify the body and answer some questions. They had no leads and hoped Carl could prod the investigation along. In the end they ruled it a mugging gone wrong.

I frowned and said I was sorry. It wasn't nearly adequate. We sat in awkward silence, neither of us knowing the right words. It was uncomfortable and Carl eventually left.

There was still no sign of Reece. I don't know if the cops had freed him before me or if he was still dealing with Drake. I was glad he wasn't around because a police precinct is bad choice of location to strangle someone. I got up and stumbled out before those detectives changed their minds.

Outside the cop shop I found Carl in his van. He was crying. I asked him if he was okay and he said no. He had a revolver in his hand. It was a .38 special and it was loaded.

Lovely.

"What's that for?" I asked.

"She's gone, and I can't live with myself anymore. My son has no mother."

"And losing his father is supposed to help?"

"I won't feel so bad."

I snatched the gun out of his lap. He didn't try to stop me. I placed the gun in the plastic bag with my wallet and turned to leave. Last thing I needed was to hang around with a piece so close to the cops.

Carl got out of his van. "Where are you going, Grady?"

"I'm starting to sober up and I have to stop it before it gets worse."

"How about I take you to get something to eat instead."

For some reason I said, "Sure."

In a diner downtown we ate and talked. Actually I talked and Carl listened. When I finished, Carl asked if I wanted his help to get sober. I told him not to waste his time. There was a long list of people who'd offered me help and were now disappointed. Carl said his offer stood.

Carl was happy to give me a lift back to my apartment. I passed out on the way, but not before puking all over the dash board. Carl didn't flinch and helped me up the stairs and got me settled into my couch where I blacked out. He even threw a blanket on me before he left.

SEVEN

With a blinding headache, I awoke on my couch still wearing my puke stained shirt. No one yelled at me or pointed out the many ways I was a loser. No one had cleaned up the wrappers or pizza boxes and no one explained how disappointed they were in me. That meant Marin wasn't home. It was going to require some major sucking up for her to ever come back.

Luckily I'd had practice.

To stiffen my resolve, and drown my conscience, I sat down with a bottle of rye. I drained the first glass before the ice had cooled it, burning my throat and warming my blood. I finished my second glass and my headache subsided. I stopped using the glass and drank right from the bottle. When it was empty it was time to call Marin.

Pulling my cell out of my pocket was harder than it should been. Dialling wasn't any easier with big fingers and little buttons. Rye is great for the nerves, but crap for co-ordination. My call to Marin's cell went straight to voicemail. I tried her home number and the cordless rang beside me. Rye doesn't make you smarter either.

I replaced the first bottle with its doomed sister and drained a third of it before I had the nerve to try Marin at her father's house. I mumbled silent prayers as the phone rang that either Marin would answer or the machine would pick up, anyone but Hank Semaniak. My luck held and the old bugger answered.

"Hey, Hank, it's me Grady."

"*I hope this wasn't your only call,*" he said and hung up.

Cancer took her mom when Marin was fifteen. Marin

had told me that no child in the neighbourhood went hungry or missed Christmas on Janet Semaniak's watch. She was, in Marin's words, an angel. No doubt her greatest act of charity was marrying a crusty son of a bitch like Hank Semaniak.

I called the old man back. "Is Marin there?" I asked when he picked up.

"*They gave you another call?*"

"Who?"

"*The cops, dumbass. Isn't this your one call?*"

"What one call? I want to talk to my wife."

"*My daughter isn't here. Aren't you in jail?*"

"No, I'm at the apartment."

"*I thought you'd gotten arrested. I'd heard you finally killed someone.*"

I love ex-cops, they're never out of the loop.

"I was only questioned and my lawyer got me released."

"*You'll be back in soon enough.*"

"I'm glad you're keeping the faith."

"*We all have dreams. Anyway, Marin's not here, not that she'd talk to you if she was,*" he paused. "*I can't believe I'm saying this, but I'd like you to stop over here so we can chat.*"

"As much fun as that sounds, I've got other plans."

"*Like what?*"

"Pulling out my finger nails," I said and hung up.

I'd have to beg Marin later.

My clothes were ruined with blood and puke so I stripped and tossed them in the trash. I took the bottle of rye with me into the shower. The water ran red at my feet from the dried blood on my face and the soap stung the cuts on my wrists left by the cuffs. I would have stayed in the shower until the water ran cold, but the bottle was empty.

The mirror revealed the welts, bruises and cuts on my face, but I didn't look so bad. It's my charm that gets me by anyway. I dressed in jeans and a plaid work shirt. The bag with my personal effects was by the front door, and I stuffed my wallet back in my pocket and slipped on my watch and wedding band.

Out of habit I stripped Carl's revolver, cleaned it using my kit and put it back together. The smell of the solvents brought me back to the army, and as much as that was the last thing I wanted to remember, old habits are a bitch. After reloading it, I hid the gun in the drawer of my nightstand. A little extra protection never hurt anyone.

Out of booze, I grabbed the little cash I had and left for the nearest Liquor Store. I stumbled down the front steps of my building and tripped along the sidewalk my head lost in a warm fuzzy fog.

The bell jingled as I walked into the LC. I made straight for the back fridge and found the beauties I was looking for. I slammed a case of Lucky Lager on the counter, and the clerk's face soured. I followed her gaze to the man behind me.

It was Davis Parsons. He pushed my case of beer aside and put down two bottles of Talisker Single Malt Scotch. At over four hundred bucks a bottle it wasn't my personal poison because it's hard to act prissy with a five-dollar haircut.

"I'm not paying for that."

"It's on the old man," he said. "No one ever expects you to pay."

"And yet you're here anyway."

The clerk put the bottles in a paper bag while Davis dropped ten crisp brown one hundred dollar bills on the counter and told her to keep the change. After she rang us through, the clerk was smart enough to find something to do in the back room.

You sober, Grady?"

"Am I ever?"

Davis grunted. "I stopped by your place. Where's Marin?"

"She's at her Dad's."

"Again?"

"Mind your own business Davis or I'll stuff my foot up your arse."

I opened the case, cracked a beer and took a drink.

Davis shook his head. "That, right there, is your problem, Grady."

"What, booze? Look in the mirror Davis, you're miles ahead of me on the race to that grave."

"I meant your mouth. The sad thing is you're smart enough to know better."

"You're the only one that thinks that."

"The old man wants to see you."

"I'll pass."

"That ain't an option. You just have to decide if you want to walk or be dragged through the door."

I took a drink and watched Davis over the bottle as I tilted it back. He wasn't going to fight me, it wasn't his style. Besides, we both knew I'd bust him up bad if it came to that and then he'd have a dozen guys hunting me all over Winnipeg. I couldn't fight everyone, and Davis worked for a man you just don't cross.

Jacob Poole is *the* drug dealer, when it comes to Winnipeg. Money from the sale of all the cocaine, marijuana and heroin in the city finds a way into his pocket. Most of his competitors are forced to buy product through Jacob, eventually most realise it's easier just working for him. Safer too. The ones that don't, Jacob doesn't allow to breathe for long. Davis' job is to make sure Jacob gets paid and he's very persuasive.

"I'd have thought you'd be more accommodating since I got you that lawyer," Davis said.

"I didn't ask for your help."

"That just shows you what a swell guy I am."

"If you're so swell then you won't mind if I go my own way."

"I don't give a fuck to be honest, but Jacob would mind very much."

"What the hell does he want with me?"

"Does it matter?" Davis poked a finger in my chest. "You owe him and that means when he says show up you show up."

I knocked Davis' hand away "No, it doesn't."

"Do you really want me to tell Jacob you're backing out of your deal?"

I grabbed my beer and headed for the exit. Davis followed.

"I don't have the fifty grand."

"He knows," Davis said as he opened the door.

"I lost it playing cards."

"He knows that too."

Davis led me to his black Jeep, opened the passenger door and I climbed in. I rested the beer case on my lap. "A real friend wouldn't have let me borrow that money, Davis."

Davis closed my door and squeezed into the driver's seat. "Quit your whining."

"Is this going to end with me in some dark forest digging my own grave?" I asked. "Because I'm not digging shit, so just shoot me now."

Davis drove out of the parking lot. "You done? Jacob wants to talk, that's it. Now pretend you haven't lost all your dignity and drink your fucking beer."

We drove the rest of the way to Jacob's condo in relative silence. I sulked in between beers while Davis sang along to some country CD. They were going to torture me after all.

Jacob's condo was on the top floor of the most expensive building in the most prestigious area of Winnipeg. Judges, investment bankers, and the president of an insurance agency also made their homes on Wellington Crescent. The neighbours included a local media magnate, NHL heroes, the CEO of a financial firm, and of course doctors and lawyers.

Then there's Jacob Poole, the biggest drug dealer in the province. The wealthy were publicly outraged at Jacob's very existence; privately they created Jacob's fortune with their secret habits as much as the homeless addicts wandering Portage Avenue.

We pulled into the underground parking lot and got out of the SUV. Davis made me leave my beer behind as we headed to the elevator. I didn't protest; there was plenty liquor where we were going.

We reached the top floor, the elevator doors opened and Davis led me through the two oversized oak doors and into Jacob's living room. With twenty foot ceilings and polished black granite floors with Tibetan rugs made of silk strewn about, it looked like a museum. The far wall was made entirely of glass and overlooked a human terrarium of the rich and prosperous.

We found Jacob in his study, perched on a stool. Two glasses sat on the table in front of him along with a nearly empty bottle of Scotch. Davis placed the two new bottles beside Jacob and motioned for me to take the other stool. Davis sat in one of the leather chairs and read the paper. It was as much privacy as any one got with Jacob.

Jacob's grey suit pants and vest were pressed, his blue shirt open at the collar. Diamonds sparkled at his cuffs. His thin grey hair receded back from his full fleshy cheeks. Jacob wasn't fat, but he was getting there. The big gold ring on his right hand clinked against his glass. His eyes were rimmed in red and his upper lip glistened with sweat. The man had his own voices to quiet and like me, he did so with the bottle. He was just better at keeping it together.

He poured me a glass and I took it. Jacob cleared his

throat. "I hear you've been stirring up all sorts of trouble."

"I'm sure you know what happened."

"I'm not fishing. I want to hear it from your mouth."

"I got in a bind with the cops."

"I want the story, not for you to gloss over it."

"Nothing to tell."

Jacob snorted. "Harris Watson and two others are dead. I hear you made them that way."

"You sound like the cops."

"Do I look like the cops? I said you did it; well you or that fool Reece."

"Who was Watson to you?"

Jacob swirled his scotch in his glass. "We had an arrangement. He was a good customer and I never worried about him. I like people like that. People unlike you, Grady."

My mouth went dry. "Jacob, if you brought me here to make a statement about ...."

"Save it. Watson wasn't a friend. Had he been, you'd be dead already."

Jacob refilled our glasses and I told him about all of it, every bloody damn thing. I left out the nightmares about all the dead bodies because I doubted Jacob would care. I finished and we both agreed I'd been fortunate to get away without being charged. "It was all because of the lawyer," I said. "That Drake was something else."

"We'll see how long you keep thinking that," he said and took a drink. "So you made friends with Shamus Gray, did you?"

Davis peeked out from behind his paper. "The word is Grady kicked the shit out of him at Watson's place."

I smiled. "We've met."

"That guy is crazy," Davis said.

Jacob nodded. "He's worse than that. Shamus once raped the wife of a man who wouldn't pay his debt."

"That's nothing," Davis scoffed. "This guy was selling

product on Shamus' turf, so Shamus crushed the head of the guy's dog with a sledgehammer, and his kids found it in the driveway on their way to school."

"Shamus cut off the fingers of some fool who had stolen money from him," Jacob said.

"Word is they transplanted the guy's toes," Davis added. "But it still sucks."

I shrugged. "He didn't seem that tough to me."

"I never said he was tough, I said he was crazy," Davis corrected.

"The worst story regarding Shamus is the one I know is true," Jacob continued. "Shamus suspected his wife of cheating. She'd been staying out late, trying to hide phone calls and been seen meeting the same man regularly. Shamus was sure of her infidelity. He drugged her and tattooed the word "whore" on her forehead."

"Best part is, the guy she had been meeting was the caterer for the surprise birthday party she planned to throw Shamus," Davis added.

I shook my head. "He must have felt like an ass."

Jacob smirked and drained his glass. "Well, to make things right, Shamus killed her. He couldn't bear the thought of his wife walking around like that. It might embarrass him."

"And now he's got issue with me?"

"I'm afraid so."

"If they'd let me and Reece leave then none of that bloody mess would have happened..."

"I didn't ask you here for a review of Shamus incompetence, or yours." Jacob stared into his glass for a long time. "All I know is Shamus is in a rage about some deal of his you messed up. Tell me the truth, did you happen to relieve poor Shamus of either money or drugs in all that chaos?"

"All I thought to do was grab my brother and get the

fuck out of there." I filled our glasses. "I didn't take a dime from that house."

Jacob smiled. "Of course not, or you'd have given it to me."

Actually, it would have gone to rent, but I wasn't going to argue. "So what do I do about Shamus? Could you tell him to back off?"

"I could and he would," he said. "But why would I want to help you? You still owe me fifty large."

"If I'm dead I'm not paying you."

"There is that, I suppose. Plus, I find you amusing and would miss you."

"Should I be blushing?"

"See, you're funny. You should offer me something, so I won't feel the need to have one of my boys cripple you."

I took a drink, not just because of the need but I wanted a moment to think. The harshness of the Scotch bit my throat before the calmness settled in. "So what do you want me to do?"

"That's my boy." Jacob clinked my glass with his and made a silent toast. "The situation is simple, really, something was stolen from me. Something very valuable, irreplaceable and vitally important. I want it back."

"What is it?"

His hand shot out, and Jacob latched onto my wrist. There was surprising strength in the old man. "I need you to listen to the next words out of my mouth very carefully and believe them in your very soul." He paused and licked his lips. "It's none of your fucking business what was stolen. I'm not going to tell you, no one is, and if you're smart you'll never, ever, try to find out."

I pulled my wrist free, and if Jacob had been anybody else I would have punched him until he was a bloody puddle on the carpet. But he wasn't anybody else so I took another drink to cool my anger. "How the fuck can I help you if I don't know what I'm looking for?"

"Do you take me for a moron? Find me who took this item and I'll make sure the thief tells me in exacting detail where my property is."

"So do you have a name for me?"

Jacob cleared his throat. "It was one of the girls from Watson's whore house. We need to find her fast."

I said nothing and stared right at him.

"What? Are you surprised some whore was able to steal from the great Jacob Poole?"

"No, that's not it. You're just the fourth person who's asked me about this girl from Watson's." I shook my head. "So let me guess, you don't know who she is, what her name is or what she looks like. The only one who did was Watson and now he's dead."

"You're a smart boy, Grady, I've always known that. Now find her fast, I need my property immediately. If I were you I'd start by interviewing everyone from Watson's house that night, even that teenage girl you dragged out with you. Her mom was a working girl, she might have told her who stumbled on some fortune, bragging about getting rich or hitting it big."

"Why do you need me for this?"

"This is delicate and I need this done quietly. The last thing I want is to make a lot of noise and scare off the girl who stole from me and have my property lost forever."

"I'm not exactly known for being subtle."

He patted me on the shoulder. "You may be a drunk, Grady, but you're smart and were in the army. You'll follow orders like a good little soldier and not double cross me, because you understand if you did, I'd kill you."

Jacob poured himself another drink, my glass he left empty. "In the mean time, you can get started on your little assignment. Go down to The Rub with Davis and meet your brother. Apparently Reece has stumbled upon one of the girls you need to talk to. Figure out what she knows and then if she's not the one we want, deal with her accordingly."

"Accordingly? Are you saying what I think you're saying?"

He lifted his glass. "If you know what I'm saying then I don't have to say it."

EIGHT

The sidewalk rocked and swayed under my feet as though the concrete was laid over marbles. Each step was an adventure as fire hydrants, street lights and newspaper boxes popped up out of the ether and slammed into me. The city lurched and reeled as though Winnipeg was at sea.

The Scotch had hit me hard and I was well past pickled.

"Straighten your shit out, Grady," Davis said. "Jacob has given you zero room for fucking up here."

"Then he shouldn't have fed me all that Scotch."

Stopping in the middle of the sidewalk, I pulled out my cell phone and dialled. Davis held open The Rub's front door for me. "You coming or what?"

"Obviously I'm phoning someone."

"Make it quick," he said and stepped inside.

I rang Marin's cell but my call went to her voice mail. *"Hey it's Marin, sorry I can't take your call. Leave a message and I'll get in touch as soon as I can,"* the message said. *"But if this is Grady, I don't care if you're sorry, no we can't try again and yes you'd screw it up if we did."*

I pressed END on the phone. It was better not to leave a message and pretend I hadn't called.

A squad car pulled up beside me, souring my mood. Sergeant Quill climbed out and stepped onto the sidewalk, between me and The Rub.

I smiled. "Miss me?"

"Drunk already, Grady? That's sad."

"What do you want?'

"Get in the car, I want to talk."

"Not fucking likely."

"I've been reviewing the case files on the Watson murder and had a poke around the crime scene, I've made some observations I want to talk to you about."

"You arresting me?"

"There are just some oddities I'd like you to clear up."

"Then call my lawyer."

"This is just an informal talk."

"Then kiss my ass."

His eyes narrowed. "I got something you'll want to hear, so quit being an asshole and get in the damn car."

"You want to talk then let's do it right here."

"Fine." Quill barred his teeth. "For starters, the coroner says Watson had enough drugs in his system that he was basically incapacitated."

"I wouldn't know. I wasn't there."

"Let's cut the bullshit, we both know you were. So maybe it was your brother Reece that killed those people, not you."

"If you're looking for a rat, you've wasted your fucking time."

"Will you at least explain to me how a loser like you has a lawyer who charges a thousand dollars an hour?"

"He charges what?"

"I like things that make sense," Quill said. "This doesn't. You're no killer, you're not even a criminal. You're just a drunk, and I think you've been set up."

"Nobody plays me."

"Then why kill three people when you could have just run away?"

"I told you I didn't."

"Does it make sense that Reece, a guy who's never been convicted of anything, shoots an unconscious man in the face? Who ordered the hit on Watson?"

I didn't answer because I was too busy laughing.

Davis wouldn't have sent Reece to kill anybody. If it had

been a hit on Watson, they would have found someone more capable than my brother, like a donkey.

Those people were dead because they'd been in the wrong place when Shamus attacked us. Bad luck, nothing more. Reece was an addict and I was a drunk and something got fucked up. It happens. Quill should read the papers.

I gave the cop my best smile. "I think that knock to the head has made you loopy, officer, because nobody told us to kill anybody."

"How about you just tell me what happened to one specific person. A girl. Her name is Nyah and she's only sixteen years old," the cop said. "She had no business being at that place or around that kind of mess."

The blonde girl again? What was with this girl? "How many ways can I tell you I wasn't there?"

"Listen Grady, she's my buddy's kid. I just want to make sure Nyah's safe."

"What kind of father let's his kid hang out at a whore house?"

"Yeah, well he's dead and it was her mom who got killed when you and your brother shot the hell out of that place. So where is the girl, Grady?"

"You're asking the wrong guy."

Pushing my way past the cop, I stormed into The Rub, slamming the door shut behind me. I needed to drink. With Jacob, the cops, and even Marin pulling at my nerves, the last thing I needed was to worry about some girl. I didn't need the guilt. Alcohol was always kind enough to fog everything over and at The Rub I drank for free.

The Rub sits right in the middle of the exchange district, which was once home to garment manufacturers during Winnipeg's early years. They'd closed down one by one and the buildings sat vacant for years until the city tried to breathe life back into the area. Developers remodelled the beautiful old buildings, and law firms and plastic surgeons now had offices there. A day spa sat two doors down from the Rub, so upper class ladies stopped by for a dozen or two martinis after their facial.

I used to own The Rub with a douche named Zack Hammell, but his ex-wife, Daria, took over his share when Zack left her and their son, Will, for Vegas and a redheaded stewardess. Daria bought my half when I needed money to pay off Jacob Poole the first time Reece ran up his tab. Daria was nice enough to let me stay on and tend bar. It probably had something to do with the fact I married her sister.

For the record, Marin told Daria to fire me.

Even though it's no longer mine, I love The Rub. It's all class. Black and white photographs were hung on the walls of exposed brick and dark wood paneling. I spend my shift behind a solid mahogany bar, the glass shelves behind are back lit with neon lights so that the bottles shine.

There are two dozen high tables with stools, and the bar is stocked with the usual spirits and a long list of beers to keep the most discriminate snob happy. There are booths, and in the corner, couches. Daria has a small office in back with a pull-out I've crashed on the many times Marin hasn't welcomed me home.

Davis had found Reece and some woman at the bar with an army of empty glasses in front of them. Davis nodded at me, got up from his stool and headed towards a table for privacy; he dragged Reece along behind him. The woman finished her drink, added the glass to the others and followed. I'm no prince, but her thick make up couldn't mask the ugliness beneath. Her store bought boobs spilled out of her dress, which was two sizes too big, and her skinny and ravaged frame would need a dozen buffets to gain the weight needed to be anywhere near attractive.

She and I locked eyes. Hers were black and empty.

I remembered her. Even through the makeup and without a sweaty fat man rutting on top of her, I recognised

Sara Silo.

Sara Silo, the ugly whore the cops said had given a statement against me and a survivor that Jacob said I had to interrogate. She and I had a lot to talk about, but before I dealt with her I had a personal matter that demanded attention.

I intercepted my brother and dragged him to the back room. Reece tried to pull away, but I dug in harder and he yelped. Daria stepped in front of me just as I opened the 'employee's only' door.

She looked mad enough to stab me. "So you kill people now? Is that your new thing? Do you even have the slightest idea what this is going to do to Marin?"

"I'm sure you're going to tell me," I said.

"Grady, I can't run a bar like this. More importantly, I can't watch you do this to my sister anymore."

"Just give me two seconds," I said and pulled Reece into the back.

The stock room smelled faintly of sour booze. I threw Reece onto the floor in front of a towering wall of beer cases. The liquor and wine were kept in another small room to the right and Daria's office was to the left. I stayed in the main room where there was more space to throw things.

Things like Reece.

I picked him up by the collar and slammed him into the brick wall. "Why did you have to go flapping your fucking yap to the cops?"

Reece covered his face. "I was scared, man, so I told them what happened."

I bounced his head off the brick. "Did you tell him you did it?"

"It all happened so fast, who knows man?"

"Did you tell them I did it?"

"I was scared, man, I'd have told them anything."

I slapped him hard across the face. "You're a real piece

of shit, Reece. I save you from Jacob how many times? I take on your debt so he won't kill you at the cost of my marriage and you do this to me?"

"That's why I did it, man. You're tougher, smarter and I knew you could handle that shit, man."

"Is that supposed to be a fucking compliment?" I slapped him again. "You did it because you're a coward. That Shamus psycho killed those people but you know the cops don't believe that so to save your dumb ass you told the cops I did it. That's worse than being a rat, Reece. You lied."

"I go to prison I'm gonna get raped and bitched out, man. That's a fact. It ain't right but I'd sell out the Pope to stay out of there."

I let him go and he slid down the wall. "I can't trust you anymore," I said. "You and I are finished."

"Don't say that, man, we're brothers."

"We're brothers? You only remember we're brothers when you want something. We're done. We'll let the lawyer do his thing and afterwards you're on your own. Don't call me to pay your debts. Don't ask me to save your ass anymore. Jacob Poole wants to cut off your hand because you owe him for drugs? Tell him you're a lefty."

My brother stood up, brushed off his pants and extended his hand. "That's fair, man, I understand. We cool?"

"Sure," I said and punched him in the mouth. He dropped to the ground and I kicked him twice in the ribs. "Do that to me again, Reece, and I don't care that you're my brother, I'll kill you myself."

I was back out into the bar before he answered. I took a seat across the table from Davis. The black, empty eyes of the hooker had been on me from the moment I'd emerged from the back room. Sara Silo shifted her chair away from me. Smart girl. Davis poured me a pint from his pitcher and I downed the first glass and poured another. I was still fired up, and the way I saw it Davis owed me.

I held Davis' gaze and nodded to the girl. "How we gonna do this?"

He shrugged and drank from his glass. "It's your show, just like Jacob said."

Sara lowered her glass and placed it on the table, freeing her hands. She pushed her chair back, giving her room to move. Her eyes grew wide, and her legs were shaking. She was scared. "What's going on here boys?"

"Do you remember me?" I asked.

"Should I?"

"Look at my face. Do you know me?"

"You look like shit."

"Courtesy of Winnipeg's finest."

"What'd you do with Reece?"

"I gave him a life lesson. You're up next."

Sara shot to her feet and held her trembling hands out in front of her. "You're making me uncomfortable," she said. "I'm going to leave now. This party is over, boys."

"Sit down. You're going to answer our questions."

Tears rimmed her eyes. "I'm not saying anything."

Davis leaned forward, his elbow on the table, and pointed across the bar. "See that big fucking dude over there?"

The hooker and I followed Davis' finger to big mass of humanity seated at a table in the corner. The man had boulders for shoulders and his hands dwarfed the pitcher of beer he was draining. A scar cut clear across his face from his left ear to the bottom of his jaw. His head was so big the baseball cap he wore looked like it was going to pop off his head. He was a scary looking dude, but he was also pissed drunk, swaying in his chair and blurry eyed.

"Yes." It was barely a whisper.

"Do you want to talk to Bert, or us?" Davis asked.

She sat down hard. When she raised her eyes, they were

clear. "Yes, I know you," she said. "You were there the night Delores died."

"We'll get back to that," I said. "Now, I'm going to ask you this question only once, did you steal from Jacob Poole?"

Something flashed in her eyes and it forced her to look at her feet. "I meet lots of men, and I don't always get their names. Even the faces run together."

Davis laughed. "Are you kidding me? Jacob Poole? You're not that dumb, sweetheart."

"Yes, I know Mr. Poole." She licked her lips and lifted her head. "I'll tell you one thing, if I was ever dumb enough to steal from Jacob Poole I would run so far, so fast I'd never be found again."

"You sure about that, honey?"

"What good is money if I'm dead? I know the man, but I've never met him and I have no idea who would be crazy enough to steal from him. So if you don't mind, I'm going to leave now. Tell Reece I'll be waiting outside."

"Fine," I said. "Just one more thing," I paused. "I know you told the cops I killed those people."

"So now you're going to tell me not to talk to the cops?" she said. "You going to beat me for that?"

"Beat you? No, I'm not that type of guy. In fact, you can talk to the cops all you want, just tell them the truth. We both know it was that short fuck, Shamus, who was doing all the shooting."

"Is that it?"

"Yes, as long as you're honest."

"So you work for Jacob Poole, right?"

"In a way."

"Then that's really interesting that you want me to tell the truth," she said and left.

Davis raised his glass and sighed. "Well, that didn't go so great. You should have pressed her harder."

"She didn't do it."

"You really believe that?"

"She was too scared to be anything but honest." I straightened in my chair. "Now that we're alone, it's time you and I had a talk."

Davis swayed slightly in his chair. "What the fuck did I do?"

"You sent me to get my brother, knowing full well shit would go crazy. You played me."

"The Hell I did." He did his best to look indignant. "If I played you would I have gotten you a lawyer?"

"How did you know we were jammed up?"

"I heard. You and your idiot brother killed a dealer. Every junkie in the city is talking about it. I knew you two were busted before they slapped the cuffs on you. You're lucky I like you."

"I didn't ask for help much less a damn lawyer."

"Well, it saved your ass."

I took a swig of my beer. "You should have told me you wanted Watson dead."

"Do you have Alzheimer's? I told you that I was worried about your brother and that you should go find him. That's it."

"What did you tell Reece?"

"He was supposed to bring Watson to see me, and the moron couldn't even do that."

"Nothing more? Did you know about this Shamus guy?" I took a drink. "He tried to shoot me by the way."

"What do I gain with you getting killed? Christ, you guys are a couple of bumbling idiots and somehow it's my fault?" He shook his head. "Listen, I just wanted to talk to Watson about this fucking girl we need to find."

Reece emerged from the back room, his face already bruising. He grabbed drinks off the tray of a passing waitress and told her to put them on his tab. He held up a glass. "To Reece Fisk, the man who fought the law and fucking won, man."

I shoved him into his seat. "Shut your fool mouth."

Reece threw up his hands. "For what, man? Do you know who our lawyer is? Ain't nobody gonna touch us, man."

"You want to visit the store room again?"

"Forget that, man. All I want to do is party."

"Quit being an idiot and understand how close we were to big jail time."

Reece smashed his glass on the floor, stood and kicked over his chair. "You're such a fucking killjoy, man." My brother quickly scanned the bar. "Where did that bitch Sara go?"

"We were done with her so she left."

"Man, you just killed my good time." He spotted her smoking out on the sidewalk in front of The Rub's huge bay windows. "There's still a chance yet, man," he said, and stumbled out of The Rub.

I turned to Davis. "My brother would be smart to stay away from her"

"Give the kid a break. He thought he was going to be raped on a daily basis."

"We aren't going jail. That's his damn break."

Through the big bay window, I watched my brother take Sara Silo's hands in his and pull her toward him. He kissed her cheek and she laughed, playfully pushing him away. Reece ran his finger down her neck and hooked the neckline of her dress, pulled it open and pretended to peek down it. She slapped his hand away, giggled, and then kissed him full on the mouth.

"Only an addict would be stupid enough to flirt with the hooker who was trying to send him to prison," I said.

"Are you sure she isn't the girl we're looking for?" Davis asked.

"I don't think so."

"I'll call Jacob."

The phone to his ear, Davis hurried after my brother. He cut the addict off mid smooch and pushed him back on the sidewalk. Davis handed the phone to Reece. My brother nodded and smiled as he listened to Jacob. Hopefully the old man talked some sense into him.

Sara Silo put on an impressive pout, arms crossed and lips pursed. What bizarre world had I entered? Hadn't she just admitted that she was lying to the cops about us killing people and now she was trying to party with my brother.

Hopefully, Jacob would deal with it.

Davis' pitcher was empty so I pulled a cold beer from behind the bar. The bottle had just touched my lips when Daria stormed over beside me. She wanted an apology. I had none to give so I made her wait. I slammed the empty bottle on the bar and made a show of wiping my mouth with sleeve.

"Are you going to bother working today?" she snapped.

"I have nothing else to do."

She grabbed my face in her hands, her fingers digging into my cheeks. "This is your very last chance, Grady. You pull anymore crap and Marin will be identifying your body."

"I'm not fired?"

Daria pointed to Davis' thug. He'd passed out, his head down on his table and a dozen or so shot glasses strewn in front of him.

"This isn't a hotel, tell him to sleep it off at home," she ordered.

"You're heartless."

"He isn't spending money passed out like that."

"He's friends with Davis."

"If I'd known that I wouldn't have let him in. Is he a friend of yours too?"

"Nope."

"Then you won't care about tossing his ass out."

Who was I to argue? I tapped the guy on the shoulder. No response. I cuffed him in the back of the head, but he didn't move. I grabbed a hand full of his hair, lifted his head and dumped beer in his face. He jumped up and flailed around.

"What the Hell?" he sputtered.

"I ain't got a lot of patience, not that it's your fault. The owner wants you out of here, buddy."

He made some fists and tried to look menacing. "Do you know you the fuck I am?"

"I don't really give a shit."

"You don't want to fuck with me."

"What I want is for to leave, now beat it."

Bert rolled his shoulders and flexed his pecs. He was trying really hard to be scary. "Let's do this, asshole."

"Did you even notice Davis is now outside? Aren't you supposed to be watching his back?" Bert's face went white. "Go be a good boy and face the music. Tell Davis you're a moron. You'll be convincing, trust me."

"I'm going to fuck you up and shut that big mouth of yours."

Bert took a wild swing at me. Stupid bastard. He was slow and I dodged it. I smacked him in the jaw, drove my knee into his ribs, clamped on a headlock, wrestled him to the door and launched him out onto the side walk. Bert jumped up and came at me swinging like a crazed baboon. I side stepped him easily and swept his feet out from under him. His head smacked off the sidewalk.

Sara wanted no part of the fight, and moved quickly across the street. Reece, having already gotten his ass kicked, followed her. They stood in front of a barber shop that had been closed sometime in the 80's when even guys started going to hair dressers. Some hipster kid had renovated and reopened it. It even had a red and white barber pole spinning on the brick front. They sold cigars, whisky, and had musicians and poets stop by to perform. Word was the guy gave a good shave with a straight razor.

Bert tried to pick himself up, but his legs were weak, and the right I landed on his chin sent him straight into the pavement. Davis tried to be the hero and intervene, but it was an empty gesture. Bert was dumb, but he knew when to stay down.

"Grady, just go back inside." Davis was shielding his wannabe bully. "I'll call you about our next move."

I said fine and ducked back into the bar not feeling particularly proud. Daria nodded and headed to the back room, no doubt to call Marin. I poured myself a draught. Outside, Bert lifted himself up, threw his hat on the ground and kicked it. Davis rushed over and picked it up, handed it back to Bert and started consoling the poor slob.

Davis reached into his coat and pulled out a wad of cash. I choked. He gave it to Bert, who listened and nodded in agreement with whatever crap Davis was telling him. What the Hell was going on? Bert gets his ass handed to him and then gets paid? If Davis would have given Reece that kind of cash for fucking up, maybe I'd still own The Rub.

Bert climbed into his truck, a Ford Ranger. Bert driving was a bad idea, neither the alcohol or likely concussion was going to help him on the road. He revved the engine, pulled out into the street and cut across both lanes of traffic heading straight for the Barber Shop. Bert floored it, blue smoke poured out the tailpipe as he sped right at Sara and Reece. The glass slid from my hands and I broke for the door.

Sara just stood there, watching the truck close in. Reece side stepped quickly, moving clear while seemingly pushing Sara back. She held her hands up and screamed. The truck didn't brake as it smashed into her. My brother, rolled away untouched. I ran out of The Rub, my brother and Davis stood together, surveying the carnage.

Bert was dead. He'd been launched out the windshield. Glass shards were embedded in his face and his neck rested at an odd angle as he lay there across the hood. There was blood everywhere and much of it was Bert's.

Sara hadn't fared much better. She'd been crushed, but was still alive. Barely. The truck had taken her at chest level and pinned her against the wall. Blood trickled out of her mouth. She'd been ripped open, all sorts of bone, organ and muscle hung out of her. She'd burst, and I tried to hold her together. Warm sticky blood oozed over my fingers, and I felt her pulse slowing. She caught her breath, and it made a rattling sound. Her eyes focused on me, growing wide right before the light inside went out.

I tried CPR and put my mouth to hers. I gagged with the taste of blood. I breathed for her, but it was useless. The air rushed through her and the blood bubbled in her chest. Sara was too broken. I stumbled back, covered in blood, sat down on the curb and waited.

The sirens approached, and a crowd had gathered. First the ambulance and fire trucks arrived, then the police. By then Davis and Reece were long gone. Daria came out to check on me but I told her to stay inside, there was no reason to get her involved. Daria was adamant that I'd done all I could and it wasn't my fault they had died. I knew that was a lie.

I just couldn't say why.

They loaded the bodies into the ambulance and drove off. I was numb. Some constable took my statement. After a while I was pushed back as the cops taped off the scene and the lab guys showed up. Eventually Daria took me home. For once she didn't blame me for anything.

NINE

Her fingers stung as though needles were being pressed into them. Her face was tight and raw, the wind felt like it was ripping the skin off her bones. Nyah's toes were numb and her knees and elbows throbbed as the cold set in deeper. It was only November, not yet winter, but it was already cold and bleak. Every Winnipegger knew it was only going to get worse. Temperatures plunging into the minus 50's with the wind chill, frostbite setting in after five minutes with hyperthermia right behind.

In winter the trees were pretty, sparkling with frost while snow blanketed the ground. Now, the trees were bare, the gold and red leaves had long been raked away. The grass was brown and rough, the air silent as the birds had left for the south. Only the grey remained. The city looked desolate, barren and depressed.

Nyah was tired, the weariness, like the frost, crept up her bones and left her hollow and hungry. It had only been two days since she lost her mom.

The first night she'd slept in the tree house, the second she'd scored a bed in the rooms above a soup kitchen on Princess Street. She'd been offered hot food and drink, which chased the chill away. A nice elderly woman took her to the bunk beds. Eight girls crammed in a room meant for two. But the bed was clean, free of bugs and not on the street. The blankets were warm, dry and smelled like soap, completely opposite of the other girls she had to bunk with. These were girls like Nyah. Girls with no money, no home and no parents.

Girls who had no hope.

Most couldn't have told you if their fathers were alive

much less what they looked like. Their mothers were out of the picture too, be it from drugs, jail, death or disinterest.

The fight was started by a girl twice as wide and a foot taller than Nyah. She was full of scars. Her knuckles covered with those from fighting, and her forearms adorned with thick ropey ones she'd given herself.

When they demanded she empty her pockets, Nyah refused and backed up against a wall. They didn't believe her when she said she had nothing. The big girl rushed her first, and Nyah barely ducked under her big looping right hand. Nyah punched the girl in her stomach and when the air let out of her, Nyah thumbed her in the eye.

She'd learned that from her Dad.

He taught her to do as much damage as quickly as possible; she was too little to trade punches. She broke the next girl's nose with the heel of her palm but her kick missed the third girl in. Then they were on top of her. They pulled her hair, gouged her eyes and kicked at her. She curled into a ball as they tore her pockets while they beat on her.

The old lady had heard the noise and broken it up. Nyah was bleeding from her nose and lip, but other than a few bruises she'd managed to protect herself. Nyah didn't want to think what would have happened if the fight had gone on much longer. One of the girls hid a pair of scissor behind her back.

Nyah tried to explain what happened but the old lady hadn't wanted to hear it. It was their word against hers, and Nyah was new. So Nyah was thrown back out on the street.

She spent the night at the outdoor hockey rink near the house she had grown up in. There was an old barn used to house the Zamboni, hoses for flooding and other equipment. It was too soon for ice, so the place was deserted. She'd made a bed out of practice jerseys and cried herself to sleep.

Finding Grady had taken longer than she had guessed.

The phone book had been useless. Nyah spent hours at the Millennium Library downtown searching the internet. They made it look so easy in the movies, all she had to do was Google his name and Grady's whole life popped up on the screen. Nyah was not so lucky. In newspaper archives she found arrest records, though there were even more of those for his brother Reece. One article proclaimed the opening of Grady's bar, and another not long after revealed he had sold it. There was a wedding announcement for Grady and a woman named Marin, who Nyah thought was too pretty for him. There was nothing on where to find him.

Grady was no druggie, but she had smelt enough whiskey on him to start asking at all the liquor stores in town. The clerk at the LC on Prichard told her that Grady lived just down the street. That's how she ended up outside the coffee shop on Burrows Avenue, watching Grady's building. She hadn't seen him yet and she was so tired of being cold, exhausted by looking and finished with being alone.

What was she going to do with Grady now that she'd found him? The problem of finding him had taken so much energy she hadn't worked out the next step.

Four years earlier Nyah would have gone to her Dad. He would have known exactly what to do. Jim Tynes could fix anything. He repaired her bike when she blew a chain, bandaged her knee when she skinned it, and scared away the monsters from under her bed. Nyah was never truly worried while her Dad was still alive.

But he wasn't. He was dead.

That was the root of all this mess.

Shuffling from foot to foot, trying to stamp out the cold, Nyah spied on what she hoped was Grady Fisk's apartment building. It would be nice if she actually caught sight of him soon so she'd know if she was wasting her time. Nyah felt the fear feeding on itself inside her mind. The last time she went inside the coffee shop, the guy at the counter started asking questions about who she was waiting for. Was he going to call the cops? She was exposed standing on a busy street corner, who knew who would drive by and see her?

Nyah checked her watch, decided to give Grady fifteen more minutes when a blue minivan pulled up in front of the apartment building and Grady got out. A woman slid out of the driver's side and joined him on the side walk. His face was decorated with fresh bruises and there was blood all over him.

Who was that woman? Nyah knew it wasn't his wife. She was pretty enough, but there was no affection between them. The woman helped Grady into the building and not even five minutes later came back down, leaned against her van and took out her cell phone. She was waiting for someone, most likely an ambulance.

A silver Honda Civic pulled up behind the minivan. Nyah recognised Marin as soon as she got out of the car; she was beautiful, if a little frazzled. Marin hugged the other woman. Their conversation looked intense, but their anger wasn't directed at each other. After another hug, Marin went into her building, and her sister drove off.

The cold finally ate away at the last of her perseverance. Nyah had to get off that sidewalk before she froze to it permanently.

At least she had found Grady. That was a start. She'd wait until the morning to talk to him when things had settled.

The only thing left for her that night was to swallow the last of her pride and go beg for scraps at the soup kitchen. Nyah finished the last of her hot chocolate and tossed the cup onto the pile of empties she'd built in the trashcan. Burrowing her hands deep in her pockets, Nyah put her head down against the wind and started the long trek to humiliation and warm blankets.

She crossed the street, trudging right past a red pickup truck. Fear ripped through her body and pushed the frost out. The skeleton sticker in the back window. The dent on the front fender from hitting the garage. It was Vern Hashen's red pickup.

She ducked into an alley, hoping to cut through to the street on the other side. It was a dead end, leading instead to the rear of a small strip mall. She tried a few of the exit doors, but they were all locked. She ran for the mouth of the alley and there was Vern Hashen blocking the way.

He was drunk, tripping over his feet while he tried to stand. Nyah shrank back into the shadows and hid behind the garbage bins. But her movements caught Vern's eye, and he turned to face the parking lot.

"Is someone there?" he screamed. "Mother fucker, I saw you."

Nyah held her breath, willing herself to disappear.

"You going to rob me, asshole?" Vern yelled. "I've been to prison, Mother Fucker!"

Vern had a long greasy pony-tail and tattoos on his arms, which along with his handle bar moustache, made him look like he might be trouble. He wanted to be a biker. He wore tight jeans, black boots and a leather jacket. He tried very hard to look the part. Even if he was tall, Vern was terribly thin, and he was a coward.

Prison hadn't been kind to Vern. As he was a total piece of shit, Nyah hadn't been surprised to learn the other inmates had treated Vern like one. On a night when Vern had been drunker than usual, he'd been screaming and fighting with her mom. The whole street probably heard. Nyah had opened her door to come out and call the cops. But then she heard Vern crying, saying he was sorry. He told her mom that it wasn't his fault. Jail had messed him up, and he drank to forget.

Nyah stayed in her doorway listening to what they'd

done to Vern up at Stony Mountain Penitentiary. The inmates had found out that Vern liked to beat women and sell drugs to little kids. Vern told Delores that he'd gotten into a few fights because of it. Later he confessed that the other cons beat on him relentlessly every chance they got until he begged the guards to put him in protective custody. Vern's nose was so crooked the tip almost touched his left cheek and his lips and forehead were a road map of scars.

Vern also wouldn't go into detail about what happened to him in the shower, except that it had been horrible. Nyah had seen enough movies to guess what went on.

Stumbling into the mouth of the alley, Vern bent down to look under the lone parked car. "Are you a fucking coward? Come out and fight!" Vern paused, listening for a response. He got none. "Stupid dogs. Should all be put down."

Turning to leave, Vern lost his centre and stumble tripped to the left. He tried to right the ship and his feet got tangled, and he completed the ungraceful panic fall drunk dance and crashed into the back door of a pawn shop. The security light blazed on and lit up the alley with enough wattage to land a plane, and illuminated front and centre was Nyah, in her suddenly horrible hiding place. Vern pushed off the door and shuffled towards her, a big goofy grin on his face. He held out his hand for her to take, but Nyah ignored it. She rose and stepped away, ready to run.

"Well hello, sweet Nyah," he slurred. "I've been looking for you. I've been worried."

"No you weren't," she said.

"Don't be sour, Nyah, I was too. So what's new? How ya been?"

"What are you doing here, Vern?"

Vern stumbled backwards even as he held out his arms to her, as if he wanted to hug her like a real father would.

"I got worried about you when I heard what happened

at Watson's place. He was a good shit, shame to go out like that... And Delores too, of course. I really miss her and stuff. She was a good broad, your Mom."

"Don't talk about her. It's your fault she was even there."

"Delores was my wife. My woman." He pounded his fist into his chest. "I didn't want her to die."

"You turned her into a whore. She's not your anything."

"Listen, I really just wanted to find you. I want to make us a family, Nyah. That's all I want, it's just you and me now, so I want us to be a loving family."

"You're not my Dad," she said. "So you can go to hell, douche bag."

His face changed. The goofy grin slid off his face and the angry, hate filled mask was revealed. "You're going home with me, you little bitch, and that's the end of it."

He lunged for her but she slipped out of his reach. He swung, but she easily avoided the punch. He was too drunk and the alley was too big. Even Vern realised that, so the smile made its return.

"Come home, we need to talk," he said.

"Just leave me alone."

"Listen you little bitch, where is it?" His face erupted in red, his teeth bared. "Give it to me, and I won't hurt you."

"I don't know what you're talking about."

"Such a little dirty liar. I'll smack the truth out of ya."

Nyah ran to the alley entrance, but he cut her off. Nyah tried to cut back around the other side, but Vern anticipated that too. He couldn't catch her, so he began to hem her in.

"No, don't touch me," she screamed.

"I'll do worse than touch you if you don't give me what I want."

Nyah took a step to the left, feinted, and tried to run around Vern to the right. Vern slipped, but gathered his feet in time to lunge. He grabbed her by the arm. Nyah shrieked as he spun her around. She clawed his face, seeking his eyes with her nails. He slapped her. Hard. Nyah's head felt like it was going to pop off her neck and her teeth rattled in their sockets.

There was a loud crack. Vern's eyes went wide, and he released her and fell down on his knees. Behind him stood Marin, a piece of wood in her hand and her hair back lit by the street lights. Nyah had never seen a more beautiful woman.

"Leave her alone," Marin said.

Vern swayed back to his feet. "Mind yer own business."

"Get away from her," Marin said. "I'm not joking."

"Me neither." Vern touched the back of his head and winced. His fingers were bloody when he pulled them away. "You're going to pay for that, bitch."

Marin let the two by four fall from her hand and from her purse she pulled a snub nosed revolver.

"What the hell." Vern jumped back. "You wouldn't use that."

"Without hesitation, I would." Marin dropped her purse and brought her left hand up and adjusted her grip. "My Dad was a cop, by the way, and he only taught me to shoot to kill."

Vern paused. His feeble brain trying to work out how things had gotten so bent so fast. Defeat filled Vern's eyes, and his shoulders sagged. Now it was his turn to back away. As he did, he pointed a finger at Nyah.

"This isn't over," he said. "I'll find you again and you'll give it back."

Marin didn't lower the gun until long after Vern's red pickup truck had driven out of sight. Marin smiled at Nyah and let out a long slow breath. Marin reached out and brushed the hair out of Nyah's face. "Are you okay?" she asked.

Nyah hugged her then. She couldn't help it. Then she started to cry and Marin hugged her back until the tears were done.

TEN

When I got home I left the lights off and the shades drawn, I sought darkness. It was bad enough I smelt the blood; I didn't need to see it. My shirt and pants were soaked, and my hands were sticky and tight where the blood had dried. It was Sara's blood.

I got the shower going as hot as I could take, and scrubbed myself raw to ensure no trace of Sara was left. My clothes went in the trash on top of those covered in puke. The garbage man was going to wonder what kind of kind parties I had.

As soon as I slipped into bed sleep embraced me, but when I woke, I felt worse for sleeping. I took aspirin with a beer chaser. There was no part of me that wanted to get out of bed. I finished my beer, wringing the last drops from the bottle. I prayed the aspirin would take root quick. I stood the bottle next to the procession of empties on my night stand. If I was going to stay drunk it wasn't going to be in bed, so I got up, dressed and headed for the kitchen.

As I crossed the living room, I flicked through my phone for Davis' number. That bastard and I needed to have a chat about what had happened with Sara and Bert. For his sake, I'd better like his answers or I'd punch him until I did.

Marin's laugh made me forget all about Davis. It was her real laugh, deep and from her belly. Not the fake titter she used when she was uncomfortable or when being polite with Reece's jokes. She was at ease, so I dropped the phone and felt my heart start to sing.

My wife was home.

The urge to bound and skip into the kitchen singing and tossing flowers was strong, but I had to keep some pretence of cool. At least until the begging started. Marin sat at our wobbly table in one of the mismatched chairs, stirring milk into her tea.

I went to my wife, brushed away a loose strand of hair from her face, leaned in and kissed her. She reached up, took my head in his hands, and broke our kiss. She held me there, her eyes assessing the new bruises and cuts I'd acquired.

In my excitement at seeing Marin, I'd missed the fact we weren't alone. My eyes drifted to the person seated across the table from my wife and my joy was short lived. Her legs curled underneath her and a warm cup of tea in her hands, little Nyah from the bloody house of Watson was now in my kitchen. The fog of confusion filled my brain as I tried to imagine how this little tea party had come about.

"Are you okay, Grady?" my wife asked.

I said nothing as my brain floundered. I stepped back and leaned against the counter.

"Grady, are you drunk? What's wrong with you?"

"Sorry, babe, just woke up. What are you doing here, Nyah?"

Marin placed her cup on the table in front of her, centering it on the place mat. "Well, it's an exciting story," Marin began. My wife then went into great detail of the events in the alley. "So after saving Nyah from her crazy Dad we came up here, made some tea and had just started chatting when you walked in."

"Vern is not my Dad," Nyah said.

"Are you out of your mind?" I glared at her. "You don't take out your gun unless you are ready to use it, Marin."

"I would have," Marin said. "I wasn't going to let him hurt her. Vern had been looking for her, he wasn't going to leave because I asked sweetly."

"Looking for her? Must be something in the air..."

"What foolishness are you going on about?"

"People have been looking for the girls who were at Watson's that night. In fact, Jacob Poole is really desperate to locate one girl in particular."

Nyah stiffened and her feet hit the floor. "What girl?"

"One of the girls who worked at Watson's I guess. It's not important."

Marin held up her hands. "Wait. What? What's all this about Jacob Poole and Watson's and some girl? Someone better start talking."

I looked down at Nyah. "You didn't tell her?"

The blonde girl shrugged. "It didn't come up."

"You've been talking all night. How'd that not come up?"

"We were talking about life and how men are idiots," Marin said. "Thanks for providing such a great example. Now, who's going to explain how you two know each other?"

"Just remember that you told me to go get Reece," I said before I started. I took a deep breath, and as I exhaled, the whole bloody story of Watson's whorehouse came tumbling out. I even told her about Sara dying outside The Rub because once I got going I couldn't shut up.

When I finished my mouth was dry. I grabbed a beer from the fridge, cracked it open and guzzled half of it.

Marin reached out and took Nyah's hands in hers. "I'm so sorry, my girl, that's awful. I lost my Mom too, and I know how much that hurts."

"I think she was lost a long time before that," Nyah said.

"So this guy Vern, who's not your Dad, why is he looking for you?" I asked. "Are you a runaway?"

"It's not like that."

"Are you living at home?"

"I spent the last two nights in a barn. I got kicked out of a soup kitchen because some girls tried to rob me. The night before that I slept in some kid's treehouse."

"Well your home has to be better than all that," Marin

said.

"Not always," I said.

"Not everyone is like your dad, Grady."

"Enough are."

Nyah lifted up her sleeves and showed the rainbows of bruising on her arms. "Vern is worse than most."

Marin's eyes blazed. "Grady, we're not giving her back to that monster."

"When did I say we would?" I smiled at Nyah. "How old are you? Sixteen?" She nodded. "Why aren't you in school?"

"Because that's the first place Vern would look for me."

"You have no one else to go to?" She shook her head. "Well, for starters, you can't stay here."

Marin leapt to her feet and shoved a finger in my face. "If you think for one instant I'm turning this poor sweet girl out on the street, you have another thing coming Grady Fisk. I'll see you living under a bridge before I let this girl..."

"Settle down psycho," I said. "I just meant she can't stay here because this Vern obviously knows where to look for her."

"Oh, sorry." Marin blushed and sat back down, but the instant her butt hit the chair she sprang back to her feet. "Wait, I have just the place." She smiled at Nyah. "I know an old cop and I know you can stay there if I ask."

"An old grumpy cop." I snorted. "If it was me I'd prefer the gutter."

Nyah's brow furrowed. "What is this place?"

"Trust me," Marin said. "There's nowhere safer."

Marin wouldn't let me finish my beer and I'd had to eat a stale bagel as I drove my Chevy to Marin's idea of a safe house. Will's bike lay on the lawn of the two story brick home in St. James. The training wheels were gone. When had that happened? My nephew was eight, and I'd already missed so much. He deserved a better uncle.

I rang the doorbell, a Superman sticker book for Will

tucked under my arm, hoping Hank wouldn't answer. A strange SUV had parked across the street. It was a black BMW, fully tricked out. It didn't belong there, not in front of Hank Semaniak's house. Daria's van wasn't in the driveway next to Hank's jeep. I couldn't see anyone inside the SUV.

Will burst through the front door, a gigantic smile on his cute little face and I forgot about the BMW.

Little Will is chubby, wears glasses, has no athletic ability to speak of and few friends. It's not nice to say, but my nephew is a nerd.

Of course, he's probably the sweetest kid ever, and he treats his mother like gold. Grandpa Hank adores him and even with what I've said, I know he'll be fine even without a father.

The kid is smart. Will spends most of his time reading or on the computer. He's not only playing games either. Will's eight and already designing online fan sites for Superheroes. I'm an adult and can barely sign into my email account.

So Will may be a little different, but I'm not worried about him. I don't care that he can't throw a football or isn't a strong skater. It doesn't matter that he's not popular. I knew kids like Will when I was in school, and yes, I teased them.

They're all driving Porsches now.

Will's blue t-shirt had a picture of Superman flying over the earth. He was polite when I gave him the sticker book. Normally I'd have gotten a high five or even a hug, but the little guy had his baby blues fixed on Nyah. It didn't rub me raw since Aunty Marin didn't even get a hello.

Will finally tore his eyes from Nyah and looked at Marin and I. "Who's she?"

"She's Auntie's friend," Marin said.

Nyah bent down on one knee and held out her hand for

a high five. "Hi, I'm Nyah."

Will smiled and slapped palms. "Do you want to play?"

"You know any cool games?"

His smile grew so big Will ran out of face to contain it. "I've got lots of games for my computer and on my PlayStation. Or we can play on my iPad..."

"Why don't you show Nyah the backyard?" Marin suggested. "She can push you on the swing or play tag. I bet Nyah is awesome at hide and seek."

Nyah grinned. "I've had practice hiding lately."

Will reached out and took Nyah by the hand. "Let's go play in the backyard for a little bit, *then* we'll play some video games."

"Deal."

I watched my nephew walk hand in hand with Nyah until they disappeared around the side of the house. "Wow, Will and an older woman, that boy is smooth."

"He totally has a crush on her." Marin sighed. "I guess you can wait here, Grady, while I go talk to Dad."

"You don't trust me to handle him?"

"It's going to be delicate. He doesn't know Nyah or the risks involved. The important thing is that Nyah is safe, and I don't want you messing it up."

"It'll be fine, Hank likes kids. He hates adults, but he likes kids."

"The girl is scared, Grady, we have to make sure this is the right situation."

"That girl is strong and she'll be fine. You're the one that needs to relax, Marin."

"And you're the one that needs to be responsible for once."

"It's not like I try to make you upset."

"Sometimes I doubt that," she said. "So where are you taking Will and Nyah while I talk to Dad?"

"I don't know why I gotta take them anywhere."

"We're talking about my Dad here. There's a good chance there'll be yelling."

"I was thinking of taking the kids to the zoo."

"Just make sure Will doesn't touch any of the animals and you keep him back from the cages," she instructed. "And don't give him too many candies at the theatre. Don't forget to..."

"We're going to the zoo?" Will ran up to us and flashed his big blue eyes. "Can I play with the polar bear?"

Nyah trailed up behind. "Sorry, I told him we were going out with Grady this morning and Will got excited. He's a quick little guy."

Marin laughed. "That's fine, Nyah, Will's got a mind of his own."

"Okay big ears." I tousled Will's hair. "We'll see if the polar bear's up for it."

"Grady, no!" Marin cried. "Will is not to go near the polar bear or any other animal."

"When did you stop being any fun, Marin? I was joking."

"Even you aren't that stupid," Hank said. He had joined us on the porch. "Luckily they have procedures to keep idiots away from the animals."

The man was seventy-two and built like an oak tree. Everything about him was square, from his grey brush cut to his jaw to his shoulders. Authority oozed from his pores. He was born a cop, and it made me uneasy.

"If I'm okay with the moron taking my grandson you should be," Hank said. "Hell, even Daria agreed, and she hates his guts."

Marin nodded. "Okay, Dad."

Hank nodded in the direction of Nyah, but didn't look at her. "Who's this?"

"This is Nyah, Dad. She's a friend of ours."

"Grady has no friends, just accomplices. She's a little

young for you to be chumming with, Marin."

"We need to talk, Dad. In private."

"That's just your way of saying you want me to do something that I'm not going to want to do."

"Dad, just hear me out."

"So you can explain to me how I just have to help this girl?" Marin's eyes bulged and jaw dropped, and the old man laughed. "I'm old not dumb, I can see where this is going. So quit beating around the bush and tell me why she's going to be staying with me."

"Who said anything about that?"

"Please Marin, the only way it would be more obvious is if she had luggage."

"I wouldn't ask you if it wasn't important. Really, do you expect me to believe you'd just leave her to the street?"

"I'm not running a halfway house here, Marin. You come and go as the mood takes you, your sister won't leave and the only one of the lot of you I like is Will."

"Can't blame you there," I said.

"Dad! Not here, let's go inside," Marin said.

Nyah strode past us, her hand out stretched. "Hello Mr. Seminak, my name's Nyah, and I'm sorry for all the trouble."

Hank blushed and shook her hand. "Nice to meet you," he mumbled. "I apologise Nyah, but I'm not a big fan of change."

"Me either, but it happens anyway."

"Ain't that the truth."

"Marin said you used to be a cop."

"Thirty-five years in uniform."

"So was my dad." Nyah sighed. "But that's a long story."

"I think I want to hear this," I said.

"You're going to the zoo," Marin said.

"Yes, Grady, you and Will go have some fun," Hank said. "Marin, take Nyah inside and go put on some tea. The three of us will have a chat."

Marin frowned. "And leave Grady and Will alone together?"

"It'll be fine. Will is old enough to keep Grady out of trouble."

Marin scooped Will up in her arms, kissing and hugging the kid like he was being shipped off to war, not taking a day trip with his uncle. Nyah shot me a smile and shrugged before following my wife into the house.

"Thanks, Hank," I said when we were alone.

"Shut up," Hank barked. "What were you thinking getting arrested again? She has enough reasons to whoop your ass as it is, why on earth do you keeping adding to them?"

"I like the excitement."

"You're a horse's ass."

"I was helping Reece."

"You're a waste, you know that? You could make something of yourself if you tried."

"I'm happy where I'm at."

"Where exactly is that?"

There was no right answer, so I said nothing.

"Marin's just angry. Really angry," Hank said, breaking the quiet. "She had certain expectations of your life together and you let her down."

"She's right to hate me."

"I never said she wasn't, but no one is perfect and I pissed my wife off too. Not like you, but there isn't a husband born that hasn't spent a night on the couch for being an idiot. Still, it's important to remember, to ..." Hank swayed on his feet, the words stuck in his throat. "Have to remem...remem...mem..."

Hank stumbled forward, his body limp. I caught him by the arms and eased him back, propping him against the house.

"Hank, you okay?" His face was grey, coated by sweat and his eyes were unfocused. "Hank, what's wrong? Talk to me."

He shook his head and the color crept back into his cheeks. "Sorry, Grady, got a little light headed there." He straightened himself and looked back into his house. "I haven't eaten much today. I'm too old to get away with that anymore."

"Sit down while I get Marin."

"No, it's nothing to concern her with."

"You need a doctor."

He set his jaw and glared at me. "I'm going to see him today, dummy, right after I'm done getting bossed around by my daughter."

My attention was stolen by the forgotten BMW. The doors opened, and Franny Manheim stepped out, all wild red hair in a slinky black dress. Her boy toy, Shamus Gray was with her, spiffed up in a slick blue suit. The bruises on his face ruined the look.

"Hank, take Will inside," I ordered.

"Friends of yours?"

"Not even close."

"If that skinny fella is going to be trouble, I still have my old service revolver."

"Just get Will inside. Now."

It was the "now," he responded to, and the urgency of it. The old cop's instincts took over and Hank scooped up Will and got him into the house.

I met Shamus and Franny in the street. Dangerous or not, I was prepared to tear out the freak's throat to protect my family.

"Beat it, Shamus," I said. "And take the bitch with you."

A grin slithered to his face. "That's not polite, especially since you've been so disrespectful already."

"I've done nothing to you, Shamus, but that can

change."

Franny's face contorted in hate. "What about killing Watson? What about knocking out Shamus?"

"I think you'll both get over it."

"Your brother shot me," she spat. "I'm supposed to get over that?"

"You crossed the line coming here. If you don't fuck off, I'll kill you both."

"You're a slow witted drunk. I can smell you from here." Shamus opened his jacket, displaying his gun. A HK 9mm. "This says I'm not worried."

I closed the gap between us. "Here's the thing, your piece is still in its holster. You think you can get it before I break your fucking arm?" I grabbed his wrist and twisted it back, Shamus howled and dropped to his knees. "Worried now, Shamus?"

Franny's eyes went wild with fear. Women are usually smarter. "We just want what you stole from us."

"I don't have your money," I told her.

Shamus laughed. "Money? Don't play games, Grady, you know what you took."

I punched him twice in the mouth and as he collapsed I slipped the gun from him. I kicked him in the ribs as I pocketed the piece. Franny moved at me, but I waggled my finger. "Shamus deserved that for coming here. Now listen to me, I ain't got the foggiest idea what the fuck you're talking about. I was only at Watson's to get my brother, I didn't take a thing. Maybe Reece has your shit."

"He doesn't have it," Franny said. "We'd know."

"I'm still lost here," I said.

Shamus picked himself up and stumbled to the safety of the BMW. "Don't play stupid, Fisk. We know you took the file."

"File? What fucking file?"

"You have a sweet young child, and a tasty woman to

worry about." Shamus ran his tongue over his teeth. "Think about those worth saving and give us the file."

"Don't talk about them."

"Who was the young girl with your wife? Don't tell me you have a daughter too."

"I'm warning you Shamus."

"That's no child of his," Franny said. "I know that girl."

"You're going to forget about all of them," I said. "If you're even the tiniest bit smart."

Shamus sniffed. "They look so fresh, I wonder how they taste."

I lashed out, drilling Shamus in the jaw. I swung again and caught him in the nose, blood exploding from his face. Before I landed another shot, Franny pulled a gun from her purse and jammed it under my chin. "We asked nicely, you bastard. Now give it to us."

I dropped my hands and backed up. Shamus wiped the blood from his face. "I'll kill you for that, but first I'll slice your wife to pieces and feed her to my dog."

"Focus," Franny told him. "We're here for the file."

A loud voice boomed behind us. "Lady, put down that gun or I'll blow your guts out."

Hank stood on the porch with his revolver, Marin hovered behind him. Hank aimed the gun at Shamus, but his hand shook. Was he scared? Not Hank the oak. It had to be the adrenaline, but either made him a bad shot with me in the way.

"I got this," I said.

"Doesn't look like it," Hank said. "Last warning lady, drop the gun and scram or I'll put lead into both of you."

"I'll kill him first," Franny vowed.

"Never liked him anyway," Hank said. "But, young one, while you're busy killing Grady, I'll be shooting at you."

Shamus smiled. "You lie old man."

"No," I said. "He really hates me."

Marin poked her head out from behind her father. "The cops are already on the way, you better just leave."

Shamus considered this for a moment before nodding. "This is your last warning." He dug his fingers into my throat, cutting off my air. "Do you understand how serious I am?"

I nodded. It was all I could do.

Shamus released his grip and I dropped to my knees, gasping for air. Each breath burned my throat and my head felt like it would explode as the blood rushed back in.

Car doors slammed and the BMW tore off. Marin and Hank rushed to me, helping me stand. Marin checked my neck, and I shivered at her touch. Our eyes met for a moment, and everything was alright until she realised what she was doing. Marin spasmed, stepped back and crossed her arms over her chest. The shadow came back and it felt a little colder.

"Are you alright?" she asked.

"In the context of the last few days that was nothing."

"Who where those people?' Hank asked. "And no foolishness about you not knowing."

"Bad people," I answered. "Bad and dangerous." Hank held the gun at his side. His hand still shook. "You okay?" I asked.

He shot a glance at Marin. "I'm fine, it's just proof I'm getting old. Now what did they come for?"

"They said I had a file of theirs."

Marin frowned. "That you probably stole."

"They were mistaken. I told them so."

"They believe you?" Hank asked.

"No, they didn't, but I'll make sure they get the message."

"Is that what's important to you, revenge?" Marin slapped me and I stumbled back from shock. "How dare you bring those people around Will and Nyah?"

Fool Whiskey Hero

I had nothing to say, and knew I had to leave before she told me never to come back.

I staggered over to my car and got in. Ignoring Marin's shouts, I keyed the ignition and drove away.

ELEVEN

From Hank's, my liver led me like a homing pigeon to the nearest LC. I spent my last twenty bucks on a couple bottles of rye and drank straight from the bottle on the drive home. Each drink got me closer to forgetting that I almost got my entire family shot.

My head got fuzzy and I stopped caring about Jacob or the dumb woman who'd stolen from him. By the time I knocked over the garbage cans in front of my building parking the Bel Air, I'd even fogged out my brother's sudden proficiency for getting people killed. I left the empty bottle in the front seat of the Old Girl, carrying the rest of the rye up to my apartment where I drained another bottle dry, blacking out in record time.

I woke under my bed the next morning soaked in sweat and my sheets wrapped around my legs. My skull had collapsed in on my brain. Alcohol is a cruel mistress, holding tight her embrace while shielding you from pain. She represses the memories, and stems the tide of guilt. But those emotions don't go away, they build. The pressure causes cracks, and the memories and pain burst free. That's where the nightmares come from. There's always a price.

Untangling myself from the sheets, I shuffled into the kitchen, plunging my face under the tap. The cold water pulled me further into consciousness. I grabbed a beer from the fridge and choked it down. Every drunk knows it's the fastest cure. Well into my second beer, my cell rang. It was Reece.

I answered. "Quit bothering me."

"*You up for a ride to see Drake, man?*"

"I doubt it. I'm trying not to puke."

"We need to see our lawyer, man."

"You going to explain to Drake how you got Sara Silo and that Bert guy killed?"

"I didn't do nothing, man. Bert was driving, he was drunk and it was a fucking accident."

"You pushed her, Reece, I saw it."

"I panicked cause a drunk asshole was driving his truck at me."

"It's a little too convenient that a witness against us is now dead."

"You should be happy, man."

"Fuck you." I hung up.

The phone was in my hand, so I took it as a sign to call Marin. My call went straight to voicemail. I dialled Hank's place. No answer. So I dialled again and after the tenth try Daria picked up. She told me that Marin wasn't taking my calls.

"Marin needs to hear my side," I said.

"She's not interested, but you'll damn well listen to me. How dare you put my son in danger? A man was waving a gun right in front of him. He could have been shot, Grady."

"You think it's my fault?"

"Whose fault is it then? He's just a little kid, Grady, it's your job to keep him safe."

"It's not like I invited Shamus over for tea, Daria. I can't help it if he's a fucking lunatic."

"Shamus came to see you, so if you're not to blame then who, Grady?"

I had no answer for that.

"I'll tell Marin you called," Daria said and hung up.

With Shamus, things could have gotten very deadly and bloody. Will was put in danger because of me and another two beers did nothing to take away the guilt. They did start my stomach growling. My fridge held nothing but condiments and spoiled milk, so I left my apartment in search of food. Reece was waiting outside my building, leaning against a brand new black Jaguar that was so shiny it looked wet. Did I have the only shitty ride in Winnipeg?

"Where the fuck did you get that car?" I asked.

"Drake lent it to me, man. He wants me to keep a low profile."

"A druggie in a Jaguar is inconspicuous?" I sighed. "Take me to get some food."

"We gotta go check in with Drake. It's important, man."

"So is getting a pizza."

"Please, Grady, after we see Drake I'll take you anywhere you want, man."

Drake's office was downtown, on Donald Street, right across from the MTS Centre where the Winnipeg Jets play. The rink stood on the site of the demolished Eaton's building. The former department store was an old meeting spot and once the heart of the city. It was "The Big Store." Locals tried to save the building as generations had grown up shopping there. Childhoods were land marked by the visit to Santa or the bike they got for their birthday. A part of the city's soul was ripped out the day it was torn down. Well, what was left of that soul after the Jets left fifteen years ago.

Taking an NHL team out of a Canadian city could kill it. We'd hoped for an opportunity to cheer for a team in the big league again. We'd have taken anyone, and we acted like the ugly girl at the dance, but twice as desperate.

But the Jets came back. A team going bankrupt in Atlanta was bought and moved here. The Jets were reborn and the city was vibrant again.

We parked the Jag around back and hurried through the large wooden front doors to Drake's office. The air inside was warm and dry and I started sweating immediately. A secretary sat behind an immense oak desk. She was delicious. Fit with dark tanned skin, her black dress looked painted on and I savoured every curve.

Her nameplate said, "Delilah." I was in lust.

"What do you desire?" she asked.

With effort I remembered that I was married. "Mr. Drake, is he here?"

Delilah rose from her seat and led us through the office to a large red door at the end of a long hallway. Four hefty men in suits sat on couches outside the door. They looked bored and uncomfortable. I took them for body guards straight off.

What kind of lawyer needed protection?

I guess the kind that lends an addict a Jaguar.

Delilah opened the red door and ushered us inside, closing it behind us. We found Drake at his desk and he smiled and closed the old leather bound book in front of him. He gestured to the two wooden chairs facing him. We sat, and I flashbacked to my frequent treks to the principal's office.

I nodded to Reece. "Why'd you send this moron to bring me here?"

"You were summoned to discuss business," our lawyer said.

"Let's start with your fee."

"As I said, you'll find a way to cover it. However, in regards to your case, I must say that the whore, Sara Silo, dying was fortunate."

"Not for her."

"Perhaps not." Drake paused. "Reece, would you please excuse us?"

"I'll just be in the lobby chatting up Delilah," my brother said and rose.

Drake smiled. "Be careful, she bites."

"I hope so, man."

The lawyer waited until we were alone before continuing. "Grady, I'll be frank; Jacob is not pleased regarding your slow progress in retrieving his lost property."

"That's it? You're wasting my time."

"When Jacob Poole is unpleased, people tend to get hurt."

"He's lost something, no one in his army can find it and you expect me to do it in a day?"

"It's been two."

"You better watch the attitude, because if you think that just because you're a lawyer I won't kick your ass then you're mistaken."

"You forget who I work for."

"He's not here, and your goons outside won't get in fast enough. Trust me."

"Why are you angry with me?"

"Let's see, I've been in jail, witnessed five murders and Shamus Grey showed up at my father-in-laws wanting to torture my whole family. You should be shocked I haven't totally lost my shit."

"When did Shamus approach you?"

"Yesterday."

"Well, that is curious."

"I'll deal with it."

"Someone will have to," Drake said. "In the mean time, you really must talk to those girls and find out who stole Jacob's property."

"I have been. Sara Silo didn't take anything, she was too scared to."

"And you believed her?"

"I did, not that it matters since she's dead. It would really help if I knew what I was looking for."

"You don't need to know."

"So, you don't know either then?"

"Do as you're told and find the girl."

"That's the problem. What girl? It's becoming pretty fucking obvious this is a huge waste of time."

"I would think that you would be quite motivated to find her." Drake paused and pursed his lips. "Of course, I'm not the one going to jail."

"Why the hell would I be?"

"For killing Watson."

"But I didn't."

"The only one who can assure that you remain free is me, your lawyer." He sat back in his chair picked up his pen and twirled it in his fingers. "You would do well to remember that."

"You said the cops have no case."

"They'll need to pin those murders on someone."

"How about Shamus since he actually killed them?"

"Facts don't always have place in court."

"Sounds like you're threatening me now."

"Good, you're not completely stupid."

I got up and opened the door. "We're done here."

Drake set down his pen and pressed his finger tips together under his chin. "Did Shamus ever mention what he wanted?"

"He thinks I have some file."

"Do you?'

"Not that I know of."

"I doubt there is a file. However, if one should surface, contact me."

"What's the deal with this file?"

"It is nothing. I only wish for you to keep me apprised of your activities."

I said I would and left. I found Reece sulking in the waiting room. His romancing of Delilah hadn't gone well.

"It's not like she's the first girl to turn you down," I said.

"She didn't, man."

"Then why the sour face?"

"I'm not into what she's into."

"Kinky shit?"

"You have no idea, man."

We left Drake's office and as I closed the big wooden doors behind me, I took a look back at Delilah. She winked and licked her teeth. Reece was a fool. I would have tried whatever she wanted at least twice.

Fortunately, Reece and I weren't stuck walking, but this time I drove the shiny new Jaguar. I deserved it. Reece was too busy feeling sorry for himself, and I was left with time to think as we headed back to The Rub.

Maybe I would finally get to drink in peace and work out why people were so fixated on this file. Three people had called it unimportant, but they all wanted it pretty bad. The alarm bells were giving me a headache.

TWELVE

Gripping the steering wheel of Drake's Jaguar hard enough to snap it, I stamped my foot on the accelerator. The car reacted to my every movement like it was linked to my mind. Jumping out of airplanes in the army had been the greatest rush of my life. The wind ripping past us, we'd free fall for a thousand feet waiting to open our shoots. With only subtle movements of my hands and feet I'd cut through the open sky to my target. Driving the Jag was closer to that than anything else I've experienced on the ground.

Reece snored away in the passenger seat. The nasal whine and guttural rasp of his breathing frayed my nerves. My phone rang, and the distraction saved Reece's life. It was Marin.

"I thought you weren't talking to me," I said.

She sighed. "*I'm not.*"

"Calling me is a funny way to go about it."

"*Something came up that's more important than being mad at you.*"

"This should be good..."

"*Nyah went to that crack house to collect some of her things. I didn't approve but she wouldn't listen and wouldn't let me go with her.*"

"Why are you telling me this?"

"*She shouldn't be there alone.*"

"If I go check up on her, you'll forgive me?"

"*No, but I won't be as mad.*"

"I'll take it," I said and hung up.

Outside The Rub, I put the Jag into park, leaned over and shook Reece until his eyes opened.

"Go inside and drink your face off," I told him.

My brother rubbed his eyes. "Aren't you coming in to party with me, man?"

"Change of plans, little brother, I have an errand to run."

"Drake's not gonna like you taking his car, man."

"He let you drive it, how mad could he get?"

"Whatever, man, it ain't my ride," he said and got out.

Slipping the Jag into gear, I peeled out into the street. After three blocks I kicked myself for not grabbing a quick whiskey at The Rub before leaving. The need morphed into a full fledge monster and clawed at my insides. I tried to push it aside, but the beast wasn't going anywhere until it was fed.

The sign for the Liquor Store beckoned. I pulled the Jag into the parking lot, left it running and dashed inside the store. I grabbed a Mickey of Five Star Whisky and tossed a twenty at the cashier. I had the cap off and bottle to my lips as I slipped back behind the wheel. By the time I was parking the Jag a block from Watson's old house, the Monster was smiling and had withdrawn its talons.

Gracefully, I drunk stumbled up the sidewalk. I'd locked the doors, but in that neighbourhood it'd be a miracle if the Jag wasn't stolen. I snuck another drink and tucked the Mickey into my back pocket.

The street was deserted except for Nyah staring up at the curb from Watson's house. If she clenched her jaw any tighter her teeth would crack.

She addressed me without looking at me. "I told Marin I didn't need help."

I stopped beside her and joined in staring at the house. "Here's the thing about Marin, she's going to do what she thinks is right no matter what anyone says."

"Why did she send you?"

"Because I do whatever she says no matter what I think

is right. It's a vicious circle."

"Just as long as you realise I'm going in there no matter what."

"Then why are you out here?"

"Because I'm scared."

"Worried you might catch something? That carpet looked like ground zero for herpes."

"The last time I went in the house that guy Shamus found me and chased me for hours the night he killed my Mom."

Ice wrapped around my spine. "Shamus? He chased you? What the Hell for?"

"I don't know. I wasn't going to let the douche bag catch me so I could ask. That's why I stayed inside Hank's house, because I thought he was there for me."

"Nyah, this may sound random, but you wouldn't be going into that house to get a file folder would you?"

She shook her head. "Nope."

I pulled out the Mickey, took a drink and ignored the sour face Nyah gave me. "So what's so important in there?"

"I left my phone inside and I really don't want to go to the police and ask if I can have it back."

"With all the fancy yellow tape and such, I'm pretty confident this is still a crime scene. We go inside and you might not have a choice about talking to the cops."

"I guess you're here so that doesn't happen."

"Why go to all this trouble when you could just buy a new phone."

"Are you going to lend me the money?"

"Good point." I let my gaze drift from the house and sweep over the street and sidewalks. "I don't see anyone around."

She bit her lip. "So you're saying that it's safe?"

"Nope, that's not the same thing at all, but we might as well get what we came for."

Tripping off the sidewalk, I crossed the street. Nyah trailed behind me down the path and up the front steps of the house. I pulled down the yellow police tape that adorned the front door. It was still unlocked and swung open freely when I turned the handle. The stench of mold and rot assaulted my nose.

"So we're just going to walk right in?" Nyah asked from behind me.

"Well, I haven't worked out teleporting yet."

She grabbed my sleeve. "What if someone's in there?"

"We'll deal with it. One way or the other."

"What if it's that Shamus? Are you going to fight? Are you going to kill him, Grady?"

"I can't say off the top of my head." I twisted the cap off the Mickey and took a pull. "I'm hoping it doesn't come to that, but I promise you this; I'll do what I have to do to keep you safe."

I gave her my best smile, took one more drink before recapping the bottle and tucked it away. I stepped into the house and onto the squishy rotten carpet.

"Marin hates that you drink," the girl said as she followed.

We picked our way past the empty bottles, garbage, and dirty blankets left by the squatters who'd ignored the police tape and no trespassing signs. I stepped aside to let her lead the way. I searched the shadows for monsters or junkies waiting to attack, but if they were there they stayed hidden.

"What Marin hates about me is long list," I said.

"You can't be too bright if you'd risk losing someone like Marin."

"I know that."

"Then why do you keep screwing it up?"

"You and Hank are gonna get along great."

In her mother's old room, the girl stopped dead at the dried puddle of her mother's blood. She swayed on her feet as though something had plowed right through her. Her hand covered her mouth as the sob caught in her throat.

I was an idiot. I should have gotten Nyah to tell me where the phone was and gotten it myself. No kid should have to see where their mother died, especially for a second time. Nyah held up her arms as if shielding herself from the onslaught of nightmares. She turned her back, and waved me away when I reached for her.

"Do you realise how lucky you are that Marin even gives you the time of day?" Nyah asked as though our conversation hadn't been paused. "Any other woman would have dumped your ass by now."

"You're not the first to tell me that." The warmth of the whisky filled me as I stole another drink. "When Shamus found you here, did he say what he wanted?"

"I didn't stick around to find out."

"And you're positive you didn't take some file of his?"

"I never saw him before he shot my Mom."

She yanked open the closet door, crouched down and jimmied the baseboard, exposing her little hidey hole. I'd had one myself as a kid. There was a loose floorboard under my bed where I'd hid some money, hockey cards and a knife from my Dad. The old man would have learned about the knife if he'd touched my Mom again. Least that's what I told myself, but I never grew the balls to do it.

Nyah stood and held her phone in one hand and a box of trinkets in the other. "Got it," she said, tucking the box under her arm. "We can go now."

"So that's all you want, just the phone and the box? You don't want those clothes or nothing?"

The girl let her fingers trail over the dresses her mother had left behind. "There's nothing else here I want to remember."

Tears traced down her cheeks as she walked past me and out into the hallway. She'd already powered on her phone and was busy flicking through it by the time I caught up. Flicking and tapping, Nyah had her face buried into her screen. The house around her had effectively disappeared, except for the wall she almost walked into.

"Dammit, Nyah, you've had that thing in hand for two minutes and you're already lost to the world," I barked.

"Relax, I'm just checking to make sure I didn't lose any data. You're such an old nag."

"I learned it from Marin. Now can you think of any reason why Shamus was poking around?"

"Maybe he was looking for you? Did Shamus mention me when you two were fighting at Hank's?"

"No, he didn't, but he was pretty busy threatening to kill me."

She tucked her phone into her pocket. "My phone's fine and everything is here, so we can go home now."

"Works for me," I said and led the way out.

To celebrate our second, and much less eventful, visit to Watson's house, I took a drink of whiskey. We made our way down the sidewalk and when we finally stopped at the Jaguar, Nyah's eyes nearly popped out of her head.

Is this your car?" she asked.

"No, it belongs to a friend."

"You mean you stole it."

"Did they clone Marin to create you? No, I didn't steal it, my lawyer lent it to me." I keyed the door and opened it for her. "Now get in big mouth."

Nyah took a step back. "I'm not driving anywhere with you."

"What, you're going to walk to Hank's?"

"You've been drinking."

I tossed Nyah the keys. "You drive then."

She tried to hand them back. "Are you serious? I can't drive. Well, my Mom was teaching me on her car before..." She looked away. "I don't have my licence yet."

"So you have your learner's permit?"

"Yes, but..."

"Christ, my brother drives and he's a complete moron. Who do you want behind the wheel, me or you? It's your call."

Nyah ground the gears and destroyed the transmission turning from Burrows onto McPhillips. The Jag bucked, stalled and cried out in pain as she restarted it and got us moving down the road. I took a drink and the whisky dribbled down my chin as she jumped the clutch.

"Can you stop drinking until we get home? I need help here," she said.

"It's to steady my nerves," I said. "Your driving is giving me a heart attack."

Nyah stopped at a red light, waiting to turn onto Notre Dame when a black BMW pulled up beside us. Some big goon with a shaved head sat in the passenger seat and Shamus Gray was behind the wheel. I locked eyes with Shamus and his jaw dropped while my heart rate tripled.

Shamus screamed and spittle flew out his open window. Our window was closed and the stereo was cranked so I couldn't hear a word. The goon pulled out a gun and aimed it at my head. That I understood.

Stunned into the void, Nyah froze. The goon fired a shot and our windshield shattered, covering us with glass. Nyah woke up and got us the fuck out of there.

We were nearly creamed by a bus and cars slammed into each other in our wake. Nyah mashed the gas pedal into the floor, pushing the needle far into the red, and I had to pinch her to shift gears.

Shamus was right on our ass with his goon hanging out the window blasting rounds. Nyah was completely out of control and we weren't going to shake them. We sped from back alleys to side streets and through bike paths. Our route was direct and simple to follow. We'd eventually get a bullet in the arse.

Nyah tried to cut through a parking lot. It was a dead end so she slammed the Jag into reverse, the tires squealed as we spun around. Shamus was a block away, rocketing towards our only exit.

I jumped out, ran around the car and shoved Nyah into the passenger seat. I climbed in, threw the Jag in gear and tore out. We met at the entrance, Shamus swerved and we clipped bumpers, spinning us out into the street and Shamus into the parking lot.

We flew down the street while Shamus lost time manoeuvring out of the lot. I took a left, then the next right, taking streets at the first opportunity. With no sight of Shamus in the rear-view mirror, I was positive we'd lost him. After five minutes, I brought the Jag back to civilian speed and took a breath.

It was a short reprieve.

The BMW slid around the corner behind us and was right on our ass with the goon spraying us with bullets. Our rear window exploded.

With both feet, I stomped on the brakes and Shamus smashed right into the back of us. The airbag exploded in my face and Nyah grunted as her seat belt dug in and caused her head to snap forward. Both cars locked together and spun in a tight circle. The goon tumbled through the air past us, his arms and legs flailing.

Our Jag slid to a stop.

I scrambled out, my legs wobbled as my brain reset itself. Nyah was fighting to hang onto consciousness, her face full of blood and her eyes glazed. My nose ached from the airbag's kiss, but wasn't broken.

The goon lay motionless in the street. His knee bent the wrong way and his foot was twisted right around. Most of his skin had been grated off from body surfing across the asphalt. His face was a lump of bloody, raw meat and he was barely breathing.

Nyah fell out of the car then used it as a brace to stand. The Jag was trashed and Nyah slowly, painfully, surveyed the carnage.

"Oh my God, look at the car," she gasped. "We should both be dead. Your friend is going to be pissed."

"Relax, it's over."

The BMW was crumpled and easily four feet shorter. Shamus wasn't in any better shape. His nose spread across his face and a long gash split his forehead. The grip of his Glock 9mm was visible in his waist band. I took it before hauling Shamus out of his seat by the neck and tossing him on the ground. He couldn't rise off his knees.

Nyah stumbled behind me. "What are you going to do to him?"

"Back in the car, Nyah."

"He just tried to kill us."

"Nyah, get in the car."

She shook her head. "He tried to kill us, Grady. He killed my mother and he's an asshole. Shoot this piece of shit."

I had the gun to Shamus' head, my finger on the trigger. I could imagine it; the muzzle flash, the blood spraying and Shamus' skull and grey matter splattering the pavement. The asshole deserved it.

My hand tightened around the gun as my fingers teased the trigger. The reasons why not to shoot grew quiet.

With effort I lowered the gun. I wasn't that guy.

"Stay away, Shamus, this is your last warning," I said. "I see you again, I'll kill you."

Shamus nodded and mumbled as blood bubbled from his lips.

Nyah tried to take the gun from my hand. "If you're such a coward, I'll do it."

I grabbed the girl by the arm, and threw her to the

ground. Sirens wailed in the distance. "I'm leaving, so if you want to stick around and explain this, fine."

The sirens came from all directions. It sounded like the whole force had been deployed.

Nyah took a deep breath. "Fine. Let's get out of here."

We hustled to the Jag. Surprisingly it started, and we tore out of there. I kept to the side streets until we were well away from the crash. We talked about where to ditch the car. After a quick phone call to Drake, which involved a lot of swearing and even more threats, my lawyer promised one of his goons would handle it. We only had to get it to the ditch point.

THIRTEEN

The mangled Jaguar looked like it had fought a tank and lost. In the parking lot of the Polo Park mall, among the Minivan's and SUV's, we were miles from inconspicuous and slightly out of place. I didn't care. The adrenaline had burned through me and I was starving.

We stopped for burgers on way to the mall. Nyah wasn't hungry and stared out the cracked windshield. I sat beside her with bag of take out on my lap and the grease from the tasty double patty, fully loaded bacon monstrosity dripping off my chin. After gobbling up the last of my burger and chasing it with a handful of fries, I pulled a second burger out of the take-out bag and offered it to Nyah. "You sure you don't want one?"

"I can't, my stomach's in knots," she said. "And watching you eat isn't helping. You're like a wild animal."

"I'm not far off, that's for sure." I took the second big juicy heart attack on a bun and bit into it. "You change your mind I'll get something later."

"I can't believe that just happened." She shivered. "All the shooting, crashing cars and the blood..."

"It's not something you'd want to do every day."

"I was crapping my pants and I'm still trying not to barf and you're just happily munching on your burger."

Burgers and fries weren't the only treats I'd stopped for on the way to the parking lot. I waggled the fresh Mickey of whiskey I'd acquired in front of her. "This keeps me even."

"So I should start drinking then?"

"Smart girls shouldn't say stupid things."

"I was being sarcastic."

"It still shows how little you know."

"Oh I know, trust me, my Mom was a full out druggie, and what I know is that drugs or alcohol doesn't help anything."

"You some sort of Doctor?"

"After my Dad died Mom turned to drugs because she couldn't deal with life. Drugs and alcohol don't keep you even, they keep you numb."

"Sometimes that's not so bad."

"Except you'll always be messed up if you don't deal with your issues. So you'll do more drinking and drugs because it takes more to keep you numb. The only way that ends is when you die."

I winced and looked away. "See, I said you were smart."

"I'm sorry," she said. "But you pushed me."

I nodded and forced myself to smile. "So, you told Hank your Dad was a cop, that the truth?"

She wiped her eyes with the cuff of her hoodie. "My earliest memories are of my Dad going off to work in his uniform. He was so handsome, and all the other kids were so jealous because my Dad was a cop."

"How did he die?"

"He was shot on the job and they never caught who did it. One night he just never came home and some other man in uniform came by and told us he'd been killed. My Mom never left that moment, I don't think."

"Sorry, we don't have to talk about it."

"No, it's okay. It was just all a chain reaction, you know? One bad thing led to the next and we just kept falling." The sob stuck in her throat. "Dad died, Mom turned to drugs which she got from Vern and that was when our life spun into total crap. But it started when Dad died."

"Vern was her dealer?"

"He'd drop off the drugs, they'd talk and eventually he was around all the time. When Mom ran out of money it became more than that."

"Then he got her working for Watson?"

"I don't want to talk about him, please, it makes me sick."

"I understand about shitty Dads."

Her eyes went cold and hard. "Vern is not my Dad."

"That doesn't make it better."

The girl turned away. "No, it's much worse."

My rusted out Chevy Bel-Air turned into the parking lot and stopped in front of us. Two of Drake's bodyguards stepped out. The only set of keys to the Old Girl were in my pocket, but growing up with Reece, I was aware of the multitude of ways to steal a car. At least they hadn't broken the steering column and jammed a screw driver into the key slot to get her going.

Nyah and I climbed out of the Jag and limped towards my car. I tossed the keys to Drake's busted ride to one of the goons, slipped behind the wheel of the Chevy and waited until Nyah secured her seatbelt before driving out of the parking lot and onto Portage Avenue.

"You dropping me off back at Hank's?" Nyah asked.

"I have to run an errand first," I said. "I need to pick up a gun."

"You already have the one you took from Shamus."

"I have no idea what it's been used for. I get picked up by the cops and they run it, the next thing I know I'm on the hook for half a dozen murders."

Nyah raised her eyebrow. "Kinda like you are now?"

"Funny girl." I sighed. "Anyway, I have to get a clean one. Good news is I got a guy."

"I thought you weren't a crook."

"I'm not."

"Then why do you have a gun guy?"

"Listen, I'm not a doctor either but I know where the hospital is."

She rolled her eyes so fast I thought they might spin out

of her head. "You know that's not the same thing."

"A gun is a tool like anything else. Are you going to argue that we don't need one?"

"Fine, but if you can help it I'd don't want to get shot at again today."

"Not sure I can promise that."

From Henderson Highway, I pulled into the little suburb of Prichard Farms. It sits just outside of Winnipeg and is home to the newly rich who wanted to build million dollar mansions but wanted no part of Tuxedo and where Jacob lived. For one homeowner, that was on purpose. Basil Bray wanted to keep his distance from Jacob, and not out of fear.

The houses were modern monstrosities sprawling over huge two and three acre lots. In the end, I guess, that was the appeal. Sure Tuxedo had the status, but in Prichard Farms you built the mansion you wanted, and had the huge yard to go with it outside the cramped quarters of the city. In Tuxedo, you bought someone else's vision of luxury and were usually forced to spend almost as much renovating.

But those are rich people problems and not my concern.

The Old Girl glided onto Basil's driveway and stopped at the gate which barred us access from the stone laid roundabout and Basil's manor. The house loomed over us, and I watched Nyah's jaw drop at its magnificence. Done completely in stone with gigantic windows, one of which was stain glass above the oak double doors, Basil's place looked ripped from the middle of an English countryside. I pressed the intercom button and waited.

"*No one asked for you to come, Grady,*" an angry squeaky female voice chirped at me.

"How'd you know it was me, Gabby?"

"*I can smell the booze on you from here,*" Gabby snapped. "*What do you want?*"

"I have an appointment with Basil."

The intercom clicked off and the gates opened. I pulled the car through slowly and headed for the house.

"Who was that?" Nyah asked.

"Gabby's my biggest fan."

Nyah laughed. "Isn't everyone? So how do you know this gun guy?"

"When I got out of the army I needed to make quick cash. A guy I served with pointed to me to Basil. I did a few jobs for him, but in the end it didn't work out."

"Did it have anything to do with you being drunk?"

"Basil said I wasn't trustworthy, but, it's the same thing. Regardless, I can go to him if I ever need anything."

"Like a gun?"

"Among other things." I shook my head. "You always ask this many questions?"

Crossing her arms, she turned and found something to stare at out her window. "No."

I followed the roundabout until I came to the garage, which was bigger than the house I grew up in and had a large glass door wide enough to fit four cars at once with plenty of room to spare. The door opened and I pulled in and parked beside a black Cadillac Escalade. Nyah and I slipped out of the Chevy, and I was careful not to ding the Escalade's door with mine.

The garage door closed behind us, the door to the house opened and Gabby Bray stepped out. "You really going to park that piece of shit in my garage?" she demanded.

The lady was firm and fit in her cargo pants and pink turtle neck. The combination of her dimples, the fact she was short, slim and didn't have a whole lot of curves would lead someone to call her cute. But Gabby would stab you if you said that to her face, most likely in the neck. Gabby was Basil's little sister and his right hand.

"I didn't come here to be insulted, Gabby," I said. "I'm here on business."

"Well, then you got the bonus plan," Gabby said. "Grady Fisk, you have to be the dumbest guy I know."

"Is that a compliment?"

"Sounds more like a statement," Nyah offered.

I turned to the blonde girl. "Gabby doesn't need help."

"Don't sulk, Grady, this girl probably can't figure you out either," Gabby said.

"I'm hardly complicated," I said. "I drink and I fuck up, usually in that order."

"You're a drunk, Grady, I get that," Gabby said. "What I don't get is why you keep covering Reece's debts? The first time it happens I understand. He's your brother and when he owes his dealer a couple hundred bucks for coke, and is going to get his arm broke if he doesn't pay, you step up and help him out. That makes sense. But what kind of idiot owes over fifty grand because his brother can't stop using?"

"I'm not your average idiot."

Nyah grabbed my sleeve. "You owe that much for your brother?"

I nodded.

"She's right, you're a super idiot," Nyah said

"Figure it out, Grady, Reece isn't going to stop and you can't afford it anymore." Gabby shook her head. "Seriously, you couldn't afford it when you were at ten large. Now you've ruined your life over this and for what?"

"He's my brother, what else was I going to do?" I asked. "Let him get killed? But you'll be happy to know if he owes Jacob anymore cash he's on his own."

"Do you actually mean it?" Gabby asked.

I sighed. "No, I don't."

"Maybe instead of covering his debt you should have let some dealer break his legs," Gabby said. "It's harsh but maybe he'll learn his lesson."

"Reece would just wheel his ass to the nearest crack house."

"We can't choose our family," Nyah said. "Or help them even if we try."

"I like this one." Gabby pointed at Nyah. "It's sweet you look out for Reece, Grady, but family shouldn't be that much of a burden."

"Basil has you doesn't he?" I said.

A shadow emerged behind Gabby and filled the doorway. Basil stepped beside his sister and into the light. Basil is a very large, bald man. A shaved ape. With muscles on top of muscles, the t-shirt he wore under his leather coat looked painted on. Basil is full blooded Cree, and had a thunderbird tattoo on each forearm and four tear drops inked under his left eye. He's the last guy you'd want as a cell mate.

The big Cree was the biggest importer in Manitoba, not that you'd see his name on a sign or in the yellow pages. If you need something shipped without the police knowing, Basil is your man. He's smuggled drugs, stolen cars and even a rare silver Indian Cobra some reptile nut just had to have. However, Basil's big love has always been guns, and he's made a fortune from that love. His guns are clean, reliable and untraceable. The holy trinity for the lawless. Basil is the best. Period.

Gabby smiled at Nyah. "What's your name girl? Fisk was too rude to introduce us."

"I'm Nyah," the blonde girl said. "Grady said you're Gabby."

"I am, and you look too sweet to hang out with a waste like, Grady." Gabby sighed. "Anyway, this guy is Basil, my brother. No need to be scared of him, he's just a big teddy bear."

"The bear part I believe," Nyah said.

The big man led us into the kitchen, where the girls and I sat at the island, and I rested my elbows on the granite countertop. Basil got a pop each for the girls and I was lucky enough to be offered a warm glass of tap water.

Basil thumbed in Nyah's direction. "You into kidnapping now?"

"Marin asked me to give Nyah a hand with a little situation she's in."

"Marin's helping this girl?' Basil nodded. "Makes sense, Marin's good people."

"Except for her shitty taste in men," Gabby slipped in.

"Grady's got his flaws, but Marin could do worse," Nyah said sheepishly.

"Ah, you've met Grady's brother," Gabby laughed.

"Speaking of the Brothers Fisk, I've heard a lot about you two lately," Basil said. "What's going on with you, Grady?"

"Getting by, same as always," I said. "But I came here today because I need a piece."

The big man frowned. "No, you don't."

"I wouldn't be here otherwise."

"Bullshit. What do you need a gun for?"

"It's personal."

The big man arched an eyebrow as he looked down on me. "Does Marin approve of this?"

I slammed my fist into the granite counter top so hard the whole kitchen reverberated. Gabby and Nyah jumped in their seats. "Why the fuck does everyone ask me the same shitty questions?"

Basil held my gaze for a long moment. His face was blank and his eyes dead. "Okay, Grady, just relax," he said finally. "What exactly are you looking for?"

"Just a gun," I mumbled. "A pistol, nothing fancy, just reliable."

Basil turned and looked at his sister. Gabby ever so slightly tilted her head in Nyah's direction and shrugged. Basil drummed his fingers against his chin for a moment before nodding. Only once his sister returned his nod did

Basil speak. "Gabby, please take Nyah into the other room and watch some TV until Grady and I are done here."

Gabby hopped off her stool and held out her hand for Nyah. The blonde girl looked at me for reassurance and I gave her my best smile. "It's fine, you'll be okay as long as Gabby doesn't make you watch any of that reality crap."

"There's a reason no one likes you," Gabby said. "And it's not just because of the smell."

Nyah laughed as the two of them exited the kitchen arm and arm. They could have been normal high schoolers, except, Nyah had watched her mom fall from widow to addict, to hooker and then murder victim. And Gabby? Even if she didn't look it, she was long past high school. She sold guns and would slit your throat if you looked at her sideways.

Not sure who I was more scared of.

Basil left me alone in the kitchen while he went off to his personal armoury. I checked my cell phone. There were two texts from Davis wondering what I was up to, and another three from Drake. I deleted them all. My brother had also left a text, telling me to get back to him ASAP. Him I answered, but only to tell him to fuck off. I did, however, shoot Marin a quick message letting her know that everything was fine and not to worry that Nyah was safe with me. I hit send knowing how silly that sounded.

When Basil returned, he had a small, hard black case in his hand. He placed it on the island in front of me. I reached for it, but stopped short because Basil hadn't released the handle. My hand hung in mid air for a moment before it became awkward and I returned it to my lap.

"What now?" I asked.

"You want this piece? You tell me what's going on with you first," he said.

"I need it for protection."

"From who?"

"That's my business."

"You made it my business when you showed up here asking for a gun," Basil said. "Lots of stories going around about you, Grady. You've been arrested for killing a bunch of people and now I hear Shamus Gray is on your ass. Tell me what's up or no gun."

"And you heard all this how?"

"You think I'm some fucking punk in back alley selling dime bags? I know you and people know I know you so they tell me about the stupid things you do."

"It's no big deal, Basil, honestly."

Basil slid the case further away and leaned his elbow on it. "I guess you don't really need this then."

"What if I fight you for it?"

A smile spread across Basil's face. "Even you aren't that stupid. Imagine how hard it is to hold a gun with broken hands or to shoot while you're in a coma."

"You're a bully."

"I learned from my sister. Now quit being a princess and just tell me your fucking story."

What choice did I have? None. I told Basil every dirty drunken detail of what happened at Watson's and at Hank's with Shamus. I even went over Sara Silo and how that truck smashed the life out of her.

"Somehow none of this surprises me," he said when I'd finished. "You've always been a fuck up."

"I lay my soul bare and you insult me?"

He shrugged his massive shoulders. "Nyah was right, you should have killed Shamus. That lunatic isn't going away and the next time you might not have a choice."

"I'll deal with that then."

Basil pushed the case in front of me and opened it up. Sitting in a cushioned cut-out was a nickel plated Beretta 92F with three fully loaded magazines beside it. I took the pistol out of the case, feeling its heft in my hand. I worked the slide, finding it oiled and ready for use. I expected no less from Basil. I pocketed two of the clips and slapped the third home in the Beretta and racked the slide putting a bullet in the chamber. I slipped the gun into my waistband in the small of my back and adjusted my coat.

"If I didn't know better I'd say you knew what you were doing," Basil said.

"Handling a gun was the only useful thing I learned in the army."

"Look at you being modest. We both know what you're capable of."

"That was another man in another time, I'm just a fuck up now."

"Won't hear me arguing." He held put his hand. "Now fork over my two grand."

"I'm a little short," I mumbled.

"How short?"

My eyes dropped to my shoes. "All of it."

"Give me the piece."

"I need it for protection."

"Protection from me if you don't hand it over."

I backed away slowly. "It's not just for me, I've got Nyah to worry about too. What if Shamus comes for me again and I'm with Nyah and Marin?"

The big man's gaze drifted from me to the living room where the girls were laughing and having a great time. "Really? Bringing the girls into this? You've no fucking shame," he said. "Keep it for now, we'll work something out later."

"Thanks, I appreciate it."

"You know what I'm gonna do to you if you fuck me on this, right?"

"You know I do."

"Then say it."

I was saved from answering by the chirping of my cell

phone. It was a text from Reece. It said *"I need to see you, man. It's about the girl. Life and death, man."*

I showed it to Basil. "I gotta go. Can you keep an eye on Nyah while the girls hang out and then see she gets home?"

"You know, Grady, this whole deal is getting too big for you. Shamus is a bad dude and Jacob will swallow you whole," he said. "You need help, Grady, and for Nyah and Marin I'm willing to give it to you."

"Just watch the girl and then we'll talk," I said.

"Don't be a hero, Grady," he said. "This ain't the movies, in the real world, heroes get dead."

"I'm too tired for that bullshit. I just want this all to go away," I said and left.

FOURTEEN

My Chevy Bel-Air isn't the prettiest girl at the dance, but she's always been good to me so there was no reason for the ugly looks the Old Girl got as we waited at Basil's front gate to turn onto the street. Two BMW's and a Mercedes Benz crawled by, the driver's glaring at me as if our mere presence brought their property values down.

The way cleared and I eased the Bel Air out and headed towards Point Douglas, and whatever idiocy my brother stirred up. Reece didn't stop by to say hello, he came with his hand out for money. We never met up for coffee; he needed bailing out of jail. He never asked how I was, just if I could save his ass. Reece was a relentless wanting machine.

Red and blue lights flooded my car the moment I turned onto Lagimodière Blvd. A police cruiser filled my rear-view mirror. That Berretta felt enormous tucked into the small of my back, like I was sitting on a whale. I pulled over and the cruiser tucked in behind me. The Berretta had morphed from my ticket out of trouble to my ticket back to jail.

Quill tapped on my window and I obediently rolled it down.

"This is borderline stalking," I said. "I wasn't speeding, so is this because you miss me?"

He crossed his arms on my window sill. "Where's the girl, Grady? I know you were with Nyah."

"Are you imagining things now?"

"My sources tell me you've been hanging around with some kid." He reached into the Bel Air and clamped his hand onto my jaw. "The last time we chatted you swore you didn't know Nyah. Lie to me again, asshole, and you'll be drinking your dinner through a straw."

The pain exploded in waves from my jaw to the base of my skull, like Quill was drilling there with his fingers. I wanted to fight back, smash the cop's face with my boot, but that fight would go bad, even if I won. "I told you don't know any fucking Nyah."

Using both hands, Quill squeezed so hard his forearms shook. "Who is the girl, then?"

I grabbed his wrists, pulling them down and relieving some of the pressure. "Stop being a fucking prick."

The cop's face was red from the effort, a bead of sweat tracked down his nose. "Last time I'm going to ask, what is her name?"

Pressing my thumbs into the back of his hands, I peeled his grip off my face. The relief in the back of my skull was instant. I held his wrists, and looked the cop dead in the eye. "Sally," I said. "The girl's name is Sally."

Confusion swept over Quill's eyes. "What's her last name?"

"No idea."

"The Hell you mean no idea?"

I relaxed my grip. "Listen, she's Marin's niece." The lies were flowing freely. "I don't know if she took her Mom's name or her deadbeat Dad's."

The cop pulled his arms free, and wiped his hands on his pants as though my skin had soiled him. "Looks like I'm going to have to have a word with my source."

"And get your shit straight before interrogating me."

"It's a murder investigation, dummy, that's what we do, we investigate the suspects."

"Except not Shamus Gray, the guy who actually killed those people."

"You're still saying he was the one?"

"I'd bet my life on it."

"All you're missing is the actual proof."

"You need me to do your job for you?"

"If you ever do see Nyah, give me a call." Quill pulled a business card out of his shirt pocket and tossed it on my lap. "I'll be sure to see you around."

The cop turned on his heel and left.

My phone chirped. It was Reece calling. *"Where are you, man?"* he demanded when I answered.

"On my way to meet you," I said. "Read my fucking text."

"Damn, this is important, man. I need you here now."

"What did you do?"

"Nothing," he mumbled.

"Never, ever in your life have you ever done nothing."

"Whatever, man, we'll talk when you get here," he said and then repeated the address before hanging up.

I pulled into the parking lot of the Mushroom plant on Archibald. The plant's a hulking mass of steel and grime, and could easily double as a nuclear blast bunker. As ugly as it is, the real affront came from the smell. No way around it, mushrooms are grown in shit and the aroma hung in your nostrils for miles after the plant was in your rear-view mirror.

A group of workers were milling around their vehicles after shift, drinking beer from coolers in their trunks. A few girls were with them. Working girls. I don't know how low you have to be in the prostitute hierarchy to chase after the guys who work at the mushroom plant, but I guess their money was as good as the next guy's. Still, you'd think the prostitutes could have found less stinky johns to lay under.

My brother was leaning against a pillar in the shadows of the front gate watching the workers; those in a union and those not. I stopped the Old Girl beside him and held my breath as the addict opened the passenger door and hopped in.

"So what's the issue, Reece?"

"We gotta handle our shit, Grady."

"Damn it Reece, what the hell are you on?"

The addict shrugged. "Bunch of shit, man. Some Tramadol to even me out, Ritalin to keep me focused and a little coke to keep me on point, man."

"For what? You want to farm mushrooms now?"

"We gotta fix our fuck up from the other night before we get ended, big brother."

"What other night? At Watson's?"

Reece's eyes burned like hot coals in their sockets. "You have no idea, do you, man?"

"Explain it to me then, because you of all people owe me the truth, Reece."

"Whatever, man, but I went to Watson's place because the fucker was supposed to point out some girl who's linked to a friend of his..."

"Skip ahead. I already know that Watson knew which of the hookers stole from Jacob."

"That ain't the half of it, man. And the half you do know ain't all true either, big brother."

"I don't want to hear your bullshit, Reece. I'll start smashing your face if don't start talking."

"Okay, okay, it all started with some guy..."

"Names, Reece."

"I swear, man, I got no idea, but Davis found this guy who used to work with Shamus, and you know Jacob and Shamus are killing each other to control the drugs and shit, right?"

"So I've heard."

"Okay, man, well this friend of Watson's was holding some shit for Shamus. I don't know what it was, but Shamus was supposed to use it against Jacob."

"Is this the mystery thing that Jacob has me looking for?"

"Damn right, man, and before you ask, I don't have a

clue what it is except Jacob is spitting fucking nails to get it back. But I guess you know that too, right big brother?"

"I noticed."

In the parking lot, a few of the workers had left, most likely for home, supper and the wife and kids. Those that remained were now five beers deep and the only place they were looking to go was to bed with one of the whores.

"But the guy who was holding this thing for Shamus was a junkie," my brother continued. "And this dude got greedy and decided to fuck Shamus over."

"Imagine that, an addict you can't trust."

"Yeah, well, fuck you too," Reece snapped. "Anyway, this junkie called up Jacob and made a deal to give the thing back for some dope and cash, but some chick snatched it before the deal went down."

"So how the hell do you fit into all this?"

The union men and working girls were pairing off, drifting towards their cars to trade cash for the chance to catch herpes.

"This dude was supposed to meet me at Watson's to point out the thieving hooker and I was supposed to get Jacob's property back. Easy as cake, man..."

"Except Shamus showed up."

"And everything went to shit, man."

"I didn't see this friend," I said. "You and I were the only guys who didn't get shot."

The addict held up his hands. "He was supposed to be there, I guess Shamus spooked his ass."

"So why not tell me all this over the phone?"

"That's easy, big brother, you're here to help me out."

"Reece, whatever you got going on in that little drugged up brain of yours you can forget it."

Reece pointed towards the group of hookers still separating their prey from the herd. "What I got going on is her, man."

I followed his finger to a greasy haired girl with enough mascara and eye shadow to make a raccoon jealous. Tattoos covered every inch of visible skin, which was saying something because her dress was little more than a black nightie.

"What about her? I got no time..."

My words trailed off. I knew that girl. The first time I'd met her she'd offered me a blow job for drugs. I scanned the parking lot and found her old man lurking in the shadows off to the side. It was the same dude she had been riding when I'd walked into Watson's. According to the cops, they were Jenny and Mark Banks.

Mark scratched his face and arms continuously, tearing at his skin.

"What kind of filth sends his wife to hook?" I asked. "I bet he wouldn't get on his knees and earn their next fix."

"That chick was at Watson's." Reece grabbed handfuls of his hair and groaned. "Seriously, dude, we gotta get her to talk, beat her ass if we have to, but we gotta find Jacob's shit, man."

"And you want to do that in front of all these people? In front of her husband?"

"But Jacob said..."

"I'm not his slave, Reece." I reached across my brother and opened the passenger door. "Get out of my car."

"I'm not going anywhere, man."

"Like you got a choice dumbass."

Grabbing my brother by the shirt, I shoved him out of the car and onto his ass. After slamming the passenger door shut, I locked it. The addict dragged himself to his feet and dusted off his jeans. Grabbing hold of the handle, Reece gave the door a tug like he actually expected it to open. When that didn't work he kicked the door. My car. He kicked my Old Girl. I threw open my door and before I even had one foot on the concrete, Reece had scurried off for the shadows.

I closed my door and keyed the engine. Reece had wasted enough of my time. If Jenny or Mark Banks had stolen something of Jacob's, it was long sold and the proceeds snorted up their nose.

The Bel–Air rumbled as I shifted into drive the same moment Reece shambled into the crowd of drinkers and hookers. What was he doing? Was there even one functioning neuron in his head? It wouldn't take but the slightest offence for that bunch of factory workers to kick his ass. Let's get it straight, mushroom farming isn't like mining. If you want to keep all your teeth in your mouth, you don't fuck around with miners because they'll fight just for the sake of it. Miners or not, these mushroom guys weren't going to back down from a scrawny drug addict. I put the Old Girl back in park.

Reece dove head first through the workers, straight for Jenny Marks. He bumped some men and spilled their drinks. Their faces contorted with anger, eyes narrowed in aggression.

The first thing Reece did when he reached Jenny Banks was grab her by the arm, pull her close and yell in her ear. The second thing he did was fall back on his ass when one of the workers punched him straight in the mouth. The workers swarmed him, throwing wild punches and kicks. Mark Banks sprinted from the shadows, racing towards his wife. When my brother managed to get to his feet, he was holding a gun.

He fired twice. The first bullet shattered a truck window. The second sent a spray of blood from one of the worker's legs. The other girls screamed and the hookers ran into the night at impressive speed given the height of their heels. The men grabbed their injured buddy and made for their vehicles, dragging the bleeding man behind them.

Reece fired once more into the air. People scrambled in

every direction, vehicles ripped out of the parking lot and there was screaming, crying and confusion. Mark grabbed Jenny and they were in full sprint when Reece spotted them. His gun out in front, Reece took off after them firing wildly at their backs. Windshields and radiators exploded around them.

Jumping out of the Bell Air I tore after Reece. The couple was headed for the street, but Reece was going to catch them before they made it across. Cars sped past me, racing to get away from all the bullets. I jumped to the side, narrowly missed by a pickup truck and had to dive and roll over the hood of a station wagon, landing face first in the dirt. I got to my feet, and sprinted as fast as I could, closing the gap between Reece and I.

Now only a few feet away, I flung myself in the air, driving my shoulder into my brother's ribs. Reece grunted as the air went out of him and we tumbled into the ground. His gun fired as we hit concrete. A bullet slammed into Mark's back and blood burst out his chest. He stumbled, tripping over his now useless feet and skidded to a stop on his face. The blood spread quickly on the back of his shirt.

Mark Banks wasn't moving, not even with Jenny pulling desperately on his arm. Jenny wailed, her knees buckling under her as she tried to run for the street. She looked back one last time at her husband and tripped, pirouetting into the street and into the path of a city bus.

The girl was smushed and the bus dragged her fifty feet. Car horns pierced the night, and the passengers on the bus screamed and pounded on the glass. The driver got out and ran to help her. Jenny was dead. Her legs had landed ten feet from her body and the blood was emptying from both halves.

I looked down at my brother, wrapped my hands around his neck and screamed in his face. "What did you fucking do?"

He tried to pry my fingers off. "Just wanted to talk, man."

"You fucking shot at them! You killed that girl. You didn't want to talk, you had a fucking gun."

"I was supposed to scare her, man. Jacob's desperate; I didn't know what else to do when she ran, man."

"So you started shooting everyone? That was your first idea? You killed two people, Reece."

"Jacob's going to kill us, Grady. I don't give a shit about anyone else," he said. "The cops are coming, man, hear them sirens? We gotta get out of here, big brother."

"You killed those two just like you killed Sara."

"You think I paid the bus driver, man? You're bat shit crazy," he said. "We gotta run, man, the cops are coming."

I bounced his head off the ground. Once. Twice. "That. Was. No accident," I hissed. "You shot at her, I saw it, and you're going to tell the cops what happened."

Reece dropped the gun and held his arms up defensively. "They're not going to believe it was an accident."

I smacked him in the mouth. Hard. "That's because it wasn't."

Tears streamed down his cheeks. "Just please stop hitting me, man, you're just like Dad."

My stomach went cold, and all the rage deserted me, leaving me hollow. I let go of Reece and stood, my knees trembling beneath me. "It's not like that," I whispered. "I'm not like that."

Ignoring my hand for help, Reece picked himself up off the ground. Blood trickled from his lip and nose. The swelling distorted his features. I looked away to the crowd that had gathered around what was left of Jenny. It was growing, and many were pointing back into the parking lot where it had all started. Reece and I were the only two people left, and we drew all their attention.

Wiping the blood off with the back of his sleeve, Reece sighed. "Dad, never believed me either, man."

"Don't ever compare me to him." I drove my finger into his chest. "This ain't about you tracking mud into the house or having your damn music too loud. You just killed two people, so me smacking you is the least you deserve."

Reece backed away. "It was an accident, man. I can't go to jail, I..."

The addict spun on his heel and took off into the parking lot, away from the crowds, the approaching cop cars and the two dead bodies.

"Reece get back here!"

"You want beat me, man, then come get me," he called out. "But you gotta run, man."

"Not with you," I said and took off in the opposite direction to my Bel Air.

The Old Girl roared to life the first try and I slammed her into gear. Stones flew as peeled out of the parking lot. I jumped the curb and pinned the gas pedal and flew down the street. Fire trucks, ambulances and a half dozen cop cars passed me going in the opposite direction. Not one of them slowed, and eventually I couldn't even see their lights in my rear view mirror.

FIFTEEN

The pink arm chair swallowed Nyah up like a plush carnivorous sponge, whispering promises of dreams and sleep. The girl curled her legs up under her and laid her head on the armrest. The temptation to succumb to the chair's charms was high. Shopping with Gabby had turned out to be a high intensity workout, not the pampering session Nyah expected. Over four hours in and no end in sight, Nyah was spent.

Lazily, Nyah let her eyes wander through the store. It was trendy like all the others they'd visited. The racks were filled with creations by designers Nyah hadn't heard of. Some were local, others just emerging but all on the cutting edge. At least that's what Gabby kept telling her as they stormed the stores in Osborne village. It was another world from the mall, where Nyah originally assumed Gabby was taking her.

The girl had passed through The Village often, headed to other parts of Winnipeg, never spending much time there. Now, she couldn't imagine hanging out anywhere else. It was alive; artsy, brash, soulful, and earthy all at once. The sidewalks vibrated with possibility. The buildings were old, some erected in the early 1900's but they'd been renovated, made fresh with enough of their charm left to display a beautiful dance between the old and the new.

On street corners musicians played, some violins, others drum and guitar. Artists painted in front of cafés, some bringing to life murals on the buildings themselves. The restaurants offered food from all over the globe and the bakeries would make you stop and drool at their offerings sinfully displayed in their front windows. Tattoo parlours were sandwiched between pottery stores and jewellers. Nyah had stopped to watch a woman blowing glass bowls and goblets in her shop, amazed at how raw and beautiful it was. More music exploded from the pubs and bars, by local established bands and those hoping to catch the ear of one of the producers of the recording studios nestled in The Village.

In Osborne Village, the soul of Winnipeg, surrounded by expression, art and creativity, Nyah had that feeling again. That beautiful feeling of being young.

No worries.

No cares.

No stress.

No fear.

No sadness.

For a moment here and there Nyah even forgot that both her parents were dead.

When she did remember, guilt for having fun sliced through her, worsened by the shame for the all the clothes she bought. Correction, that Gabby had bought for her. Coughing up the cash for even one of the outfits that filled the bags piled around her feet would have been impossible, but Gabby gladly picked up the tab, making a run at buying out every shop in The Village. Even though Gabby could afford it, given the mansion she lived in, Nyah felt guilty and tried to refuse the gifts. Gabby was insistent, and no one told that short girl no. Not successfully anyhow.

A garment tornado of shirts, shirts, skirts, pants, silks, cottons flew over the top of the changing booth as Gabby had Nyah try on outfit after outfit. Nyah couldn't recall what she'd bought, and doubted she'd live long enough to wear it all. Finally, Nyah had been allowed to rest while Gabby took her turn in the change room.

The blonde girl had been content watching TV with Gabby after Grady had run off. She'd been able to let her guard down more and more since meeting up with Marin, Grady and their friends. Nyah hoped Vern would show up just to see what Basil would have done to that slime for sullying his doorstep. Probably squash Vern under his foot, if Gabby didn't slice Vern's throat first.

Nyah just had to be careful. If she got too used to feeling safe, that would be when the monsters came for her. Nyah would put her walls back up and arm the alarms after she enjoyed the day out and had some fun. Paranoia would wait.

They'd left the mansion right after Basil had taken a call. He said it was business, and he didn't want Nyah around when whoever it was came over. Nyah understood. It was no different when her Mom had been working.

Her Mom.

She was having fun and her Mom was dead.

The sharp edge of guilt slid its blade deeper into her. There was nothing more than threads keeping her from turning in on herself and losing it completely.

She needed to keep focus on the moment so the darkness remained out of sight.

Basil had sent Nyah away just like her Mom used to do and for the same reasons. It wasn't because they didn't want her around or they hated her. Basil just didn't want her to see that dark side. Nyah was okay with that. Basil might not be out selling himself, but she was still better left ignorant of the details of Basil's business. Still, she doubted she'd ever cry herself to sleep over what Basil and Gabby did. Unlike with her Mom.

It had been for her protection too, and they'd been tactful about her temporary banishment. Besides, although exhausting, Nyah was having fun shopping with Gabby.

She remembered what it was like being a normal kid, back when her parents were alive. She caught a glimpse at what her life should have been like. If she was careful she could be happy.

Back and forth, happiness burst through the sadness only to have the grief pull her back into the pit again. Would the pain ever disappear? Would she ever really feel happy? Nyah promised herself that one day she'd smile and not feel guilty for it.

The dressing room curtains parted and Gabby emerged wearing a slinky black dress. It had splashes of blue, orange and yellow like a painter's drop cloth. Gabby spun slowly in front of Nyah.

"Do you like it?"

Nyah nodded. "It's so pretty."

Moving to the mirror, the short girl arched her back and stuck out her butt. Gabby ran her hand down the front of the dress, a straight path as her breasts were as flat as her stomach. "I don't think I fill it out right," she said.

"You don't have an ounce of fat on you and I'd die for your legs," Nyah said.

"I just wish I had some curves." Gabby sighed. "You're half my age but you look older."

"I bet that won't be a problem when you're forty."

"Ain't that the truth."

The cute red headed sales girl returned, balancing a tower of clothes in her arms. The girl was sweating already, and her smile was strained. She was in line for a huge commission if she lasted, but Nyah was betting the girl was twenty minutes from being run off her feet. The red head might sell clothes for a living, but she wasn't in Gabby's league.

"I'll try on these last few outfits and then we'll get going," Gabby said as she ducked back behind the change room curtain. "Basil should be done his meeting and he might need some help."

"What, with counting bullets?"

Gabby pulled the curtain back and cocked her eyebrow. "Aren't you the cheeky girl?"

"I know what Grady came to you for."

"Yes, but there's no need to let the whole world know."

"I won't, I'm sorry."

"Don't worry about it." Gabby paused and stared at Nyah for a long moment. "Listen, honey, are you okay being with me? With what we do?"

"It's better than what my Mom did. At least no one is hurting you."

"I can't imagine how your Mom or any of those other girls fell so far to have to sell their bodies, but don't think about it, you're too good to fall into that trap."

"Does any girl deserve that life?"

"No, I guess not."

Nyah looked away. "Sorry, it's all still really raw."

Rushing over from the change room, Gabby bent down and hugged the younger girl hard. "It just happened, girl. You're not going to be right for a long time if ever."

"It's not just that she died, but how people are going to remember her. She was so much more than some hooker, you know?" Nyah wiped her eyes with her sleeve. "At least she used to be."

"What you remember is all that matters, right?" Gabby kissed her cheek. "After we're done here let's go get something to eat."

"Okay, that'd be good."

"Where do you want to go?"

"I dunno, McDonald's?'

Gabby wrinkled her nose. "Uh, no way. I'll take you anywhere you want, even to the most expensive restaurant you've ever heard of."

"You've already spent too much."

"Why do what I do if you're not enjoying the money?"

"You don't need to do all this, I'm not a charity."

"I know that, but I want to and I'm having fun. Besides, we'll charge it to Basil's card anyway." Gabby dipped back into the change room. "I'll rip through the rest of these clothes and then I'll take you for the best Thai you've ever had."

There was no use arguing, so Nyah returned to her chair's warm embrace. She pulled her cell phone out of her back pocket, entered her lock code and thumbed through her various screens. She opened a file that she'd buried deep into folder after folder. Someone would have to know exactly what they were looking for to find it. The file was a video. She clicked it and watched the short clip for the thousandth time.

The video opened with three men standing in a dimly lit back alley. The video wasn't the greatest quality, and even when she zoomed in the faces remained blurry. One of the men she knew instantly, it was all in the way he stood and talked with his hands. Nyah would know that man anywhere.

Each time the clip ended, Nyah's heart was ground under foot all over again. This was no movie and those weren't actors. What happened in the video was all too real. She'd been dealing with the consequences of what she was watching for years and she'd keep dealing with it the rest of her life.

If she had the equipment, Nyah could enhance the quality of the video. Maybe then she could make out the faces and figure out who was there. She needed help, but who could she trust? Was Grady going to be able help her? How could she ever trust anyone with something this big?

Whatever his skills, Grady was no computer geek. Nyah would have to find some way to figure out who the men were in the video. Once she had the names then those men could be dealt with like they deserved.

The crazy thing was, Nyah had found that someone to deal with it.

Luck was a funny and fickle thing, but she'd finally found some.

It was about time.

She deserved some luck after all the crap she'd been through.

SIXTEEN

It was all I could manage to keep the Bel-Air on the road and pointed in the opposite direction of the blood, bodies and cop cars. Dead bodies. Plural. They were really starting to pile up. Foot on the gas, hands on the wheel and try not to run anyone over. Simple, straight forward, and about all I could handle.

What the fuck had Reece done?

There was no explaining away what happened. Reece had killed Jenny and Mark Banks. That was the truth in its entirety, and anything different out his mouth would just be more lies.

That poor girl had been cleaved in two, her blood and entrails smeared over the cold concrete. All the dead, six and counting, had done nothing wrong save crossing paths with Reece. Six dead faces, their bodies ripped open by bullets, filling my eyes and monopolizing my thoughts.

The Old Girl always pulled me back from the darkness. Like she knew the way, the Bel-Air pulled up to the front doors of The Rusty Nickel Pub on McDermot Avenue.

Every day I woke up and made the same decision: *Today I'm going to get as drunk as I can.* It was a special occasion because it was one of the few times I actually deserved it.

The lights inside The Rusty Nickel were so heavily coated with dust they barely glowed and it took a moment for my eyes to adjust to the darkness. The walls were plastered with yellowed posters and fly paper. There were few tables and only a handful of booths. None of the chairs matched. There was no dance floor because no one would use it. The pub hadn't survived because of the ambiance, people came to hide in the shadows, drink their troubles into tomorrow and disappear for a time.

I was among my own.

Peanut shells crunched under my feet as I made straight for the bar and took a seat. I wasn't confident in my choice of stool. It wobbled enough to cause motion sickness. Some guy played guitar in the corner for free drinks. He didn't so much sing as mumble in key about how he'd lost a woman and his youth. I didn't know the song but I'd heard it before.

The big fat bartender, in a sweat stained shirt and piss poor comb over, poured me a beer and a shot of whiskey. I downed those immediately and told the bartender to leave the bottle of whisky. I poured faster myself.

Through the drunken cloud of rye, nothing seemed to connect. First off, Reece was no killer; but suddenly he's hunting people down and firing bullets like a mad man. But what niggled at me, even in my stupor, was that I was searching for these girls because they had stolen from Jacob, except I only had his word that they'd stolen anything.

My mouth soured and I chased the taste away with another shot. Was I the patsy here?

Logic and good sense wouldn't have to be stretched very far to see that the goal was to find these girls and kill them. The mysterious stolen object story was nothing more than an excuse to get me to go along. And it wasn't even a good story.

Deep into the bottle, it all made sense. Jacob wanted the girls dead and he made sure I was there when it happened. He was setting me up for an indefinite stay in a four by eight room in the concrete hotel.

But I figured it out. This dumbass wasn't going to jail for anybody.

To celebrate my awesomeness, I filled my glass and

raised it for a victory drink. An iron hand covered with thin wrinkled skin grabbed my wrist and stopped the rye inches from my lips. Hank stood at my shoulder, his jaw clenched and eyes full of disappointment. He let go of my wrist and I set the glass down on the bar.

"You've had enough, Grady," he said.

"Hank, I haven't even gotten started."

"I thought we had a talk about you getting your head out of your ass," he said. "My daughter needs you and you head right for the bottom of a bottle?"

"You come here to just lecture me?"

"No, I came to talk."

I poured him a shot and pushed it in front of the old cop. "You want to talk, you drink."

Hank took the stool next to mine and pushed his shot away. "I can't drink with my new meds."

"My brother would say different." I threw back his shot and then mine. "What are the pills for?"

"That's no concern of yours."

"So we can talk about my shit but not yours? Typical." I refilled my glass. "How'd you find me?"

"Your rusted out piece of crap is parked outside." He sighed. "You have that look again, Grady."

I tossed my shot back and wiped my mouth with my sleeve. "What look is that?"

"The one you get before you go into a deep dark hole and pull the earth down over yourself."

"You're talking out your ass." I refilled my glass.

"I've seen it before," he said. "And a rabbit gives you flowers for donkey races."

"What the hell does that mean?"

His cheeks burning crimson, the old cop stared down at the floor. "Sorry, I get a little confused when I'm tired."

"You're that way a lot lately."

He ignored that comment. "What I meant, was that all

booze gives you is trouble."

"That ain't even close to what you said." I swirled my drink in the glass. "So when are you leaving?"

"I came to have my say."

"Then have it and then beat it."

He frowned. "Marin needs you, Grady, and that girl needs you too, but not like this. Not drunk off your ass."

"Nyah has you now, Hank, and we both know you're a better role model."

"I'm not going to be around forever."

"I wish that were true, but you'll be there pissing on my grave, Hank."

A shadow passed over his face. "Guess we'll see about that. Grady, please think about what I said." He rose off his stool and put a hand on my shoulder. "One more thing, do you know what Nyah's last name is?"

"I'm pretty sure it's Tynes, why?"

"No reason, except you said her Dad was a cop. I'm wondering if I knew him." He shrugged. "Maybe it'll come to me," he said and walked out.

I toasted his departure and drained my glass. Damn that old bastard knew how to ruin a good drunk. Pushing myself away from the bar I stumbled to the washroom to take a leak.

Hands down, The Rusty Nickel had the most disgusting bathroom I'd ever been in, and I'd been to jail. The floor tiles were black with grime and the grout had something fuzzy growing in the cracks. The sinks were green with mould and there was crud an inch thick on the faucets. It stunk like every shit taken in there had lingered.

Standing as close to the urinal as I dared, I unzipped and took relief. As the booze rushed out, some asshole bumped into me and I pissed all over myself. I cursed and zipped up, a dark wet spot spread across my crotch. My hands clenched into fists, I spun around ready to beat some manners into the poor jerk that'd bumped me.

Standing there in his four thousand dollar suit, Jacob Poole didn't belong in that toxic dump of a washroom, but there he was with Davis flanking him. Two big ugly fuckers with scars on their knuckles and steroids coursing through their veins stood between us.

"Hello Jacob," I said. "I wouldn't have thought this was your type of place."

"I'm not here for small talk." Jacob's nose wrinkled. "Christ, the smell in here. I'm going to have to burn my clothes after this."

"Who pushed me?"

"What the fuck does it matter?" Davis sneered. "We're here because Jacob wants answers."

"He'll get them," I said. "After I get mine."

Davis snorted. "Fine, it was me, okay? What are you going to do about it?"

"You'll find out, trust me."

"This is childish, Grady," Jacob said. "I am furious with you for forcing me to hunt you down here."

"You could have called."

"Have you figured out where to find the whore that stole from me?"

"Not a fucking clue."

"Are you even looking for her?"

"No, and that might be my problem."

"Why the hell not, you cheeky fucker?"

"You're a smart man, Jacob, and I'm not so dumb," I said. "You're killing these girls, and I want no part of it."

Jacob's face erupted in rage. "You think you're better than me?"

"We're both drunks, Jacob," I said. "But I ain't going to kill girls for you, and the sad thing is you can't do it yourself."

I expected one of the two goons to hit me right then.

Even a little part of me thought Jacob might be mad enough to do it himself. What I didn't anticipate was Davis smacking me right on the jaw with a decent hook before backing up behind the others. It wasn't a great punch, but I hadn't seen it coming, and it rocked me.

The goon on the left lunged and I kicked his knee as he planted, driving my heel right into his kneecap. He buckled, all that muscle crumbling down on his busted joint. I spun around, driving my elbow into Davis' face slamming him back into the washroom wall. A left to his stomach and then a quick right hook to the ear sent him to his knees. The second goon grabbed me in a head lock, squeezing me tight with those massive arms. I drove my heel down on the tender top of his foot, he cried out and I threw my head back, his teeth crunching against my skull. I twisted in his grip and hammered away at his face with punch after punch.

Only the feel of steel against my temple made me stop. I raised my hands and stepped back. Jacob kept his gun levelled at my face. It looked like a 9mm Glock, but it was hard to tell that close up.

"That will be enough, Grady," Jacob said.

"They hit me first."

"Leave us," Jacob ordered his men.

The goon with one good knee was helped to his feet by the goon with the broken teeth. They limped their way out of the bathroom. Davis pressed his back against the wall and tried to stand. His lip was split pretty bad, and the blood ran down the front of his shirt. When he found his feet, he followed the other two out of the room and fell in with the parade of shame.

Jacob waited for the door to close behind them before speaking. "For the record, they only did as I ordered," he said.

"Next time you might want to find guys who can

actually fight, not just look like they can," I said.

"I'll have to choose more carefully." He kept the gun in my face. "Now, I must not have been clear before when I told you to find the girl who stole from me because you don't understand how important it is to get my property back."

"I understand. I just don't like what happens when those girls get found."

"You'll like it even less if you fail me," he said.

"Do you really expect me to find anything if I don't know what I'm looking for?"

"Christ, we've been through this already. Find the whore and it'll be simple enough after that."

"I doubt it."

"Pardon me?"

"Shamus is looking for this mystery thing too, so it's not your grandfather's watch or grandma's silverware. So I'm telling you, if you want my help tell me what it is."

With his free hand, Jacob lashed out and slapped me. I saw it and let it happen. That only made him angrier. "What, you're too good to fight an old man?"

"I'm just too smart to fight Jacob Poole," I said. "I might as well slit my wrists."

The old drunk smiled. "Fine, it's a piece of incriminating evidence. Shamus stumbled across it recently, and is using it to gain control of some of my interests. I've recently learned that he lost it and now I need to find it before he does. It's important, I want it, and I'll kill for it. That's all you should focus on."

"So this big important piece of valuable evidence is such a big fucking deal every crook in the city wants it?"

"Yes."

"So how the hell did a hooker get it?"

"I've told you all you need to know," he said and left.

SEVENTEEN

No one in The Rusty Nickel moved or drank as I stumbled out of the washroom to find my stool. Some didn't even breathe and the guitar player kept his strings quiet. The patrons had seen two big monsters walk in with Jacob and Davis, only to have them limp back out. The fat sweaty bartender replaced my empty whisky bottle with a fresh one full of liquid gold. Whether out of fear or respect, he refused my money. I was too broke to argue. I filled my glass and threw back the whisky.

Eventually, the people grew tired of watching me drink and returned their attention back to their glasses. The hum of conversation began to build, the guitar player found his voice and strummed softly, singing more to himself than for anyone else's benefit. The pub slowly crept back to normal.

I was left alone with my thoughts and my whiskey.

Along with bruised knuckles, I'd gotten a little info about what Jacob was looking for. But what the hell was this evidence? Fingerprints? A gun Jacob had used to off some punk? Maybe pictures or some note Jacob had signed? Whatever it was, this evidence had allowed Shamus to survive while Jacob wiped out every other competitor in Winnipeg. No wonder Shamus wanted it back, he was dead without it.

Near the end of my bottle, I grew tired of sitting centre stage at the bar while the clientele drank hunched over their tables, shooting furtive glances in my direction. I downed the final drink and walked out of The Rusty Nickel.

The Old Girl was still out front, waiting for me. The whiskey had come on at full force, making it hard to maintain my balance as I searched my pockets for the keys.

I put one hand on my car for stability while I patted myself down with the other. The second time I checked my front pocket I found them, but dropped them on the street when I pulled them out. My head smacked against the car door when I bent over to pick up the keys. Stars filled my eyes and I fell back on my ass. It took me longer than it should have to pick the keys and myself up off the ground.

I scanned the street to see who had caught my slapstick routine.

A silver Jaguar idled in the parking lot across the street. Except for the colour, it was an exact match for the one I'd trashed days before. Same make, same model. I wondered if it also belonged to Drake when the passenger door opened and Davis got out. The fresh swelling on his face made him uglier than usual.

I stepped back behind the Bel-Air and into the shadows of the alley beside The Rusty Nickel. Davis tucked a package into his jacket pocket and waved to the driver before walking away. The Jaguar sped off in the opposite direction and the choice of who to follow was easy. Besides being slower, Davis and I needed to talk.

As much as I wanted to catch up and punch Davis' teeth down his throat, I hung back and followed him from a distance. I wanted to see what errand he was running for Jacob. Davis wound through the streets at random, searching. He crossed Portage and Main, risking the traffic at the city's busiest intersection. He continued through Winnipeg's downtown, and turned into an open alleyway. The stench of sweat, booze and decay hit me as soon as I entered a minute after.

Homeless men, bums, squatted in the dirt and muck, their backs against the building. Some shared a bottle. Others passed a bag back and forth, their mouths and noses covered in the paint they were sniffing. They stopped long enough to ask for money. Ignoring them, I moved on.

The far end of the alley opened onto Hargrave Street, where a dozen hookers had set up shop, dressed in booty shorts, leather skirts with fishnets and cheap plastic shoes with eight inch heels, their coats open to display the menu.

The women flocked to Davis as if his pockets were lined with cocaine. He chose the worst looking one. Not the ugliest, but the girl who was too wasted to stand. A junkie for sure; track marks peeked out from under her sleeves. She was young, which was still obvious in spite of the wear. The drugs had ripped the fat away and left her skin loose and yellowed and hair thinning and stringy.

Each and every needle was killing her just as sure as wrapping her lips round the barrel of a gun. It was a race. It could be the junk, AIDS, Hep C or some pissed off john, but something was going to kill her. It was just a matter of time.

I knew that girl. She was Tammy Smalls, the young hooker who'd offered herself to me in the hallway at Watson's. Davis had been hunting, and he found himself one of the girl's from that night. This girl was in trouble and she didn't have a fucking clue.

Tammy Smalls arched her back, stuck out her bony chest, and beamed up at Davis. She was shaking from withdrawal and begging him to pick her. Davis whispered in her ear and she nodded hungrily.

Davis led the blonde junkie off by the arm, like he was escorting her to the ball. Reeking of jealousy, the other girls stared after her. I followed them to a house on the north side of Ellice. It should have been condemned, the rot had won, and it leaned hard to the right. People littered the steps; bottles and joints were shared freely among those who'd not passed out.

It was a crack house, a way station for addicts and hookers to wait for fate to give them their ticket. Some were headed to prison, others the morgue.

Davis led his date into the house. With all the dealers

and addicts, who knew how many guns there were? If I was smart I'd have waited for a better opportunity. Since I wasn't, I followed them inside. The men on the stairs moved over to let me by, barely looking up from their liquor and weed. They knew me for one of their own. A drunk is just an addict on a liquid diet.

In the entrance, the floor was spongy under my feet and my weight threatened to snap the joists. What carpet that was left had been burnt and the walls were a collage of torn wallpaper and graffiti. I drifted from room to room, where people were shooting up, screwing or sleeping off their recent high. In the bathroom, two guys were bottling moonshine stilled in the tub. I declined a taste test and went upstairs.

Davis' voice echoed down the hallway from the last room on the right. There was a hole in the wall next to the door. Given the blood splatters, it was probably the work of a shotgun.

Through the hole, I peered into the room. Davis leaned against the far wall, unable to look at Tammy Smalls sitting naked on the bed, looking lost among the dirty sheets. She was ravaged, her collarbone and ribs threatened to tear through her skin. Her breasts were small and sagging and thick ropey scars marred her wrists. The only color came from her red chipped nail polish.

The junkie and Davis weren't alone.

A tall lanky fucker was setting up a video camera on a beaten up wooden chair, his long thin fingers skittering over the controls. With arms and legs too long for his torso, the man moved like an insect, in quick halted bursts. A cigarette dangled from the creep's lips as he fiddled, keeping one eye on the girl.

"We ready, Lyle?" Davis asked.

"Absolutely," the tall creep said.

The camera's red recording light blinked on and Lyle

slinked to the foot of the bed. He loomed over the girl, and Tammy wouldn't meet Lyle's black eyes. In his outstretched hand, he held a baggie of white powder, dangling it in front of her like angling for trout. The junkie knew the hook was there, but still wanted to bite.

"It's too much," she slurred. "Let me save some for later."

"All." Lyle's voice was slick and wet. "That is the deal. Do it all or do none."

She spread herself before Lyle. "Do you want me first or after?"

"Not at all. My friend explained what I desire."

Davis pulled out a small black leather case, unzipped it and laid it open on a dresser. He withdrew a spoon, syringe and lighter. Tammy pulled her knees up under her chin and watched greedily as Davis poured the heroin into the spoon and heated it with the lighter. It bubbled and he filled the syringe before handing it back to Lyle. The lanky creep held up the needle, allowing the light to shine through the liquid, and bounce off the steel. He offered it to the girl. It was over eighty units. He might as well be holding a gun.

Tammy reached out and closed her fingers around it, but Lyle wouldn't let go.

"I need you to say it," he said. "I give you this and you tell me everything you know."

She lowered her head and her shoulders sagged. Her hand stayed firm on the syringe. "My word, I'll tell you everything. I'll bare my soul," she whispered.

"Good girl." Lyle released the syringe.

The girl held it delicately like a flower, before straightening her arm and lowering the needle. The steel touched her skin and I couldn't let it go further. Ripping open the door, I burst into the room. Lyle turned from the girl as she plunged the needle into her flesh. I bent my legs, ready to launch myself at her, but Lyle's arm flashed out. I slipped the punch, and had a clear shot at Lyle's jaw. I planted and swung, but I'd forgotten about Davis. His hand swung out, holding a black leather sap. It connected with my skull and then everything went to black.

I came to, sprawled at the foot of the bed. My brain ached. The girl's head hung off the edge of the mattress above me. She was foaming at the mouth and her eyes had rolled back in her head. I sat up and checked her neck. There was no pulse.

A dozen, red circles were burned into Tammy Smalls' left arm. Oozing and puckered, her skin was marred with cigarette burns. I swayed on my feet, my head throbbing. She'd been tortured. The poor girl had lit cigarettes pressed into her skin. My hands curled into tight fists.

Lyle watched me with interest.

"Did you actually think you could stop this?" Davis asked. "You're such a loser, Grady."

"What have you done? You're a fucking monster, Davis."

He shrugged. "She was nothing, just a sack of garbage."

Grabbing Davis by the throat with one hand, I punched him in the mouth with the other. He held up his hands to block, but I swiped them away, landing blow after blow. I wanted to dismember him, disfigure him, so he'd remember the girl he had played with and killed. I drove my elbow into his nose, and he dropped to floor.

I raised my foot, ready to stomp Davis dead. Lyle reached into his coat and pulled out an old revolver. A six shooter, straight out of a western movie. It looked odd in his hand. He pulled back the hammer with his thumb, and shoved the barrel right in my face. His eyes held no anger or malice. I froze, my boot suspended over Davis' head. I lowered my foot, backed up to the wall and stood perfectly still. I didn't move. Not an inch.

Lyle nudged Davis with his foot, he was still out cold.

Lyle put his pale face inches from mine, crazy danced in his eyes. "You're either brave or a fool, Grady Fisk. I've been ordered not to harm you, however, if you continue to be a nuisance that will change."

Davis stirred, and Lyle lifted him from the floor to a chair in the corner. Davis' eyes rolled in their sockets, and he took a moment to regain his senses. When the fog lifted, Davis glared at me and bared his teeth.

Flying off the chair, he lunged, fists ready to pummel me. Lyle restrained him with some effort. Davis was real tough, knowing that with the gun on me, I couldn't fight back. I blew Davis a kiss and he thrashed in Lyle's grip.

"He smashed my face, Lyle," Davis cried. "I'm going to kill him, I swear."

"Davis, ease back," Lyle said. "He is not for you. Go, clean up, and Jacob will speak with you once you have rested."

Davis took a swipe, trying to land at least one punch, but he missed my face by a good foot. Lyle turned the gun to him, and Davis shrunk back, his face red with hate and embarrassment as he slunk from the room.

"You are all pathetic," Lyle said when we were alone. "This should have been my task from the beginning, I've already learned the names of all the girls."

"Girls?' I asked. "There's only one."

"See, you have no clue. There were more girls employed by Watson than those you and your brother saw the night the two of you wrecked havoc." Lyle took the camera off the chair. "The prostitute told me everything, all the names of any female who'd ever set foot in that house, where they live, where they frequent. Everything."

"So now what? You're going to kill me?"

The creep shook his head. "No, Jacob still has need of you. But after this is all over, who knows?" Lyle stepped towards the door, and paused, his hand on the door frame.

"I'm leaving now. Count to one hundred and then I suggest you leave before the police arrive. But not before one hundred, or I may have to shoot you."

Finally, I was able to breathe normally when the freak closed the door behind him. A smart man would have dragged his ass home to wallow in his failure, but I wanted that camera. It wouldn't change anything; Tammy would still be dead. But if Jacob got that camera, and the names on it, more girls would die. I couldn't let these hired monsters keep killing. If I did nothing there'd be just as much blood staining my soul as if I'd killed the girls myself.

Racing out of the room, I plowed over a junkie on the main floor and tripping over those strewn about on the front steps. I kept running and spotted the freak up ahead of me. He'd crossed Ellice, heading back to Portage.

I cut down a side street hoping to pop out ahead of him. I sprinted down the sidewalk and when I came out at Portage, my lungs pleading for air, Lyle was only a block away heading right for me. He glanced behind him, making sure he wasn't being followed. I blended in with the crowd and walked right for him. I bumped some fat University kid who had his nose glued to his Smart Phone into him and Lyle stumbled. Lyle and the kid started shoving each other and the crowd trying to pass them by jostled them, and bumped them together again. In the confusion I reached into Lyle's pocket and snatched the camera.

It wasn't slick, but I'd gotten a block head start before Lyle screamed my name. He pulled out his gun and fired, the crowd around him dropped to the ground. Bullets whizzed past but I kept running, stuffing the camera into my pocket, and forcing my legs to move faster as Lyle gave chase.

I bobbed and weaved in the crowd along Portage and cut across Main. I snuck a peek. Lyle threw people out of his way, with no regard for raising suspicion. My lungs were on fire and my throat sore as I fought to get in enough oxygen. It felt like I was running in water, and my legs got heavier with every stride. But I kept running.

I just wanted to find somewhere safe. It was a mantra that beat in time with my pounding heart. But as I turned down Market Avenue, and saw the Rub ahead of me, I realized what a bad idea that was. It was a bar, not an armoury. And my gun was sitting uselessly in my Bel Air at The Rusty Nickel. So unless the plan was to get him drunk, I'd need another idea.

Lyle was closing and Market Ave was deserted. There was nothing between the freak and me but air and inevitability. I veered from The Rub into the alley beside the church. Lyle was right behind me and breathing hard, but his feet sounded lighter and faster than mine. A bullet ricocheted off of one of the walls. I pulled trash cans down as I ran, leaving the stink of garbage and rolling bins in my wake.

Emerging in the parking lot at the far end of the alley, I ducked as the window of a Ford Ranger exploded beside me. I threw myself to the ground and felt the rush of air as a bullet passed right over my head. I rolled under the truck, scurrying on my knees and elbows for cover. The ping of metal hitting concrete echoed in the parking lot, unmistakably the sound of empty shells hitting the ground. Lyle stormed to the truck as I came out the other side. He snapped shut the cylinder of his freshly reloaded revolver. He aimed over the truck bed, the barrel level with my face. He motioned with his gun, and I moved around the truck until we were both out in the open, no more than fifteen feet apart.

"Give me the camera you stinking sack of meat," the freak roared.

"You're going to have to take it from my cold dead hands," I said.

The bullet sent up gravel and sparks inches from my feet. "That's your last warning. Jacob will forgive killing you given the situation."

I took the camera from my pocket and held it out. "Come over here and take it from me."

A slimy grin spread over his face. "Put the camera on the ground, and back away. This is just business, Grady, this doesn't need to get personal."

"Tell that to Tammy Smalls."

I let the camera fall through my fingers. There was a crack as it hit the concrete. Lyle screamed and rushed forward. I raised my foot and brought it down hard on the camera, once, and then twice, shattering it under my heel.

Lyle dropped to the ground, trying to scoop up the broken pieces of the camera. I surged forward, planting my knee squarely on his chin. The gun fired as he fell back, and the Ford Ranger's taillight exploded behind me. I dove on top of Lyle, driving my fist into the side of his head. We scrambled, fists flying wildly. He caught me across the side of the face with the pistol. My eyebrow spilt and blood ran into my eyes. I dug my thumb into his eye, pushing it in far as I could. Lyle howled, and punched me hard enough to take off my jaw and then grabbed me by the neck. He pulled my head close to his gnashing his teeth, desperately trying to bite my face. I smacked him hard, his head bouncing off the concrete, and I pulled myself free.

I found my feet as Lyle squirmed on his back, clutching his eye with one hand while trying to centre the revolver on me with the other. I drove my heel into his face, smashing his teeth down his throat. He raised his arm to shoot, but I latched onto his wrist, twisted it while straightening his elbow. I braced his arm over my knee and pulled until I heard his joint snap

Rolling and shrieking on the ground, blood pouring from his eye, Lyle cradled his ruined arm. I bent down to pick up his gun.

"That wasn't business," I said. "You tortured that poor girl and you loved it."

"My eye, my face, I can't see. My arm, shit, fuck, it hurts," Lyle wailed. "I'm going to kill you for this. I'm going to kill your whole family for this."

"That was just the beginning," I said. I put a bullet in each knee. They exploded in blood. The third bullet ripped through Lyle's stomach.

Lyle's screaming made him hoarse.

Gathering up the pieces of the camera, I carried them to the alley. I righted a trashcan and filled it with paper and cardboard before lighting it on fire. I fed it until the flames were two feet out of the bin, then I tossed the camera and revolver into the blaze. I left the alley, walking past Lyle and through the parking lot. I wanted to avoid The Rub. The cops would be by soon after all that shooting. I wondered if Lyle would be alive when they arrived.

I found I didn't care.

There wasn't enough of him left to worry anyone anymore.

EIGHTEEN

Leaving Lyle to bleed out in the alley, I hiked back to The Rusty Nickel and my Bel Air. Cop cars passed by, sirens blaring and lights flashing, but none stopped for me. The whiskey and adrenaline had beaten me down to where I could no longer drive. Curling up in the back seat, I slept until the morning sun slapped me awake. Assaulted by a migraine, I drove home and found Marin's note. She was staying at her Dad's until Nyah was settled and I stopped being an ass.

Shuffling into my bedroom, I toppled into my sheets and buried my face in the pillow. It was well past lunch when I surfaced again.

My face was stuck to the pillow case, adhered by dried blood. I peeled myself free and went to bathroom and flicked on the light. It looked like I tried to pick my nose with a scalpel; the blood was smeared over my mouth and chin. Filling the sink, I washed up, only to reopen my wounds. I dried off, bloodying the towel, before dabbing the deepest cuts with some stinky ointment.

All cleaned up, I was pouring my first drink of whiskey when the phone rang. The call was from Carl.

"*I hope this isn't a bad time, Grady.*"

"It depends," I said. "Are you in a bath tub about to slit your wrists or have a noose around your neck and want someone to kick out the chair?"

"*Well, no, I'm just calling to apologise for what happened outside the police station.*"

"Forget it, I didn't do anything."

"*My boy would be an orphan if it wasn't for you. When you found me in my van, I had full intentions of using that*

165

gun. *I want to repay you.*"

"No need."

"*I sort of already did,*" he said. "*I saw Marin at the mall today, and I got the impression things are rough between you two. I told her what you did for me, and she beamed with pride. Take it from me, if you don't want to lose your wife now is the time to call her.*"

"I think I owe you now," I said and hung up.

When I called, Marin didn't slam the phone down in my ear. That was progress.

"I love you and I miss you," I told her. "I'm stupid and I'm sorry, just please come home."

My wife sighed. "*If I did, would it be any different than the last time?*"

"I know I've been a crappy husband but I promise..."

"*I won't do this over the phone, Grady.*"

"Then come home and we can talk."

"*How about we go for dinner?*"

"Like a date?"

She laughed. "*Is that too much to ask?*"

It wasn't. We agreed on *Gerald's*, a bistro down in St. Boniface, Winnipeg's French quarter. The restaurant sits at the foot of the Esplanade Riel, a bridge over the Red River that connects St. Boniface to The Forks, giving *Gerald's* a Hell of a view of the river.

I pulled up to the house and Hank answered the door. I felt sixteen again, and ready for Hank to make me watch him clean his gun and remind me of his daughter's curfew.

"She'll be a minute," he said.

As Hank led me to the sitting room, he tilted left and walked into the wall, bumped off it, righted himself and kept going like nothing happened.

"First day with the new feet, Hank?"

"Piss off smart ass, I'm just old." He took a seat in his old armchair and I sat across from him on the couch.

"Sometimes parts of me forget how to work. So, can I get you a drink?"

"Sure, I'd love a ..."

"Don't say beer."

"I was going to say a glass of water."

Hank blushed. "I didn't mean anything by it, Grady. Just with you seeing Marin tonight, it's best not to have booze on your breath."

"Really? I'd have thought you'd be dousing me in whiskey to keep me away from Marin."

"I've charged a bit lately."

"Charged?"

Hank frowned. "I mean changed. Changed," he repeated, his mouth working over the word. "Sometimes things change you."

"But you said..."

"Never mind what I said."

Hank fetched us water from the kitchen. A glass in each hand, the water sloshed over the sides from his trembling as he set them on the coffee table.

"You okay, Hank?"

Hank sank into his chair. "I'm fine, why?"

"You're shaking like a leaf."

Hank stole a look up stairs. "It's not the time to talk."

"About what?"

"I'm just having a moment."

Hank took a bottle of pills out of his pocket and shook out two big enough to gag a horse. Hank popped them back and washed them down with water. The old cop acted as guilty as an addict about it.

"What're those for?" He ignored me, but I could be stubborn too. "What are those pills, Hank?"

"What pills?" Marin asked from the stairs.

Perfection in a soft blue dress, Marin's smile weakened my knees. Her lips begged to be kissed, but I was smart enough not to.

"You are gorgeous," I told her.

"And you look like someone was using your face as a catcher's mitt," she said. "What happened?"

"The polite thing to do is say thank-you when you're complimented," I said. "I got in a disagreement with the wrong guy."

"Were you drinking?" she asked. "Are you drunk now?"

"I swear I'm not." I held out my hand, which trembled. "That's why I'm shaking. That and I'm nervous, this feels like a first date."

The hint of a smile crossed Marin's lips. "What are you wearing?"

I looked down at my suit and shrugged. "I thought I'd dress up."

"Take off that hideous tie," she ordered. I did, she untucked my shirt and ruffled my hair. Marin smiled. "Much better." She turned to her father. "Did the doctor give you new pills, Dad?"

"They're for heart burn," Hank snapped. "It's the price of having daughters."

"So funny, Dad," Marin said. "We need to be going, Grady."

I jumped to my feet and met her at the front door. I wasn't going to argue to stay.

"I meant what I said, Grady," Hank called out. "I have a fever we need to discuss."

I stopped. "Fever? I'm no doctor, Hank"

He frowned. "I mean favour. I need a favour."

"From me? You must be sick."

Concern cloaked Marin's face. "You okay, Dad? I can stay home if you need me."

He waved her off. "I'm just tired. You kids go have fun, and I'll call you later, Grady."

I closed the door behind us, thankful my phone had

caller ID.

The car ride to the restaurant was strained, but Marin let me hold her hand as we walked into *Gerald's*. Avoiding the lounge, we claimed a table in the restaurant for privacy, which was at a premium. *Gerald's* layout was an open concept, enabling you to look into the kitchen as the chefs worked. Whatever they were doing was magic because the aromas that hit me caused my stomach to gnaw on itself.

A jazz combo was playing in the lounge, and the melodies jived right with the vibe of both the restaurant and the customers. I did not belong.

To be smart, I ordered water with the braised beef and mussels. Marin thought she'd enjoy the salmon in a red wine reduction. She asked for water too, in deference to me.

The elephant was still in the room.

I reached across the table and took her hands in mine. "So here we are again."

"And where is that?"

"Me asking you to come home."

"Has anything changed? Our problems are still there."

"Maybe you and I should move away from here and start over."

"Anywhere we go you'd still find a bar."

"I'm just saying that I'm willing to try anything."

"Is that true?"

"I swear."

"Then you'll finally consider adoption?"

Marin got pregnant ten years ago, right after I'd got kicked out of the army. I was finally going to be home instead of off in some foreign desert playing hero and our relationship would finally be stable. We decided to bring a baby into the mix. It'd be a precious little life we could screw up in our own unique way.

It was an uneventful pregnancy; Marin didn't even have morning sickness. The doctor called the nine months textbook. When Marin's water broke, she started to bleed. I have nightmares about all that blood.

We lost our daughter in delivery. The doctors tried, but there were complications, which is just fancy doctor talk for things went to shit. Now Marin can't have babies, and I know enough not to adopt. Guys like me shouldn't have kids.

I ordered a double whisky.

Marin's eyes blazed. "Grady, I'm trying to have a serious discussion with you."

"Trust me, I need it."

"I need you sober."

"One of us is going to be disappointed."

She pulled her hands away. "I want the man I married back."

"We both know I'm not going to change. You should leave me. This is going to keep happening."

Tears streamed down her cheeks. "You don't want that."

"But you should."

"What I want is you." She wiped her eyes with a napkin. "I'll take poor, or even homeless, I only want you sober and safe. I need you safe." She paused. "And I want a child. Is that too much?"

I didn't know what to say. I scanned the restaurant, searching for the right words, and possibly an escape route. There were three men sitting at the bar, and the sight of them made my heart freeze. Reece and two big bastards were perched on stools and downing drinks. They were Drake's men, the same two who picked up the wrecked jaguar. I scolded myself for not seeing them come in.

Marin's brow furrowed. "What is it?"

"Nothing."

"Another secret?"

"I'm just scared of what kind of kid I'd raise."

"What's that supposed to mean?"

"Look at my family," I said. "When my Dad wasn't kicking the crap out of me he was rotting in prison and Reece is an overdose waiting to happen. Being a loser is in my blood. Hell, I'm the shining success of the family and I'm a broke drunk."

"What about your sister? She's good to her little boy, Andy."

"She won't talk to me," I said. "She married that low life who beat up on her and it's me she won't have anything to do with."

"And you got him sent to jail so he'd stop hurting her," Marin pointed out.

"That's why she won't talk to me," I said. "See how fucked up the Fisk's are?"

"Now hold on, your mother is a sweetheart."

"I know, she's just like you, and look at the shit we caused her. Trust me, I wouldn't be a good father. I wouldn't know what one was like."

"You can learn, maybe from my Dad."

"I'm never going to be Hank."

"He's not all bad, Grady. You just need to be kind, patient and be there for our child."

"I'm not the 'be there' type," I said. "I'm better at letting people down."

"You're looking out for Nyah, aren't you?"

"I didn't say I wouldn't risk my life for a kid, that's not the point."

"Then what are you saying?"

The words were right there. I didn't want a kid to hate me like I hated my father. I knew myself too well. I'd drink, stir up trouble and do all the messed up things I've done all my life and then the kid would feel about me the way I felt about my Dad. That would kill me.

But how do you say that to the woman you love and not

171

have her look at you like a monster?

As I fumbled for my voice, a pretty blonde in a short plaid skirt and a tight black shirt with a tantalizingly low neck line burst through the front doors of *Gerald's*. It was Emma James, and Reece didn't look like he was holding a grudge for her snorting all his coke that night at Watson's. When a key witness in the murder investigation against you walks into the restaurant you're in, smart people run and hide. Idiots, like Reece, call her over for a drink.

Me? I almost shit myself.

"Grady, what's wrong?" Marin asked.

"I know some people over there."

She turned and spotted my brother and his friends at the bar. Her eyes narrowed in disgust. "Reece." It sounded like a curse. "I suppose you want to go over and say hello?"

"I'd like to strangle him, but that'd ruin our date." I sighed. "I'll be right back."

"This is how it starts."

I stormed over to the bar. Reece had his arm draped over Emma's shoulders. The pretty blonde, accepted a fresh martini and gave Reece a kiss on the cheek before she drank. This girl had no clue. I dragged Reece to a corner. I wanted to smash his head into the wall.

"What the fuck is wrong with you?" I demanded.

Reece straightened his new silk shirt. "Hey, Grady, you're being the asshole, man. What's got you so bent?"

"Like you don't know. That chick you're with is Emma James. We need to get the fuck out of here."

"She's an old friend, man, and always up for some fun."

"Like the fun you had with Jenny and Mark Banks?"

My brother's eyes dropped to the floor because he couldn't look me in mine. "It was an accident, man," he mumbled. "I was just gonna talk with them."

"You shot at them, Reece, which makes for less of a convincing argument," I said. "You're a murderer."

Something hard and round dug into my ribs. It was the barrel of a gun, which was being held by a large man in a suit. He was one of Drake's goons. Even his muscles had muscles. He smiled without contempt or malice and without egging me on or challenging me. He looked amused. The fight went right out of me.

My brother shrugged and smiled sheepishly, before scurrying back to Emma. The goon and I stood staring at each other, each waiting for the other to move. We both knew I had no real options.

"Don't ever touch me again, asshole," I said without conviction.

"Grady Fisk, you should go back to your wife."

"I'm not done with that idiot."

"Let it go." He shoved a thick fold of bills into my shirt pocket. "Your dinner is on me. Please walk away."

Was this worth getting shot over? Maybe the situation was harmless. After all, Emma had sat at the bar willingly and maybe she and Reece really fancied each other. I've seen stranger things. It was stupid, but harmless. I walked away, not believing my own lie.

I sat down at our table not as tough as when I'd left it. The food had arrived, but the smell of it turned my stomach sour. Besides, I was full from swallowing my pride.

Marin's big blue eyes helped a little.

"Is everything fine?" she asked.

"We'll see." I sipped my water, wishing it was a whiskey.

Marin peeked over her shoulder at Reece, who'd gone back to drinking. "That didn't look like a pleasant conversation."

"It wasn't, and our next one will be much worse."

"When are you going to wise up and cut him out of your life?"

"Now you sound like your Dad."

"He wants what's best for his daughter," Marin said.

"Family is important to him, and he's had it rough. He expected to grow old with Mom and her dying crushed him. Maybe if we gave him a few more grandkids it'd ease his pain."

"I haven't agreed to one kid and you're talking about a few?"

"I don't want an only child."

"I should just concede defeat."

Marin smiled. "I said you weren't stupid."

I took her hands in mine and kissed them, wanting to hold the moment forever. I tried not to guess how I'd screw it up.

I didn't have to wait long.

Reece and his crew were leaving the lounge. They'd put on their coats and were downing the last of the tequila. My liver was jealous, but I'd be glad to be rid of them. Too bad Emma James decided to tag along.

Marin stroked the back of my hand. "So you'll agree to adopt?"

"We can look into it. No promises."

"I'll take that."

Emma wobbled off her stool and into Reece's arms. She kissed him on the cheek and it would have been sweet if the goon with the gun hadn't used the moment to slip something into her drink. Glasses were raised, a toast was given to the night, and drinks were downed. Emma cheered after draining her glass.

The two of them left arm in arm and I played the scene over in my head. What the fuck had just happened? Had they just slipped her roofies? Poison?

I told Marin I was going to the bathroom and didn't wait for her response. I nearly knocked over two tables and upended a waiter as I rushed off.

Outside of *Gerald's*, I couldn't pick out Reece or Emma among the bridge full of people. I'd lost them. Had they gone back towards St. Boniface or on to The Forks? I panicked.

Jacob's goons were huddled a few feet away, obviously not about to help.

I guessed and ran along the bridge towards the Forks. I got lucky. Emma and the idiot were just up ahead. She giggled, swayed and Reece held on, keeping her from nose diving into the pavement, erasing any doubt she'd been drugged.

Following as they weaved through the crowd, pedestrians passed between us and I lost them. Rushing ahead, I gave elbows and curses, and received threats in return. I found them leaning against the railing, laughing so hard their faces were red and they fell into each other. Emma seemed willing and it almost looked harmless.

Almost.

The addict and Emma were joined by Davis, who had come strolling up the bridge. My brother gave him a hug and introduced him to his date. Davis' face was obscured by the huge bandage covering his broken nose, and he had matching black eyes. He had a flask that he passed freely between himself, Emma and my brother. Only Emma actually took a drink. My brother and Davis faked it well, but it was obvious they swallowed nothing.

They were going to poison Emma just like they'd done to Tammy Smalls. Whatever the goon had slipped into Emma's drink and whatever was in that flask was going to be the end of her. I had a full set of nightmares about all the girls Reece and Davis had found from that disastrous night. Each one dead moments after they'd been found. I couldn't let it happen again. I'd failed with Tammy, but I wasn't going to watch another girl die.

My cell rang and I looked at the display. It was Marin. Bile rose to the back of my throat. If I answered she was just going to yell. What would I tell her? Our date had gone to shit.

When I looked up from my phone, Emma was standing on the railing. Davis reached out for her but Emma danced away. A crowd had stopped to watch and a woman shouted for her to get down. Emma took another step and slipped. Reece lunged but Emma pitched backward.

She screamed as she fell.

Reece and Davis were leaning over the railing as I sprinted up, the crowd closing in behind us. Emma hadn't made it to the Red River, she'd crashed into the base of one of the bridge's supports. Her dead eyes stared up from her crumpled form, her face a mask of blood.

Another girl dead.

I bent Reece backwards over the railing. "What did you do?"

"I dunno, man, I dunno. She was here and then..."

"The drunk bitch fell," Davis finished. "We were having fun and she took it too far."

"So this was another accident? Just like when you killed Tammy Smalls?"

"She OD'd, you were there, you saw it."

I let go of Reece and grabbed a fist full of Davis' shirt and jammed my finger into his chest. "You tortured Tammy and then you killed her, sure as if you'd shot her in the head. Does Jacob know what a sicko you are?"

"Jacob knows about that and the camera," he said. "He isn't pleased, which you'll figure out when he catches up with you."

Sirens blared from the street. The cops had arrived. The crowd was bathed in red and blue flashing lights, as officers pushed through, closing in on us.

Reece's face was wet with tears. "Please, Grady, let's get the fuck out of here, man."

"Not until Davis tells me what's going on."

"Do you want to be standing here when they see the

girl?" Davis asked.

The crowd collapsed in on us and the shock dissipated as the fingers of blame began to point our way. No one had seen anything, but we were closest so we had to be guilty. I knew the cops wouldn't think any different.

Reece was the first to run. Typical. I followed with Davis close behind. We raced across the bridge and down the path along the river. Reece peeked over his shoulder as we fled along the water's edge, he had a step on me and tried to lose me around a corner, dip out of sight and hide among the bushes.

But Reece is slow.

I caught up and tossed him to the ground. He curled up, tucked his knees to his chest, and covered his head with his arms.

"I'm sorry, man, so sorry," he sobbed. "I was scared, and I didn't mean it, man. I'm sorry, Grady."

Davis reached us, breathing hard and his face crimson. "We don't have time for this."

I swatted him away and he stumbled. "I want answers Davis, no more fucking games."

"Don't you ever lay a hand on me again or ..."

I drilled him in the face and he dropped beside Reece. "I'll keep hitting until you tell me why Sara, Emma, Tammy and Jenny and Mark Banks had to die."

Davis gingerly touched his nose and he winced. "That was your second fuck up, Grady. I'm protected."

"Not from me. Not here, not now," I said. "You don't talk I'm going to kill you."

"You're going to have to. If I say anything, I'll get worse than that."

"From who?"

Davis stood and brushed himself off. "Open your eyes, Grady. Witnesses are being erased, do you think that's luck?"

"So Jacob is getting rid of witnesses to keep me out of jail?"

"Who says they're witness against you?" Davis asked.

I had no answer to that, and didn't stop Davis from disappearing down the trail. Reece was still curled up and bawling. I helped him to his feet. "What is Davis not telling me?"

He shook his head. "You don't want to know, man. It's so messed up." He sobbed. "What's going to happen to me?"

"You'll go to jail, probably die of an overdose, who knows? But it will be sad and pathetic," answered a voice behind us. Sergeant Quill was on the path a few feet away. "Here I am, canvassing the area to see if anyone saw a girl swan dive off the bridge and I find you two. Do I even want to know?"

"I was having dinner at *Gerald's* with my wife."

"Was Reece was dining with you?"

"He was drinking in the lounge. I'm just making sure he makes it home."

"Such the responsible big brother. I suppose you don't know anything about the girl."

"We saw it happen."

The cop's eyes grew hard. "Who did it?"

I shrugged. "She fell. I only looked up when she screamed."

Quill turned to Reece. "What about you?"

Reece's eyes never left his shoes. "Same here, man. I couldn't do nothing about it."

The cop scanned our faces for lies but couldn't find them. Quill ordered us back to the bridge to give our names and statements to the officers there. He'd insisted on escorting us so we wouldn't get lost.

Quill stayed behind us as we trekked back up the trail. "The girl that fell was Emma James," he said. "But I bet you already knew that."

I stayed quiet.

"Did either of you two speak with her?" the cop asked. Again my only answer was silence. "I'm not playing games here, Grady. Did the girl give you anything before she died?"

"Are you talking about drugs, officer?" I asked.

"Don't be a smart ass," Quill snapped. "

"Why are you asking?" I demanded.

It was the cop's turn to go mute.

We climbed the stairs from the trail and walked out onto the bridge. "Several witnesses say it was a suicide. She apparently got up on the railing, crying about some old boyfriend. They say she screamed his name when she jumped," Quill said when he found his voice.

My jaw dropped. "What witnesses?"

Quill motioned to Jacob's goons, who were giving statements to another cop. The gorilla who'd talked to me earlier winked at me.

Strings were being tied to me by unseen hands. I was a puppet. I felt myself being made to dance.

"What's the matter? Isn't that what you saw?" Quill asked.

"I just heard her scream."

The cop smirked. "Another witness is dead, and none of their deaths looks like an accident. So anytime you want to discuss theories just give me a call," he said and walked away.

I looked around and Reece had split, my answers disappearing with him.

Marin had left fifteen messages on my cell, her anger growing with each until she was screaming. Where had I gone? How dare I leave her with the bill? Was I that scared of children? And finally don't ever call her again.

For the moment, my priority was hunting down Davis and Reece. Four witnesses dead and those two were with them all in the end. That wasn't coincidence and it wasn't bad luck. If I didn't figure this out soon, there'd be no one left to testify.

No wonder Drake guaranteed my acquittal.

I trolled the streets. Reece and Davis didn't answer my calls and there was no luck at their apartments or any bar they'd ever frequented. I checked with every dealer Reece had ever scored off of and came up empty.

I was wasting gas and had given up when my cell rang. It was Drake.

"*I hear you've had an eventful night,*" my lawyer said.

"Did Jacob's steroid monkeys tell you that?"

"*They keep us informed.*"

"You know about Emma then."

"*I do, but you would be wise to concern yourself with those whores that are still alive.*"

"Meaning?"

"*Do I have to spell it out for you?*"

"I'm kinda slow."

"*Jacob has given us each a task,*" he said. "*Yours is to find his missing property and mine is to keep you out of jail. If you won't do yours then I will cease doing mine.*"

"Is that a threat?"

"*It is, and you need to take it seriously. Jacob feels you lack proper motivation and wanted to send some of his boys to visit your wife, but I managed to talk him out of it. For now.*"

"What kind of fucking lawyer are you?"

"*The successful kind,*" he said. "*You have run out of chances, Grady Fisk, so listen to me very carefully, if Jacob finds you before you find the whore and his property he will make you pay with your blood.*"

"How about you go fuck yourself?"

Drake sighed. "*Another can do the deed if you will not.*"

"Another, really? How did that work out when you used Lyle?" I asked.

"*Don't pat yourself on the back too hard, Grady,*" my lawyer advised. "*Jacob has more tools in the box than you can fathom and you don't want him to find you empty handed and use them on you.*"

He hung up before I said another word.

I wasn't finished. I drove to Drake's office to shove the lawyer's threats up his ass. Davis' jeep was parked outside when I arrived. I'd be able to deal with every idiot at once. There's nothing like being efficient.

I'm dumb and I was angry but I wasn't crazy. Drake would have his thugs with him so I'd need back up before I burst in and started kicking ass. I gave Basil Bray a call.

"*You better be calling because you have my money,*" Basil growled.

"I need a favour."

"*Of course you do, it's not like you'd ever call just to say hello.*"

"Listen you big ape, you're the one who told me that I could call on you for help."

"*What did you call me?*"

"Don't worry about it," I said. "But I may have found a way to figure out what the Hell is really going on."

"*Seriously? What happened?*"

"That's why I need you. The guy with the answers needs persuading."

"*Tell me where you are and we'll be right there.*"

"What do you mean *we*?"

"*Gabby can be very convincing, especially with her knife.*"

"Lovely," I said and hung up.

While I waited for the cavalry, I decided to scope out the building. The lights were on, but the shades were drawn. I crept closer. Davis' jeep was unoccupied which meant everyone was inside. I slipped down the alley towards the rear to check how many cars were there to have a rough idea on how many we'd be dealing with.

Halfway down the alley, a blinding pain erupted in the back of my head. I hit the ground and rolled over, my arms up to protect myself. My vision blurred. A man stood over me, raised his arm and delivered another blow to my head. Everything went black.

NINETEEN

The crowd vibrated as theories, questions, and best guesses were thrown about with increasing frenzy. People spoke of the shame, horror and waste, yet tingled with the thrill. Death always brings excitement, even the death of a young girl. Nyah did not share in their exuberance.

She'd been in the shadows when the girl fell. The girl was Emma, and Nyah knew her.

Pulled from the darkness when Emma slipped from the railing, Nyah was drawn forward by some base need to see the girl topple over the edge. People didn't do that. They didn't tumble off bridges into the Red River. That's the movies, not real life. Her curiosity pulled Nyah out into the middle of the sidewalk not twenty feet from Reece and Davis. They hadn't seen her. Even Grady hadn't noticed her when he ran by close enough for Nyah to touch him. He had been preoccupied with catching Emma and then chasing after the other men.

They were no different than the crowd that continued to swell around her; everyone's attention focused on the railing Emma had fallen from. The part of the bridge where Emma was, right before she wasn't anymore.

Nyah was invisible.

Nyah was background.

Anonymous.

Alive and therefore unimportant.

They only saw Emma because she was dead.

The lights from the cop cars washed everything and everyone in reds and blues. Nyah enjoyed feeling people around her, being together and alone all at once. She had made sure to phone home earlier. She'd only spent a few days at Hank's, and already thought of his house as her home. She'd called to check in with Hank just as she used to do when her Dad was alive and her Mom still cared.

The old guy was kind, though tired and slurring his words. Hank wasn't a drinker; Nyah knew enough of those to tell. Hank had told her about Marin and Grady's dinner date at *Gerald's,* so she popped by to spy, hoping to catch a glimpse of them happy. Peeking through the front window, Nyah watched Grady and Marin at their table smiling and holding hands. The moment was destroyed with Grady's fight with Reece and the other big scary men.

Nyah had retreated to the shadows.

The night turned cold and Nyah had been about to leave when Grady burst from the restaurant right before poor Emma fell from the bridge.

The excitement and adrenaline was draining from the crowd and she'd lost Grady to the night, so there was no reason for her to stay. Except for the cop. Dozens of officers drank coffee, took notes and held back the crowd as the firefighters retrieved the body. Only one concerned Nyah. Bigger than most, he was thick across the chest and shoulders, his hair shaved close to his scalp. He was a Sergeant, Nyah knew from the stripes on his shoulders and because her father had been one too.

As a kid, there were always cops in Nyah's life, and each of them she'd called uncle. She spent time with them at picnics, soft ball games and Christmas parties at the rink. Each one had been on her Father's squad, but this broad shouldered cop didn't bring her back to those days.

She knew his face and Nyah searched her mind for his name. Nyah pushed forward for a better look, maybe hearing him speak would remind her.

Nyah had to stop kidding herself.

She knew the cop, and without question she knew from

where. More importantly, Nyah knew what he had done. Her heart raced, fueled by fear and excitement. She needed his name.

How would she find that out? Bump into him and read his name tag? That would be suicide. What if he recognised her? It would be over for her and Nyah couldn't allow that. This whole mess had to end on Nyah's terms, and she was finally inching towards a conclusion. The next inch would be gained by learning the Sergeant's name, and there had to be a way to do that without being discovered.

Nyah had learned that no matter what you needed, there was always a way. Money? Love? Drugs? Food? There was a way. Even learning the cop's name. But as with everything else, the only hitch was the cost.

For the name, the cost was to go home. Not to Hank's place but her Mom's, Vern's, actually. Once it had been her home, a place where Nyah felt safe, and her Mom and Dad had made it that way. Funny how all it took was for Vern to move in for that to change.

Back at the house which wasn't a home, Delores hid an old album along with other mementos from when Nyah's Dad was still alive. The pictures from picnics, soft ball games and Christmas parties. Those pictures proof that Nyah had once been happy and her family had once been whole. Those pictures were full of cops, and Delores always taped a note listing the names beside each one. Those notes were going to give Nyah her answer and move her that little bit closer.

Nyah kept her eyes on the Sergeant as the other cops pushed the crowd back. Time to go home, they said. There was nothing to see, which was true.

It had already happened. Emma was already gone. She'd already jumped and she was already dead. There'd be no replay.

The crowd dispersed, wandering back into their lives.

Nyah blended in and disappeared, letting the crowd take her with them.

Nyah caught a bus and it let her off a block from Vern's. As she walked up to old home she scanned the street. There were no cars around, Vern's or otherwise. Nyah slipped around back, and found that the old screen door had been removed since she'd last been home and replaced by a locked iron gate.

Alone in the backyard, Nyah stared at her house, the most dangerous place in the city for her to be. She'd seen enough movies to know you shouldn't look for the monster in his cave. Nyah ignored common sense and kicked in the basement window. The girl slid through, surprisingly not cutting herself, and moved through the house.

To protect her precious things, Nyah had kept them hidden at Watson's place. Her Mom had few treasures left since Vern sold anything of value he found and destroyed the rest. The photo albums had disappeared from the bookshelf right after Vern tossed the family pictures on the mantel into the fire. Her mother burnt her hands snatching the pictures from the flames. There'd been a huge battle, and Vern had accused Delores of loving her dead husband more than him, but Delores had been smart enough to deny the truth. The screaming stopped once Vern passed out. The next day there wasn't a trace of her father left in the house. All the photos, diplomas and mementos had vanished. That had been her mother's work.

Her father kept a hidden safe in the house for his service revolver so Nyah wouldn't stumble upon it. She suspected her Mom hid birthday and Christmas presents in it when she remembered when Nyah's birthday was. If her Mom had kept the albums from Vern, they would be in the safe.

In the hall closet that led from the living room to the kitchen, under a pile of shoes and a couple of gym bags,

Nyah lifted the loose piece of carpet and revealed the safe. Her father had sunk it in the floor, and if someone curious had ever been down in the basement and looked behind the furnace, they would have wondered why there was a large steel box bolted into the ceiling. Vern had never been that ambitious.

The safe was locked and in the middle of the door was a key pad, but Nyah had no clue what the code was. She closed her eyes. What number would her Father have used? What would he know he'd always remember? His wedding date? His badge number? Nyah ran her fingers over the keys. Her mother knew the code too, what would be special to them both?

Nyah punched in her birth date and the safe popped open.

Inside the safe was an envelope with a few hundred bucks she wasn't too proud to pocket. Secured with elastic bands were dozens of her school report cards. A velvet box with her Dad's badge, and the medals he earned came out next. Nyah pulled out baby books, awards she won and a few crafts Nyah vaguely remembered making in kindergarten. Memory after memory she lifted from the safe until she uncovered the photo albums.

In the second album she tore through, Nyah found a group photo taken at a softball game. In the second row, with his arm around her father, was the cop from the bridge. The note taped beside the picture had the name she needed. Another inch gained.

Nyah grabbed a grocery bag from the kitchen and emptied the contents of the safe into it. She closed and locked the safe and replaced the carpet as keys jingled at the front door. Nyah stood and moved to the living room. There was a shadow in the window shade of the front door. The deadbolt turned, and then stopped. The shadow dropped the keys and cursed, bending over to retrieve them.

Vern was home.

She needed out of the house. Now. But Nyah would never make it to the basement; she'd have to pass by the front door. Vern had his keys and again fumbled with the lock. She scrambled to the kitchen at the back of the house, grabbing the grocery bag and album on the way. Throwing open the back door, she stood face to face with the iron gate. It couldn't be opened from the inside either, it had been padlocked. Nyah would need a blowtorch to leave that way.

Voices screamed in her head.

Vern is coming.

Run.

He's going to find you.

Get out.

There's no time.

Hide.

Doubling back, Nyah dove into the closet, shutting herself in just as the front door opened. She pulled jackets and boots over herself, trying to disappear. The house shook as the front door slammed closed. Vern let a groan, and moments later there were two thumps as his shoes hit the floor. Nyah remained perfectly still as Vern crossed the living room, let out a roaring fart and stumbled into the hallway.

Vern stopped right outside of the closet. Her breathing was too loud, her heart thundered in her chest. She was sure he'd hear her. She clamped her hand over her mouth to keep from screaming. The fan clicked on in the bathroom across the hall. Vern burped and laughed. He was drunk for sure.

He threw the bathroom door open, and it ricocheted off the tub. Vern slammed the toilet seat up, and peed for longer than Nyah thought any human should. She smelt it from the closet. So gross. The drunk pig didn't flush before shutting off the fan and continuing down the hall to the kitchen.

Equal parts brave and stupid, Nyah cracked the closet door and peeked out. Illuminated by the refrigerator light, Vern swayed as he reached in and pulled out a beer. He cracked the cap and put the bottle to his lips, draining it in one gulp. Vern grabbed a second bottle and closed the fridge. Nyah ducked back into the closet as Vern turned and headed back towards her. The couch groaned as Vern plopped down and the flicked on the TV. The familiar theme song of "Cops" drifted towards her; Vern's favourite show. He yelled at the crooks for being stupid enough to get arrested, like he was some criminal mastermind.

Nyah leaned back and got comfortable. Vern was no amateur; he could drink a brewery dry before passing out, but eventually the asshole would fall asleep, even if it took until morning. She just had to wait him out.

There was a knock at the front door and Nyah bolted upright. She held her breath as Vern swore and turned off the TV. Vern and the couch moaned in unison as he rose and shambled to the front door.

"Better not be fucking selling anything," he growled. He opened the door and even tucked into the closet Nyah heard him gasp. "Oh, it's you," he said.

"Going to invite me in?" the visitor asked.

"Yes, for sure, Shamus, of course."

Shamus! The girl bit down on her hand to keep from screaming.

The front door closed and the men entered the living room. "Have a seat, Vern," Shamus ordered.

"What's going on?" Vern asked weakly.

"Have a seat, I said."

"This is my fucking house, don't tell me... Whoa, what the fuck, Shamus?"

"I'm not in a good mood, Vern, I had a little car accident and I'm in some pain so don't fuck with me right now."

"What the Hell, Shamus? Put the fucking gun away."

Ice cold fingers tickled Nyah's spine. A gun? She'd spill no tears if Shamus shot Vern, but would he then look for witnesses? If she had left a few moments before she wouldn't have these problems.

"If you don't want me to use it you'll sit the fuck down."

"Okay," Vern croaked, and the springs of the couch squeaked.

"Now, Vern, am I crazy, or did we have a deal?"

"We did, we did..."

"Well, maybe you're too stupid to get how these things work, but when I pay you for something I expect you to actually fucking give it to me."

"I told you it's gone, it's not my fault."

"You took my money, Vern."

"I told you it's gone."

"Or maybe you're trying to screw me."

"Never, I fucking swear."

"I don't believe you, Vern, but if I hurt you enough the truth will fall out of that lying mouth of yours."

"I'm telling the truth, Shamus, I promise."

"You better go over it again because I must be missing something," Shamus said.

"I had the video, I swear it Shamus. It was on my computer, I hid it with some movies and music so no one would notice it. After you paid me I came home to make a copy like we agreed, but it was gone. My old lady told me the girl got a new iPhone and downloaded everything off the computer and then wiped it clean just to piss me off."

Nyah smiled so big her cheeks hurt. She had the video all these big bad men were going crazy for, and she'd tricked them all. She couldn't get too cocky, she was still trapped in a closet.

"And you only had the one copy?" Shamus asked.

"I was going to make more when I came home and

found everything on the fucking computer erased."

"And now it's on some dumb girl's iPhone with a bunch of movies and music?"

"Yeah, so when we find Nyah we find your stuff."

"Thanks, moron but I worked that out myself. So how do we find this Nyah?"

"That's the fucking problem, I can't."

"Well, you better figure it out because time is against me. Jacob is looking for it too and as of right now the fact that it's the only copy is a bad thing."

"Why is it the only copy?"

"It wasn't. There were five, but Jacob has destroyed four of them. He found my lawyer who held the first copy and killed him after torturing the weak bastard and learning the other locations. Then he paid off the manager of the bank where the safety deposit box held the second. Jacob's boys broke into my mother's house and took the one I'd hidden in the attic then trashed and burned the condo I'd stashed the fourth in."

"What about the last copy?"

"You had it you fucking idiot! The last copy I kept on my computer so I would always have access to it. That computer was in my office at the garage I own on Watt Street. Jacob had his boys busted in to search for it, but that computer wasn't there, was it?"

"No, I guess not," Vern stuttered.

"You're fucking right it wasn't, because that computer had already been stolen by the fucking addict I had working there doing oil changes. That loser sold that computer to you to pay for his crack."

"Yeah, I didn't know it was your stuff, Shamus, I really didn't. When I saw that video and heard you were looking for it I put it all together and got in touch, didn't I?"

"You're a regular fucking genius, Vern, but now you went and lost it."

"I didn't mean to, honest, but when we talked you never mentioned Jacob Poole was looking for it."

"Are you brain dead? Of course, dipshit, you saw it, every fucking hood in the city is after it."

"Wow, if it's that important, there must be some big reward for it."

"Are you for real?" Shamus screamed. There were half a dozen smacks in quick succession. It sounded to the girl like steel hitting flesh and Vern cried out. "You planning on screwing me over?"

"No, no, I'm just saying," Vern sobbed.

"I know what you said and I know how that pickled brain of yours works," Shamus said. "Now, I need to get some facts perfectly fucking straight."

"For what?"

"To find the girl, you dumb fuck, what else? Why aren't you looking for her?"

"I have been, I told you that on the phone. She's a tricky little bitch."

"Seriously, I'm surrounded by morons... We've got to find her before the video is lost and everything I've built goes down the shitter. No video means no leverage and nothing protecting me from Jacob, and that means nothing keeping you alive."

"I don't know where to find her, Shamus."

"She's your damn daughter and you don't know her?"

"The brat's not my kid. She fucking hates me, and is disgusted by what her mother did. Of course, she blames that shit on me too."

"So she's not stupid, which means you might be outmatched, Vern. This is going bad for you."

"Even if I find her, don't mean she'll give it to me."

"Pain makes people do surprising things."

"She's a kid, Shamus, she's a little bitch but she's still a kid..."

"Find the girl, Vern, or you'll be the one in pain."

The front door slammed shut and Vern waited a while before releasing out a long sigh. There was clinking in the kitchen and Nyah knew Vern was primed for a bender. He mumbled to himself when he returned to the couch, polishing off beer after beer. "Fucking bastard, fucking Shamus," he said. "Maybe I'll talk to Jacob again, and see how Shamus likes that..."

Nyah hugged her knees, wrapped in a tight little ball. The fear paralysed her, knotting her in on herself. Her brain was frozen from the threats. These men wanted her dead. They were more than she could handle. What had she been thinking?

Then, as the seconds became minutes, logic crept in. She knew what they were capable of because that was the entire reason she was doing what she was doing. These men had already shown her how violent they could be. Their violence had brought her back in their crosshairs the moment she found the video on Vern's computer. It was her choice to bring things full circle and it was time to stop acting the scared little girl and finish what she started. Digging deep into her strength, she forced herself first to relax and then to get comfy. She was going to be there awhile waiting for Vern to pass out, which was fine, it would give her time to plan.

TWENTY

Consciousness returned in sluggish waves, momentarily breaking the surface only to submerge again. I don't know how long I drifted, but I awoke in a chair, my hands bound with thick ropes behind my back and my ankles latched to the chair legs.

I was also naked.

My chair, a table and a couch in the far corner were the room's only furnishings. The carpet had been stained with blood. Knives of various lengths, crochet needles, a leather strap and a ball peen hammer were lined up neatly on the table.

I'd seen enough horror movies to know someone had vicious plans and being naked did nothing for my confidence. I thrashed against my restraints and the ropes dug into my skin. My shoulders ached and my head screamed and throbbed, but there was no give in the ropes.

The door opened and Davis Parsons limped in, his face even uglier than usual. His nose hadn't been set properly after the second time I'd broken it after the bridge, and fresh stitches closed the gash on his forehead. Some big no necked fucker with scars on his face and red hair shaved close to the wood filled the doorway behind Davis.

Jacob sauntered in last with a glass of whiskey in his hand and closed the door behind him. He plopped down on the couch, lit a cigarette, crossed his legs and glared at me.

Davis was even uglier close up. "The princess is finally awake. Not so tough now with your little worm hanging out."

"I'll bet Jacob likes the show."

Davis chose a long thin knife from the table, testing the

point with his finger. "Imagine all the places I could put this."

"You're a kinky bastard."

"All we want is the name of the hooker that has Jacob's property."

I nodded to the big fucker. "Are they cheaper when they're that ugly?"

Davis held the tip of the knife under my chin. "Let me be clear, Morris is here to hurt you, how bad is up to you. Co-operate and give up the whore or you'll be gutted and left to die."

"That's counterproductive. You won't get shit then, dumbass."

He punched me. Pain shot through my skull and lightning filled my eyes.

"Give us the girl and this ends quickly."

"Are you seriously this fucking stupid or do you practice?"

Morris' hands rained down like sledgehammers, crushing my ribs and smashing my face. His elbows nearly knocked my jaw right off. Morris stomped on my toes and kneed me in the stomach when his hands got tired. I prayed he'd knock me out.

But no matter how many times Davis asked about the girl and that mysterious stolen evidence, I couldn't say anything because I didn't know anything.

Davis eventually pulled Morris off me; the monster was sweating, taking deep breaths to pull the oxygen into his lungs. My eyes were heavy with swelling, and my body vibrated in pain with every movement.

Jacob watched from the couch, smoking, drinking and saying nothing.

"Having fun yet?" Davis asked.

I shook my head.

"Maybe now we can be social and you can give up the

girl," he said.

"I don't have a clue who she is."

"Morris, get us a couple buckets of water."

The behemoth nodded and left the room.

"What are those for?" I asked.

"If you tell us where the evidence is you won't have to find out," Davis said.

"I told you already, I don't have it."

"Then it's still with the girl, and we know you have her."

"Are you brain dead? What hooker do I have?"

"When did I say hooker, Grady? I said girl, and we know what's going on."

Morris returned, and set two large buckets of water on the carpet. They easily held forty litres each.

"What are those for, Davis?"

"They're to help you remember. I'd love Morris to beat on you all night, but Jacob's impatient. He thinks this will be quicker and more unpleasant."

"To be honest, I really don't give a fuck what Jacob thinks."

Davis clenched his jaw. "You never learn, you dumb shit."

He grabbed my hair and yanked hard enough that I teetered on the chair's hind legs. Morris lifted a bucket and poured it in my face, slowly and carefully making sure every drop covered my nose and mouth. I fought to keep my mouth shut, forcing my lips together but I finally succumbed to the need for air.

I gasped and the water rushed down my throat. I choked, it was too much and I still couldn't breathe. As I fought for air I took in more water. I was suffocating, battling to inhale oxygen, which brought the water deep into my lungs. It burned, and panic engulfed me as I thrashed in my chair. My lungs felt like they were going to explode and the room turned black.

Then it was over. Morris tossed the empty bucket aside and Davis released me. I pitched forward, coughing, gasping and snot streaming out of my nose. But there was air, sweet beautiful air.

"Did that jog your memory a bit?" Davis asked.

"I don't know anything." My throat burned with each word.

"I'll settle for where you're keeping the girl."

"What girl? I don't have any girl."

"We got a phone call a few hours ago from someone telling us you've been seen with the girl who stole from Jacob," Davis said.

Jacob took a long pull on his cigarette and blew the smoke out his nostrils. "You've been holding out on us, Grady. We know you found the girl and my property. I get it, you got greedy and thought you'd turn your miserable fortunes around. That's understandable, but it was foolish."

"You're not making sense."

"Maybe you'll understand this," Davis said before pulling my head back.

Morris picked up the second bucket. I took rapid breaths, taking in as much air as possible, waiting until right before he poured the water to hold my breath. Morris the mute kicked me in the shin and I groaned. He dumped the bucket into my gaping mouth. It was worse than the first go round, and I choked the water into my lungs. The pain and panic overwhelmed me and I was willing to die to end it.

Mercifully the water stopped, and I coughed, hacking phlegm all over myself.

Jacob flicked his cigarette on the carpet. "If he doesn't tell you now kill him, Davis."

Davis shook his head. "The prick was right, he can't tell us a thing if he's dead. It's time for real pain."

He held up a six inch piece of metal with a sharp tip for

me to examine. It looked like a knitting needle. Where was he going to stick me with that? Eyes? Ears? My balls?

It was almost a relief when he plunged it three inches deep into my leg, until the pain came. I screamed, trying to free my arm and pull it out. Each movement brought new waves of agony as cold sweat poured off me.

A machine sat on top of the cart Morris rolled in from the hallway. It was a generator. Davis flipped a switch and the machine hummed, my skin prickled as the current built. He clipped one of the leads to the end of the metal spike in my leg and I screamed again.

"Ever been electrocuted?" Davis asked. "It's quite the experience."

"Take that fucking thing out of my leg!"

"As the electrical current passes through the body, the skin and organs burn, literally cooking you. The current forces your muscles to contract with such force it could snap your bones. Wouldn't that be something to see?"

"I'll take your word for it."

He put his hand on a dial. "Unbroken skin offers some resistance, but that is in your leg and your skin is wet. There is a very good chance it will stop your heart, but luckily, this machine could restart it with another jolt. We can keep going for hours."

"Why are you telling me this?"

"Anticipation of pain usually makes a man talk," he said. "But I'll give you a taste first then we'll discuss the girl. This is going to hurt like a bitch."

I had no time to beg before he flipped the switch and the current hit me. I convulsed, my muscles flexing, threatening to burst through the skin. My thigh was on fire, right through to my balls and into my stomach. My jaw snapped shut, and the pressure on my teeth was enough to shatter them. But the leg was the worst. The metal felt as big as a bus and hot as the sun. It felt like my skin was melting and the pain was everywhere.

I tried to convince myself there was no pain, this wasn't happening. It did not hurt, I was fine. But the pain was real, it was horrible and I wanted to die.

Davis flipped the switch and it stopped. The pain receded reluctantly as though saddened it had not broken me completely. My leg was still on fire and my muscles cramped. I shook from exertion.

"Please, never again, I can't take it. I can't do that again."

Davis' fingers teased the dial. "You should tell me about the girl now," he said. "This is only going to get worse."

"Please, I don't know who she is."

Jacob jumped up from his seat, and stormed over. "I've had enough of this bullshit, Davis. I'm not going to burn for a waste of skin like this." He ripped the metal rod from my leg and stabbed it into my chest. "Let's see if he likes this."

I started to cry. "Please, not again, please. Just stop."

Jacob spat in my face. "Shamus Gray has been using that video to protect himself. He's selling his drugs on my streets to my customers and lining his pockets with my money. The word is he stashed that video and it fell into the hands of a whore who was at Watson's that night. We searched the house, we've killed the hookers who were there but there's no video."

"That's not my fault, Jacob, please..."

The old man frowned. "But the phone call we received today was enlightening. It wasn't a hooker we were looking for but a girl. A young girl and she stole the evidence. And since you have her that means you have the video."

"What fucking video?"

Davis sighed. "Shamus had a video of Jacob doing something highly illegal, and was threatening to give it to the cops if Jacob got in his way."

"You didn't say that. You didn't tell me it was a video."

Jacob's smile was genuine and he caressed my face. "So you have it?"

"And this girl, she's young, like sixteen, blonde, pretty?" I asked.

"Yes, yes, that's her," he cried.

I closed my eyes and felt dread envelope me like a slimy cold blanket. I knew the girl. I had been too stupid to figure it out. Everything made sense. The trip back to Watson's. The running from Shamus. Her phone. The moment the puzzle snapped together, I immediately wished it hadn't. I may be one of the biggest pieces of shit wasting oxygen in Winnipeg. I might be a drunk, a lousy husband and a useless human being all around, but I wasn't giving Nyah to Jacob.

With what pain I knew was coming, I prayed to be strong enough to keep my mouth shut.

"We want the video," Jacob said. "And the girl who took it."

Davis toyed with the dial. "Remember the situation. This isn't about you, the video is what's important and it's all we want."

I shook my head. "All those other girls dead, and just for a fucking video."

Davis snapped his fingers. "Focus, Grady. That video is more important than your life. Where is she?"

"I put her on a bus to Saskatchewan."

Jacob's face went crimson. "What?"

"She was just some kid who needed help so I bought her a ticket," I lied. "You told me I was looking for a thieving hooker."

The old drunk levelled a gun at my head. "Tell me exactly where the girl went or I'll round up your wife, mother and anyone else you've ever loved and kill them in front of you."

I didn't answer because I was distracted.

The door behind Jacob opened and light spilt into the room. A figure entered, she was small, delicate, and held an Uzi loose at her side. The fairy rushed in and a gorilla followed close behind. The guns in his hands looked like cannons.

The fairy and the gorilla raised their weapons and opened fire.

Basil's first shot took out Morris, his head exploded and splattered Jacob's face. Gabby caught Davis in the leg and sent him spinning to the floor. Bullets filled the air, and hissed as they flew past. Jacob ducked behind me for cover and I have no idea how I wasn't ripped to shreds.

Davis crawled across the room and Gabby sent a torrent of bullets up his body slicing him in two. Davis lay motionless in a pool of his own blood.

Jacob screamed, leaving cover and shooting wildly at Gabby. The guns bucked Basil's hands and Jacob' chest was torn apart, dropping him in a heap. The roar of gunfire echoed in my ears.

Basil and Gabby came to me and I started to cry. The big man cut me loose and held me tight as Gabby eased the metal spike out of my chest and dropped it on the carpet.

Gabby found my clothes and handed them to me. "Hurry up with your pants, you're creeping me out."

With Basil's help I dressed myself. When I tried to stand there was no strength in my legs. My jeans turned crimson where the metal shank had pierced me. Basil helped me hobble over to Jacob.

My tormentor writhed on the floor, chest cleaved open, and his mouth working, as blood seeped out of it. He wasn't dead yet, but it was close. I hoped he felt every bullet.

"What is on the video?" I asked. "Why was it so important?"

It took him a long time to find the words. "It show how... I ... stayed... out of... jail...," he said. "Why I own...

the..."

"Own who? Who?" I asked.

Jacob convulsed twice and the light left his eyes. He was dead, and it should have made me happy. I felt hollow. What had been so important that he had to torture me like that? I needed a reason.

Basil sat me down on the chair, while Gabby looked me over. I winced when she touched my ribs and cried out when she probed my leg.

"Sorry," she said. "I'm guessing you're just bruised, badly, but nothing looks broken."

"You just wanted to feel me up."

She winked. "I do like a man who can handle pain."

"Enough," Basil snapped. "Grady, what the Hell was this about?"

I told him everything. All of it, every bloody damn thing. Even Basil winced when I described being electrocuted. I only kept the girl out of my story. I wanted to talk to her first. "It was all over that fucking video," I said. "I just wish he'd told me why."

Basil squeezed my shoulder. "We'll figure that out later, right now we gotta get out of here."

"I'll need help," I said.

Basil flung me over his shoulder and carried me out. It was almost romantic, except for the tears I shed from every step.

"How did you find me?" I asked when he helped me into his SUV.

"Davis took your car and the moron parked it out front."

They'd kept me in a rundown house in the North End. It was probably a crack house and I'm not sure the neighbours would have been bothered by gun fire.

Basil wanted to take me to his personal doctor, but I demanded to go to my apartment. Basil relented; Gabby bitched the whole way.

Curling up in the back seat, I buried my face in my hands and sobbed. Basil turned up the stereo, and Gabby reached back and stroked my hair and held my hand. Neither of them said a word because there were never going to be the right ones.

I'd been broken.

TWENTY-ONE

A beating can rip huge chunks from your memory, and getting knocked out sends your recall on vacation. Shock can force your brain to erase the scary parts to protect you from the pain and humiliation, keeping you ignorant of the fact that you, as a human, are vulnerable.

But not for me.

Every second of being electrocuted, nearly drowned and every moment Davis tortured me is seared into my memory. Add that to my many blessings.

After I passed out in my apartment and couldn't protest, Basil and Gabby dragged me to Basil's doctor. With trembling hands the old saw bones stitched me up. The quack sent me home with a bottle of pills, never saying if they fought infection or numbed the pain. All I know is they knocked me on my ass.

Basil put me to bed and sleep overtook me, held me down, and refused to let go. I flowed in and out of consciousness for the next three days. I'd wake up, eat a little, swallow a few more pills and then pass out again.

Marin came home. She wiped my face with a cold cloth and rubbed my back while I puked. I became close with the toilet, cradling it for hours. I can't say what was worse, sobering up or the agony of my injuries, but the combined misery was near unbearable.

Through the clouds of my concussion, the haze of drugs and waves of pain Nyah's face emerged. The tears streaked her cheeks and rolled off her chin falling onto my face. She said she was sorry. Over and over she repeated it as she ran her thumb over my brow. I wanted to tell her it was okay, but the words weren't able to find their way from my brain to my mouth. I drifted back into the clouds and she was gone.

Eventually my eyes opened and the fog dissipated. Marin sat in the bed beside me, feet tucked under her and a smile dancing in her eyes as she read. When she realized I was awake the smile disappeared.

"Hello beautiful," I said.

"Go back to sleep."

"I've done enough of that."

"Good." She picked her purse off the floor. "See you around, Grady."

"You're going?"

"You're awake now so there's nothing more for me to do."

"Please, stay and talk."

She shook her head. "I'm only here because Basil, of all people, asked me to be your nurse. My shift's over."

"Marin, listen, I'm sorry, I..."

Marin held up her hand. "I don't want to hear it, not after the lack of respect you showed the other night." She closed her eyes and sighed. "My father said he still wants to talk with you." She waggled a finger at me. "And before you argue, you're going to hear my Dad out, it's important to him. That much you owe me for cleaning up your vomit."

I tried to stand but my knees buckled and I fell back into the bed.

Her brows furrowed. "Who did this to you, Grady? I want the truth."

"You won't believe me, but it's why I never made it back to the restaurant."

"With you it's always a story."

"Forget it, just go."

"What happened?"

"You don't want to know."

"I wouldn't have asked otherwise."

For the first time since I met her, I told Marin the truth. I must have had a concussion. I told her every bloody thing that'd happened and when I finished, we were both crying.

"Why do you hate yourself so much, Grady?"

"I don't have an answer, but I've realized I can't do this anymore."

"What? Drink or get beaten up?" Marin asked. "Most people don't to go to such extremes to learn that lesson."

"I'm talking about Reece," I said. "Everything I've done for my brother hasn't made one bit of difference. He's still a druggie and what did trying to save him get me? Nothing but arrested and tortured."

"I'm so sorry." She hugged me tight and I didn't mind the pain. "How do we keep you safe? Do you really think these men will let you walk away?"

"Jacob is dead, Davis is dead, and so is any debt I owe them."

"What about their lawyer?"

"He doesn't have a client anymore."

"And this Shamus?"

"Apparently Shamus wanted this video to use against Jacob. It'd be pointless for him to hunt for it now."

"Does Shamus know that Jacob is dead? What if he keeps looking for the video?"

"Word will get out about Jacob if it hasn't already, don't worry about that."

My wife nodded, went silent and turned to the window. The setting sun cast a red haze over the buildings and trees as it dropped down past the apartments across the street. "Tell me this is over," she said.

"I hope it is."

"That's not convincing."

"We're going to have to wait and see how this all shakes out."

Marin reached forward and caressed my cheek. "We're

in this together, I promise. I know the police aren't your biggest fans, but maybe my Dad could get them to help you."

"The cops are begging for an excuse to lock me up. Besides, it's not safe for you with me until I know where everyone stands."

"I don't care. I'll do whatever I can to help out of this mess and get you away from these people."

"If I know you're safe then I can handle myself."

"How is this going to end?" she asked. "Is it over when you are in jail? When more people are dead? When is it finished?"

"Honestly?"

"Yes, of course."

"I have no fucking idea."

"That's not very comforting."

"If you want me to lie, I can. Just believe that once I get my hands on Shamus, one way or another I'll rip the truth from his lips, and then, I'll know the way out."

Marin climbed under the covers, snuggled in and I drifted off to sleep. When I woke, she was gone. She'd left a note on her pillow.

"Be safe and call when you can.
Try not to be too stupid.
I love you,
Marin."

The reflection in the bathroom mirror paid me no compliments. My body was a mass of bruises and my skin red and angry where the metal rod had pierced it. Purple stitches held me together. My face was hollow and stretched tight; my eyes ringed in black. I looked like Hell.

In the shower I scrubbed myself as hard as I could. The hot water poured over me and my joints cracked and groaned, but I felt loose and mobile by the time I towelled off. I dressed in jeans and a t-shirt and walked to the kitchen for some water.

Marin had left a plate of food covered in tinfoil in the fridge. My stomach rumbled. I ignored the bottles of beer that surrounded it and removed the plate. It was spaghetti, and I ate it cold. Shovelling in one forkful after another, sauce covered my face and I clenched my teeth to keep it from coming back up.

I put my dishes in the sink and then opened the fridge to stare longingly at the lovely rows of beer. The bottles called to me and begged me to drink them. Their pull was strong and not even the fear of what Marin would do if I started drinking again could dull it. A knock at the door saved me.

It took effort to close the fridge, but I did. My liver whimpered as I crossed the living room and opened the front door. Marin was there, leaning against the frame, head down staring at the floor. She raised her face to meet me, her brow lined with worry. It suddenly occurred to me that my wife may be telepathic.

"I wasn't going to drink," I said. "They were just sitting there and I was only looking."

"Drink what?"

It was a bad place to go so I stopped. "You know you have a key."

"I know, but I wasn't sure I actually wanted to come in."

"What happened?"

"Since I left here I've been driving around, thinking on what you said, running through your story, trying to make sense of it."

"I don't like where this is heading."

"You left something out of your story," she said. "I didn't notice it at first, but you're holding out on me again."

"I told you everything you can handle."

"I guess we'll see about that." She tucked her hair behind her ears and stood up straight, crossing her arms over her chest. "The thing is, you told me about all those dead girls, the psychos chasing you, Reece and all that other mess, but you never mentioned if you found out what was on the video."

"Because I didn't. Jacob never said, Davis neither. They were too busy trying to find it."

"How about who has it?"

It was a long minute before I answered. "I have an idea."

My wife waited for me to continue. I didn't. She held my gaze before reaching out, taking my hand and interlacing her fingers in mine. "Tell me."

"I think it's Nyah. At least I'm pretty sure it is."

"Dad told me he remembered her, well, Nyah's father anyway. He was a cop, just like she said. He died. My father said he was killed on duty."

"I know all this. I've even heard the rest," I said. "Her mom turned to drugs, became a hooker and then got killed. Nyah is alone."

"If she has that video she's still in danger."

"It's over Marin, Jacob's dead, there's really no point anymore."

"Is it over? You sure? Would you risk her life on it?"

"Jacob said the video was evidence to be used against him."

"And you take him at his word? You trust him?"

"Of course not."

"Exactly. What if he was lying?" She let go of my hand and rubbed her eyes. "The point is, Grady, I think it'd be safer to have Nyah with us until we figure out where we're at and not take chances."

I had no argument so I gave none. "Where is she?"

"I tried her at Dad's but he said she went out. I sent her a text." My wife held up her phone so I saw the exchange. "Nyah said she went to her Mom's grave. Oh, that reminds me, we buried Delores and had a service while you were healing."

"And like an ass, I missed it."

"Nyah understood, you nearly died." My wife sighed. "I didn't tell her about the video, I didn't think it was wise until I came back here and confirmed it with you, but Grady, we need to talk to her and if she has it we need to see it so we know what we're dealing with."

"We also have to consider the fact she may have run off, if she felt threatened or unsafe."

"Exactly, so you need to go get her now, bring her home safe and we can handle whatever we have to. But us standing here guessing isn't going to accomplish much."

Not for the first time, I thought how smart my wife was. "Okay, which cemetery is she at?"

TWENTY-TWO

St. Andrew's cemetery was no place to hang out. According to horror movies, no cemetery was. The cemetery had manicured lawns, perfectly pruned trees, and an explosion of the prettiest, most vibrant flowers around, but it also featured thousands of tombstones and was ground zero for ghosts, zombies and every creature born of nightmares. The graveyard didn't bother Nyah; she was already living her worst nightmare.

The wind had a bite to it. Even with her hoodie zipped up, the cold air sliced through Nyah's skin and cut deep into her bones. The girl tucked her legs under her and leaned back against her Mom's tombstone. The cemetery was quiet except for the wind, empty except for the ghosts, and as far as the living went, Nyah was alone. The earth was still fresh beside her where they had covered her mother's coffin with six feet of dirt. The moon and sun were both in the sky together, passing each other as they changed shifts.

Nyah first traced the words etched in her mother's headstone with her fingertips and then those on her father's headstone beside it. Finally, her parents were back together. Her father would have words for his wife about how she'd been behaving since he'd died, but in the end, wherever they were, Jim would be happy to have his Delores back.

Tears tracked down Nyah's cheeks. She felt closer to her Mom than she'd had in a long time. It was morbid but now she could remember her Mom like she wanted. Her old mom, how she was when dad was still alive.

She could remember when her Mom baked cookies and they went for walks together. Nyah could forget they'd ever

213

met Vern or her Mom snorted coke and turned tricks. She could just remember when Delores was her Mom in all ways, not just in name.

From the front pouch of her hoodie Nyah pulled out her cell phone. Tears dripped from Nyah's cheeks onto the screen of her phone as she pressed play.

The video begins with two men talking in an alley at night. The older one is dressed in a suit, his grey hair slicked back from his face, while the other wore a leather jacket. They passed a bottle of booze back and forth between them. The alley lights up from the headlights of a car. Both men shield their eyes as the car comes into view. It is a cop car and it parks a few feet from the two men.

Tossing the bottle off to the side, the two men move to the passenger side of the squad car. The bottle explodes as it hits the concrete. An officer exits the vehicle, the same cop Nyah recognised from the bridge where Emma was killed. The cop approaches the two men and shakes their hands. The younger one in the leather coat reaches into his pocket and pulls out an envelope and hands it to the cop who makes it disappear into his jacket. Blue and red lights illuminate the screen and a second cruiser pulls up. The cop that exits this vehicle is her Father, the other men don't look pleased to see him.

Especially not the other cop.

There is yelling, finger pointing, and her Father pushes the other officer when he steps between her Father and the two men. Those men decide to run and her Father draws his service revolver, shouting orders for them to stop. They do, raising their hands and walking back to the squad cars. The other cop is pleading, begging her Father to let the men go. It is clear the cops aren't on the same page, especially when he takes out his gun and points it at her Father. The yelling turns to screaming, and her Father turns his gun towards the other officer. They are screaming at each other and forget about the other two men.

The criminals.

The man in the suit has his own gun, and when he takes it out from his waist band at the small of his back, he doesn't hesitate. He fires three times and blood spurts from her Father as he crumpled to the ground. Nyah sobbed as her Father crawled across the ground towards his car. The man in the suit hands his gun to the other cop, yells and points at her Father. The other cop shook his head no, but the man in the suit won't accept that answer. Finally the cop took the gun and fired twice more into her Father, and he stopped crawling, the pool of blood spreading from him in a slow dark circle. The two men rush off, and after a moment, the cop left too, driving away in his cruiser leaving her Father alone on the screen.

Again and again, Nyah played the video. Maybe this time the men aren't in the alley or the other cop doesn't show up. Maybe her Father doesn't arrive or when he does he isn't betrayed. Maybe he isn't shot or doesn't die. Maybe this time, her world doesn't end.

Each time she prays it turns out different.

But it doesn't, it never does.

Nyah lost count how many times she watched that video while leaning against her mother's tombstone. So it may have been the fiftieth or hundredth time that night she watched her father die when she heard the gravel crunch under someone's feet behind her. Instantly Nyah was ripped from the alley back to the graveyard.

"Watcha watching?" A voice slurred.

Nyah knew that voice. Her stomach tightened, and her throat went dry. She stood and turned, tucking the phone into her rear pocket. Vern stood on the path, about a dozen feet away, his long greasy hair was half in and half out of his usual pony tail. Sweat beaded down his crooked nose, and into his moustache. Vern took a step toward her and he stumbled to the left, but it had nothing to do with his damaged leg. Vern was drunk.

"What do you want Vern?" Nyah demanded.

"Enjoying some fresh air. Now, watcha doing here, Nyah?"

"I'm visiting my Mom."

"Isn't that sweet? Crying over your poor dead Mommy. Probably bitching to her too, I bet. That's you, Nyah, always bitching and whining."

"You're such an asshole, Vern. My Mom is gone, can't you leave me alone?"

Vern stumbled a few steps towards her, his hands deep in his pockets. "But I'm responsible for you now, see."

"I'm fine on my own, and I don't need you." Backing away, Nyah tried to maintain the distance between them. "You should just forget about me."

"I wish I fucking could, but I can't, not after what you done." Vern moved forward and was mirrored by Nyah moving backward. He stopped and smiled at their little game. "Saw you at your Mom's funeral. So what, did you go find some new family? I know they don't know your mom from shit."

"They were paying their respects. Something you wouldn't know anything about."

Vern ripped his hands out of his pockets. They were balled into tight fists as he lunged closer. "Listen you little bitch, I gave everything to your Mom."

"Especially drugs."

"You're nothing but a brat and should have been a better daughter."

"Because I wouldn't watch you ruin her and not say anything?"

Nyah moved away, keeping an open escape route behind her. Vern was drunk, old and slow, but she wasn't completely sure she could outrun him. Nyah would hate to be wrong about that.

"Ruin her? Don't make me fucking laugh, she did it all to herself." He wiped his nose on his sleeve. "So, Nyah, you never said what you was watching."

The girl kept the tomb stones between her and Vern while she stole glances for someone to help. "Just some junk on YouTube."

"We both know that's a fucking lie."

"Then why bother asking?"

His eyes blazed in anger and his face contorted with rage. "That video was mine, you stole it from me. You took it from my computer and erased the only other fucking copy."

"This video is of my Dad so it belongs to me. It's mine, not yours."

"No, you're wrong. Dead fucking wrong. That video, it belongs to an important man. A scary man. He'll hurt you if you don't give it to me."

"I know he'll hurt you if I don't."

Vern's head snapped straight like he'd been slapped. "What did ya say?"

A smile drifted onto Nyah's face. "I'm not such a dumb little girl, am I? I know about Shamus and I hope he kills you like he did my Mom. You're the one who deserves it."

Vern growled and rushed forward, head down and hands out reaching for Nyah. "Give me the fucking phone. Give it to me. You've caused enough shit."

The girl dipped to the side, spun and stumbled out of the way. "I'm not done yet. There's going to be a lot more trouble, Vern, a lot more."

Nyah dug deep and sprinted for the path. Vern dove and latched onto her hoodie, spinning her around. "Give me the phone," he said as he pulled her closer.

Panic filled her as she clawed and punched at Vern, trying to break free. The dirty drunk slapped her and the girl's head snapped back. Nyah could taste the blood from her cut lip. Vern snatched at her pockets, ripping them, searching for the phone.

Remembering a lesson her Dad had given her years before, Nyah dug her nails into the side of Vern's face and jammed her thumbs into his eyes and hard as she could. Vern screamed and punched her flush on the jaw. Again her head snapped around and stars filled her world. Her face felt like it'd swelled triple. Vern tore through her pockets, and finally found her phone. He pulled it free and held it up to his face.

"There it is," he said. "About fucking time."

Nyah reared back and swung her leg with all she had. The top of her foot connected flush with Vern's balls, and the girl swore she felt them squish. Vern groaned, his eyes rolled back in his head, and he pitched forward, vomit erupting from him and spilling down the front of his jacket.

Nyah snatched her phone off the grass from where Vern dropped it and ran off. She peeked over her shoulder.

Vern had stood up and reached into his jacket.

Nyah pumped her legs faster.

Vern pulled out a gun.

The girl's legs burned as she raced through the tombstones.

There was a crack.

The bullet whizzed by Nyah's ear.

Nyah ducked behind the little limestone chapel near the centre of the graveyard. The girl kept her head down, scrambling through the flower bed that encircled the rear of the chapel. The two stain glass windows at the side of the building exploded behind her. Nyah felt the scream stuck in her throat as she pulled out her phone and sent a quick, desperate text.

The sent confirmation appeared and she tucked away her phone. There was another gunshot, and she could hear

Vern stumbling around the chapel so she took a breath and dashed off towards a thick grouping of trees and hid behind them in the shadows.

"I've got all fucking night to find you," Vern screamed.

Nyah peeked out, and looked for her next hiding spot. She'd stick to the shadows, keep to cover and just pray she could hold on long enough.

Pulling her head back just in time, Vern bumbled past her towards the front entrance. Nyah snuck out and stayed behind him. Close enough to follow but with enough space to hide. If she kept him in sight, from the rear, he might stay stupid enough to never find her.

"Just give me the fucking phone you bitch," Vern screamed. "Think about it, Nyah, it's just you and me and there ain't anyone to help you."

But there was. Vern was wrong, she had help. Nyah just hoped he got there fast enough.

TWENTY-THREE

Blood rushed to my head as I bent over to tie my boots in the entrance to my apartment, and the pressure built making me dizzy. Because Marin was watching, I fumbled through it, too proud to sit on the couch. With my boots finally laced up, I stood, the pressure receding as I did, and I narrowly avoided ruining the carpet with half digested spaghetti.

My coat hung looser than I remembered. It might have been from the ten pounds I lost from my quasi coma and not drinking. Although, I was sober for the first time in months and everything looks different without whisky lenses. I plucked my car keys off the small table beside the front door and Marin gave me a deep, full kiss on the mouth.

"Be quick and don't wander," she said.

I snorted. "Wander? What am I, a fucking dog or an old man?"

My wife caressed my cheek with her fingertips. "Are you telling me you can't find trouble?"

"Fine, I'll grab Nyah and be right back."

"You better be," she said. "Oh, and I left the Bel Air at Garret's lot."

"Greasy Garret's? That's no way to treat my girl. That lot is just a front to run drugs, there's probably a kilo of coke hiding in her trunk right now."

"Suck it up, darling. It's the cheapest lot around, and could you have afforded the tow if I left it on the street?"

"I can barely afford to breathe."

"Exactly." Marin gave me a small peck on the cheek and closed the door behind me.

Exiting the building, I stomped down the front steps as

221

an icy gust of wind shredded me. I zipped up my coat and stuffed my hands in my pockets. It was ten blocks to Greasy Garret's parking lot; I'd have to thank Marin for that.

There is no explaining wind chill; you have to experience it to truly understand. Everyone knows Canada can be cold and even fathom temperature in the minus 30's and 40's. But to feel a wind that makes the temperature drop another ten to twenty degrees colder is a lesson in the brutality of nature. Winnipeg is home to that type of wind. It rips through you, ice slicing nerves and frost tearing flesh from your face. It will take the breath right from you, causing your lungs to collapse, frostbite crystallising any skin exposed in less than a minute.

In winter, those winds are at their worst, like the icy breath of death. On a fall day, it's a slap to warn what's on its way. As my feet reached the sidewalk, that wind sent a spastic shiver through me.

Flashing red and blue lights announced the squad car that pulled up and blocked me from crossing the first of many intersections on my hike back to the Old Girl. Officer Quill sat behind the wheel in his puffy parka, warm gloves and toque. Quill rolled down the window and the heat blasted my face. Shuffling from foot to foot, I shivered from the ice creeping up my spine as his ass was all toasty in his pig mobile.

"I haven't seen you in a while, Grady, and I've been worried. A lot of people coming and going at your apartment though." Quill shook his head. "Interesting friends you have, especially that Basil Bray."

"Basil? I doubt he'd say he's my friend."

"I don't blame him. Get in the car, I'd like a word."

"You're very needy, Officer. I'll get in if you give me a ride to my car."

"Isn't the whole point of owning a car not having to walk?"

"Explain that to my wife."

He laughed. "Where'd you leave it?"

"My wife put it in Greasy Garret's lot, she didn't want to leave it out on the street and risk it getting towed. You know what huge pricks cops can be."

"We're the worst." The cop waggled his finger at me. "I really didn't like not being able to get a hold of you, Grady."

"I was drying out and that takes awhile."

"I'm surprised you had anything left once the booze was gone."

"Are you going to give me a lift or not?"

"I'll drive you as long as you answer my questions."

I slid into the passenger seat. "Fair enough."

Quill drove away from the curb, south down Main Street. "What happened to your face?"

"I walked into a door."

"How many times?"

"Funny."

"And here I thought you led a charmed life, vicious attacking doors notwithstanding."

I rolled my eyes. "My life's so great I want to shoot myself."

"That makes sense since you've shot just about everyone else."

"How's that again?"

The cop shrugged. "Well, first you shot Watson, but that's old news."

"It's also not true."

"Then of course there been all these prostitutes ending up dead. There's a pattern developing here."

"I'm sure I don't follow."

"Someone is crossing the names off the witness list. It'll be a short trial if there even is one."

"What do you want me to say? I didn't kill anybody."

"And now Jacob Poole and Davis Parsons have been

executed."

"If you're waiting for me to cry about that, you'd better get comfortable."

"It's well known that you owed Jacob Poole a large whack of cash, but I guess that's done with now, isn't it?"

"Look at you trying to cheer me up."

"You know, Grady, one thing you learn as a cop is that the person with the most to gain usually committed the crime. Everyone who's died was a potential witness against you. That's not a coincidence." He shrugged. "Either way, it's easy work for your lawyer."

"What do you care?"

"I don't like all these dead bodies. Not in my city." The cop finally pulled the cruiser to the curb outside Greasy Garrett's. "Some cops write tickets, sitting at speed traps drinking coffee all day going numb. Some beat up drunks and young punks because they think they're better, and others try and keep their nose clean, and move up the ladder to a higher pay grade and a desk job. Me? I want to keep people safe. I want these killings to stop."

"If it makes you feel any better, I'm confident this whole mess is finished." I opened the passenger door and swung my legs out. "Thanks for the ride, officer, but this is the last time we'll ever need to talk."

"What about the girl?"

I paused, half in and out of the cruiser. "What girl?"

"Don't play stupid, it just pisses me off, Grady. I've talked to you about Nyah a couple of times. Ever run into her again?"

"Why are you asking?"

"Nyah still hasn't turned up and I'm concerned. No one has seen her since the night Watson was killed."

"How is that my problem?"

"Please, Grady, no more games, it's very important that I find her."

"If I see her I'll tell her you're concerned," I said. "Maybe I'll even tell her she should give you a call."

Or maybe I'd tell Nyah to build a spaceship out of marshmallows and go colonise Mars.

"That would be smart of you," the cop said. "And if you do find her, she may have something for me and I'd appreciate any help in getting it to me."

"What could you want from a girl?"

Quill reached out and grabbed my sleeve, pulling me closer to him. "The girl has something I need. A file..."

My heart froze mid beat, and sweat soaked my back like a hose had been turned on. "A file?"

"Yes, a file, or a thumbnail drive, or something with some data that I really need to get my hands on." Quill's left hand remained on my arm, but his other had drifted to his gun. "The police department really is interested in it. What I need you to do is either take it from Nyah when you see her, or keep a hold of her until I get there, but either way we need that file."

The cop's eyes were wide and frenzied. He was desperate. I'd seen that look too often lately, and for the same reason. "What's on this file?"

"None of your business," he snapped. "What's important is I get a hold of it."

"I bet it is. See, the funny thing about this mystery file you're looking for is I think I know..."

My cell phone chirped and I paused.

"Think you what?" the cop prompted.

"Heard that this file..." I pulled out my phone, read the incoming text and my words left me.

Quill's knuckles whitened as he gripped his gun. "Spit it out, Fisk."

I reread the message. It was from Nyah. "*Help, Grady, I'm at St. Andrew's graveyard. Need help now. Vern's here and I'm scared.*"

"Fuck me, I gotta go, now," I barked.

"What?"

"I got to go, it's an urgent problem."

The cop tightened his hold on my sleeve. "What's going on Grady? I know you know Nyah, but what do you know about the file?"

I tried to pull my arm free, but Quill wouldn't release my sleeve. "No games, cop, this is going to go badly for you."

"Answer the damn question."

"Let go of me now. My friend's in trouble and I've got no time for this bullshit. Let go or this gets very ugly."

Quill actually laughed. "I'm the cop and if this gets ugly for anyone, it's you. Now tell me what I want to know and maybe I won't go to the next level here."

"Next level? Are you going to shoot me? Because that's what it's going to take to stop me. A friend is in trouble so I'm leaving. I'll fight you if I have to, but if I do it won't go well for you, Quill."

"Are you actually threatening me? A cop? You are fucking crazy? I'm the one with the gun."

"And it's in your holster while you're sitting in a car. I guarantee I knock you the fuck out before you have a chance to draw it." I let that sink in. "But I don't want to go there. It's nothing personal but I have to go."

"We're talking here, Grady, and I'm not done."

"Trust me, I want to finish this conversation as much as you do, just not now."

Quill let go of my sleeve, and both his hands latched onto the steering wheel. "If I don't hear from you by tomorrow I'm hunting you down."

I climbed out of the cruiser and Quill drove off.

TWENTY-FOUR

The fifty bucks to get car out of the lot wasn't exactly free, but it was a shit load cheaper than a ticket and impound fees. Not that it mattered, because if I didn't have the cash I'd have punched Greasy Garret in his sweaty, oily face and taken my keys out of his hands if I had to break his fingers to do it. I didn't have time to negotiate, not that I'd learned to do that in the army anyway. There's no need to bargain when you're pointing an M-16 at someone.

As soon as the lift gate with its chipped orange paint rose, I mashed the pedal into the floor of Bel Air and tore out of parking lot. The Old Girl protested as I ripped down Main towards the Perimeter Highway, with St. Andrew's cemetery laying on the outskirts of town.

I pulled off the highway onto a gravel road and eventually parked beside a beat up old red pickup outside the gates of St. Andrew's Cemetery. The pickup was dented and rusted enough to make my Old Girl look cherry. Some asshole even pasted a sticker of a skeleton giving the double finger in the back window of the truck. I was betting it belonged to Vern.

The big iron gates were open and as I walked through, I half expected them to slam shut behind me. No Demons sprang from the bushes and evil spirits didn't rise from the graves to laugh maliciously as they circled, ready to tear me to shreds.

Can't say I was disappointed.

St. Andrew's is a big, rolling, graveyard. There were more people planted there than populated the town of St. Andrew's itself. The headstones were in neat rows, the grass was recently mowed and the limestone chapel in the back corner looked well cared for. There were flowers on most of the plots, and pictures and cards adorned others. Clusters of trees separated the different sections. The leaves had changed colours and started to fall, and it was simply beautiful. It reminded me of an old English country side, if you didn't consider the graves, I guess.

What I didn't find were people, Nyah, Vern or otherwise. Standing on the path near the entrance, I listened, but no yelling, screaming or sounds of bloodshed drifted in the wind. I'd expected to arrive and find Vern dragging a limp and bloodied Nyah across the well groomed lawn. The fact that I didn't find anyone, most of all Nyah, scared the shit out of me. Had I got there too late?

Finally, on one of the paths that led off the main road I found someone. It wasn't Nyah, but some ugly, dumb looking biker wannabe with a crooked nose that announced to the world he couldn't fight but was dumb enough to piss people off enough to punch him.

Held low and tight to his leg, the ugly bugger held some heavy and dark object in his right hand. I couldn't make out what it was, but he definitely was walking with a purpose. What the Hell was he carrying? A tool? Was he a grave digger? The caretaker?

Mr. Ugly was so engrossed in searching the shadows, that he nearly walked into me by the time he realised I was even there. He stopped and tucked his right hand further behind his leg. His beady dull eyes looked me over, considering me. Because I didn't know what else to do I stared right back. I could see the pain on his face as he tried to get his brain to work and jumpstart that lump of fat between his ears. He slid his hand behind his back to conceal it.

The guy wiped the drool from his chin. "You got a problem dickhead?"

"I might, and I'm thinking it's you."

"You some kind of asshole?"

"Only on my good days."

"You some sort of fucking comedian? Beat it, asshole, you're not wanted here."

"Anyone ever tell you that your manners need some work?"

Pulling his hand out from behind his back, the guy made sure I noticed he was holding a gun. A Luger P08 as far as I could tell in the dark and the guy's hand covering it. No matter, it wasn't a good thing.

One thing they teach you in the army is... Well, they teach you lots, but one of the things is never go in unprepared. I must have gotten hit harder in the head than I realized. I came storming into this rescue with nothing. No blade, no piece, not mace, nothing. I hadn't even brought a knife to the gun fight. It was so dumb a move it's not even worth an idiom.

"I know who you are, Grady fucking Fisk. Thinks he's some tough guy, but you look like a pussy to me." He spat on ground. "I know you're in this with her."

I took a slow step towards him, like we were just chatting. "Who is this *Her*?"

"Stay the fuck there." He raised the gun but aimed at some point beyond my right shoulder. "I'm talking about Nyah, don't pretend you don't know her."

Holding up my hands, I moved closer. "Don't be stupid, we're just talking buddy. I don't even know who you are."

"I'm Vern, and I bet you know all about me from that brat."

"Hello Vern, I'd say it was nice to meet you, but you know, you're apparently a big piece of shit, so I won't."

"Fucking comedian, I heard that about you."

"Is that so? Who's been talking?"

"None of your business just like this is none of your fucking business. This is between me and my daughter. It's family shit."

"Her Dad is dead and we all know you've been nothing like a father."

"I raised her like my own. I fed the brat, put fucking clothes on her back and treated her damn well."

I shrugged and shuffled closer, cutting the distance between us again. "So, where is Nyah?"

"Not going to tell you again, asshole, mind your fucking business."

Three feet away and I was close enough to smell him, which was awful. It was booze intermingled with rot and it hurt my nose. Did I smell like that?

"Nyah is my friend, so this is my business."

The gun jumped up and down as Vern's hands shook. There's nothing more dangerous than an anxious guy with a gun.

"Back the fuck off or I'll kill you. Don't matter what Shamus said, he'll live with it if you don't give me no choice."

"Shamus? Did you say Shamus? Like Shamus Gray?"

"Stop fucking talking or I'll shoot you."

There was a shout from the bushes behind me. "Don't! Please, don't!" It was a girl's voice.

Nyah emerged from the bushes, gently pushing the branches back as she stepped from her hiding spot. She stayed in the shadows, but her big eyes shone bright. She was nervous, but there was a lot of that going around. She wrapped her arms around herself, and shuffled from foot to foot.

"Don't hurt him, Vern, please just let him go," Nyah said, her voice wavering.

Vern grinned so hard he nearly split his face. "Will ya look at that, the big man gets saved by the little girl."

"Nyah, don't worry, I'm fine," I said. "Go wait for me by the front gate."

"She ain't going anywhere until I get her fucking phone," Vern snapped.

"Wait. What?" I shook my head. "Her phone? Why the Hell would you want her phone?"

"She's got a video on there that's mine," Vern said. "The little bitch stole it from me."

Nyah flinched and sunk further back into the shadows.

"This video, is this THE video that has been fucking up my life the last few weeks?" I asked her.

The girl shrugged and lowered her head. "I can't say, there's lots of videos out there. Besides, Marin told me that you are drawn to trouble and make bad decisions and can't control your ..."

I held up my hand and cut her off. "I get it, I get it. I'm talking about the video Jacob, Shamus and every damn criminal in Winnipeg has been looking for. So I guessed right, you do have THAT video?"

She nodded. "Sorry, I didn't mean to get you involved."

"If you're talking about this moron," I said and thumbed towards Vern. "Don't let him get you flustered, he's as scared as you are."

Vern waggled his gun at me. "Do you want me to fucking shoot you? Just shut your mouth, this is none of your fucking business."

"See, you keep saying that, but I've been through a lot. I've been beaten, tortured, pissed on by cops, and I've fucking had it up to here with that video. So trust me, all you assholes made it my business, Vern."

Vern shoved the gun in my face, and the barrel blocked out the rest of the world. "I'm serious, Nyah, give me the phone or I'll fucking kill him."

From her back pocket, Nyah whipped out her phone and held it out in front of her like an offering. She stepped from the shadows into the lamp light and towards Vern. I saw her face. Her jaw was bruised and swollen. Her eyes were red from tears. I could still see the faint handprint of where she'd been slapped.

"What happened, Nyah?"

"I'm fine Grady, I'll give him the phone and it'll all be over."

"Nyah, you're hurt. Who did that?"

Vern snorted. "She got what she deserved. What did the little bitch expect when she stole from me?"

I surged forward, the barrel of the gun pressed into my forehead. "You hit her?"

"Gotta... Gotta keep her in line," Vern croaked as he backed up.

"You hit, Nyah?"

"Back off man, you're fucking crazy." Panic coated his voice. "I'll kill you. I swear, I'll do it."

The girl cried out. "Grady, no!"

Vern turned to Nyah and allowed his hand to dip as he looked away.

That was his mistake and my opportunity.

I latched on to his gun arm with one hand, and drove him twice in the face with my right. His knees buckled, and as he swayed I drove my elbow right up under his jaw. He pitched backwards and fell onto his ass. I followed him down, landing on top of him, driving my fist into his face over and over until he dropped the gun. He covered up, crossing his arms over his face as I continued to smash him with my fists.

"You hit a fucking kid? A girl?" I screamed, punctuating each word with a strike. "You loser. You scum. You piece of garbage."

Vern cried out, begging me to stop. He squirmed underneath me, trying to break free while his right hand grasped and pulled at his front pants pocket.

"Pussy, weak little snake." I could feel the skin on my knuckles spilt as I punched. "You can't even fight you coward."

Nyah rushed forward, grabbing my shoulder. "Please, that's enough. He's not worth it."

I landed punches at will, his face turning lumpy and bloody. Vern's one hand wasn't enough to protect him, but when his other escaped his pocket, it held the knife he'd had stashed there. Vern swiped at me, the knife slashed my forearm. The blood flowed over my wrist and between my fingers.

The pain was sharp and intense, but my arm still worked. I lunged forward, grasping for the arm that held the knife. I missed and Vern scrambled, kicking and flailing. The blade slashed towards my face and I pulled back, letting it pass harmlessly past me, but Vern used the moment to bumble to his feet.

My eyes steady on the knife as Vern wobbled back and forth, I rose, ready for another attack. My hands in front of me, we circled, I feinted to my right, and Vern gasped and cowered, throwing his arms up. I swung from my heels, caught him with a left hook and felt his jaw crack. He crumpled to the ground while I lost my balance and tripped over him, rolling off the path.

My mistake left Vern between me and Nyah. He leapt up and rushed towards the girl, his blade out in front of him. She screamed and took off, but he had the jump on her and was closing. I took off, grabbing a stone flower pot off a tombstone as I raced past. The pot had a stone angel perched on top, and weighed about ten pounds. I gripped the angel like a handle. Vern's free hand had only just grasped the hood of Nyah's sweater when I brought the stone pot down on the back of his head. I smacked him again, and the pot made a slurping, wet sound as the blood burst from his head. The third blow cracked his skull open and Vern dropped face first on the ground. I was covered in blood and Vern wasn't moving. Bits of brain and more blood dripped from the flower pot, I dropped it beside Vern's feet.

With eyes wide, Nyah's face was white save for the bruises and cuts. The girl was shaking and I went to her and put my hand on her arm. "It's over," I said. "You're safe."

Nyah wrapped her arms around me. "I thought he was going to shoot you. I was so scared."

"And you saved me. You distracted him and that was what I needed."

Releasing me from the hug, Nyah stepped back and shoved her hands in her pockets, casting her gaze down at Vern's body. "I almost got myself killed."

I shrugged. "Helping sucks."

"Grady, is Vern going to be okay?" she asked. "Do we need to take him to the hospital?"

"He's dead."

"No. Really? Oh my God, are you serious?"

"Pretty sure, since his brain is spilling out." I checked his pulse. "Yep, he's gone."

Crouching down, Nyah moved close to Vern's face, staring deep into his lifeless eyes. She tilted her head, and considered him for a long moment. "Am I awful if I don't feel bad?"

"I don't think so, but I'm hardly the one to ask."

Nyah nodded and stood, moving away from the corpse. "He was nothing but an asshole and mean to me. I'm glad he's gone."

"From what he put you and your Mom through, I can't say I blame you." I rubbed my face in my hands. "So this is all about that video on your phone. I know Jacob Poole was on it and he was powerful and very dangerous but now he's dead. What I don't understand is why Shamus would send Vern for it if Jacob's not alive to blackmail with it anymore."

Nyah furrowed her eyebrows. "You thought this was about one guy? This Jacob Poole? Because he's not the only one on the tape."

"I really need to see this video."

"You do, and then we need to figure out what we're going to do about everyone else on it."

"I agree, but first, we take care of Vern."

"I thought you did that with the flower pot."

"Well, no one likes a mess."

TWENTY-FIVE

The graveyard was quiet. Only the sound of the shovel breaking the earth disturbed the night. Perched in the trees, a dozen crows silently watched our progress. The grave took three hours to dig. Working with flashlights, Nyah and I took turns. My back ached and hands blistered from the effort. The crappy thing about digging a grave is that once you've dug the damn hole you had to fill it back up.

The small private plot of graves behind the stone Chapel hadn't been used in over forty years because they'd run out of space, but we managed to squeeze Vern in by the old Oak in the far corner. We used an old, worn stone cross for a headstone. Nyah had found it in the shed next to the church when we broke in to grab shovels. After the hole had been filled, we replaced the sod, scattered leaves and did our best to hide the disturbance.

Once Vern had been planted, we conducted a quick service, just the two of us, faces streaked in soil, sweaty, and fatigued. Nyah told Vern she hoped he got better than he gave in life, but suffered enough for what he did. I spit on the grave and hoped he'd rot in Hell. The service was nice, I guess, as far as that goes.

Before we buried Vern we'd emptied his pockets of his cell phone, wallet, car keys and knife and dumped them in the stone pot. Surprisingly, the pot wasn't even cracked, although it was covered in brains and blood. I carried the pot to the gate as Nyah followed.

"What are going to do with those?" Nyah asked. "It's a little creepy to keep souvenirs."

"Funny girl. They're evidence and I'll toss them on the

way home."

Popping the trunk of the Bel Air, I stuffed the pot and its incriminating contents inside, along with my shirt, which was covered in Vern's dried blood. From a duffel bag I keep for just such predicaments, I grabbed a clean shirt, then pocketed Vern's cell phone and a removed a flat head screw driver from my tool box before slamming the trunk closed.

With the screw driver in one hand, I picked up a rock from the parking lot and smashed the driver's side window of Vern's truck. I knocked the jagged little pieces of glass left in the window frame with the screw driver. After opening the door, I slid behind the wheel, and popped the steering column open with the screw driver. I fumbled with reconnecting the wires properly, and struggled with jamming the screw driver into the ignition, and in all, it took me two minutes to get the truck going.

"Where'd you learn to do that?" Nyah asked.

"It's the one thing my brother Reece is good at and he would have been embarrassed at how slow that was," I said.

Nyah arched her eyebrow. "You know we took Vern's keys, right? Why would you break the window when we could have used the fob?"

"Because I'm an evil genius."

"Genius?" The girl giggled. "You hide it pretty well."

"You've been hanging around Marin too much."

"Or any woman you know?"

I slammed the door shut and left the truck running. "Now, when the cops find this, rewired, smashed up and out of gas, they'll assume some punks took it for a joyride and then ditched it when it ran empty."

"And what about Vern?"

"Who's going to miss him?"

"Not me."

"Anyone who did will probably assume one of the many

people who he's pissed off finally did him in."

"You sure?"

"I'm surprised it hasn't already happened."

Bloody, bruised, and blistered from digging down six feet and back again, Nyah and I fell into the Bel Air. I put the Old Girl's tires on the asphalt of Highway 8 and pointed her toward Winnipeg. We were alone on the road, and that suited me.

The girl leaned over and rested her head on my shoulder as I drove. "Thanks, Grady. I'm glad you came for me."

"That's what I do for friends." I sighed. "Actually, I normally borrow money and break promises."

Five minutes into the city I turned off Main onto Chief Peguis Bridge. I pulled over, popped the trunk and carried the stone pot and its blood smeared proof to the railing overlooking the Red River. Dangling it by the Angel carving, I opened my hand. The pot tumbled into the rushing water, lost to the current. When I climbed back into the Bel Air, Nyah was fast asleep.

The Old Girl lucked into a spot right outside my building and Nyah snuggled in as I carried her upstairs, my body groaning with each step. Marin opened our door and relief stemmed her tears. She helped me carry Nyah to our spare bed and covered her with an old afghan blanket. My wife brushed the hair out of the girl's forehead and gave her a quick kiss.

"You brought her home safe," she said.

"I told you I would."

"You did good, Grady."

"Not exactly, it got messy. The thing is..."

Marin stopped me with a kiss. "Nyah is safe, and that's all I need to know for tonight."

The next morning I stared out the window as the sun came up. My nightmares had stolen sleep from me. Vern's face had joined the others in the screaming chorus, so I watched as the streets below me slowly and grudgingly inched to life. The commuters were headed for their cubicles, children were off to school and the drunks on their way to bed.

Eventually, the need for coffee forced me to put on some pants and leave my room. Caffeine addiction isn't as demanding as booze, but it's still a good motivator.

At my kitchen table I found Hank drinking coffee, while Nyah sat across from him working on a plate of pancakes and bacon. Marin was at the stove cooking some more. I poured myself a cup of coffee, leaned back against the counter and savoured that glorious first sip.

"About time you got your ass out of bed. Nyah wasn't telling us a thing without you," Hank snapped. "And when are you going to stop blocking with your face?"

"I got my licks in too," I said.

"That's your problem, if you aren't going to punch at least bite because licking isn't effective."

"You think insulting him is going to get Grady to tell us what happened, Dad?" Marin's one hand was on her hip, the other shaking a spatula.

"There's not much to tell," I said. "I found her and brought her home, pretty simple, really."

Marin rolled her eyes. "I find that doubtful."

Nyah's eyes twinkled. "Basically that's what happened."

"Cute, he's got her in cahoots." Hank said. "You didn't show up here till the wee hours so there's a story here."

My wife nodded. "I'm not going to pretend I don't see the fat lip and bruises either, Nyah."

The blonde girl's eyes lowered to her plate. "Vern found me."

Throwing down her spatula, Marin grabbed our cordless phone. "That's it, I'm calling the cops."

"That's probably a bad idea," I said. "We don't need to

make their suspect list for them."

"Oh, no, Grady." Marin covered her mouth. "What did you do?"

Raising her head, Nyah held my wife's gaze. "He saved me and how he did it is not important. I'm just glad it's over."

Marin considered for a moment before nodding. "I guess I can live with that." She turned to me. "So, were you right? Is this about the video?"

"Yeah, Nyah had it on her phone."

"And have you seen it?"

"Not yet."

"Nyah, you know, that video has caused a lot of trouble," Marin said.

Nyah's lower lip trembled. "You have to believe me that I didn't mean to."

"We could have protected you if you'd just come to us and been honest," Marin said. "Now my husband is hurt, people have died and our lives have been threatened. Damn it, Nyah, you almost got yourself killed."

Tears streamed down the girl's face. "I didn't want any of this, but I had no choice."

Hank gently squeezed her arm. "I'm afraid there's always a choice."

"Hey, go easy on her," I said. "It's not like they made an after school special about what to do if killers and gangsters are after you, so cut her some slack."

"Well, look who's all grown up and responsible." My wife gave me a wink. "How about we all have a look at that video now?"

Pushing her empty plate away, Nyah took her cell phone from her pocket and thumbed through various screens until she had the video cued up. She handed me the phone and moved so Marin and Hank could see the screen as well.

The video was grainy and dark, but I recognised the two men drinking in the alley. Jacob and Davis passed a bottle back and forth, working their way towards drunkenness. A cop car pulled up and the officer exited the vehicle. I tensed, my hand gripping the phone tighter. I knew that cop, and the bile rose to the back of my throat.

There was a pay off, the thick envelope changes hands. Now I knew I'd been set up. Jacob played me like a fool and I'm embarrassed to say I didn't even know it was happening.

Marin and Hank were watching expectantly, waiting for the big event. They wanted to see what's so important that people would kill for this video. I know, really, it already happened.

A second cop car arrives, and the officer who exits it looks angry and ready for a fight. Jacob seemed even less thrilled the second cop showed up. The first cop looks scared. While the second cop looks like his daughter.

I could already guess what happened in the rest of the video. I look up to see Nyah crying softly at the kitchen table. I know this isn't going to end well.

Back on the screen there was fighting, yelling and the two cops laid hands on each other. One cop pulled a gun and then so did the second. The interesting thing was that the cops were pointing their pistols at each other. Jacob, ever the opportunist, took out his own gun and shot the second cop. Three times Jacob fired.

Jacob shot Nyah's Dad, but he didn't kill him. Jim Tynes crawled for his car, the will to live strong, making it harder to watch.

Never to be confused with a dumb man, Jacob forced the first cop to put two more bullets into Officer Jim Tynes, ending the cop's life and destroying Nyah's. The job done, Jacob and Davis leave, driving off the screen.

Officer Quill stayed behind for a moment, standing over

the corpse of a fellow cop. Then Quill, the backstabbing liar left too. The screen went black and the video ended.

Marin took the phone from me and she and Hank watched the video again, trying to get it all straight. Me? I'd already seen enough. I know I'm fucked.

That bastard Quill lied to me. He lied to my face. He dragged me into this shit just to save his own ass. Both he and Jacob used me. The same Officer Quill who spouted off about doing the right thing, saving Nyah and keeping people safe was taking bribes, killing other cops and the reason Nyah was unsafe to begin with. I should have seen this coming.

I went to Nyah, and she wrapped her arms around me and buried her face in my neck. Her tears, wet and warm, soaked my collar.

"You saw it? You saw?" she demanded. "They killed him. Shot him. They left him there."

Stroking her hair, I held tight. "I know. They'll pay, I promise."

She lifted her head, her big tear filed eyes narrowing. Hardening. "Will they? How?"

"Two of them have paid already. Jacob, the old guy in the suit and Davis the asshole in the leather jacket are dead."

"Are you sure?"

"I watched it happen myself."

"And the other cop?"

We let go of each other and I stepped back. "He's going to be a problem."

Hank held out the phone and pointed to the screen. "I remember both of these officers, I actually trained them. Your Dad, Nyah, was a good cop and I remember him coming to me and saying he was on to something big. He had some informant who swore some cop was on the take, but I'm ashamed to say I never believed him."

I tapped Quill's face on the screen. "That must have been who he was onto, obviously. And that guy? This piece of shit? I know that guy."

"How do you know him?" Marin asked.

"He's the cop that busted me for this bogus murder rap and apparently he's also been fucking me over."

Slipping her hand into mine, Marin gave me a squeeze. "We can deal with this Grady. We'll figure it out together. I know you're angry but…"

"Angry? It's just not that simple, Marin. I'm scared. Truly scared. You don't fuck with cops. Ever. They're bad enough when they're legit and just want to bust you. But this guy? This Officer Quill? This lying murderous snake is crooked, and there's nothing more dangerous than a bent cop. He's the reason Reece and Davis got away with killing those hookers. He's the reason no one's been arrested. He's controlling everything right now. He can take a guy like me out and make it look legal. He's not scared of the law because he is the law."

"But we have this video. This horrible, awful video," Marin pointed out. "Can't we just go to the police?"

"He is a cop," I said. "We can't do that."

Hank frowned. "I'm sad to say he's right, dear. We have no idea who we can trust in the department."

"Think he still wants the phone?" Nyah asked.

"If I was him, I would," I said. "Jacob dying doesn't help him."

My wife threw up her hands. "Well, we can't just sit around waiting to find out."

"Fuck, I don't know what to do. This is too much for me. Maybe we just give Quill the video and end it."

"He may not be satisfied at getting the video because, unfortunately, we've seen it," Hank said. "I know what I'd do if I was him, cut all loose ends."

"Well we can't give it back." Nyah slammed her fist into

the table. "He killed my Dad. He can't get away with it. He just can't."

Crouching down beside Nyah, Marin embraced the blonde girl. "I can't imagine how much it hurts, but you have to ask yourself if revenge is worth dying for?"

"I've got nothing left because of them," Nyah said.

"Oh honey, you have us now, and we aren't going anywhere."

Pressing her clenched fists against her eyes, Nyah's body shook. "I loved my dad more than anything, and because of greed, that man took him away from me. He has to pay for that."

"What are we going to do, Grady?" Marin asked.

"This is beyond me," I said. "I don't want to run away, because Nyah needs us, but we can't take on the cops. The thing is, Hank is right too, if we give Quill the video he'll kill us for having seen it."

"Okay, so we figure out how to deal with this Quill, cop or not, he's just one man," Marin said. "We have to be able to handle one man."

"But it's not just Quill. There's Shamus too. Even with Jacob dead he's still coming for Nyah. Here we are stuck in the middle, and we're going to get crushed."

"So there's no hope?" Marin said. "We're just going to lie down and let them kill us? I don't believe that you'd let that happen Grady. That isn't you."

"What do you want me to say? Quill and Shamus are like two trains headed right for each other and we're stuck on the tracks. I mean the only chance we have is if we can side step them and let them smash head on without us..."

I trailed off. Somewhere, deep inside my booze soaked brain there was a tiny thought.

"You have something," Marin said. "I can see it in your eyes."

"I may," I said. "It's just an idea. Give me a little bit, I have to talk to some people."

"Okay, you go do what you need to do," Marin said. "I'm going to take Nyah to have her checked out. I don't like the look of her bruises."

"Going to a hospital is a bad idea," Hank said. "This Quill is a cop and it won't be hard for him to keep an eye on the patient lists. He's probably got her flagged."

My wife nodded. "I have a friend who's a nurse. She'll be good enough, and if she says it's bad we have no choice but to take Nyah to emergency."

Hank and I agreed, mostly because Marin would have done it anyway.

The girls left the apartment first and it was just me and Hank. We sat in silence for a long time, both of us eating and lost in our own thoughts and troubles. The only sound the scrapings of forks on our plates and the clinking of our glasses as we drank. When the food was all gone, we cleared the table and were forced to acknowledge the other was there.

"So do you really have a plan?" Hank asked. "Or were you just telling my daughter what she wanted to hear so she wasn't shit scared?"

"I don't have the details worked out, but I know what has to happen," I said. "I've just got the 'how' to work out now."

"So just the most important part?"

"Listen, I'm trying here. I didn't ask for this and for once it's not my fault."

"Are you saying it's Nyah's?" The old cop sighed. "I'm going to ask again, what are you going to do?"

"Whatever it takes to keep them all safe."

Rising out of his seat, his water glass still in hand and sloshing its contents over the side, Hank's face was contorted. "Not good enough, Grady, not good enough." The cords on his neck bulged out. "That's my daughter and a sweet young girl. We need a plan. A smart one too! None of this crap you're selling now. So don't be vague with me and then run off like a damn drunken vigi... vigi..."

Hank groaned, let go of the glass, and fell back into chair and grabbing his head in both hands. His face was grey and dripping in sweat. I jumped out of chair and dropped to his side.

"Hank, Hank, what's wrong? Are you in pain? Are you sick?"

"I'm just a little dizzy," he moaned. "My sight went for a second. I must have pushed too hard. Give me a moment."

"Dizzy my ass." I dialled 911 on my cell. "I'll get an ambulance. Just stay with me, you're having a heart attack!"

Hank grabbed the phone out of my hands. "Shut your yap," he hissed. "You're going to get yourself all worked up."

"Hank, this is serious, you're dying."

"Not yet, don't get all excited."

"This is no fucking joke. You're having a coronary."

"My heart is fine dumbass." He rubbed his face in his hands. "It's my head, Grady, I have this little tumour. But I'll be around to keep your ass in line for awhile yet."

"How bad is it? And I want the truth or I'm going to tell Marin. I bet she has no idea about any of this."

"If you tell her, you'll need the ambulance." Hank had regained colour and rose to his feet. "Honestly? It's not good. It's cancer. The tumour's sitting at the front of my brain. There's nothing they can do for it either. They gave me pills for the pain but I stopped taking those because all I wanted to do was sleep," he admitted. "The migraines are unbearable and my memory and speech come and go. I think you've noticed that. My vision's now leaving me and I've been told to expect seizures. I'm not going to last much longer, which is why you have to make things right between you and Marin," he said. "Marin needs you, and she still loves you."

"Don't talk like that, Marin needs you, not me. Jesus, Hank, all I do is let her down. In fact, if it was up to me I'd trade places with you. Marin, Nyah, Daria and Will all need you."

"Even if you could, I wouldn't take the offer. I lived my life, loved my wife and tried to do right by my kids. I worked hard and made do with the blessings I received. It's all I could ask for. So when it's my time, it's my time."

"Have you seen a doctor?"

"You think I diagnosed myself?"

"Why don't they cut it out of you?"

"It's inoperable," he said. "I didn't go get myself checked out until it was too late. Now the tumour's too big and too wide spread."

"Then we go get you some chemo."

"No, we don't. I'll be damned if I'm going to let those pill pushers hook me up to some machine and pump poison through my body. It's worse than death; believe me I went through it all with Janet and had to watch my wife die by inches. I don't want the last thing the girls remember is me wasting away, shitting myself, puking and too far gone to remember who they are. When death calls for me, I'll go willingly." He took a deep breath, and wiped his eyes. "Now stop being a horse's ass and keep your mouth shut about this around the girls."

"I just wish…"

"That's your problem, you're wishing instead of doing. Wishing is for the lazy, and I'll tell you something, it ain't worth it unless you worked for it and earned it."

"Don't turn this on me, you're the one with the problem."

Grabbing his glass, Hank took a long drink of water. "I get it, but no matter what we do it's not going to make me better. We need to focus on Nyah and that damn video. We gotta solve that without getting you killed because I need you for a favor."

"You need me? For what?"

Hank opened his mouth but was interrupted by a phone ringing. Nyah had left her cell on table, but it wasn't hers ringing. Or mine. It was coming from my jacket hanging on the back of my chair. It was Vern's phone.

Taking the phone out of the pocket, I checked the display. I didn't recognise the number, but then I didn't really expect I would. I pressed TALK and said, "What?"

"*Don't you 'what' me you piss brained, useless sack of mucus,*" the caller said. "*You better be drunk to be talking to me like that.*"

"I'm sober but I'm an asshole either way," I said.

The caller's breathing quickened. "*This isn't Vern.*"

"You may be a genius, even if you're sensitive."

"*Who is this? Give me your name, asshole.*"

"Or what?"

"*I'll kill you.*"

"How you going to threaten me with that if you don't know who I am?" I snorted. "Maybe you are dumb."

"*Jokes over, dickhead. Give me your name now.*"

"You first."

"*This is Shamus Gray. Are you scared now, motherfucker?*"

"I'm so glad it's you, Shamus, I've been meaning to speak to you again."

"*Enough games, where's Vern?*"

"He's gone."

"*Where?*"

"All the way gone, as in not ever coming back."

"*Dead? Vern? Bullshit. I don't believe you.*"

"You shouldn't have sent him for the girl, Shamus."

Shamus' laugh was cold. "*Grady Fisk, I wondered when we'd meet again. So, you killed Vern, did you?*"

"Look who figured it out."

249

"*So you saved the girl and are the big hero now. Do you think I won't send others for her?*"

"Leave her alone, Shamus, or I swear..."

"*I don't have to kill her you know,*" Shamus continued, cutting me off. "*I could do worse. You should meet some of the sick bastards I know. When they get done with her, the girl will wish I killed her.*"

Hank regarded me warily as he sipped his water. I turned my back to him and lowered my voice. "What the fuck do you want, you little ugly troll?"

Shamus growled. "*Cut the crap. We both know you have my property.*"

"If it was yours you'd have it."

"*No games, you know what I want.*"

"The video."

"*Exactly, and you know I'd risk killing the girl to get it,*" he said. "*Is it worth that to you? Give it to me and I'll leave you all alone.*"

I walked to living room and sat on the couch. "Why should I believe you?"

"*Trust me, Grady, this has been a huge pain in the ass for me. So believe me when I say I'd kill your wife, family and anyone you ever cared about to get that video. It's that important to me and it'd be so much easier if you just gave it to me.*"

My hand clamped down on the phone so hard I'm surprised the screen didn't burst. "If you think I'm just going to hand over the phone you're fucking crazy. And if you ever threaten my family again, you're the one who's going to be hunted down."

"*Okay, jackass, we can threaten each other all day here and that's not going to get us anywhere. So just make me a deal. What you want?*"

"Let me think about it."

"*I don't have time, Grady. I'm under huge fucking*

pressure here."

"Just give me a day, Shamus, so nobody does anything they'll regret. I promise by this time tomorrow I'll call you and work something out."

The line was silent for a moment. *"Fine, one day, and then we meet,"* he said finally. *"Don't cross me on this, Grady. I don't hear from you I send my boys hunting."*

"Fair enough," I said and hung up.

Hank had followed me, and there was genuine concern on his face. "Was that phone call about these people giving Nyah trouble?" he asked.

"I'm working things out."

"Doesn't sound like it."

I checked my watch. "I have to meet someone."

"Now?" Hank frowned. "You and I need to finish talking."

"If this is more about your cancer, it'll have to wait," I said. "I'm not trying to be an asshole here, Hank, but I've got to worry about Nyah right now."

"I understand that, Grady, I'm not that self centred," he said. "And no more cancer talk, well, not exactly. Thing is, I need a favour from you."

"Listen, I can't fit anymore shit into my to-do list right now, Hank."

"Just hear me out."

"What could possibly need from me?"

"I know you have to take care of things, but eventually you'll have to eat. I'll help Marin fix a nice supper and we can eat a meal as a family and then you and I can go for a walk and talk."

"Really? Like I have time for this right now?" I stifled a scream. "I have to keep people from killing my family, so I'm not so sure I'll make it back for supper. I don't even know where I'm going to be five minutes after I meet this friend of mine."

"We'll save a plate," he said. "You live here so eventually you'll come back. When you do, you can eat and I can talk. Sound fair?"

"I guess I gotta eat," I said.

TWENTY-SIX

Up until a few weeks ago, I was killing myself one drink at a time, riding shot gun on the whiskey wagon to hell, heading straight for liver failure, divorce and homelessness. I was two steps away from begging for loose change on the corner, toothless and feet full of gangrene.

Now sober, I wasn't exactly in a better place. I'd been blindsided with responsibility. For no good reason, Nyah and Marin thought I was some vigilante protector. With Shamus trying to kill me, the cops out to bury me and my addict brother doing his best to get me charged with murder, I was less optimistic. To top off that messed up sundae, Hank was dying.

Didn't they know that I'm a fuck up?

Sitting on the steps outside my apartment building, I thumbed thought the contacts in my cell phone. I selected Basil and sent him a text.

"Meet me in Kildonan Park. My spot. We need to talk."

His answer was almost instant. *"What do you want?"*

"Tell you when I see you."

"What do you want?"

I sighed. *"Meet me there. My spot. 20min."*

"Better not waste my time."

Hefting my battered carcass off the front steps, I limped down the sidewalk towards the Old Girl. A dark blue Nissan Sentra, pulled up beside me, blocking the Old Girl in. My brother got out from behind the wheel, leaving the screw driver jammed in the ignition with the wires hanging out below and twisted together. With Jacob dead, I guess the free rides were over.

My brother looked like shit, even for him. Reece's face

was thin and gray, his cheeks hollow and sporting about five days worth of stubble. Hands jammed into his coat pockets, the addict shuffled over. "Hey big brother, watcha up to man?"

"I don't have time for you."

"I come to see you, my only brother, and right away you treat me like shit, man."

"Maybe because the last time I saw you, a girl was pushed off a bridge."

"Man, I told you, that was an accident."

"The time before that, you shot and killed two people."

"Listen, Grady, I was in deep to Jacob, and it was either them or me, man."

"Time before that some hooker got crushed by a truck." I poked him in the chest with my finger. "Do you see the pattern? I don't want you around, because when you are around, people die."

"What about, Lyle, Davis, Jacob and all the people you put down, man?"

"Fine, we're both assholes. Doesn't mean I want to see you."

"Grady, I'm serious, man. I came here to help you."

"Are you fucking kidding me? Help me with what?" I waved him away. "Jacob is dead so your loan is squashed. You got a clean start, Reece, and that's my last gift to you."

"I am clean, asshole. That's why I look like I just got shit out a dog's ass, man." He turned and spit on the ground. "I'm straight, man, and it feels like my brain is trying to eat its way to my stomach. I'd feel better dead, man."

"It's not fun," I said. "Trust me, it gets better."

"I ain't here for a pat on the back, man, I want to help you. I heard Shamus is still gunning for you, and I got your back."

"It's my concern, not yours. I'm fine. We're fine. Besides, I'm not sure you're on my side."

"We're brothers, man, we're always on the same side."

"No, you're on Reece's side. Always have been."

My brother nodded. "I know, man. I'm that guy, selfish, like you said. I fuck things up, that's true too. You know better than anyone what I am, what I'm like. You know me, Grady, so can't you see this time I'm telling the truth?"

"Why are you really here, Reece?

"The needles calling me man, it's fucking relentless. All I think about is getting high every second of the day, man." He pressed his fists against his eyes. "I need a reason to say no, a reason to ignore it, man."

Every piece of common sense I had inside me was screaming to tell Reece to go fuck his hat. But the idiot was my brother and sometimes that blood bond makes you stupid. Like I needed the help.

"Okay."

"Okay what, man?"

"Okay, you can help."

A smile exploded on his face, and there was the little brother I'd lost long ago. "What do you need from me, man? I'll do anything."

"Give me some time. I just have to meet someone then I'll catch up with you later."

"Promise?"

"I swear."

My brother stepped forward, his arms wide, ready to hug me, and despite the smell, I let him. Reece hopped into the stolen sedan and drove off before I could change my mind. Like I wasn't already handicapped enough, I might as well mail the video to Quill and then go shoot myself in the head. I'd save everyone a whole lot of time.

Popping the trunk of my Bel Air, I hid Nyah's phone in a plastic bag under the spare tire, then drove the Old Girl to Kildonan Park and through the front gates, nestling her into a parking space between two minivans near the entrance.

Kids had overrun the play park, chasing each other up the monkey bars and racing down the slides, their laughter and screams musical. Was I ever like that?

Keeping to the park paths, I walked past the gardens, benches and picnic areas. I checked my watch, Basil would be there soon. Deep into the park, I left the groomed stone path and followed an overgrown dirt one towards a large cluster of trees. I pushed past the branches and bushes and emerged in a clearing. This was my spot, where I'd smoke pot and drink as a kid.

The wind stirred up the leaves and swirled them around my feet. The birds, those not yet headed south, sat in the trees staring down at me. Perhaps they smelt death on me and waited for me to drop so they could have one last meal before the big trip. I was sweating, still shaking the last of the booze out. It had soaked in deep and my hands trembled; another present the drink left behind.

The clearing was at the edge of the Red River. The trees around it formed a tight ring, and the clearing was tucked away and forgotten at the edge of the park. The small gardens had been left unattended and the grass hadn't been mowed in years. The empty beer bottles, food wrappers and forgotten clothing told me some kids looking to party had found it. An old stone bench covered in moss sat facing the river. I sat and the breeze off the river flowed over me, and I was gifted a moments peace. The leaves rustled and branches creaked as someone pushed through into the clearing.

It was Quill.

The cop wasn't in uniform. He wore a ball cap, windbreaker and cargo pants. His boots were his issued 511's, Police SWAT boots, with steel toes perfect for either running or shit kicking. The bulge under his armpit told me where he'd hid his gun. He was ready for battle.

The army has its own way of teaching you a lesson. I

screwed up lots in the army. Mostly, I spoke before filtering myself, and sergeants do not like being called ignorant sacks of garbage by a private three weeks off basic training.

I was punished for every mistake and disciplined for each moment of insubordination. I ran several marathons in five and ten mile stretches, often I ran till I puked. The amount of pushups I did deserves an entry in Guinness. If it was dirty I cleaned it, and if you could eat it I peeled it. I spent one night in the rain holding two full buckets of water in each hand, my arms out wide. When my arms gave out, I was told to run. I'm not a quick learner, but I did pick up one thing, I never fucked up the same way twice. So I can learn, most times the hard way, but I learn.

When I met up with Vern in the cemetery I was without a gun. Things got messy. I took my H & K 9mm with me when I left to meet Basil because you just never know. I mean, I went looking for Nyah and ended up killing a man, things happen.

Now Quill happened, and I was right. Too bad the pistol was tucked into the back of my waistband. Of course, the cop's piece was stuffed in his jacket so maybe we were even.

Lowering my head, I stared out at the river watching a handful of kayakers get in their last few runs before winter. I didn't look up as Quill approached and didn't acknowledge him when he sat down next to me.

Turning from the river, I looked out into the clearing, my gaze passed from tree to tree. In no hurry to talk, I was content to enjoy the fresh air. Quill finally broke.

"You look like shit," he said.

"I get that a lot."

"You've alive, I suppose that's something."

"What did you want to see me for?"

"Who says I wanted to see you?"

"You're here now, aren't you?"

"I told you, I'm worried about the girl. She was my

friend's kid and I'm trying to look out for her. I made him a promise and I plan to keep it."

I turned to face him then. "Your buddy's kid? You made a promise?"

He held my gaze. "That's what I said. We were close, he had an accident and died. I gave my word I'd be there for her."

"Accident? Really, that's what happened?"

"Yeah, like I said."

"You sure?"

"Why?"

"Well, it's a funny thing to call it when you kill a guy."

The cop's eyes narrowed. "I guess we're done playing games," he said. "I guess you saw the video."

"Obviously, dipshit."

"Then be smart and give it to me."

"Not a chance. You killed your partner and I'm going to give it to you because, what? I'm a moron?"

"You think I can't get to you, is that it?" He raised his eyebrows. "This is the crucial moment, Grady, the moment where you decide how this is all going to play out, make a mistake and bad things are going to happen."

"Is that why you showed up, dressed to fight and packing a gun?"

"I had hoped to reason with you, but if that doesn't work I'll be taking this to that whole other level I told you about."

"Just give me some time to figure out what I want here."

"What you want? Are you for real? I'll tell you what you want, you want to live. Get it? You want to live, stay out of jail and have nothing to happen to your wife. That's what you want and that's why you're going to give me the video."

"I'm real fucking tired of assholes threatening me and my family. It's making me want to smash someone."

"And you want to try something with me?" He pointed

his finger in my face. "I dare you, buddy. I'm the one in control here, Grady."

"If that were true you'd have the video."

"Guess I can't argue with that." He shrugged. "So I'll give you the courtesy of asking one last time, give me the video and just walk away."

"I'd have your word nothing would happen to my family?"

There was only one answer to that question, whether he meant it or not. He should have said yes. Instead, he looked away. I knew the truth, and Hank had been right, Quill was going to kill us the second he had the video. The cop reached into his jacket and I smashed him in face.

Quill's hand was still stuck in his jacket, I punched him twice more. His nose and lip were smeared with blood. The cop pulled his hand out empty, and swung back, his fists driving into my face. We traded punches, grabbed and clawed, the two of us eventually falling from the bench to the ground.

I landed on top and drove my left elbow into his throat as I pounded on him with my right fist. Quill reached down and grabbed a solid handful of my balls and gave a violent twist. I screamed and rolled off him, prying his hands free. Quill jumped to his feet, reared back and kicked at my head. I blocked it, grabbed his foot and brought him back down to the ground. We tumbled over each other, trading punches, no one gaining an advantage. I threw a wild punch and I lost my leverage, and Quill latched on a headlock. He tried to choke me but I threw him off and we both scrambled to our feet.

He pulled his gun and I pulled mine. We stood there, looking down our barrels at each other. Too close to miss, the first to blink would end up with a bloody crater in the middle of their forehead. We had a standoff.

"I swear, Grady, if you don't put that gun down I'll kill

you," he said.

I backed away, headed for the entrance to the clearing. "You do that and there's no video for you, asshole."

"Really? Without you Nyah would be defenceless."

"Don't be so sure."

The branches dug into my back, the entrance was right behind me. A few more steps and I could turn and run for it. He wasn't going to come out shooting in public. I could lose him quick enough in the crowds.

"Stop it right there, Grady, or I'll kill you."

"If you were going to shoot, you'd have done it already."

A big engined vehicle pulled up right outside the bushes on the other side of the entrance. The doors opened and closed and I could hear footfalls coming towards me on the path. I immediately recognised their voices. My heart slammed into overdrive.

"Give me the video, or I'm coming for you," the cop said.

"You need to stay away from my family or I'll be coming for you."

"With what?" He laughed. "What could you do against me?"

I couldn't answer. An arm wrapped around my waist and pulled me through the entrance. I was ripped through the bushes and tossed into a vehicle before it sped away.

TWENTY-SEVEN

The nurse, Megan, had been gentle and thorough, disinfecting and bandaging the blonde girl up just as Marin said she would. Megan had brewed sweet tea for Marin to sip, and put out cookies and dainties for Nyah to snack on.

But along with kindness, Megan had been full of questions. The nurse was subtlety relentless, repeating and rephrasing her queries as she worked on Nyah. Megan never came out and said that she didn't believe the story that Marin had given her, but it was easy to tell the nurse didn't think things added up.

That's quite the cut under your eye, Nyah.

You say it was from tennis, Marin?

No, my mistake, you did say softball practice.

Wow, there's bruising in so many places.

Seems big for a soft ball.

Sure it's not from a bat, Nyah?

And this happened today?

Yes, you did say yesterday.

Which team do you play for, Nyah?

Isn't it late in the year for baseball?

Finally, Marin had told Megan to mind her own business. The nurse nodded and did just that. The nurse had asked them to stay for lunch, but didn't seem disappointed when Marin said no.

Hank was at the apartment when the girls arrived home. He and Marin went to the kitchen table and whispered while the blonde girl vegged out on the couch, scrolling the TV for something to watch. Nyah's daydreams were pushed away by a knock at the door. She and everyone else in the apartment froze. Hank grabbed his revolver from his jacket and Marin pulled a carving knife from the drawer by the stove. Nyah left the couch, grabbed a blade of her own and holding it low at her side, joined the adults in the kitchen.

Leaving the others to watch, Hank walked silently to the door and leaned forward to look through the peephole. He turned back and shrugged. The old cop opened the door and stepped back. A gaunt, well groomed man in an expensive dark brown suit and overcoat stood there with a leather briefcase at his side. His broad, toothy smile didn't quite meet his dark eyes.

"Who the hell are you?" Hank demanded.

The man in the suit extended his hand. "My name is Connor Drake," he said. "I am the attorney for Grady Fisk."

Hank looked at the lawyer's outstretched hand, but as his own still held his revolver, he didn't shake it. "I'm Grady's father-in-law," he said.

Like his smile, the frown on Drake's face seemed rehearsed. "I'm sorry, but I have come as the bearer of bad news."

Leaving the kitchen, pointing her knife at Drake, Marin stormed up beside her father. "Grady told me all about you," she said. "You're in Jacob Poole's pocket."

"Do you all have weapons?" The lawyer's amusement seemed genuine. He dropped his brief case and raised his hands. "Look, nothing up my sleeve."

Hank raised his gun and held the barrel in the lawyer's face. "I don't take kindly to people messing with my family," he said. "So if you're just Jacob's stooge than you can see yourself out."

"I did work for Jacob Poole, that is true, but he is dead and I am still on retainer for Grady." The lawyer paused. "And so you are aware, the bill has been paid and you owe me nothing else as of yet."

"And you are no longer looking out for Jacob?" Marin asked.

"The fact is, the dead don't pay, Mrs. Fisk, and like I've explained, I work for who pays me. Surely you've heard that about lawyers before." Drake laughed and flashed his toothy grin. "So please, just hear me out and afterwards I'll leave if you wish."

Hank exchanged a look with his daughter and shrugged. "Let him say his piece, Marin, what can it hurt?"

Marin rolled her eyes. "Fine, but as soon as you're finished, Mr. Drake, you will be leaving."

"There's no nice way to put this, so I'll just come out with it." He straightened up and stared right at Marin. "Grady's been hurt. From the reports I have received, your husband was beaten severely by persons unknown. Currently he's in hospital undergoing treatment."

Marin gasped. "Oh no, please no."

"Which hospital?" Hank asked.

"Health Sciences Centre," Drake answered. "He's in the ICU."

"Are you sure it's Grady?" Hank asked. "How bad is he? What happened?"

The lawyer frowned. "Sadly, I am positive it's Grady and he's alive, but as I understand, his situation is precarious."

Marin walked over and laid her knife down on the coffee table. "Dad, Nyah, let's go," she said, her voice wavering. "We need to go see, Grady."

The knife slipped from Nyah's fingers and clattered, spinning on the kitchen linoleum. "This is all my fault, if I hadn't come to ..."

Rushing to Nyah's side, Marin held the girl's face in her hands and wiped away the tears. "Whatever happened to Grady, whatever mess he got into, it was of his own doing. So we'll cry over him later, but for now, we have to go see that he's alright."

"Thank you for passing on the message," Hank said to the lawyer. "You'll have to excuse us now, but we're obviously leaving."

"I expected as much," Drake said. "I have a car waiting for you all down stairs."

"Thanks but no thanks," Marin said. "We won't be going with you."

"No offense, but we don't trust you an inch," Hank said.

"None taken, but you would be best served accompanying me," the lawyer told them. "What you don't understand, Mrs. Fisk, is that you won't be getting anywhere near Grady without me. Grady has been arrested and there are a dozen officers surrounding his hospital room. The three of you won't even be allowed on his floor let alone his room."

"Oh no, not now." Marin took a step back like she'd been slapped. "What did he do?"

"It's a long story and it would be a waste of time going over it here when I can tell you it in the car on the way to the hospital," Drake said.

Hank turned to his daughter. "We don't need this lawyer. I'm an ex cop and I know people, I'm sure I can talk to one of them and get us in to see him."

"You can talk to whomever you wish, but it won't help," Drake said. "Grady is in serious trouble and has had some severe charges laid against him. I am his lawyer, and I promise I can get you in."

Her purse tucked under her arm, Marin faced the lawyer again. "So if we want to see Grady, we have to go with you?"

"It's only way I'm afraid." Drake pointed at the revolver still in Hank's hand. "Best not to bring that, it could make things awkward."

Hank nodded and hid the gun in a kitchen drawer next to the fridge. Nyah didn't know where she would have put it, but that seemed an odd first choice to her. The young girl and the old cop got their jackets on and joined Marin at the front door.

The three of them followed the lawyer down stairs and out onto the sidewalk where a black stretch limo waited. Drake held the door open as the others climbed into the limo and slid across the leather seats so they could all fit. Drake got in last and closed the door after him. Nyah flinched when the door locked.

It was dark inside the vehicle and it took Nyah a moment to realise they weren't alone. Sitting across from them was a gorgeous red headed lady in a tight black dress. Beside her was a short man with spiky blonde hair and a broken nose. Nyah recognised Shamus and Franny immediately.

"You," Hank gasped.

"What's going on here," Marin demanded.

The young girl didn't ask. She didn't say a word. Nyah knew what the presence of her mother's killer meant and that was why she was scared enough to pee her pants.

It was over.

They were going to hurt her.

And her friends.

They'd torture her.

There'd be no vengeance.

There'd be little she could do dead.

Marin pointed at Franny and Shamus, her face so red Nyah feared it would explode. "What are you doing here? What's this game, Drake? Where's Grady?" Marin demanded in rapid fire succession.

Leaning forward, Shamus clasped his hands clasped together. "Funny thing, we were actually hoping you could answer that for us."

"Isn't he in the hospital?" Marin asked.

"Surprise, the lawyer lied," Franny said flatly

Driving his shoulder into Drake, Hank tried to push him through the door. "Let us out of here, you bastard."

Bracing himself against the door, Drake tried to shove back. "I can't do that sir. Just listen to what we have to say, and if you're smart this will be over quickly."

Reaching over her father, Marin slapped Drake across the face. "You want us to trust you?" Marin asked. "All you've done is lie since we met you."

Shamus waggled his finger and Marin and her father. "That will be enough of the hitting."

"And it was only a partial lie." Drake massaged his reddened cheek. "I told you Jacob was no longer my client. That was true, as my new client is Mr. Shamus Gray here."

Giving a quick wave, Shamus smirked. "Hello," he said. "Listen, this all can be over in moments because we all know what I want, right Nyah?"

"How do you know her?" Marin demanded.

"Because I'm smart," Shamus said. "She's Vern's girl."

"I'm not Vern's anything," Nyah cried.

"Whatever, I don't care who the fuck you are except you took my video and caused me a shit load of grief," Shamus said. "But I'm willing to overlook that if you give me the video and your phone."

Her face red, Nyah looked away. "I don't have it."

"Do you think we're stupid? We know you took it," Franny snapped. "Vern told us all about how you took our only copy off of Vern's computer before you erased his whole hard drive."

"If it was so important why only have one copy?" Hank asked.

"Listen, there was a reason, copies could be stolen, fall into other hands," Shamus explained.

"Isn't that what happened?" Hank pointed out.

"Clearly that was a mistake," Shamus said. "But now would be a bad time for any of you to question my fucking judgement."

"We don't have it on us," Marin said. "Feel free to check."

"I will," Shamus said. "But just for laughs, who does have it?"

Nyah looked at her feet, and was pleased to hear her new family all grow silent.

There was a click and when Nyah raised her head she was staring right down the barrel of Shamus' Glock 9mm. "I'm not asking again," Shamus said.

Marin won the race to speak. "Grady, my husband, has it."

Lowering the gun to his lap, Shamus nodded. "I believe you, it makes sense."

"If that's true it means we have a problem," Franny said.

"What kind of problem?" Hank asked.

"Technically, it's your problem," Shamus said. "Because we're going to have to keep you until Grady brings us that video."

"What are you going to do with us?' Marin asked.

"Honestly?" Shamus shrugged. "We'll take you somewhere, tie you up and hold you in the dark until Grady gives us the tape. Then we'll let you go."

"And if he doesn't?" Hank asked.

"Then I'll ship random pieces of you to him. Or maybe I'll send Grady a video of my own, one where I'm whipping the skin off your backs," Shamus said. "Perhaps I'll just behead one of you and leave your skull at his door step, honestly I really haven't thought it though."

"Let them go," Nyah pleaded. "It was me that took it."

Franny laughed. "Oh, our sweet little hero girl."

"Now, why would I do that?" Shamus asked. "Aren't three bargaining chips better than one? What if I accidently killed someone? Then I'd be left with nothing." He reached behind him and tapped on the driver's privacy glass. "Let's go."

The limo pulled away from the curb. Nyah's lungs cramped as the panic overwhelmed her. She had to do something. She had to stop Shamus from kidnapping and hurting her friends. But she didn't know what to do, so she sat there helpless and scared as the limo drove down the street, leaving the apartment behind.

The driver paused at the stop sign two blocks from the apartment before moving on. It hadn't even cleared the intersection when a blue sedan smashed into the driver's door. The limo jumped and spun. The five people in the back seat tumbled over each other, arms and legs all tangled. Nyah tried to focus, but her head was floating, unable to clear.

"Get off me, get the fuck off me," Shamus groaned. "What the fuck was that?"

"Nyah, Dad, are you okay?" Marin asked.

"I think I'm fine," Hank said. "Where did that com..."

Hank's words were lost as the sedan smashed into the limo again, this time crumpling the hood and engine in on itself. The sedan was spinning its tires, trying to reverse so it could dive bomb the limo again, but its fender was caught on a shorn piece of the limo's hood.

"Some lunatic's ramming us," the limo driver called out.

The sedan driver gave up trying to separate the mangled vehicles, jumped out and emptied his H&K 9mm into the engine block of the limo. Nyah, Hank and Marin covered their heads and ducked down lower between the seats. Shamus had the opposite instinct and climbed out of the mass of arms and legs and opened the door and spilled out into the street, firing his own gun blindly in the general direction of the sedan. Franny was out of the limo right after Shamus, her own gun in her hand, screaming as she unloaded.

With two less people to contend with, the four remaining in the back seat managed to right themselves and get up off the limo floor. Drake adjusted his tie and pointed at the others.

"You three stay in your seats," he said. "If you even think of..."

The lawyer's words were cut off by Hank's right fist. Drake's head snapped back and his mouth filled with blood. Hank's next punch dropped the lawyer out cold, and Drake slouched in his seat, eyes rolled back in his head.

Outside the limo, the gun shots had stopped and the shouting and screaming increased. First Hank, then Marin and finally Nyah jumped out of the limo. What awaited them was complete chaos. The driver of the limo was hanging half out of his window, a large bullet hole just below his left eye, blood and torn tissue covered what was left of his face. There were two empty pistols on the street, being kicked and knocked around as three bloodied and crazed people wrestled over a third gun, which Nyah guessed was still loaded.

The young girl suspected she had suffered a concussion, because if she hadn't, she was watching Shamus and Franny wrestle with Reece over a hand gun. Grady's brother was punching and biting as he tried to keep a hold of his gun while Shamus kicked and swung at him and Franny tried to gouge out Reece's eyes with her nails.

"Reece? What the hell are you doing?" Hank asked.

"Saving you, man," Reece cried. "Run, all of you run. I got this, man."

The distraction was enough for Shamus to land a solid hook to Reece's temple and send him sprawling on the pavement. The gun went spinning under the crumpled blue sedan and Franny dove after it. Shamus ran after Marin, who was pushing Nyah towards the alley. Hank swung at

Shamus missed, and off balance, tripped right into Shamus' punch and fell limp on the side walk. Marin screamed and turned back, right into Shamus. He pinned her arms down as she struggled to get to her dad.

The young girl was halfway down the alley, arms pumping, legs driving and lungs burning. She peeked over her shoulder and saw Marin and Shamus wrestling in the mouth of the alley. Her pace slowed, and then she turned back.

"Don't stop, Nyah," Marin screamed.

The girl obeyed, but only because Reece had regained his feet and was pulling Shamus off of Marin. They'll be alright she told herself. She had to get away and tell Grady. Digging deeper, Nyah surged forward, just a few yards from the exit and well out of Shamus' grasp.

But there was a gun shot. Then there was another.

Nyah turned and stumbled, looking back from where she came, Nyah fell backwards on her ass. She didn't try and break her fall; she didn't even know she was falling. She was transfixed by the sight of Franny standing behind Reece, holding the lost gun in front of her. Reece was spinning, blood spreading over his shirt from the gaping hole in his chest.

Blood sprayed as he fell. Reece crumpled into the pavement and went limp. Nyah had seen that before, it was just like her dad. Reece didn't move and the blood puddle spread out from him.

Her dad. Reece.

Franny turned the gun from Reece's corpse to Marin. "That's enough," she screamed. "Get off my man."

Letting go of Shamus' hair, Marin raised her hands and stood. Shamus picked himself off the ground and wiped the blood from his nose. Nyah scrambled to her feet and backed down the alley.

"Get back here you little bitch," Franny called out. "I'll

kill this woman if you don't get that little ass back here by the time I count to ten."

Her feet took root, and Nyah neither took the exit nor headed back. Her brain froze as solid as her legs, and she couldn't decide what to do.

Franny took the choice away from the young girl. Stepping forward, Franny pressed the barrel of the pistol hard into Marin's cheek. "Six seconds and I blow out her skull."

Right then, Nyah knew it was done. She walked back down the alley and back to Shamus. Back to those who would hurt her.

TWENTY-EIGHT

The green, yellow and orange blur of foliage as the trees whipped past my window, made it feel like the Escalade was about to break the sound barrier. Joggers on the path next to the road dove into the bushes for cover. Oncoming cars drove into the ditch to avoid a collision.

We flew past the Play Park, and I was surprised driving as fast as we were the kids weren't clutching the monkey bars with their feet kicking in the air as their little fingers held lest they be sucked into the wind vortex left in our wake.

With the accelerator mashed to the floor, the Escalade burst out of the gates to Kildonan Park, tires screeched and the stink of burnt rubber filler the air as she headed for downtown.

"Fuck, Gabby slow down," Basil snarled.

The crazed pixie cut through a narrowing space between two delivery trucks. "That cop's on our ass, I'm not taking any chances."

"I left Quill standing there in the clearing, he'd need a rocket to catch up," I said.

"I'm still waiting for you to say thanks for saving your ugly ass," Gabby said as she zipped through the next intersection.

"I was doing fine on my own."

"By having a shoot out with a cop?" Basil asked.

"There were no shots fired, we were just talking," I said. Gabby popped up on the sidewalk briefly to pass a car before coming back to the street. "Can we please slow this shit down? We're safe, I fucking swear it."

My face smashed into the back of the passenger seat as

the Escalade's tires screeched and the back wheels lifted off the ground. Gabby must have been standing on the brake. She eased the Escalade back into the flow of traffic. "Happy? You're such a baby, Grady,"

"I'll be fine once my brain moves back into place."

Basil turned in his seat to glare at me. "You're worried about your head? Look at your face, you keep taking these beatings you're going to move from ugly to disgusting."

"I'm tired hearing about my looks."

"Then get a new face," Gabby said.

"You're so funny," I said. "How'd you know Quill was a cop, anyway?"

"We spotted you walking in the park with that cop on your ass," Gabby explained. "We hung back to watch and then when shit went sideways we scooped you out of there."

"Okay, but I still don't get how you knew he was a cop," I said.

"Isn't the first time I've seen him around," Basil said. "I know that bastard and he's no good."

"That's a fucking understatement."

"So what was that all about?"

"It's about Nyah, like I told you, all of this is about her," I said. "But it's gotten way out of control and I need your help."

The big man cocked his eyebrow. "You need to catch us up to speed before we agree to anything."

"I will, I promise, but first I need you to watch something," I said.

A few blocks ahead I had Gabby pull the Escalade into the parking lot of a Carpet and Flooring store. It was next door to a Jeep dealership, and was busy. The stream of customers in and out of the lot was constant and we wouldn't be noticed. Gabby killed the engine and I queued up the video on Nyah's phone. We huddled around the small screen and watched.

I pointed to the first two on the screen, drinking in the alley. "That's obviously Jacob and Davis."

"And they are dead so they no longer matter," Basil said.

"Yup, and the first cop is Quill, the douche bag from the park," I added.

"That crazy fucker killed his partner?" Gabby said.

"And his partner was Nyah's Dad," I said. "That's what this has all been about." I explained everything as I knew it to be, not even leaving the smallest detail out. Throughout my story, even Gabby was quiet. "So now I'm caught between Quill and Shamus," I said when I'd finished. "Both want the video, and I thought about making copies and just lying to them both, but they also want Nyah and me dead for seeing it. Also, there's the fact that Nyah wants revenge for her Dad." I took a deep breath. "It's probably not healthy, but I'm no parent, I gotta say I want to help her to make things square."

Her eyes fierce and hard, Gabby nodded. "No, that's what needs to happen," she said. "She's a sweet kid, and those bastards almost ruined her."

Basil nodded. "She's already two thirds of the way there with Jacob and Davis dead. Now all that's left is that Quill."

"We just have to remember there's still Shamus to deal with," I said.

"There's only one choice," Basil said. "We gotta take them both out."

Tucking Nyah's phone back in my pocket, I leaned back in my seat. "I agree, so now we have to come up with how."

"Wait, what? You ain't got a plan?"

My phone rang, and I checked the display. It was Hank. I held up a finger. "Give me a second."

Gabby snorted. "He's stalling because he doesn't have an answer."

I ignored the crazy pixie and answered my phone.

275

"What's up, Hank? Everything okay?"

"*No, Grady, everything is very far from okay,*" Hank answered.

"What happened?"

"*Not over the phone, Grady,*" he said. "*Where are you?*"

"Damn it Hank, what's going on?" I demanded. "Are you in the hospital?"

"*No, but I probably should be.*"

"I've got no time for this, Hank, tell me what the problem is now."

"*Meet me at your apartment,*" he said and hung up.

I sat there, staring at my phone, turning it over in my hands.

"Who was that?" Gabby asked. "Shamus? Quill?"

"It was Hank," I said. "And whatever the fuck is going on it's bad."

"How can you be so sure?" Basil asked.

"Because if everything was fine, Marin would have called," I said. "Get me home, now."

Nobody asked anymore questions. Gabby pinned the gas pedal to the floor mat, and was weaving in and out of traffic, cutting off cars and scattering pedestrians. The Escalade burst through intersections and ignored traffic lights.

Sliding the ass end of the Escalade as she made the corner, Gabby turned onto Burrows Avenue. My street. Again Gabby hit the brakes hard. Basil and I were snapped forward and I gave the back of the driver's seat another smashed kiss. I wiped the fresh blood from my nose and looked up. I didn't have to ask why she stopped. There were a dozen cop cars two blocks down my street, lights bathing the buildings in red and blue.

Slowing the Escalade to a crawl, Gabby took the first street to our left. Through the rear window I could see the squad cars had circled the scene of an accident. A limo and a sedan had collided hard enough that it was tough to tell where one ended and the other began.

I guided Gabby down the back lane towards my building. There wasn't a cop to be seen, and no one bothered us as she parked the Escalade at my building's back door. Basil and Gabby were right on my heels as I raced up the stairs and burst into my apartment.

We found Hank on the couch, his face a mass of cuts and bruises. He was holding an ice pack to the back of his head.

"Holy Hell, Hank what happened?" I looked into the kitchen, there was no one there. I opened the door to my bedroom, only to find it empty. The spare room was also unoccupied. I stormed back into the living room. "Where are Marin and Nyah?"

"Sit down," Hank said.

"No," I said. "You only get bad news when you sit down."

Hank dropped the ice pack on the cushion beside him. "Do what you want, it's bad news anyway."

"What the fuck happened, Hank?"

"He took them."

"What? Who?"

"Shamus."

"Shamus Gray? Are you saying Shamus took Nyah and Marin?"

"Yes, I'm afraid so."

"No, that isn't right, Nyah's just a kid," Gabby said.

"I don't think that Shamus cares." I turned to Hank. "Why didn't you try to stop him?"

Hank buried his face in his hands. "I did try, but I'm too slow, weak and old. But I tried..."

"Not good enough. What happened? What did you do, exactly?"

"What I could. I fought but it wasn't enough."

Basil put his hand on my chest, easing me back. "Leave it, Grady. It's done. We need to let him tell us what happened."

The old cop looked up, way up, at the big human. "Who the Hell are you?"

"I'm a friend."

"Good, we need the likes of you I think," Hank said. Then he told us what happened with Shamus, how they been tricked by Drake and what Reece had done to save them. "That brother of yours tried, he did what he could."

"My brother? Reece?"

Hank nodded. "He fought like Hell and gave us a chance, even if I fouled it up in the end. When I finally woke up, the girls were gone."

"They probably thought you were dead."

"You're not helping."

"Do you know where Shamus took them?" I asked Hank.

"I was laid out cold, Grady, I have no idea what happened after that."

"But they're alive?"

"I'd have to say so or they'd have been lying next to me."

"What about Reece? Where's his body?"

"I believe the cops took him away about five minutes before you got here. At least that's what I could tell from your window. I didn't want to stick around once the cops showed up. I told them I was a passerby; they took my statement and let me go."

"You just left him there?"

"I'm sorry, but he was already dead, Grady. I was worried about Marin and Nyah and if I stayed and said I was involved they still would have shipped him to the morgue and kept me downtown interviewing me for hours. I'd have been no use to anyone, so I stayed out of it so I could help."

My head started to pound and the room began to spin. "Sorry, I just need a minute."

Stumbling to my bedroom, I shut the door behind me. I made it to my en suite in time to throw up in the toilet. When I finished I rinsed my face in the sink. I could barely look at my reflection in the mirror. It should have been me.

I have hated and loved Reece alternately all our lives. I'd wanted to kill him at times, but there were also moments when I wanted to hug him till it hurt. He was my brother. Reece was there for all my favourite moments as a child. He was beside me for every beating the old man ever laid on me. We were linked. I knew no matter what he'd always love me and need me.

Every moment I had ever been mean to him came back, and I wanted to crawl inside myself in embarrassment. In his last moments, Reece was more of a man than I'd ever be. He saved Hank, and he sealed his fate in trying to rescue Marin and Nyah. I have called Reece every despicable word there is in every language I know. I believed him less than human at times, and treated him so.

I was wrong, and my shame would never wash off. I never deserved Reece as a brother.

Basil opened the door but stood aside to let Hank walk in. The old cop door glared at me from across the bedroom. "Care to explain what you're going to do about the fact a psycho has just run off with my daughter?"

"Not really," I answered as I closed the bathroom door behind me.

"Wasn't a choice dumbass."

"I don't want you to panic."

"Do you think anything you got to say is going to shock me now?"

I sighed. "Fine, but you're going to wish I hadn't."

"I'm already up to speed," Basil said. "I need to grab

some stuff from my place and make a few calls before we meet up and get started."

"We'll stay in touch," Gabby added as she appeared behind her brother. "Don't go anywhere without letting us know."

"How long until you're back?" I asked.

"About an hour," Basil said. "There's some cash and equipment I need to grab. This is going to get messy so I also have to wipe my computer, and do a sweep of the house to make sure there's nothing there the cops can use against us in case we get arrested."

"Make it an hour and a half," Gabby said. "I need to get ready too."

I smiled. "So this is a makeup run?"

"I'm probably a few hours away from driving straight into a shit storm. Those bastards took Nyah, and I like that girl. In case you haven't noticed I don't like many people and even less like me back. I plan on slitting that fucker's throat if she even has a stubbed toe. So maybe I want to look good for that."

On her way out, Gabby squeezed my arm and whispered. "Those two girls are coming home."

I doubt she believed it herself. The sibling assassins left Hank and I alone, and it felt oddly intimate.

"So what do we do now?" Hank demanded.

"I expect I'll be trying very hard not to drink."

"How about saving your wife? Or the girl? Did either thing cross your mind?"

"So where do we find them? Can you tell me that? Winnipeg is too big, and the hiding places in this province are too many to waste my time looking. Shamus has Marin and Nyah now, and we have to wait for him to come to us. Besides, even if we found her, what are you and I going to do against all his guys? We're going to get fucking killed, that's what, and so what am I doing right now? I'm waiting for Basil."

"Okay, but while we're waiting that doesn't mean we can't try and come up with something."

"I guess I can't stop you from thinking."

"Exactly, so let's see, what are the issues here? Shamus wants the video and he says if he gets it he'll give the girls back. But let's be honest, he'll probably kill us once he has it."

"That's my take."

"And if not Shamus then we give it to Quill and most likely the same result. We need both out of the way, but if we make a deal with one the other will come for us." Hank paused and the scowl left his face as a smile spread like sunrise.

"You have an idea," I said.

"I do, and it'll solve all our problems, I just need to use the bathroom first."

"Seriously?"

"I hafta crap, and I'm no use if I'm pinching my cheeks together. Besides, I do my best thinking on the throne."

Hank didn't wait for me to argue. He tucked a newspaper under his arm and marched to the bathroom. He at least had the decency to turn on the fan.

With nothing to do but wait, I stared out the window and wondered where Marin was. She had to be scared and alone. I prayed those were her only problems.

The toilet flushed and Hank emerged from the bathroom. He tossed the paper on the table and joined me on the couch, a smirk firmly on his lips.

"Good dump?" I asked.

"At my age, the fact I can still go makes it a good one."

"I'll take your word for it." I sighed. "You know any plan you came up with while taking a shit is worthless unless we find Shamus, right?"

"You were right, we can't find him," Hank admitted.

"But we can definitely get in touch with him."

"Ah, I'm an idiot, we still have Vern's phone."

The old cop nodded. "That son of a bitch will answer it when you call."

"I guess there's just one problem," I said. "We still need a plan. I can't just call the fucker and start yelling and threatening."

"I just told you I had an idea. Which one of us has the brain tumour? Stop interrupting and let me get it out." Hank cleared his throat. "I have a way to fix everything and get that bastard. All we need to do is..."

I cut him off. "Wait, stop right there. There's no *we*."

"What the Hell is that supposed to mean, *there's no we*?"

"You're old and sick. This is going to be dangerous, and no offence I get you're twice the man I am, but at the moment you aren't up for this."

"I was a cop for thirty-five years and I know my way around a gun. I can be useful."

"You don't get it, do you? Marin will kill me if I let you die saving her."

The old cop slapped his knee and cackled. His shoulder shook and his face went red as he howled with laugher.

"Did I fucking say something funny?" I snapped.

"Yeah, you did." Hank wiped the tears away with his sleeve and caught his breath. "It's funny that you'd be worried about me."

"Because I'm too much of asshole to care about anyone? Is that it?"

The old cop sighed, and the wrinkles on his face deepened. "Remember how I've been bugging you, saying I needed a favour these last few days?"

"I'll tell you straight off, you need a kidney or something, mine's ruined. Same goes for my liver."

"Do you know how I know I'm old, Grady? I'm

attending more funerals for my friends than birthdays. Hell, the only time I see my friends is in the hospital. They're full of pain and nothing but shadows of the men they were. My father died of Parkinson's and all I remember is him laying in that big, white sterile hospital bed. My wife had the cancer, and she was like everyone else, spent her last days in that same hospital bed wishing, praying for death to come end their pain. Do you know what they got? Some doctor keeping them alive with drugs, wringing the last painful drops of life out." He shook his head. "Who wants to put their kids through that? What would that do to Marin and Daria? Every time the phone rings they'll be dreading it's the hospital calling to say I died. Eventually they'll be hoping. I watched my father die by inches, and my wife stolen by the pain, and I won't go on like that."

"Hank, that sucks, it really does. Not to be an ass, but what does that gotta do with me? I'm no doctor."

Hank took a deep breath. "I was going to ask you to kill me."

I blinked. "That's not going to fucking happen, Hank."

"Call me a coward, but I think I've earned the right to bow out early on this. I'm not greedy, I'm not asking for more time. I just want to end it before the pain gets too bad and before my children have to watch me suffer. I need your help to do that, suicide is a sin. Besides Marin is smart, she'd know even if I tried to hide it."

"And if I killed you? She'd figure that out too."

"I had an idea, we'd make it look like an accident, set it up so you wouldn't be a suspect."

"You're a cop, so you should know there's always evidence. Besides, if my father-in-law gets popped, who the fuck do you think they're looking at first?"

"I've thought of all that. I know the system, and the greatest advantage we have is that I'm the victim and I'll be helping you. Trust me, I got a handle on this."

"You're wasting your breath because there's no damn way I'm going to do it."

"You owe me this much."

"For what? You've been an asshole since I met you."

"So you'll get your payback watching me suffer?"

"Give me a break. You know it's not like that. I'm just not going to kill you. How can you call that a favour anyway? It's not like asking a buddy to help move."

"You've killed before so what's one more?"

"This is what I'm talking about. You're such an old dried up prick. I'm not a criminal and before a week ago I've never even been arrested. I'm just a drunk, Hank."

"Not that I thought you were an assassin or something, but what about when you were in the army?"

"That's different, Hank, and you damn well know it. I can promise you it was self-defence. But I'll tell you what, I didn't like the taste of it."

"I never said you were a serial killer."

"For fuck sakes, I'm not even a felon. I'm not a crook or a hit man or anything else other than a drunk, a lousy husband and sometimes I'm a bartender."

"You're also a hard man, and of all the people I know you're the only one who'd have the nerve to do it. My buddies from the force talk a good game, but most haven't even fired their piece in the line of duty," he admitted. "I don't think you'd enjoy it, but you're man enough to see it through."

"I'll tell you a secret, Hank, hurting a person I care about, that would never be just business, and you don't get used to killing people."

"I only hoped you'd do me this favour because a long time ago I did one for you. It was that time you got sent to the hospital with alcohol poisoning. The ambulance found you in the alley behind a bar without any pants. Marin came to me and asked what she should do. I told Marin that if she loved you and saw a good man in there somewhere, she had to try. Like her mother did with me."

"Well, shit, that's a surprise."

"So you'll do it? You'll help me end this with some dignity?"

"No, I'm sorry Hank, I feel for you, but I can't."

"Don't tell me it's because you don't have the balls. We both know you'd kill the entire city to save Marin."

"In a heartbeat."

"Then what's difference?"

"You're not her and every time I looked at Marin, I'd think about the fact I capped her father."

"Please, I'm begging you, don't let me suffer."

"You aren't some dog I could take behind the woodshed and put down."

"I have money. I could pay you to do it."

I stood up, knocking over the coffee table. "Hank, of all the things you've ever said to me, that's the first time I've ever been insulted. I'm gonna leave before I do you that favour and beat you to death."

I stormed into bedroom almost taking the door off its hinges. I flopped on my bed, pulled out my phone and checked the display. Nothing from Basil.

The urge to scream and punch holes in the walls was strong, almost as powerful as the sudden need to fill my insides with whisky. Wasn't I under enough stress? Didn't I have enough crap piling at my feet that deal with a suicidal father-in-law?

My bedroom door creaked as it opened.

"Hank, fuck off, I'm not in the mood. I'm fucking pissed at you right now."

"Mad enough to kill me?"

"You're such an asshole."

"Listen, Grady, that didn't go the way I wanted. It was a bad idea."

285

"You think?'

"No, I mean telling you, because the point is moot."

"What the hell are you talking about?"

Cautiously, Hank shuffled into the room and took a seat on the opposite end of the bed from me. "See, I only meant to ease your mind about my safety. I want to die, so you don't need to worry about anything happening to me."

"Well, that was a fucked up way to go about saying that."

"Yeah, well, it's true, so don't worry about me, if I die, it's okay." He paused and cleared his throat. "Which is a good thing to keep in mind while I tell you my plan."

"Oh, damn it, this should be good."

"Just hear me through. Don't say a word until I finish, because it's going to be a doozy."

Hank laid out his plan, and at first I was confused. After Hank explained everything in complete detail, and I understood what he wanted, I realized I felt better being confused. The scary part was I knew it would work. Our shot at salvation had been thought up by an ex-cop with a brain tumour. Who knew what part of Hank's brain the growth consumed? Guaranteed it had to do with logic.

TWENTY-NINE

I deally in the army, I'd get my packet ahead of time with recon, intel, maps and detailed mission plans. There were also nights where I'd be woken up, screamed at and forced to embark to some unknown hellhole. Either way, someone had come up with contingencies and a well conceived action plan. Unlike, for instance, Hank's crazy scheme.

Step one of Hank's brilliant tactical masterpiece was for me to go to a bar.

Me.

Grady Fisk.

In a bar.

At least the old cop had been smart enough to send chaperones. Gabby and Basil were right behind me as I passed through the doors of The Smiling Skull Pub. The bar was dark, as all the good ones are, with plenty of shadows to drink in. It had a strip down industrial feel and used to be a warehouse, the ducts and pipes were left exposed in the ceiling. The tables were once work benches in an old mechanic's shop. Motorcycles, mostly choppers and big old Hogs hung from the ceiling or were mounted on the walls in various stages of assembly. The bar itself was made up of thousands of engine parts fused together with a solid granite top. The place smelled of grease and whiskey. I wanted to drink so bad my liver cried.

As much as I loved the vibe of The Smiling Skull, I wasn't a regular. Basil was the owner and he didn't want me scaring off the paying customers. The Smiling Skull was how Basil explained to the taxman how he could afford such a beautiful house and all his toys. Basil also kept the place for times like this, when he needed somewhere public he could control.

Stepping aside I let Gabby and Basil lead me to the bar. A jarringly beautiful curly haired brunette in a skin tight metallic silver dress stood on the other side of the counter staring up at the Jets afternoon game on TV.

Basil nodded. "Hello Nancy, good day so far?"

The brunette shrugged. "It's a little slow, but this time of day the regulars are still sleeping off last night."

"Anything I need to know about?"

Nancy pointed to the back corner of the bar. In the shadows, with a bottle of rye and two glasses in front of him, Quill sat alone. No other cops in sight. "He's been waiting for you."

"For how long?"

"He walked in an hour ago bought the bottle and sat down. I told him you weren't in but he said you'd be back and that you'd want to talk."

"We do," Basil said. "Grady's got something to tell him."

I stayed at the bar while Basil and Gabby spread out, taking positions on either side of Quill, leaving three or four tables open between. Nancy motioned for her waitresses to follow suit, pulling them back, leaving a bubble of empty chairs around Quill, not another soul within twenty feet. I don't know if he noticed, as his eyes never left the bottle in front of him.

Crossing through the no fly zone, I joined the cop. I pulled a folded piece of paper from my pocket and dropped it on the table in front of Quill.

"It's an address," I said. "You'll want to stop by."

Quill slid the paper back and told me to sit down. "Unless that's where the video is, I don't give a crap." He poured a glass of rye and pushed it over. "You look like you could use this."

I took the seat opposite him and lifted the glass, I could

smell the whiskey and the desire to throw it back and feel the burning in my throat was strong. I poured the whiskey out on the floor and put the glass back on the table upside down.

Quill sat staring at me. "That wasn't polite."

"I hate to break your heart, but you and I aren't drinking buddies," I said. "I'm only here to keep things fair, because unlike you I don't sneak up on people and try to jump them like a fucking coward."

"What, that thing back at the park?"

"I'm talking about the fact you killed another cop."

Quill grunted and threw back his drink. He filled his glass again before answering. "You really know how to ruin the mood, don't you? If it makes a difference, I'd take it back if I could but there's no way I'm going to jail for it. Jim Tynes was a cop, he knew the job was dangerous."

"He wasn't the only victim, you fucked up his daughter's life too."

"That's not my fault."

"Here's a fact, if you don't shoot your partner in the back, Nyah doesn't lose her dad and her mom doesn't turn into a druggie prostitute and meet that asswipe Vern and so on and so on."

"Delores obviously had it in her to go down that road. You don't become a crackhead or a whore just because you had a bad day. Maybe I nudged her along, but tons of people have been in Delores Tynes shoes and haven't fallen down that hole."

"What the fuck happened to you, Quill? Why the hell did you become a cop? You're supposed to help people, be the fucking good guy, not this cold murdering bastard."

Staring at his glass, Quill slowly swirled the amber liquor inside. "Things happen. Things you don't expect or even dream of in the beginning. The rules change, or they weren't even what you thought they'd be. You wouldn't understand but the job breaks you down and changes who you are."

"I wouldn't understand? Do you have a clue what kind of monster I had as a father? You're asking the wrong guy for sympathy."

Quill sighed and took a drink. "I'm going to tell a story, Grady, then you tell me if you can find some sympathy." The cop waited for me to nod before he continued. "I'd only been on the force about three years when I caught this case. Some dealer in town got in a spot with some very dangerous men out of Toronto. He'd been supplying their competitor so they sent an errand boy to advise this dealer that it was in his best interest to stop. The dealer was insulted and decided to send a message of his own." He shook his head. "He had a man named Dex, not as scary as your friend Basil but he was competent. This dealer put Dex to work on this errand boy from Toronto and he ended up dead from massive head trauma. Dex tended to go overboard." Quill shrugged. "Anyway, there was a price on the dealer's head. Dex was found shot three times in the face and stuffed into a dumpster. It was only a matter of time before they got their hands on the dealer."

"How the fuck does any of this matter?" I asked.

"Shut up and hear me out." Quill emptied his glass again before continuing. "Now, we were tasked with hunting this dealer down and getting him to safety. We eventually caught him and put him in protective custody. Those men from Toronto found out I was one of the cops on the case and they came after me. One day, I came home and found my wife cut to shreds in our bed, their way of letting me know I shouldn't have gotten involved. They murdered her and the baby boy she was carrying. I suffer everyday knowing they died because I was a good cop."

"That's a raw deal, Quill, no doubt about it," I said. "But that doesn't give you a pass on killing some cop who wasn't involved."

"What if I told you the department did nothing? All I got was a bunch of we're sorrys and a month paid leave. That's it. The dealer gets to be a witness and is kept safe in protective custody while my family gets slaughtered. I was supposed to be the good cop, lick my wounds and come back to work. That was supposed to be the end of it."

"But it wasn't."

"We couldn't pin my wife's murder on the fucks from Toronto. They used a third party and there was no proof linking them to it. So I was told to let it go. I was told to let Karma handle things. I was told justice would come our way eventually."

"So what did you do?"

"I took my leave like a good soldier. I went on vacation." He laughed. "I took a trip to Toronto, and found those guys. I guarantee the last thing they expected to see was me. Some I shot, others I used a blade, but in the end I killed every last one of those fuckers."

"The department must have known you did it."

"Maybe, but no one could prove it, and how hard was anyone going to look at the deaths of some criminals anyway?" He chuckled as he took another drink. "But someone knew. The dealer whose ass we saved knew. A month or so later, that dealer came to see me and handed over an envelope full of cash. He was paying me for taking care of his problem. It wasn't about the money, but I took it anyway."

I shook my head. "And that's how it starts."

"I didn't care anymore, so when that dealer asked for favour, I did it. It made me money, kept me comfortable and I got to take some of that rage out. I mean, being a cop meant nothing to me, not after how the department, fucked me. So one job turns into another and before I know it, that's my life. It's who I am and that's how I got here."

"Who was the witness?"

"Jacob."

"I figured, but I still had to ask. That's some story."

"You don't sound moved."

"Well, I get the whole killing the assholes from Toronto thing. They murdered your loved ones, so they deserved to be slaughtered. That's fair enough. But whole rogue, crooked cop routine? That ain't because of your family."

"Then what's it about genius?"

"Just like you said about Nyah's mom, it's always been there. You're a piece of shit because that's what you are. Your wife's murder just gave you the reason."

"Watch your mouth, Grady, talk about my wife again and they'll be the last words you use." Quill leaned back, pulled open his coat and showed me the gun strapped under his arm. "I'll kill you right there in your fucking seat."

"No, you won't, not one on one, and not with Basil and Gabby here."

The cop frowned and slumped in his chair. "Alright, I'm too old to play games, Grady. We can play coy and dance around a bit, but my knees hurt when I polka." He laughed. "Here's the deal, give me the video and let's just end this."

"I have to ask, how the Hell does this video even exist?"

Quill sighed. "The alley was behind an Autobody Shop, they had a security camera. We didn't even know about it until a year ago. The shop's owner was into drugs and kept it as an insurance policy in case he ever got into debt. Except when he did, it was Shamus he owed money to. So he gave it to that psychopath and all this chaos and killing started. Now it's going to end when you give it to me."

"Not likely, because I'm going to give it back to Shamus."

"And you brought me here to tell me that?"

"I'm just giving you a heads up."

"But why Shamus?"

"He has my wife and Nyah. I have no choice, I have to make an exchange."

I push the folded piece of paper towards him again. "The address written here is a farm house out in the town of Stonewall."

"Why are you telling me this?"

"Like I said, I'm just being fair."

"It sounds like you're setting me up."

"A set up? Maybe." I smiled. "But not for you. Once the exchange is made, and my wife and the kid are with me, what you do to Shamus is your business."

"And you just walk away?"

"Is that going to be a problem?"

The cop shrugged. "Well, you saw the video, and I don't like that. I worry you might think you have influence over me then."

"I do have influence," I said. "And in case you're wondering, I will use it against you if you don't stay away when this is done."

With the cop staring at me, his glass half raised to his mouth, I turned and left. Basil and Gabby followed me out the front door and into Basil's Escalade. The first part of Hank's crazy plan was done. There was no going back now.

THIRTY

The thing to cling to, if Nyah and Marin were to escape the cess pool they'd been dragged into, was the fact they were still alive. Were they dead, everything else would be irrelevant.

The stone bench on which Nyah sat was perfectly smooth with no discernible flaws or marks. Nyah sat absolutely still, focussed on controlling her breathing and slowing her heart rate. Her throat was sore from screaming. She had nothing to show from her hysterics other than a runny nose and red puffy eyes.

Nyah took stock of the certainties of their predicament. They were still handcuffed, held captive by a mad man. They were going to die; the only question was if they would be tortured first. The list was short and disheartening.

Sitting opposite Nyah on top of an old teacher's desk, hands folded in her lap, knees together and ankles crossed, Marin couldn't get her hands to stop shaking. The young girl couldn't blame her. They were being held in old abandoned high school. Years before, during the spring melt, Winnipeg had flooded, and the school was among the many homes and businesses that had been damaged by the high waters. The damage was so extensive the school hadn't been worth repairing. It had been cheaper to build a new school a mile down the road.

There were desks piled in the corner of the classroom where they were sitting. The windows had been boarded up, and most of the fluorescent lights overhead had burnt out. The few that did work were covered in dust and bathed the room in a yellowish glow. Paint had bubbled and peeled from the walls where the water had sat three feet deep during the flood. What was odd to Nyah was that the blackboards still had writing from the lessons on them and there were still motivational posters, notes and memos stapled to the bulletin boards around the room.

On the floor in front of the jumble of desks, discarded food, pop cans and other trash had been pushed into the corners. A growing community of beetles, ants and silverfish crawled over and around each other, covering the floor like a vile rug. Nyah hadn't seen any yet, but she was quite certain there were rats scavenging there too. The rustling and scratching sounds they made picked at her nerves.

When that asshole, Shamus, had deposited them in the school, he'd left Marin in that room and brought Nyah to one further down the hall. Nyah had been handcuffed in what was once the Science Lab and left at one of the work stations. There were broken test tubes, rusted Bunsen burners and Petri dishes everywhere. The sink at her workstation had mould and other things growing in it, Nyah had wondered if it had been an experiment that had been forgotten and outgrown its container.

When she'd been left alone, Nyah alternated between sobbing and screaming. Eventually, Nyah realized no one had been left to guard her. Nothing restrained her to the desk. No rope or chain tethered her there. She rose to her feet, and no one told her to sit. Nyah took a few steps from her stool and work station and no one emerged from the shadows to stop her. Once she was certain not even the creatures in her imagination would attack her, Nyah searched for escape.

The windows in the science lab were boarded up, so she couldn't find any tool to pry them free. Nyah tried the door to her classroom and it was unlocked, and she stepped into the deep darkness of the hallway. She was at the far end and the emergency exit door had been chained shut. She tried the class room across the hall first. The desks had been scattered around the room, and books, rotten and swollen from the flooding littered the floor. The windows were also boarded up and it offered no escape. Nyah worked her way down the hallway, with the next two classrooms being no different than the first. The fourth room had so much furniture crammed into it that there was no point even entering.

Double doors with wired safety glass closed the hallway off from the rest of the school. Nyah ran past the last two classrooms, and tried to pull the double doors open, but they wouldn't budge. She threw all her weight down on the push bar and drove forward but there was no give. Kicking and screaming at the doors had even less effect.

"They've been chained shut," said a voice behind her.

Nyah spun round and back peddled, nearly tripping over her own feet. She raised her arms to defend herself as her screams pierced the air as she swung wildly with her manacled hands. When her eyes were able to focus on the figure emerging from the shadows of the classroom at the end of the hall, Nyah relaxed and started to cry. It was Marin, and the blonde girl was no longer alone.

Marin rushed forward and they embraced, Nyah buried her face in the older woman's shoulder. When Marin broke the hug, she led Nyah back to the classroom from where she emerged. Marin sat on the up on the teacher's desk and Nyah took the stone bench, the only piece of furniture she'd been surprised to find in a school.

"We need to talk quickly before they come back," Marin said.

"Shamus? Where did they go?" Nyah asked.

"Maybe somewhere else in the school. I really don't know anything except after they split us up they left and locked us in."

"I looked around and it's eight classrooms and two

bathrooms. All the windows are boarded up and the exits are chained."

Marin nodded. "We have to get out of here before they come back, but there aren't any tools to work with."

"In the lab where they put me there's some science stuff the students used for experiments. Maybe there's something we can use."

"It's better than sitting here," Marin said and hopped off the desk.

The two of them scoured every inch of the lab. They went through all the cupboards and drawers, looking for anything to pry off the boards nailed to the windows. Nyah found a protractor in the sink at one of the work stations. There was some rust on it but the metal was fine and the point still sharp. She stuck the tip into the keyhole of her cuffs.

Marin smiled. "Do you even know how to pick the lock?"

"How hard can it be? I'll figure it out."

"You're just wasting time."

"What else are we going to do?"

"We have to come up with a way out." Sitting down on one of the stools, Marin leaned back against the work station and pressed the heels of her palms against her eyes. "This is so crazy. All this over a video."

Nyah took the stool opposite of her and placed the protractor down on the table. "I'm sorry, Marin. This is all my fault."

Marin reached out and squeezed Nyah's hand. "No, you need to understand it was never your fault. It's theirs, and if it had been my Dad that..."

Her lips trembling and the tears streaked down her cheeks, Marin lost her words. "I get it," the girl said. "I know how bad it hurts."

Straightening up, Marin wiped her eyes with her sleeve.

"Damn it, I can't be crying now. You had the right idea, and maybe we can find something better to open those cuffs with."

"We also need to look for something we can use as a weapon," Nyah said.

"You want to fight them? Are you crazy?"

"We could sit around and wait for Grady, but what if he doesn't show up?"

"You know as well as I do he's hunting for us right now."

"Doesn't mean he'll find us," Nyah said. "Who knows what's going on out there? He could be in trouble himself. I think we're going to have to save ourselves."

"What chance do we have against those men? They have guns, Nyah and what do we have?"

"My Dad always said if there's no solution to the big problem work on the small problem first," Nyah said. "Let's work on getting out of here."

Marin laughed. "That's the small problem?"

"Maybe not, but it's the most important."

The sound of footsteps echoed in from the hallway. There were voices, more than one person headed towards them. They were men and they were laughing. Instinct screamed for Nyah to hide, but she had enough sense to know that would be both dumb and useless. There was nowhere to go. Instead she tucked her protractor in her pocket, and turned to see who had come for them.

Shamus stood in the doorway, a briefcase in his hands, and a greasy smile on his face. He was flanked by two men so big Nyah wasn't sure they could even fit through the door.

"Look, my two little birds found each other," he said. "Are we crying on each other's shoulders?"

"Why are you such a douche bag?" Nyah spat.

"I can't wait to see your face when Grady finds you," Marin said.

"That's the whole point, don't you fucking get it?" Shamus laughed. "I want to make him come to me."

"You say that now, but when he finds you he's going to hurt you."

"Honestly, I don't see that happening." Shamus gestured to the stools. "Now, both of you take a seat and we can talk."

"No, how about you go to hell?" Marin snapped.

Shamus gestured to the two slabs of granite behind him. "These are my friends, Otto and Zeke. Now you either you ladies sit on your own, or they will plant your asses on those stools for you."

Nyah took her seat, and Marin did the same. From the corner, Shamus grabbed a stool, righted it, and took a seat between the two women. Otto and Zeke stayed at the door. Shamus placed his briefcase at his feet, and crossed his arms over his chest.

"Do you feel like a big man, scaring the crap out of two women??" Marin asked.

"This asshole killed my mother because he can't fight men," Nyah said.

Shamus held up his hand to stop them. "I don't give a shit what you think of me. Really, I don't. I have some questions and you're going to give me the answers. And if you think you're not going to tell me what I want to know, just realise I have ways of getting what I want out of you."

From the pocket of his designer jeans, Shamus pulled out a pair of black leather gloves. He made a show of putting them on, flexing his hands and pulling them snug. He laid the briefcase on the table, opened it, and took out a 9mm Beretta, a knife and a pair of bolt cutters. He lined the tools up on the work surface, closed the briefcase and placed it on the floor. Marin wouldn't look at the objects on the table. Nyah wished she could stop.

Fear filled every inch of her.

Fear of pain.
Of being cut.
Of being ripped open.
Torn.
Sliced.
Dismembered.
Her fingers.
Her face.

"We want to leave," Marin said. "Please, let us go home."

"You are the ones who decide how long you stay." Shamus held out his arms. "You have total control. Give me what I want and you leave. Don't and you won't. It's very simple."

Jumping to her feet in an anger that surprised her, Marin slammed her fist down onto the table. "Just. Let. Us. Go."

The two behemoths stepped into the room, flanking Marin and closing the gap. Shamus shook his head and shooed them back as he gestured for Marin to take her seat.

Marin paled and returned to her bench. "Are you going to kill us?" she asked.

"Let's save that question for later and start talking about what I want to know."

"I promise I won't tell anyone about you if you let us go."

Shamus shrugged. "I am hardly worried of that. That's the beauty of it. If this goes bad no one will find you."

"But Grady would know," Nyah said. "Body or no body Grady would know and he'd kill you."

"How many times do I have to say I'm not scared of him? Where was he when I took you both so easily?"

"You're scared because he kicked your ass already and that's why I know you don't want anything to do with him."

Letting his hand fly, Shamus slapped Nyah across the

face. She rocked back on her stool, slamming into the table behind her. "I don't want any more fucking mouth from either of you, understand?"

Straightening herself in her seat, Nyah forced herself not to cry. "I understand," she said through gritted teeth.

"Now, let's get down to business, okay?" Shamus motioned to the items laid out on the table. "This is the way it works. I ask a question and you answer. I don't like your answer or you lie you get hit. Keep lying and I snip off a finger. More lies get your pretty faces cut and eventually they earn you a bullet. Just remember I don't actually need both of you to make a trade. Are we clear?"

"You're a monster," Marin said.

"Oh, lady, you have no idea." Shamus stood and moved in front of Nyah. "Let's start with you. What are your plans for the video?"

"I don't have it," she said. "Grady does."

Spinning quickly, Shamus drew his arm back and laced Marin across the face with the back of his hand. Marin pitched backwards in her chair as her head snapped back and she cried out. When Marin regained her balance and raised her head, there was a glowing red welt on her cheek.

"Why did you hit her?" Nyah screamed. "She didn't do anything!"

Shamus shrugged. "I didn't like your answer."

"But it was me, not Marin."

"I forgot to mention that I guess. If you fuck up I hurt her, and of course, vice versa. Nasty business, right?"

"I told you Grady has the video!"

"But that's not what I asked. I already know Grady has it, you told me that in the limo. I want to know what he's planning on doing with it."

Nyah gritted her teeth. "Why don't you go find him and ask him? Maybe he'll tell you after he kicks your ass."

Stepping into it and swinging hard, Shamus' slap lifted

Marin off her stool and she toppled onto the floor. Her lip was split and the blood had already covered her chin. Tears filled her eyes, and with wobbly arms she tried to lift herself up. Shamus used his foot to push her back down on the linoleum.

"Stay right there on the floor," he said. "No one told you to move."

"You're a total bastard," Marin slurred.

"Your mouth is making me angry, Nyah." Shamus put his heel down on Marin's hand where it rested on the floor. "I've always found that the bones in the human hand are quite delicate and snap like twigs. Want to find out if Marin has been drinking her milk, Nyah?"

The blonde girl shook her head. "Please, don't."

Pressing his weight down, Shamus ground his heel into Marin's hand. She grunted, trying to push him off her with her other hand, but cuffed she had no leverage.

"I'm getting annoyed with your bullshit, Nyah," he said. "And I'm willing to bet Marin isn't liking it too fucking much either."

"I swear I don't know," Nyah said. "He didn't tell me, honest. Just get off her hand, you're hurting her. Grady didn't tell me what he was going to do."

Lifting his foot off Marin's hand, Shamus paused, letting his boot hover for a moment before driving it back down. His heel slammed into Marin's hand, crushing it. Nyah could hear the pop and crunches as bones broke. She screamed, pulling the protractor from her pocket. She swiped at Shamus, slicing his cheek. Nyah lunged again, aiming for his eye, but she missed. Shamus stumbled back against the table, his legs tangled in Marin's stool. Nyah raised her arms above her head, ready to bring the point of the protractor down into his neck when she found she couldn't move. She tried again, but she was stuck in the double vice grip of Otto and Zeke. Nyah tried to wriggle free but it was like she had been cemented to a wall.

Rolling on the ground and crying in pain, Marin clutched her crushed hand to her chest. Nyah was on her tippy toes as the goons held her tight. Zeke ripped the protractor from her hand and tossed it into the shadows. Shamus dabbed at his cheek, his hand coming away slick with blood.

"You cut me you little fucking psycho," he seethed.

"Touch her again I'll cut off your balls," Nyah said and tried unsuccessfully to kick him.

"What is wrong with you?" Shamus said as he flinched. "I should have killed you when I shot your bitch mom."

Thrashing in the hands of Zeke and Otto, Nyah spit at Shamus, a thick wad of phlegm hitting him on the side of his nose. Shamus drove his hand into her jaw, snapping her head back and buckling her. If not for the two mounds of muscle clamped onto her shoulders, Nyah would have crumpled to the floor.

Shamus picked the bolt cutters and motioned for Zeke to extend Nyah's arm. Shamus grabbed her pinky finger and slipped it between the blades. "Now I'm going to ask you one last time little girl, and if you can't answer you're going to lose this fucking finger. What is Grady planning to do with the video?"

Nyah flailed as panic exploded through her. She tried to pull free, to get her hand away from that cold sharp metal, but the men were all too strong and she cried as the blades started to pinch her. "Please, no, please don't. You don't have to do this, just stop. I don't know, I swear, I don't know."

"Wrong answer, say good-bye to your little finger."

"Wait!" Marin screamed from the floor, her hand cradled in her lap. "Just wait. Ask me. I'll play your game, just ask me."

Shamus shook his head. "That game is done, things

have changed."

"Just ask me."

"Fine. Do you know..."

"About Grady's plan?"

"Yes."

"No, I don't, but I don't know because he doesn't have one."

"What?"

Marin took a deep breath. "Grady has the video, that's true, and you're not the only one who wants it," she told Shamus. "This cop, Quill is after it too, and Grady has no idea what he's going to do. So we can't tell you about his plan because Grady doesn't have one."

Shamus lowered the bolt cutters to his side and stepped over to Marin. "Is that the truth?"

"That's how Grady is," Marin said. "He's a fly by the seat of his pants kind of guy; he's just winging it."

"What a fucking idiot." Shamus' shoulders shook as he howled with laughter. "This fucking guy has Jacob, some bent cop and me after his ass and he's just winging it? Sorry, but your husband is a fucking moron."

Marin arched her eyebrow. "He's beating you, isn't he? Jacob is dead and Grady is the one with the video, so maybe you're just not up to matching wits with a moron."

Waggling his finger, Shamus hushed her up. "Careful, don't ruin the moment by being a bitch. Okay, so Grady has no plan, that's good, I don't have to worry about that. Now, my next question is what do you think he'll do about our trade?"

Marin was saved from speaking by Franny who appeared from the darkness of the hall. She had a cell phone in one hand and a cigarette in the other. The skimpy black dress Franny wore was more the suggestion of clothes than a garment. Reaching down to Marin, Franny wiped blood from the corner of the other woman's mouth and then licked it off. "Enjoying yourself?" she asked Shamus.

"It's just starting to get interesting," he said.

"Not as interesting as the phone call I just had from Basil Bray, I bet."

"Really? He's Grady Fisk's friend, right?" Shamus asked. "What the hell does he want?"

Franny nodded. "Apparently he's acting as an emissary, the middleman for a little deal. He wants to set up a swap for tonight."

Shamus' eyes sparkled. "For certain?"

"That was what Basil said. The girls for the video, no one else present either except Grady and whomever we want to bring."

"What about the cop? He's cutting Quill out?"

"Not surprisingly, Grady wants his wife and the girl back."

Shamus clapped his hands and laughed. "I have waited so long to get back here, now I'll have that fucking video again and all the power I need over that fucking cop. I'll be fucking untouchable."

"Guess we'll have to see about that," Marin said quietly. "I don't know how, but Grady will not let go so easy."

"Oh, Grady will never be free from me, and you, sweet Marin will remember me for a long time," he said and turned to Franny. "And I swear, if he tries any bullshit, Grady Fisk will bleed at my feet."

THIRTY-ONE

I've never been good at letting other people do my dirty work. I hate leaving my fate tied to the competence of another, even someone like Basil. If things went pear shaped, I'd never want my dying thought to be, *I should have done it myself.* We were trying to play some dangerous men like puppets, and we had to pull their strings without braiding our own noose. I couldn't lose anyone else.

Buckled into the back seat of the Escalade, I listened in on Basil's phone call. It was a struggle to stay quiet and not coach him.

Basil ended the phone call and handed the cell back to me. "It's done."

I tucked Vern's phone back in my pocket. "It's all set up like we wanted?"

"You were listening."

"What did Shamus say?"

"It was that crazy bitch, Franny. But it went well, she seemed excited."

"That could be because she was talking to a man over five feet tall for a change," I said.

"And I'm charming."

"And a moron," Gabby added.

"Regardless, she agreed to the exchange?" I asked.

The big man nodded. "Naturally. That's what they wanted, right? The girls for the video. They agreed to meet on our terms."

Pulling up to the curb outside my apartment, Gabby parked the Escalade behind my Bel Air. The Old Girl shuddered and shook as it idled there, but at least she was running. I made out Hank's silhouette in the passenger seat.

Hank was eager, and I wondered how long he'd been sitting there.

I got out of the Escalade pulling a black bag behind me. The bag held an H&K 33 assault rifle with three full clips and the Berretta 92F pistol, which I still hadn't paid Basil for. The H&K was a compact weapon, and good for close range work against multiple targets. At least that's what Basil promised me when he armed me up. The Glock 9mm I'd taken off of Shamus a week earlier was tucked into the waist band at the small of my back.

Basil rolled down his window. "So we'll follow you to the place?"

"Wouldn't it be simpler to meet there?"

He looked at the Bel Air. "What if that heap of shit doesn't make it?"

"Hey, the Old Girl will be fine."

As the Escalade pulled away from the curb, Basil nodded and rolled up his window. I tucked the bag in the Bel Air's trunk, behind the spare tire. I opened the driver's door and slid in behind the wheel. Hank was wearing a pair of my cargo pants, my old brown leather jacket and a Winnipeg Jets ball cap I bought at a game last year. They were all too big on him, and the gun he was hiding weighed down the pocket on his left side.

He grunted and shook his head. "Took you long enough."

I checked my watch. "We've got plenty of time."

"Doesn't make it smart to waste any."

"Are you sure you want to do this?"

"Did your big, ugly friend call Shamus?"

"Yeah, Basil said he's in and ready for the exchange."

"Then it's already in motion."

Shifting the Old Girl into drive, the engine rumbled as I started after Basil. "Okay," I said. "Let's just do this and try not to fuck it up."

"That isn't an option."

We drove out of my area and through the city. Hank stared out his window watching Winnipeg pass by. He pointed out the parks he'd taken Marin and Daria to play at and the old apartment building he had his wife had first made their home. Eventually he grew quiet and got lost in his memories. I was smart enough to leave him there.

I pushed the Chevy to make it to the meeting place on time and the Old Girl shook with the effort. We'd made the timing tight so no one would have the chance to set up an ambush. That was Hank's idea. We needed two sites for this to work, one place to meet Quill and the other to swap with Shamus.

For Quill, we needed somewhere isolated and Hank offered his old family farm. It'd been sold when Hank's dad died and neither Hank nor his two brothers wanted to carry on. They used the money to set up Hank's mom in a condo in the city close by so she could see her grandkids.

The farmer who'd bought the place had only wanted the fields to add to his own neighbouring plot. The house he left vacant, except for hunting season when he let Hank camp there and hunt deer on his land as long as Hank let the farmer join him and brought Bailey's for their coffee. The farmhouse sat on the far side of the fields and had gradually begun to rot and sag. No one was going to disturb us.

For our meeting with Shamus, we needed a crowd for the noise and disruption, but not where we'd attract future witnesses. We couldn't be disturbed, but we wanted Shamus distracted. I didn't know a place like that, and neither did Hank.

Basil did.

An auto parts dealer used to own a warehouse just outside the city. When the owner caught his wife in bed with her masseuse, they divorced. She had a better lawyer, so the owner was forced to sell the company and the warehouse changed hands so many times no one knew who had the title anymore.

This was according to Basil.

The warehouse was normally deserted and basically ignored, except that night the warehouse would be full of drunk, high and sweaty kids grinding and dancing to techno funk. Basil knew the host of the rave. The same guy held raves all over Winnipeg and the communities surrounding it. He'd jump from one place to the next, from the warehouse to the basement of an apartment building, to an old school gym, never using the same venue twice in a row. This guy was smart enough to let Basil use part of the warehouse that night when the big man asked.

We now had the warehouse to couple with the farmhouse. Somehow I was going to be in both places at the same time. We couldn't have people at the warehouse figuring out what happened at the farmhouse or the other way around. We needed them ignorant of each other. Hank figured out how to solve that issue too, but I was having trouble agreeing.

Twenty minutes outside the perimeter, we found Basil's Escalade sitting on the beginning of a dirt road just off the highway. I turned off and followed Gabby through the trees and eventually emerged into a dirt parking lot around the warehouse. A handful of trucks were parked near the open doors of the warehouse. A crew of well muscled potheads were rolling boxes, speakers and beer kegs into the warehouse on dollies. I'm sure there were a few kilos of mind altering chemicals tucked in to those boxes somewhere. There were a few girls carting in what looked like a lighting system with strobes, projectors and smoke machines. A few bouncer types with tattoos and arms the size of my waist were helping the girls.

After parking the Bel Air beside the Escalade and a

hundred feet from the warehouse, Hank and I got out and watched Basil pull a large grey canvas bag from the back seat of his ride. It was heavy, and Basil's forearms flexed with the heft of it. Hank watched Basil intently as the big man carried the bag closer to us and set it down at our feet.

One guy separated himself from the group at the warehouse and walked towards us. His short spiky hair was dyed blue and his sunglasses and tank top were both metallic silver. Gabby whispered that his name was Knox and he ran the rave. He called himself a promoter, but he was really just a drug dealer who used the rave to find customers. He bought his product from Basil which is how my big Indian friend knew about the warehouse.

When he reached us, Knox shook Basil's hand and then Gabby's. He ignored me and Hank. Basil didn't introduce us either, and I was fine with that. I didn't want to be remembered anyway.

From his back pocket, Knox pulled out a bandana and wiped his face with it. "So explain to me again what you want here, Basil, because you all can't be looking to party tonight."

"If I wanted to go dancing I'd find a better place than a shithole stuck in the middle of the woods." Gabby snorted. "And nice hair Blueberry."

"You don't like it? I got tired of orange. But the rave tonight? The music is stellar and it's just a great big crowd of dancing happy people."

"Happy people? Try a bunch of kids stoned on E with soothers in their mouths touching each other's faces."

"And listening to music with no words made by computers," Basil added.

"Whoa, did you come here for a favour or to rip my shit apart?" Knox asked.

"This is no favour. You're doing this because you know better than to say no to me."

"We're cool, man. No need to be cruel though. Raves have come a long way since back in the day."

"Are you calling me old?' Gabby asked.

Knox smiled. "I just want to know what you need."

"Are you expecting a big crowd?"

"Absolutely. It's invite only, but I'm expecting all my crazies to come out."

"The louder the better," Basil said.

"Maybe it'll get too loud for you all?" Knox asked. "Is that why you asked for a room?"

"Never mind why," Gabby said. "We just need a place in the back that's secluded."

"I'm asking for privacy," Basil added. "No one else but us and this guy."

Basil handed over a photo of Shamus to Knox. If he recognised Shamus, he was smart enough not to mention it. Knox put the photo in his back pocket with his bandana. "I'll tell security to look out for him."

"Just make sure they stay out of the way."

"Listen, Basil, I don't want to get in your business, but I have a couple questions about all this."

"Don't piss me off, or I'll ensure no one sells to you again," Basil warned. "How many people you going to get to these parties if there's no dope?"

"Just do as you're told and we keep being friends," Gabby said.

Holding up his hands, Knox nodded. "I just want to know my people are going to be safe. We don't need to get mixed up in any crazy shit, you know?"

"Are you listening Blueberry?" Gabby asked. "You don't want trouble then don't make any."

"And remember I'm not asking, I'm telling you how I want shit done," Basil said.

"Fine, I got it." Knox turned and pointed through the open front door of the warehouse. "Go straight in through the big main room until you get to the door in the back. Follow the hallway on the other side until you get to the room at the end. It's the one with the exit door. You can't miss it."

"Good. You can go finish setting up," Basil said.

With a nod, Knox turned and walked back to his crew. A couple of the tattooed bouncers met him part way. They stopped and had a little heated discussion, the muscle heads doing a lot of pointing and flexing our way. Knox pushed them back to work before his boys did anything to provoke Basil.

Basil hefted the grey canvas bag off the ground and Hank, Gabby and I fell in behind as he led the way to the warehouse. The men and women unloading the trucks did their best to ignore us as we passed, but I could still feel the dozens of eyes on me as I crossed over the entrance into the warehouse.

Inside, Knox's people were setting up for the evening's musical chaos. Space had been cleared in the centre of the main room. Half a dozen men were laying an electronic floor that would light up as the ravers thrashed and danced about. On the cat walk over head, a few of the girls were hooking up the lights and strobes, while others put up decorations and curtains to hide the bleak walls. On the stage above the dance floor, the DJ, bald with tattoos covering his skull, was setting up his computers and turn tables. The crew was organised and efficient enough that my old drill sergeant, if capable, would have smiled.

Our convoy sailed through the double doors at the far end of the warehouse and followed the hallway past even more women carrying boxes and props. One blonde in a tank top carried a box full of stuffed animals and a red head in leather pants followed her hefting an industrial sized tub of Vaseline. The women were setting up the rooms we passed as we made our way to the end of the hall. One girl was unloading crates of vegetables and fruit on a table while another stapled plastic sheeting to the walls. I didn't ask questions because I didn't want the explanation.

We'd reached the door at the end of the hallway and Hank turned, his eyes following the women around us. "So this rave thing, it's just a big party, correct?"

"Basically, it's just a bunch of stoned kids dancing until they pass out," Gabby said.

"They're just burning off energy while making lots of dealers rich in the process," Basil added.

"Is this the best venue for us?" Hank asked.

"It's perfect. It's loud, busy and no one will remember us after they sober up."

"It just feels wrong."

Gabby casually looped her arm in Hank's. "We trusted you, so now you have to trust us."

"Marin and Nyah are counting on us and I won't accept any fuck ups," Hank said.

"Really? Hank, what part of your plan isn't fucked up?" I asked. "It's too late now anyway, so this is what we got. It will work because it has to."

There were no more arguments from Hank, so I opened the door to the room at the end of the hall and walked inside. It was bigger than I expected, deeper too. It must have been a conference or meeting room of some kind. There was a long oak table pushed up against the left hand wall. The emergency exit was on the right with a lighted sign above it. Three naked light bulbs were suspended by cords in the centre of the windowless room, equally spaced out.

Hank and I pulled the table to the middle of the room, and set a chair on one side opposite the entrance door. We wanted the exit door to be free and clear, with all the angles available to it. Basil dropped the canvas bag on the table and unzipped it and stood aside. Hank reached in and withdrew two 12 gauge shotguns, both with polished walnut stocks, well oiled and cared for. They were identical 870 Remington Wingmasters and were beautiful as far as those things go.

"These were handed down to me from my Grandfather," Hank said as he turned them over in his hands.

"Are those going to work?" I asked.

"Are you accusing me of not taking care of them?'

"I mean, will they be enough?"

"Absolutely," Basil said as he took one the shotguns from Hank. "Not my first choice, but they'll do the job."

Gabby whistled as she took the other shotgun, holding it out in front of her. "Very fancy. Not hi-tech or anything, but they're pretty."

The siblings laid the shotguns back on the table, removed the four boxes of 3.5 inch slugs from the bag and stacked them beside them. They would tear the hell out of a deer and blow a hole six inches wide in a man's chest at close range.

Basil took a small black case from his coat, opened it and laid it on the floor in front of the exit door. With a screwdriver and some long thin tool, he set to work on the lock bar on the door. Gabby hopped up on the table and unscrewed all three hanging bulbs. The room went dark, except for the red light from the exit sign. I sat down at the table and sunk into the shadows while Hank went back to the door and opened it.

"I can see that you're sitting there," Hank said to me. "But I couldn't say I knew who you were if I didn't already know."

"And I can see you in the door way clear as fucking day," I said.

"Door's done." Basil stood and tucked his case away. "The alarm is disabled and the lock is disengaged. It'll open without a sound."

"We'll be able to leave it open a crack without being noticed I'll bet," Gabby added.

"You think it'll work?" Hank asked.

"It'll have to," Basil said.

"You sure about this?" Gabby asked the old cop.

"Stop asking me sweetheart."

Gabby nodded and kissed him on the cheek. "Sorry. By the time the party is in full effect, we'll be ready, no worries."

I handed Nyah's cell to Hank. "Okay, this is it."

He put it on the table, right in the middle of the glow of the exit light. "All this for a silly phone."

"It's about power," I said.

"It always is with these people." He patted me on the shoulder. "Now don't go get yourself killed, and come back for my daughter."

There were words I wanted to say, but they didn't seem right. He wanted me safe, as I did him but we couldn't both have what we wanted. So I gave him a hug. Lucky for me Hank didn't knock out my teeth.

THIRTY-TWO

The stench in the school was aggressive. Instead of growing accustomed to the odours after the initial onslaught, the reek grew stronger. The smell had become a physical presence, and the only way to be rid of it was to burn the school down. Nyah would gladly toss the first match, especially if Shamus was still inside.

Surprisingly, even the pizza Shamus had brought them hadn't hidden any odours.

Not that Nyah was a delicate flower, she'd spent time in plenty of disgusting places.

Watson's whore house.

The alleys of Winnipeg's downtown.

The youth shelters.

The basement of a condemned house.

Vern's.

That school trumped them all.

But the smell wasn't why her pizza remained untouched and her appetite had vanished. She'd tried, but had spit up her first bite when she couldn't swallow and returned the slice to the box.

It was fear.

From the first moment Franny had come in and told Shamus about Basil's phone call the room started to vibrate. The floor was unsteady, heaving around Nyah as the walls of the small room quivered with the reverberations of her screams which were only now growing fainter as they echoed in her ears. Nyah's fear had caused her world to shake. Her hands bore the brunt of her nerves, but her brain rolled around her skull trying to process the chaos that had played out in front of her.

She had just watched Shamus beat Marin and had nearly lost a finger to him. She'd been smacked around, certain that it was only the beginning of her pain. Nyah had been trying to brace for the first cut, the first sight of her own blood when the torture had just ceased. She'd been spared right when she'd accepted that she was going to be murdered one piece of her at a time.

Nyah couldn't pretend everything was normal and that Shamus hadn't promised to kill them. It had come as a shock when Shamus and Franny had returned to the lab with a half dozen boxes of pizza. They gave one to each of the hostages and the rest to Zeke and Otto. Shamus had gone from trying to tear her apart to asking if she wanted pepperoni or mushrooms in a matter of minutes. Things had changed that fast and maybe the shaking was just her brain racing to catch up.

Sitting across the lab work station, Marin picked at the toppings of her pizza with her good hand, nibbling even though she looked as nauseated as Nyah felt. The damaged hand lay bruised and swollen in her lap.

"What do we do?" Nyah whispered for the hundredth time.

Dropping her piece back on top of the box, Marin shrugged. "We just have to trust Grady."

"They're going to kill all of us."

"Grady always figures something out."

"Are you sure he can this time?"

"No, I'm not, but it's all we got." Marin motioned to Nyah's pizza. "You should eat."

Nyah pushed the box away from her. "I'm not hungry."

"Me either, maybe if we stay here long enough we won't be so picky."

Zeke and Otto didn't share the girls' delicate sensibilities. The two man mountains were at the table closest to the door, empty pizza boxes at their feet and halfway through the next victim. The fate of the relatively two untouched pizzas in front of Marin was about two slices away from being sealed.

"Okay people, get your shit together," Shamus said as he appeared from the hallway. "It's time to go."

The twin ogres dragged Nyah and Marin through the hallways, the school's main rotunda and out the front doors, tossed them into the back of a waiting van and climbed in after them. Franny was smoking in the passenger's seat as Shamus slipped in behind the wheel.

While Nyah and Marin were bounced around the back of the van, the two meatheads were quite still in their seats. Nyah assumed they were too heavy to actually move. Zeke and Otto had forgotten their hurt feelings and turned their attention to their pistols, which they checked and rechecked with an attention that rivalled their love for pizza.

"What do you need those for?" Nyah asked.

Otto racked the slide, putting a round in the chamber. "What do ya think, smart ass?"

"If you kill us, Grady won't give you the video," Marin said.

Franny blew a ring of smoke into the back of the van. "Gag these bitches, I hate the sound of their voices."

One after the other Otto held them as Zeke tied a dirty rag over their mouths. Nyah tried to fight, but she was no match. Even much less so with her hands already handcuffed. The gag tasted of mildew and dirt. Nyah did her best to breathe through her nose, and concentrate on not allowing the bile to rise any further up her throat.

The van slowed and then stopped. Vehicles passing by blared their horns. Shamus stared off at something to the left. Franny leaned over him, squinting, trying to help him make out the shapes in the night.

"Turn here?" Shamus asked. "Are you fucking serious?"

"That's the directions Basil gave me," Franny said.

"It's a dirt road in the middle of the bush."

"Why would they lie? They can't afford for us not to show up."

Shamus clenched his jaw, and turned the van hard left. "Fine, fuck it."

Branches scraped the sides of the van, and Nyah and Marin shook into each other as Shamus pushed the van down the bumpy road. After fifteen minutes, the ground changed, there was gravel under the tires and once again the windows were free of tree limbs. Nyah got to her knees and the twin ogres didn't bother to stop her. She peered out the window into the night. They were in the middle of a large parking lot with hundreds of cars jammed in. At the far end of the lot sat a huge steel sided warehouse. Even inside the van, Nyah felt the music pumping.

Shamus frowned. "Looks like we stumbled into a party."

"I don't like this, it just feels wrong." Franny pulled at Shamus' sleeve. "There are a lot of people in there, what if they try use the crowd to separate us? What are we going to do about this?"

"What choice do we have?" Shamus asked. "Either that or we stay out here and get rained on."

Franny looked up at the dark and cloudy night sky. "It looks like it's going to get nasty," she said. "But just because it's going to rain doesn't mean we should walk into a trap."

"This isn't a trap," Shamus said. "It's Grady trying to protect his dumb ass. But he made a mistake, it'll be loud so no one will even hear a gunshot, and with that many high bastards, no one will remember us. Besides, once we get that video, the last thing we need to worry about is the police bothering us."

Pulling himself free of Franny's grasp, Shamus got out of the van and closed the door, effectively ending the debate. Franny exited her side, and taking the hint, Zeke and Otto pushed the girls out of the back of the van.

Shamus held up his finger and shook it at them. "Now, I'm going to take the gags off, but if either of you bitches say anything, try to run or cause any shit whatsoever I'm going to kill you. Are we clear?"

Without hesitation, Marin nodded okay.

One at a time, Shamus pulled the dirty rags from their mouths and let them hang at their necks. He took out a key, removed their cuffs and stuffed them in his coat pocket. Nyah felt the blood return to her fingers and worked her jaw to get the kinks out.

Shamus and Franny led the way to the warehouse. Nyah would have run and taken her chances in the woods, but Zeke's meat hooks were clamped around her slender arms. She wasn't going anywhere unless Zeke and Otto had simultaneous coronaries, because she wasn't getting out of their grasp on sheer strength. Of course, if they did collapse she'd have to avoid the ensuing fat-alanche when they toppled over.

In fact, she and Marin offered no protest at all as they were paraded towards the warehouse. They wanted to be with Grady, so why stop Shamus from taking them to him?

In the warehouse the music was blasting at near ear shattering levels. They'd definitely stumbled onto a rave. Nyah's bones pulsed in time with the bass and her heart fought to burst from her chest. The warehouse was one enormous dance floor, with smoke rolling and hundreds of laser lights flashing around in an epileptic's nightmare. A DJ feverously worked the turntables on a stage in the middle of the mob.

The blonde girl could feel the pheromones flowing from the hundreds of people around her as they danced, writhed and grinded to the music. They ripped off each other's clothes, kissed, fondled and were as close to having sex as possible without penetration. Drugs and booze were everywhere and the air was thick with marijuana and hash. There were people at tables off to the side doing line after line of coke. It was pure craziness.

Zeke and Otto shoved Nyah and Marin through the crowd. A young girl, barely out of her teens, blocked their way. Her pupils were three times the size they ever needed to be, the smile on her face was chemically induced. She grabbed Nyah's face in both her hands and pulled her down for a kiss. Zeke pushed her away and the caravan kept moving.

A man offered Marin a handful of pills. She shook her head no, and tried to move past. The pusher kept thrusting his hand in her face so Otto grabbed his arm and twisted it behind his back. The monster spun him around and swept his legs, sending the man and his pills tumbling across the floor.

Quickly, they all moved on.

At the far end of the warehouse, they came to a set of double doors. Shamus led the way through to a long, green painted hallway. There were at least a dozen doors and they were all closed. Shamus stalked from room to room.

With each door Shamus opened, Nyah was assaulted with another vision of corruption that until then was unknown to her. Shamus first exposed a group of men and women, naked and writhing over each other. Sliding from partner to partner, they were fondling, caressing and sucking. Shamus closed the door quickly, but Nyah was certain they'd been covered in cream corn.

In another room they found a woman who'd bound a man to a chair. She was pouring wax on him, hitting him, and cutting him with a long bone handled knife. A third showed men in diapers, dancing as a woman in a teddy bear costume grinded with them. In a fourth a group had a sparkle fight. Glitter and paint covered every inch of bare skin. The room after that hosted a food fight, with men and women rolling around the mess like pigs.

Room after room, a little more of her naivety was stripped away. Just when Nyah thought that between her Mom and Grady she'd seen it all, her eyes were opened further to the weirdness of people as she was pulled down the hall.

The parade ground to a halt outside the very last door. Zeke and Otto replaced the gags on Nyah and Marin while Shamus took the handcuffs out his pocket and put them back on the girls.

"Can't have you two ruining the surprise," Shamus said and then turned to Otto and Zeke. "You boys ready?"

The men drew their guns and held them out in front. "We're good to go," Zeke said.

Shamus tapped Franny on the shoulder and she opened the door as she stepped aside to allow Shamus and the rest of them to walk in first. The room was bathed in darkness and full of quiet; it took a moment for Nyah's eyes to adjust to the faint red light emanating from the exit sign on the far wall. Shamus flicked the light switch, but the room stayed black. He toggled it faster, as the rest strained to make something out of the shapes and shadows in the room.

"What's the matter?" asked a voice in the darkness. "You scared of the dark, Shamus?"

Her eyes finally adjusting, Nyah followed the red light of the exit sign as it fell across a table in the middle of the room. There was a man sitting there wearing a ball cap and a dark leather jacket. His hands were on the table, and in one he held a gun. Nyah was sure it was Grady and her heart swelled with hope.

Shamus stepped forward and squinted. "That you Grady?"

"Who the hell else were you expecting, dumbass?" the man said.

"What's the game with the fucking lights?" Shamus

asked.

"It's an old warehouse, Shamus, surprise, surprise some things don't work. We won't be here long enough for it to matter."

"Didn't we say no weapons, Grady? What's with the piece?"

"I count four guns in your little party."

Shamus nodded. "So we both don't trust each other. Now what?"

"Let's just get this over with." There was a cough as Grady cleared his throat. "I can't stand the look on your ugly face, and your bitch isn't much better," he said, nearly yelling. "The only thing uglier than you is the two meatheads you brought with you."

Blinking and squinting, trying to see through the tricks the shadows and poor lighting played, Nyah strained to see Grady's face. Something was off. His voice was gruffer, lower and his shoulders seemed smaller as the coat hung loose. As off as the voice sounded, his hands seemed the most wrong. They were too old, weathered and Nyah was sure there should have been more scars. Was it fear, was it the dark? What was going on?

"Why are you yelling?" Shamus asked.

"You're pissing me off."

"Like I give a shit. All I want is that fucking video and to be on my way." Shamus paused. "You did bring the video, didn't you?"

The man in the shadows nodded and reached into his coat. Zeke and Otto both leaned forward, their guns raised. Shamus tensed and took a half step back. The man chuckled as he held Nyah's phone on the table in front of him. He used his finger to flip through the icons and after a moment the video filled the screen. Nyah watched as her father got out of his squad car once more, approaching Jacob and Davis. Grady exited the video, and spared Nyah the ending.

"We don't need to sit through the whole thing," he said. "And I promise this is our only copy."

"All this fucking bullshit for a kid's cell phone," Shamus said.

"I was thinking the same thing. That, and how much of a dumbass you are."

Shamus growled. "Again with the insults. Why don't I..."

Grabbing Shamus' arm, Franny hissed. "Honey, relax. Let's just get to what we came to do."

His lover's words seemed to pull Shamus back into the moment. "She's right, you know. We got to stop this fucking chit chat." He laughed. "That's a woman for you; they always want to keep business and personal shit separate."

The man in the shadows shook his head. "You obviously never got the chance to argue with my wife."

Pointing behind him to Marin, Shamus smiled. "Oh, trust me, your wife and I have had plenty of time to chat. In fact, she's got quite the fucking mouth on her, not as bad as this little thieving bitch Nyah, but trust me I've had enough of the two of them. So I'd really like to give them back to you and take that phone off your hands."

"Works for me. Send the girls over and you can have the phone once they're safe."

Snapping his fingers and motioning to Zeke and Otto, Shamus took a step back as the goons moved Marin and Nyah to the front.

Grady pointed to the far corner of the room. "They can go over there."

"Why?" Shamus asked.

"Because I said so."

"They're fine where they are."

Closing his hand over the phone, Grady stood, stepped back and disappeared deeper into the shadows. "If you're not going to listen, this game is over."

"Who are you to give orders?"

"I'm the one with the phone. Now, let the girls cross the room to me and I toss you the phone as they walk."

"At the same time?"

"Yes, same time."

"I saw this in a movie once." Shamus stepped behind the girls, his head between theirs. "Once he tosses the phone you run your asses over there."

Nyah's legs wobbled as her nerves sent jolts of panic and hope through her in alternating currents. This was going to be over. It wasn't what she wanted. They hadn't got the cop and she wouldn't have the video, but she'd be alive. Nyah knew that'd be enough.

The phone seemed to leap from the darkness. It spun in the air, and Zeke and Otto released their grip on the women. Marin was the first to move, sprinting across the floor and to the safety of her husband. Nyah's paralysis broke a moment later, and the blonde girl followed in behind Marin to Grady and to freedom.

The phone passed over their heads.

Tears filled her eyes as Nyah ran around the table, fall right behind Marin and plunging into the shadows that still concealed Grady. Sobbing so hard she couldn't breathe, Nyah had but two steps until she was safe and it was all over.

She heard the phone smack skin and Franny called out, "I got it, it's ours."

Grady's hands reached out, and Nyah relaxed, ready to be embraced by both Grady and the darkness. But those hands weren't there to hug. The hands pistoned out from the shadows and drove Marin back into Nyah. They stumbled, became tangled and the next shove sent them both sprawling into the corner.

Landing first on her tailbone, a blast of pain shot up Nyah's spine, then her head snapped back and she crashed into the wall with Marin coming down on top of her. Nyah felt Marin's chin hit her knee, and her whole leg went numb as blood rolled down from Marin's mouth.

"Stay down," Grady barked.

"Open up on the fucking lot of them!" Shamus screamed.

His gun raised, Shamus' eyes blazed in fury as he let loose the first bullet. Grady took it square in the chest and he stumbled further back. Zeke and Otto surged forward and joined in. All three unloaded on Grady, and it was deafening as the bullets filled the room. Each bullet found Grady, his stomach, shoulders and neck all spurting blood. The barrage kept him upright for a moment before he spun to his right, his knees crumpling.

Nyah had seen this before.

Death had come again, embracing the man as he hit the floor. The red light found his face, and it wasn't Grady. It was Hank, and his eyes held no light. It was Hank, and it shouldn't have been him, it was all wrong. What had just happened?

Nyah's brain short circuited, unable to process anything. Marin screamed through her gag. She rushed to her father, taking his head in her bound hands and sank to the floor. Nyah stayed frozen, her ears ringing and eyes coming in and out of focus.

What had just happened?

Stalking around the table, Shamus' wild grin dropped from his face when it saw it was Hank lying torn apart and bathed in blood. His gun had been aimed at the back of Marin's head but it drifted to his side as he turned back to Zeke and Otto who were only a few steps behind him. Shamus opened his mouth to say something, but the words never made their way out because the exit door flew open, smashing into the wall, and Basil and Gabby stepped into the room. Their shotguns were raised with fingers on the trigger.

Basil moved to his left and Gabby to her right, they opened fire as one. Basil's blast ripped tore through Otto's head, and the bully crashed on his back. Gabby's first shot shredded Shamus' stomach and her second erased his face. Walking, firing and pumping out spent cartridges and loading the next, Basil and Gabby flowed through the room. Basil put two into Zeke's chest and a third hollowed out his neck. Zeke crumpled to the ground beside his brother. Gabby emptied her gun into Franny, blood and entrails painting the wall behind her. The woman landed on her back and her head rolled to the side, her empty eyes staring right at Nyah.

Only then did Nyah believe she wasn't going to die.

THIRTY-THREE

With just me and the Old Girl, it had been a lonely drive from the warehouse to Hank's old family farm. The Bel Air had a lot of character but she wasn't much for conversation. I left the Old Girl in the driveway beside a fully loaded, silver BMW X5. One of Basil's dealers had stolen the SUV and dropped it off earlier. Some soccer Mom was going to be bent out of shape in the morning, but the BMW looked like something Shamus might drive, and I wanted Quill to see them when he pulled up.

After putting on my leather gloves, I popped the Bel Air's trunk and unzipped Basil's canvas bag. The Berretta went into my coat pocket and the H&K assault rifle I slung over my shoulder. I checked and rechecked my Glock before tucking it back in my waistband. I slammed the trunk closed and scanned the darkness for movement. There was an old rusted out combine at the side of the house, and a couple of tractors laid to rest along the driveway. If anyone was hiding, I couldn't spot them.

Surprisingly the front steps didn't crumble during my ascent. The front door was locked, but the frame was rotten and it splintered with the slightest pressure. I tried the lights and was surprised to see the electricity was still on. The scattering mice and other vermin was less shocking.

I stayed in the front living room, where a few chairs and a coffee table had been left behind. It was too dangerous to risk the stairs or any other part of the house. If the whole frame gave way, I wanted to be near the door. That old house was a lot like Hank. They were broken down, and the rot had worked its way through them both. It was hard to imagine Hank growing up in that house, to picture him as a little kid running around with his toys, bounding down the stairs Christmas morning or even parking his butt on the couch to watch TV.

I pushed away all thoughts of Hank. My mind needed to be clear and I couldn't worry if he'd held up his end or what had happened to him. No way was I going to mess up my end and have his sacrifice be for nothing. I wasn't that kind of asshole.

Luckily, I'd taken shelter just in time. The skies opened up and a wall of rain fell from the heavens. I've never been to Niagara Falls, but that had to be close. Puddles formed in the yard and became lakes. Water leaked through the ceiling in dozens of places, and when the first bolt of lightning appeared the lights in the house went out. Within seconds, the mice were back.

I didn't have the balls for going to the basement to check the fuse box. I'd deal with the darkness. I pulled forward a chair, dusted it off and set it by the front widow to watch the driveway. That's the way Quill would come.

That was the hope.

Man, did I need a drink.

My little game was only going to hold up until Quill got inside the house. The story about the exchange with Shamus and the cars parked outside were only to draw Quill to me. Hopefully he'd be eating a bullet before he realised he'd been screwed.

The storm outside hadn't let up. There was a solid wall of rain and the puddles grew so fast it looked like they were trying to swallow the Bel Air. The wind had picked up and hammered against the house. I was barely able to make out the highway and the cars passing by.

Finally, a big black pickup truck emerged through the storm and onto the driveway before killing its headlights. Slinking back into the shadows, I kept watch on the truck. It had stopped at the end of the driveway, parked at an angle, blocking off any way of escape. The truck sat there. There was no movement. No one got out and it didn't move closer to the house. From where they were, my car and the SUV had to be visible. What were they waiting for? Was there back up en route? Were they waiting for those inside the house to come out? Maybe they were hoping the rain would stop, because they'd need a boat to cross the yard.

Lightning struck, illuminating the yard and everything in it. There was only one guy in the truck, sitting there and staring up at the house. We were both waiting for the other to do something. Anything. Blackness returned to the sky and I could barely make out the outline of the truck.

Again, lightning tore through the sky. It was brighter this time, and even with the distance I could tell it was Quill. What was he waiting for? If his plan was to catch us on the way out and if mine was to catch him once he came into the house, we were going to be there for a while.

Lightning flashed. It was blinding and when my eyes cleared, Quill was still in the truck. His head was bowed as he worked on something he held in his lap. The thunder shook the house.

The next strike, the yard was again lit up, the lightning forking above us. Quill had reached into the back seat of his truck, pulling a long box towards the front. In the crash of thunder, the house shifted under my feet.

The entire inside of the house lit up when the next bolt struck. The thunder was deafening. The truck was empty. The doors were closed. There was no movement, the yard looked empty. Was Quill laid across the front seat, trying to hide? Where had he gone? Panic began to swell, threatening to burst out of me.

There was still no sign of him under the light of the next round of lightning. I left the shadows and pressed my face against the front window and searched the yard. He was out there somewhere, manoeuvring through the shadows.

Fuck.

The house no longer felt safe, I'd locked myself in my own coffin. I ran around the main floor, peering out the windows for some sign of Quill in the yard. I didn't catch even a hint of movement. I had no idea where he'd be coming from and there was too much house to cover. The longer I took the better position he'd be in.

So I left. I snuck out the back door in case he was watching the front, ready to snipe me and any other clown who poked their nose out. I crouched low, strafing the back porch with my gun out just like they'd taught me in the army. My finger teased the trigger of the H&K, ready to send a bullet into Quill's face the second I saw that bastard. But he wasn't there. I closed the back door so the wind wouldn't rip it off its hinges. I took the stairs down off the porch, and the board on the last step snapped under me and I stumbled forward, losing my footing in the mud and I fell on my ass.

At least I managed to keep the rifle clean, but I was covered in muck and my shoes were water logged. I'd been outside for fifteen seconds and there wasn't a dry inch to be found on me.

Taking a wide arc around the yard, I went past the shed and then the old red barn. I stayed behind cover as the lightning flashed around me. I took each burst of light as an opportunity to scan the yard for Quill. There was still no sign of him. I ignored the fact I was standing in nearly a foot of water in the middle of an electrical storm. It'd be a cruel joke to survive everything just to get fried out there in the country.

Finally I made it to the edge of the yard and the tree line that defined the property. The bushes were thick, and the trees were long since trimmed or cared for. My arms were scraped and my face cut by the branches as I tucked in. Moving towards the front of the yard and the highway, the wet leaves stroked my skin as I ploughed through the branches and brush. I peeked out to mark my progress from the house and towards the truck, my gun raised and ready.

Where was Quill?

I finally worked around to his truck. I stayed in the bushes, tucked behind a tree and watched the vehicle. There was no movement. As low as I could get and with H&K up and ready, I rushed to the truck and flung open the door. It was empty. On the seat were empty boxes of ammo for .223 rifle rounds. There was also an empty rifle case that looked about the right size for an AR-15 assault rifle. I turned and scanned the yard. The cop could have bunkered down anywhere.

I was soaked to my skin, painted in mud and blind in the darkness. Quill could have been in the bushes ten feet away.

Spinning on my heel, I turned and dashed around the old rusted out tractor at the side of the yard. I weaved my way back to the house going around the shed and sliding through the mud to the side of the house. I pressed myself close to the siding, kept my gun ready and moved towards the back yard. The backdoor slammed just as I was jumping over the broken step and up onto the porch. I almost shit my pants and shot the hell out of the swinging screen door.

The back door was open. I had closed it.

Crouching down outside the doorway, I held my breath and listened. I heard nothing but the rain hammering down around me. I crept into the house, strafing my rifle and searching the shadows for Quill, but he wasn't hiding in the broom closet, cupboards or anywhere else. Peeking out into the hallway, my finger teased the trigger of the H&K. It was clear and I rushed through to the dining room, where the old dining room table and chairs were covered with a bed sheet now grey with dust.

Back out in the hallway I pulled open a door and found the closet empty. The door next to it led to the basement and I decided to wait on joining whatever creatures were lurking down there for the moment. From the hallway, the living room looked empty. My chair was still laying where I'd knocked it over when I first saw Quill's truck. I moved into the room, ready to clear it and move on when I heard the stairs creak behind me.

"Toss your rifle into the corner," Quill said from behind me.

I did, feeling my chances die as the H&K skidded across the floor. Raising my hands, I turned around. Quill stood on the landing, bracing his AR-15 police assault rifle on the banister, the barrel pointed at my chest. Water dripped off of Quill's black police slicker, his ball cap looked heavy with rain.

"You can drop your pistol too," he said. "Take it out with your left hand and toss it over with the rifle."

"What makes you think I have anything else?" I asked.

Quill fired. The floorboards at my feet splintered, dust flew up and I jumped back three feet. I may have pissed my pants a bit too. From my coat pocket I removed the Berretta and tossed it aside.

"Is that it?" Quill asked.

"If you want to come frisk me, asshole, be my guest."

"Just keep your hands nice and high." Quill came down the steps to the main room.

"It'd be a shame if you fell right now."

"I know, my gun might accidentally go off." Keeping the rifle on me, he stole a look around the room. "Where's Shamus?"

"He's being taken care of as we speak."

"I missed the exchange?"

"No."

His step faltered at the bottom as his brain hitched and stumbled to catch up. He blinked. "This was a fucking set up."

I shook my head. "No, not a set up. This, Quill? This is about you paying for what you did."

The cop made a face. "For what? I did nothing to you, Grady."

"We're past the point of lying to each other, I think. Since it's just you and me, asshole, how about you try the truth for once?"

"You first," Quill said. "Since Shamus isn't here, how about telling me where the phone is?"

"Trust me, you don't need to worry about the phone."

Quill raised his rifle so I was looking right down the barrel. "So what do I have to worry about?"

"The fact that I'm going to kill you." I let my arms fall to my sides. "You fucked with my life, you've hunted Nyah after killing her father and you're basically just a piece of shit. Pick your reason, but you're going to die tonight."

"If you can figure out how to do that with me holding a gun on you while you're unarmed I'll be impressed."

"See, now you're underestimating me, and you don't even realize you'll be dead soon."

Quill laughed and shook his head. "You think you have it in you to be a murderer, Grady?"

"This isn't about me. You killed Nyah's Dad and I can't let that go. I'm going to kill you because she's a great kid and you fucked up her life."

"So you're going to die for her then, Grady?"

"No, you are."

I rushed him, grabbing the barrel of the rifle and pushing it to the side just as he fired. The bay window exploded and Quill fell back on his ass. He brought the rifle up to fire again but I was already moving. Bullets ripped into the drywall behind me as I ducked into the hallway. I had my Glock out from the back of my waist band. The stupid dirty cop should have frisked me. Diving into the dining room, I slid underneath the dining room table, hidden by the cloth covering it.

With my face pressed to the floor, there was enough space to see Quill's feet as he ran past. Scampering out of my hiding spot, I chased after him, putting three bullets right in the middle of his back and he toppled through the doorway into the kitchen. Quill was sprawled on his back on the linoleum floor, but he wasn't dead. The bastard had been wearing a police issue ballistic vest.

Quill fired wildly at me and I barely managed to tear back down the hallway as the bullets sizzled past. Using the living room wall as cover I took a peek down the hallway just as Quill poked his head out of the kitchen. I fired, hitting the doorframe, the wall, some dusty family photo and pretty much everything but that damn cop. I was one bullet away from empty.

My only two options were leaving through the front door and hope to make it to my car before Quill did. Or, I could double back and try to surprise him from the other side of the kitchen. I wasn't going to kill Quill by running away from him. One shot, I'd take my chances. I ran through the living room and the hallway on the other side, past the sewing room and den. I was five feet from the kitchen door when Quill burst out. Apparently we had the same idea.

Quill tried to raise the rifle, but I lowered my shoulder and drove him to the floor. Scrambling on top, I hammered my fist into his face. His head snapped back onto the floor and blood spurted from his nose. I brought my right hand back for another blow, and Quill bucked his hips and I lost my balance. His left hook knocked me off him and we flailed around trying to grab a hold of each other.

We both managed to get to our feet and I snuck two quick jabs past his guard, knocking him back into the wall. I went for a looping left and missed. His upper cut staggered me back into the kitchen.

On shaky legs Quill advanced, his hand bringing out his service pistol from under his coat. I backed away, my hands out in front, my eyes fixed on the gun. When I saw his finger squeeze I tried to jump out of the way. The bullet tore through my thigh. It felt like my whole leg was on fire and it wouldn't support me. I hopped on the good leg, trying to create space.

"Still think you're going to kill me?" His words come in deep ragged breaths. Quill tore at his ballistic vest, the Velcro ripping as he pulled it off and tossed the vest to the side. "This is over."

"I'm not done trying," I said, trying to steady myself.

"Tell me where the phone is and we can end this, Grady."

"How about you shove that gun up your arse and pull the trigger?"

Quill's foot lashed out. His shin found the bullet hole and the pain dropped me to my knees. Quill's leg pistoned out again, and I managed to get my hands up in time to catch it. Twisting, I pulled Quill down to the ground with me. I got lucky and my wild swing caught him on the jaw and he fell back, his eyes rolling in their sockets. His gun skittered across the floor. My leg screamed as I moved and I was getting weaker as I lost more blood. I couldn't finish him, I had nothing left. I needed to get to the Bel Air. I needed to buy time.

On my hands and knees I tumbled out the back door and onto the porch. I crawled to the steps and then down them, the pain ripping through me to my soul as I hit the ground. I waded through the mud and water, like a man desperate to find the shore. My leg dragged behind me as I clawed my way through.

The back door opened behind me. I tried to move faster, but the mud and muck latched onto me, sucking me down as I tried to hurry. There were footsteps on the porch. I threw myself forward, pushing on in the mud and rain. There was a gunshot, fire erupted in my side, and I fell on my face. I tried to breathe but the water and mud filled my mouth. I couldn't move, I couldn't get off the ground and I panicked as the water entered my lungs.

A hand grabbed me by my collar and pulled me to my knees. Water and mud spewed from my mouth as I coughed, the beautiful air finding my lungs. My side screamed in pain, and my leg was useless. Blood swirled in the puddle I knelt in.

Quill stood over me, the barrel of his service pistol pressed against my forehead. The farm, puddles and mud went in and out of focus as I swayed, barely staying upright. I raised my hands, trying to surrender, but I didn't have the strength and they fell to my sides. Quill was going to kill me, and part of me wished he'd hurry.

The rain beat down around us, the droplets hammering into the puddles. The thunder was faint in the distance, as the storm passed through. There were voices, I'm not sure from where. They could have been in my head. There was a hammering sound, loud thumps that could have been my heart's last gasps.

"You stupid bastard, Grady, couldn't just do the smart thing could you?" Quill's speech was slurred, and it sounded like his nose was broken. "This is where the hero shit ends. You don't give up that phone I'll kill you, then I'll kill your wife and I'll keep killing until I have it."

"No don't. Please don't." The words were heavy on my tongue.

"And you thought you could get to me? Kill me? You're pathetic."

Behind Quill there were shadows, figures, moving towards us. My eyes wouldn't focus.

I made a grab at him, but my arms felt tied down, and Quill stepped aside. "No, please..."

The figures were right behind Quill. There were two, one much larger than the other.

Quill pushed my head back with the gun. "You're have five seconds to tell me where the phone is. One... Two... Three..."

"Don't fucking move," a voice barked. "Put down the gun, Quill, or we'll kill you."

It was Basil, I recognized his voice. The little person beside him with the large gun must have been Gabby. They split, each rounding on Quill so they flanked him, weapons pointing at the bastard.

"I wondered if Grady was going to have some of his friends show up," Quill said. "Does everyone want to kill a cop today?"

"You're no cop," Gabby snarled. "You're just a piece of shit."

He kept the gun pressed hard against my skull, and he did not turn from me. "Did one of you two bring me the phone to trade for this idiot?"

"Fuck you and fuck your video," Basil said. "Trust me, when you're dead you won't care about none of that."

"Wait, Basil, hold on, this isn't the plan," I said. "Gives us a second here."

"I got told the plan sucks," Basil said.

"Then Marin's safe?"

"She's good," Gabby said. "She's more than good."

"Nyah?"

"My girl is alright too." I could hear the smile in her voice.

"Hank?"

"Just like he wanted," Basil answered.

Some of the heaviness evaporated from me and some of the pain ebbed away. "Then make this guy dead," I said. "I'm done, just end this shit."

"Me dead? You're like a fucking broken record." Quill

laughed. "I don't think so, Grady, least I won't be dead alone because I'll take you with me."

"Kill him, Basil, don't worry about me."

"Oh they care, lord knows why, but they do," Quill said to me. "So here's the deal, your friends put their guns down or I kill you. You all got that? I'll count to five."

"We're faster than you,' Gabby said. "Don't be a tool."

"The way I look at it, I put down my gun you shoot me anyway. So the only way I stay alive is I keep my gun. You might get me first but I'll probably get one off before I bleed out." He tapped the barrel against my forehead. "I'm too close to miss. Do you want to take that chance? I'm going to count now so try and do the smart thing here. One... Two..."

Basil looked over at his sister. Gabby didn't seem to know what to do either.

"Three."

Basil lowered his pistol first, but Gabby wasn't much behind.

"No, please, no, just do it," I begged. "Just shoot this bastard."

Quill counted on. "Four."

His gun at his side, Basil turned my way but his gaze didn't fall on me. His interest was on something else behind me. I could hear sloshing and splashes in the puddles.

"Fi..."

There was a crack, as loud as thunder but from somewhere behind me. Quill's stomach erupted in blood and guts. My face was splattered with bits of his entrails. His gun fell from in front of my face to the puddle I knelt in. Quill looked down, his hands searching the gaping hole in his stomach and the parts of him that fell out of it. His eyes went dull and then he folded in on himself, crumpling into the mud.

When I raised my head Marin crouched in front of me, Hank's big old shotgun still in her hands. She was so beautiful. Tears mixed with rain drops and ran down her cheeks. I wanted to kiss her, I wanted to thank her, but the words wouldn't come. She'd saved me, and all I could do was cry. Marin let the shotgun drop and wrapped her arms around me, burying her face in my neck. I couldn't return the embrace. I tried, but my limbs were limp, no longer taking orders from me.

My words came out in a whisper. "I'm sorry."

"It's over," she said. "It's okay, I love you."

My wife released her hug, and moved back, her eyes went over me, stopping at the wound in my side. "Grady, you're bleeding..."

I looked down at Quill, dead beside me. His empty eyes stared back.

"Now she is safe." I stared at Quill's eyes and they grew bigger as they came closer. I was falling. "Now you're all safe."

My world went black. I fell down, further and further. There is a slap of cold as my face hit the water. I fell through the puddle, past the mud. Down and down I fell until it all went away into nothingness.

THIRTY-FOUR

Nyah switched positions on the chair for the hundredth time, tucking her legs underneath her. The seat cushion had been beaten into submission long ago, and barely gave any relief from the hard wooden frame. She flipped through her phone, starting and stopping the video of her father, of his death, over and over but wasn't really paying attention. It was just something to do.

Instead of cry.

Or scream.

Or puke.

Or go totally freaking insane.

The hospital room was clean and non-stimulating. The sparse décor and mint green walls did nothing to distract Nyah. There was nothing else to look at. Nyah sure wasn't going to look at him. Not anymore. It just made things worse.

What Nyah needed was to go home. She needed sleep and she was desperate for a shower. She felt gross and was sure she smelt worse. She'd been hauled around all over the place, from the condemned old school, to the drug filled warehouse, the rotting farmhouse, the creepy police station, and now St. Boniface Hospital.

She'd been lucky that a kind nurse had given Nyah some scrubs and taken away her clothes. Most likely those rags had been sent to the incinerator. They'd been soaked with blood, mud, sweat, puke and who knows what crud from the school. But even in clean clothes, Nyah still felt like her skin was crawling with bacteria and cooties. She needed to shower. She needed to go home.

But not without him. When they went home, it'd be

together.

Her thumb flipped through her apps. She couldn't find anything to look at. She needed the distraction, but Nyah couldn't bring herself to play some mindless game or read what asinine tweet a spoiled celebrity had their assistant put out there. She clicked on the video again, watching and fighting the urge to look up and see Grady in his bed. In the days since he'd been carried from the farm, Grady's bruised face had gone from red, to purple to shades of brown and grey. Like a beaten puppet, Grady was tethered to machines and IV bags by a vast web of tubes and wires. He'd been so strong, so solid when Nyah had met him, now Grady was swallowed up in his coarse linen sheets.

Marin was outside the door, arguing with the surgeon. Nyah couldn't hear what she was saying, but through the window, Nyah could tell the Doctor was struggling to answer. Marin was extracting another promise that Grady would be alright. She'd been tenacious in her fight for Grady's treatment. She'd harassed the doctors into doing all they could and all that there was left to do was wait. Marin was having trouble with that.

The detectives in the hallway were just as impatient. They would arrest Grady the moment he was conscious. They'd already handcuffed him to his bed. It was ridiculous. A useless act, meant to make the cops feel important. Marin had stopped arguing when Detective Jian pointed out it could be a whole world worse.

Two years for breaking his fire arms prohibition and assaulting the Webber brothers. Two years and that was it. Two years for the beating, the killing the stealing and whatever other sins Grady had committed in the last few weeks. Two years. The only reason he'd gotten anything was because it was still on the books from Grady's last stay in the drunk tank. Two years and if he behaved, he'd do half of that.

They had Basil's lawyer to thank for that. Gabby had called him their Doberman. The cops didn't like it, but what could they do? The whole thing was wrong. It stunk, and they knew it. No one pretended it made sense, but there was nothing the detectives could do about it. Basil's Doberman had seen to that. He had Marin, a respected retired cop's daughter. The cops believed her because hers was the only story they had.

By the time the police had arrived at the farm house, Basil and Gabby were long gone. They'd left the bodies they'd taken from the warehouse behind. The police found only a woman, a girl, a man badly injured, two dead cops and four dead crooks. All they had to make sense of it was Marin's story.

Basil had called it beautiful bullshit. Nyah liked that name.

More details would spill out in the telling and retelling, but Marin had kept it simple, and Nyah had done the same. Hank had taken his son in law hunting at the old family farm. Marin had tagged along to keep the men from killing each other.

That part always got a chuckle from the cops.

When they arrived at the old house it had started to rain, so they were about to turn around when they spotted all the vehicles parked up by the old house. So Hank, always the cop, went to investigate. Just as they were about to enter, there were gunshots and a girl screaming. Through luck, either good or bad, they stumbled on the hideout of some kidnappers, Shamus, Franny and their crew.

Every cop they'd told this part too nodded, for Shamus was very well known.

Shamus had kidnapped poor little Nyah Tynes, for what purpose Marin had let the cops surmise for themselves. But given Shamus had been present at her mother's death, and a suspect, theories from being a drug mule to child prostitution ran freely.

Hank immediately led the charge to free the poor girl. Luckily, Sergeant Quill was there. He'd been searching for the daughter of his dead partner. He'd been rousting bums, asking at homeless shelters and turning the city upside down looking for the girl. Finally, he'd found her.

Again, the cops and detectives nodded at this part, remembering Quill had been asking after Nyah.

It was fortunate for Quill, being outnumbered four to one that he had suddenly had help. Marin didn't pretend to know who had shot who, or the sequence of events once they found Quill squaring off against Shamus and his minions. It had all happened too fast, as it tends to do, and it was a blur. All that mattered was when the bullets stopped and the air cleared, Shamus and his lot were dead and the girl was safe. Sadly, both Hank and Quill had given their lives, and Grady had come close to doing the same. But the girl was safe.

It was a miracle.

It was fantastic.

It was incredible.

It was also total crap.

The detectives were now waiting for Grady to wake up and confirm the fairy-tale. Marin was busy holding them off so Nyah could be the first to talk Grady. She needed to give him the story. She needed a moment to coach him. He didn't need to know all the details, and it would probably be more believable if Grady was vague in his recollection. After all, he'd almost died; of course he'd be left a little foggy.

Their new lawyer would take care of the rest.

The blonde girl really like the lawyer. She'd never met him, and wasn't even sure if she'd been told his name, but Nyah thought he was the best either way. He'd been busy. He'd filed papers, presented motions and been filling up the courts with documents the last few days. A lot of it had been just for Nyah.

Nyah had been adopted.

Just like that.

Marin had already signed and initialled in the appropriate places, and whenever Grady resurfaced from his deep sleep, he would too. Then it would be official. She'd have a family again. Not a Mom and Dad. She already had a set, and Marin had said she wasn't looking to replace them. When Marin asked Nyah to join them, it was just to be a family. Labels were always tricky anyway, but they were a family all the same. Nyah was safe.

Nyah flicked on the video again, let run a few seconds and then paused it. She looked at the image of her father one more time and then deleted the file. She couldn't hold on to that anymore. She had so many better memories, she couldn't let that scene be the first among them.

Besides, Quill, Jacob and Davis were dead. It was over. They paid their price for killing her dad. It tore at her heart that Quill would be honoured as a hero for saving her. But Marin kept pointing out that Quill was still dead so it didn't really matter. She still hurt, and figured she always would, but she felt right about moving on. Now it was truly over.

The video was gone.

The bad men were gone.

And her fears were gone.

All that was left was to live.

With her family.

The blonde girl looked up, and found Grady looking right back at her. He was smiling. As least with his swollen face, it looked like he was. His eyes swam in their sockets as he drifted out of his morphine haze. But he was awake.

"Hey you," he slurred.

Jumping from the chair, her phone clattering at her feet, Nyah rushed to his bed, wrapped her arms around him and hugged. Grady groaned, the machines he was tethered to beeped and rang in protest, but he hugged her back and wouldn't let go.

"You okay?" he asked.

Tears streaming down her face, she nodded, the sobs stealing her voice.

"Marin?"

"She's outside," Nyah finally managed.

He lifted his hand and the cuffs rattled. "Cops?"

"There too. A whole bunch of them."

"I'm sorry Nyah."

She looked up into his battered face. His eyes were also full of tears. "For what?' she asked.

"This was all my fault."

"What? You only did this because of me."

"But I messed it up. I should have been smarter."

She carefully wiped the tears from his face. "It's all over now. Let's call it even."

He nodded, licking his lips. His mouth sounded dry and thick from the drugs. "So what's going on out there?"

"The cops are waiting to talk to you."

"Can I see Marin first?"

Nyah shook her head. "There's no time. I have to tell you something first. I need to tell you what happened at the farm house."

He laughed and it turned to coughing. The machines whooped and beeped in protest. "I was there, I remember." He looked her. "Were you there?"

"I was. But what you know isn't what you're going to tell them," she said. "Before the cops showed up we had to fix some things and Marin came up with a story. You need to listen because this is what you have to repeat."

He groaned. "This should be good."

With one eye on the door, Nyah went over the story both she and Marin had told the cops dozens of times already. When she was done, Nyah had Grady repeat it back to her. Just like Marin had told her to do.

"My wife is something else," Grady said once Nyah was sure he had it straight.

"She's the best."

"What if I fuck it up? My head hurts and I'm all hopped up on these drugs."

"Basil said fuzzy is better. He said to act like you've had a concussion or some brain damage." She smiled. "He also said he doubts you'll have to act."

"Cute. He's a real comedian." Grady smiled at her. "I'm glad it's over."

The blonde girl hugged the drunk. "Thank you for saving me."

He chuckled. "The thing is, you saved me first."

ABOUT THE AUTHOR

JT Blundell was born and raised in North Bay, Ontario. He played football for the University of Manitoba and graduated with a BA in English. He has worked in bars, a prison and an ice cream shop. He now lives, writes and works in Winnipeg.

NewPulpPress.com
or AbsolutelyAmazingEbooks.com